MERLIN AT WAR

MERLIN AT WAR

A DCI FRANK
MERLIN NOVEL

ABOUT THE AUTHOR

Mark Ellis is a thriller writer from Swansea and a former
barrister and entrepreneur.

Mark grew up under the shadow of his parents' experience
of the Second World War. His father served in the wartime
navy and died a young man. His mother told him stories of
watching the heavy bombardment of Swansea from the safe
vantage point of a hill in Llanelli, and of attending tea dances
in wartime London under the bombs and doodlebugs.

In consequence, Mark has always been fascinated by
World War II and, in particular, the Home Front and the
fact that while the nation was engaged in a heroic endeavour,
crime flourished. Murder, robbery, theft and rape were rife.
This was an intriguing, harsh and cruel world – the world
of DCI Frank Merlin.

Mark Ellis is also the author of *Princes Gate* and
Stalin's Gold, the first two titles in the DCI Frank Merlin series,
and is a member of the Crime Writers' Association.

He divides his time between homes in
London and Oxford.

markellisauthor.com
Facebook.com/MarkEllisAuthor
@MarkEllis15

MERLIN AT WAR

A DCI FRANK MERLIN NOVEL

MARK ELLIS

LONDON
WALL
PUBLISHING

First published in hardback, paperback
and eBook in the UK in 2017 by
London Wall Publishing Ltd (LWP)

A CIP catalogue record for this book is
available from the British Library.

HB ISBN 978-0-9955667-0-5
PB ISBN 978-0-9955667-1-2
EB ISBN 978-0-9955667-2-9

1 3 5 7 9 10 8 6 4 2

Print and production managed by
Jellyfish Solutions Ltd

London Wall Publishing Ltd (LWP)
24 Chiswell Street, London EC1Y 4YX

ACKNOWLEDGEMENTS

I am very grateful to Geoffrey Barclay, Jon Thurley and Patricia Preece for their detailed advice on my draft manuscripts. Thank you, Audrey Manning, as always, for your sterling work on the typing front and thanks to my copy editor, Maria Ainley-Taylor, and cover designer, Madeline Meckiffe. I am very lucky to have such great supporters of Frank Merlin as Norman Lang, Brian Murray and Gregg Berman in the USA. My family provided great support and encouragement throughout the writing process and I am grateful to Victoria and Kate for their helpful comments. Finally, many thanks to Fiona Marsh, Eve Wersocki and all at London Wall Publishing and Midas PR for their hard work and help with this book.

To David Meurig Ellis

AUTHOR'S NOTE ON CURRENCY

A pound, of course, went a good deal further in 1941 than it does today. There are different ways of analysing equivalent values but, as a rule of thumb, a 1941 pound would be worth 40 times more today. The 1941 exchange rate for dollars to sterling was roughly four to one. Thus £1,000 in 1941 would be worth approximately £40,000 or $160,000 in today's money.

PROLOGUE

Crete, May 1941

It was nearly five o'clock when the three soldiers reached the end of the olive grove. The dust-filled air shimmered in the late-afternoon heat. Their bodies ached, their uniforms were caked with dirt and sweat and they were hungry, thirsty and exhausted. The sensible thing now would be to lay up where they were for a few hours' rest, then finish the journey under cover of darkness. But there was a tight deadline to meet. The evacuation vessel was scheduled to leave at midnight and they had been warned the captain wouldn't wait for stragglers.

There had been eight of them at the start of the day. During the hard slog over 15 miles of rough, hilly terrain, the company had lost five men. Corporal Johnny Thomson had been the first. Just after 10 o'clock they had halted at a deserted farmhouse to make a late breakfast of their meagre remaining rations. Thomson spotted a rabbit on the far side of the farmyard and, despite the sudden growing engine sound, stepped out from the shade of the small verandah at the back of the house and ran after it. When the soldier was halfway across the yard, his head had exploded in a mess of blood, bone and brain matter as he was struck by a burst of fire from a diving *Stuka*. Corporal Harry Goldsmith automatically hurried to his friend's aid and was cut in half by a following *Messerschmitt*.

The captain had said they had no time to bury the bodies in case the aircraft returned. He left the dead soldiers to the swarm of insects already buzzing over them and led the way across the yard and into the trees. An hour later, they were making their way across a narrow path above a mountain gorge when Sergeant Eric Jones had slipped on some loose stones and fallen headlong the 70 or so feet between the path and the jagged rocks beneath. There being no response from below to the men's shouts, the captain had grimaced, shrugged and pointed ahead.

The other two men had been lost when the party stopped at around two o'clock for a drink in a little glade, where a clear pool of water was fed by a small mountain stream. Privates Jack Peterson and Sid Moore were very close friends. Their attachment to each other had become a source of amusement and ribaldry to the others. The two men were lying on their fronts, sleeves rolled up, bobbing their heads in and out of the pool.

Suddenly Peterson had squealed. "Oww! Something's just bitten me arm. What the…?" His friend lashed out at something green he had seen slithering into a bush. "Was it a snake, Sid?" Peterson looked down to see that his arm had started to swell and was taking on a bluish tinge. Within seconds, he was sweating profusely and his breath was coming in short starts. The lieutenant tried to help Peterson to his feet but the man's legs were like jelly. The captain gave Peterson a hard look and reached a quick decision. "You'll have to stay here, Private. With luck some locals might find you. At worse the Germans will pick you up. Someone will have an antidote."

Peterson tried to speak but his voice failed him. His panicked eyes sought out Moore.

"I'll stay with him, sir."

"No, Moore. Good of you to offer but you must come with us."

"I'm not budging, sir. Someone will come, as you say." Despite the captain's increasingly fierce commands, Moore persisted in his insubordination. "I'm staying or you can shoot me. It's one or the other." The captain briefly looked as if he was giving the shooting option careful consideration before turning on his heels and beckoning the two remaining members of his company away.

And so Captain Simon Arbuthnot, Lieutenant Edgar Powell and Private Matty Lewis stood at the edge of the olive grove. A long, wide and exposed expanse of sparse scrubland faced them. The lieutenant calculated that they had another six miles to cover before they reached the port. At the far end of the scrubland were some pine woods that he knew covered the greater part of those six miles.

"How do you want to proceed, sir?"

"I don't think there's any particularly clever way to do this, Lieutenant, do you? There are about a thousand yards of open land to cover. I suggest the three of us get out of these trees and run like the clappers for the other end. Unless you have a better idea?"

Powell found the captain cold and difficult. The two had been together in combat for several months, first in Greece and then in Crete, but he felt he knew the man little better than on the first day they had met at camp back in England. Arbuthnot was a good-looking, middle-aged man with small neat features and strikingly blue eyes. Just under six-foot tall, his body seemed to have weathered the deprivations of recent days better than his companions' and retained a certain healthy solidity.

Powell had yet to see the man smile and conversation was difficult and certainly not encouraged. In his one and only moment of unguarded conversation, Arbuthnot had let slip that he was a businessman with substantial interests and property in England and South America. Further enquiries were batted away firmly and Arbuthnot evinced no interest in Powell's own background. Powell did hear some gossip in the mess suggesting that the captain had enjoyed a reputation as a playboy of sorts back home. Whatever he was, however, Powell had realised he was no coward. Despite their antipathy, Arbuthnot had earned Powell's grudging respect.

Before the war, Matty Lewis would not have been a man you would expect to run like the clappers. As a portly young East End butcher's boy, his figure had reflected a healthy appetite for his employer's products, particularly sausages, pies and pork scratchings. Now, after the general rigours of military service and the particular rigours of Crete, he was a shadow of his former self and as capable of running at speed as any athletic – if exhausted – young man. Lewis flicked a finger of salute to acknowledge his readiness.

"Give me your binoculars, please, Lieutenant. Thank you." The captain scanned the ground ahead of them. "Do you see there is a small collection of rocks about halfway across, just to the right? "

Powell and Lewis nodded.

"The rocks look like they could provide a little cover. Why don't we make them our first target? About 400 yards. Only a quarter-mile sprint. I can't hear any engine noise." Arbuthnot scanned the horizon with the glasses again. "No movement that I can see anywhere. Shall we?" The three men paused a second for breath, then set off as fast as they could. The lieutenant got there safely first, the captain and Lewis a second behind. As they rested on their haunches and looked around, they realised that the few boulders and rocks set amidst a clump of bracken afforded little meaningful cover. The captain took a moment to recover his breath. "Better crack on then, chaps." As they got to their feet they heard a buzzing noise. The captain looked hard at his two companions. "Come on!"

They had run about 100 of the 600 yards remaining when the two *Stukas* appeared from out of the sun in the west. The buzz of their engines became a roar as they sped down on the running men. A burst of bullets from the first plane cut a neat line in the earth between Lewis and the two officers. The second plane's bullets thumped into the ground behind them.

There were 200 yards to go. The aeroplanes disappeared into a solitary, puffy white cloud ahead of them before wheeling around to attack again. One hundred yards away the pines beckoned them. The lieutenant heard a strangled cry behind him but kept on running. He felt his lungs were going to burst. A trace of bullets pounded into the ground to his left. With a gasp of relief, he reached the wood and crashed down into a bush behind a tree just as another burst of bullets rattled nearby.

Struggling to get his breath back, he looked up through the leaves to see the planes banking and then disappearing to the north. The pounding of his heart slowed and he was able to concentrate. He turned to look out on the expanse of ground he had just miraculously covered without harm. Forty yards out, he could see Lewis sprawled on the ground. He was not moving or making any noise that Powell could hear. Twenty yards to his right, under the cover of the trees, he saw the captain. He was on his knees, his head down, a hand to his chest. Powell shouted, "Are you all right, Captain?" There was no reply.

The lieutenant struggled to his feet and walked over to Arbuthnot. By the time he got to him, the captain had slumped to the ground. His breath was a harsh rasp. He was on his back, eyes closed, his arms wrapped tightly around his body. Carefully, the lieutenant pulled the captain's arms apart and was able to see the damage. It was bad. The *Stuka*'s bullets had ripped into his back and there were three exit wounds in his chest. There were other wounds in his legs and his left hand. The captain's eyes opened. He grasped Powell's wrist with his good hand and, to the lieutenant's surprise, winked at him. "Powell." The captain's grip tightened. "In my jacket. Inside," he croaked. "In my jacket. Inside. Letter. Take it."

Powell knelt down and reached carefully inside Arbuthnot's blood-stained jacket. It was impossible to do so without touching some of the captain's wounds. The captain cried out and Powell withdrew his hand.

"No. Go on. The letter. Inside left pocket. Take it. Please."
The captain shuddered with pain. "Important. Bad things
happen if letter doesn't get to…" The captain's eyes closed for
a moment then reopened. "Please… Edgar." The captain patted
the top left part of his jacket. "There… please." Powell reached
in again, this time hurriedly so as to get the task done as quickly
as possible. There was something in the inside left pocket and he
withdrew a blood-soaked envelope. The shadows of the trees were
lengthening and Powell struggled to make out what was written
on the envelope. He found a shaft of sunlight. There was nothing.

He leant back down to the captain, whose chest was making a
nasty gurgling noise. "Give it to… matter of life and death. Give
to my…" A trickle of blood dribbled out of his mouth. Arbuthnot
managed to lever himself up and mimicked a scribble with his
good right hand. Powell found a pencil in one of his pockets,
put it in the captain's hand and held out the envelope. With a
look of intense concentration, Arbuthnot managed to scrawl a
few spidery letters before he dropped the pencil and the letter.
He released his grip on Powell's wrist and fell back. With a small
sigh, he died.

Powell closed Captain Arbuthnot's eyes. He wasn't a religious
man but felt he ought to say something. He stood up and recited
the Lord's Prayer then made a sign of the cross. When he had
finished, he ran over to Lewis. As expected, he was dead too and the
insects were already congregating. The Lord's Prayer was spoken
again. He went back to the captain and picked up his letter. The
scrawled addition to the envelope was, unsurprisingly, not very
clear. It looked like 'Give to my s…' There was one other letter
following the 's'. It was hard to decipher. "Perhaps 'u', perhaps 'a',"
Powell muttered to himself. He turned the envelope different ways
in the light. "Maybe an 'o' or even an 'i'?" He grunted then pocketed
the letter, and retrieved his binoculars from another of the captain's
pockets. He would have to worry about the letter another day.

His watch showed it was five-thirty. Powell had to make the boat. After surviving this day, he really deserved to.

*   *   *

Vichy France, May 1941

The birds were chattering melodiously in the plane trees of the Parc des Sources. The two men, one in uniform and flourishing a white military baton, the other in a baggy but expensive civilian suit, sauntered out of the Hotel Splendide, followed at a distance by a small group of military men and secretaries. The outside tables at the Grand Café were crowded in the balmy late-spring sun. Several of the male customers rose to tip their hats to the strollers while as many ladies, some young, some old, smiled by way of respect.

The civilian, short and dark, with a cowlick of oiled hair and a thick black moustache, acknowledged the signs of deference with a nod of the head and the crinkling of an eye. His stiffly erect companion responded with a raised eyebrow and a baton tap of his *kepi*. They walked in silence under the café awnings towards Les Halles de Sources before turning into the park. Fifty yards on, they found a park bench in a secluded area of rhododendron bushes and fuchsias and seated themselves. Their attendant party took up position nearby, just out of earshot, beside a small clump of chestnut trees. In the distance, a brass band was playing a selection of military airs.

"So, Admiral, the marshal tells me your trip to Paris was a success."

Jean Louis Xavier François Darlan, admiral of France and the senior minister in Marshal Philippe Pétain's Vichy government, stroked his cheek. "Yes, all went as planned, Pierre, although little has been finalised as yet."

Pierre Laval, former prime minister of France and, until recently, vice-president of Vichy France's Cabinet of Ministers, chuckled and patted his companion on the knee. "The marshal mentioned no qualifications. He told me you had got everything he wanted from the Germans. Said you had got the occupation costs to us down from 20 million reichsmarks a day to 15 million, the return of nearly 7,000 of our best people from the German prisoner-of-war camps, and a considerable improvement on the current restrictions in our dealings with the other France."

"By the other France, Pierre, I take it you mean occupied France?"

"Do not be a pedant, my friend. You know that is what I mean. We need to free up the limitations of our trade so that the French state can benefit to the maximum from our partnership with the Germans."

The admiral pursed his lips. "You use the word 'partnership' Pierre. Others use the word 'collaboration', which has a less satisfactory ring."

Laval rose stiffly to his feet and circumnavigated the bench. When he regained his seat, Darlan noted the unhealthily red flush on his cheeks. "Partnership or collaboration, what does it matter? We were in a mess and we have found a way for some kind of France to survive. At least *Herr* Hitler provides us with a bulwark against a worst danger."

"And, pray, what worst danger is that, Pierre?"

"Why, Bolshevism, of course. The local Bolshevism, which we had to combat before the war, and the greater Bolshevism represented by that maniac Stalin. Hitler is by far the lesser of two evils in that context."

"Those Frenchmen languishing currently in Hitler's camps would find it hard to agree with your analysis, I think."

"But you are gradually getting many of those Frenchmen home, François. That is part of the deal you have just struck, is it not?"

"In return for, among other things, allowing Germany access to our military facilities in Tunisia, Syria, Lebanon and our possessions in west Africa. No doubt 'access' will prove a polite substitution for 'control.'"

Laval stroked his moustache thoughtfully. "And what is so bad about that in the overall scheme of things, if we can recover a much greater level of independence for Vichy France and further the cause of reunification with 'the other' France?"

The admiral removed a handkerchief from his jacket pocket and mopped his brow. The May sun was now at its highest point in the heavens and was beating down from a now cloudless sky. "Perhaps you are right, Pierre, although I somehow doubt that *Herr* Hitler fails to realise the strength of his negotiating position and the weakness of ours. Dealing with your friend the German ambassador in Paris is one thing but… Of course, *Herr* Abetz was a fine host and I have to say I was impressed by the restraint with which, under his leadership, the German occupying forces go about their business in Paris."

The two men sat silently for a while, enjoying the warmth of the day, the mild relieving breeze and the mingled music of birdsong and trombone. For a moment, the heavy burdens on their shoulders lifted and a different France, the old France, took shape around them. Their brief reverie was interrupted by one of the admiral's men, who ran over to deliver a note. Darlan read it and sighed. "The marshal wants to see me again at four. When do you think you will be regaining your place in the council, Pierre?"

Laval smoothed some of the creases in his baggy pinstripe trousers and shrugged. "I serve at the marshal's discretion. As you know, there are voices speaking against me. It is tiresome but I can handle it. Sooner rather than later is the answer to your question, I believe."

"The marshal still values your advice above all others."

"Indeed, François. But back to those agreements with Abetz, the Paris Protocols I understand we must now call them. What next?"

Darlan slowly rose to his feet. "They must be ratified by Berlin and by us. Although I have negotiated the protocols myself, I am not completely happy with them. As for Berlin, who knows how long they will take?" The admiral looked up to the sky and sighed. "Such a beautiful day to be discussing these uncomfortable matters."

Laval stood. "Before we go back, François, have you been briefed recently on the activities of Monsieur de Gaulle and his so-called 'Free French' forces in London?"

Darlan looked up, distracted for a moment by what appeared to be a fierce disagreement among the pigeons. He returned his eyes to Laval. "I see the same security reports as you, no doubt, Pierre."

"And what about the intelligence on the activities of the so-called Resistance here in Vichy and elsewhere in France?"

"I believe I am up to speed. As yet these people appear to pose only a minor threat to us or the occupiers."

"So the cabinet report says but I have my own sources. I understand from them that the anti-government forces here are going to be receiving direct assistance from abroad."

"From abroad?"

"From England. In fact, according to my sources, the English secret services have already sent agents over here."

"Two agents, perhaps three, I understood, Pierre. Is that anything to be particularly concerned about? Naturally, the British will deploy intelligence and counter-intelligence agents as the war proceeds. I would guess that the SS and other German agencies will be well on top of such problems."

Laval shrugged. "As you say, the Germans should be on top of this. Meanwhile, our own people will be vigilant and I am happy to know that we have our own viable sources here and abroad.

Now, my friend, I believe we have time for a quick bite. If we return to my rooms at the hotel, I'm sure my people can rustle up a nice bit of beef and a fine burgundy to accompany it. Shall we?"

The two men retraced their steps to the marshal's seat of government at the Hotel Splendide, acknowledging the renewed greetings of the people again in dignified fashion.

PART 1

CHAPTER 1

Thursday 5 June 1941

Cairo

An inter-services game of cricket was in progress in the lush grounds behind him as Powell made his way through the grand portal of the Gezira Sporting Club. It was a hot and humid day and Powell was dripping with sweat. A fellow officer had given him a lift for part of the way but he had had to walk the last mile. Uniformed Egyptian attendants bowed and guided him through the lobby towards the bar, where he could see his host with a drink already in hand.

"Edgar, there you are. How the hell are you? So glad to see you made it back safely."

"Thank you, sir."

"Oh, you can forget the 'sir' stuff in here. Relax. Can I get you one of these very refreshing gin slings? You probably haven't had a decent drink inside you for a while. You look like you could do with a towel as well."

Powell opted for a whisky and soda. The drink and small towel were supplied swiftly and, after Powell had wiped his face, he clinked glasses with Major Rollo Watkinson, his second cousin.

"Chin-chin, old chap." The major was a stout man of medium height, whose red face was dominated by a large, pock-marked drinker's nose. "So, Edgar, tell me all about it. How was Crete? Fearful, no doubt."

Powell related the tale of his company's retreat to the east of Crete under relentless attack by German planes, and his final fraught journey to the evacuation point of Sphakia.

"My God, you were lucky. The only survivor of your company. Christ! Well, the whole thing was a bloody disaster. As I understand it, everything began swimmingly. At the outset the Germans suffered very big casualties but, through some cock-up, we allowed them to overrun the airfield at Maleme. They used it to fly in reinforcements and everything went wrong from then on. Air superiority proved decisive. The CO in Crete – Freyberg – is a damned good soldier. I understand he wanted to spike all the airfields before battle commenced but was thwarted by some old farts in the Middle East Command. That might have made all the difference."

"Maybe, Rollo. It seemed from early on that there were German paratroopers and planes coming at us from all directions and we didn't really have a hope in hell."

Watkinson finished his drink and ordered again for both of them. "Water under the bridge now. We'll just have to regroup. Things were going a little better out here with Wingate taking the battle to the Italians in Abyssinia, but it looks like a different story again in Libya. That fellow Rommel is not going to be a walkover, I tell you."

The major's rheumy eyes stared off grimly into the distance for a moment until the arrival of a fresh gin sling perked him up again. "And despite everything, you're feeling good in yourself, Edgar? Apart from looking undernourished, sunburnt and a little thinner on top, you look much the same. Still got those odd different-coloured eyes and the old turned-up nose, eh?"

Powell knew he looked a fright. He managed a little chuckle before sipping the whisky, which he guessed would go straight to his head.

"Who was your company commander again? I didn't quite catch the name?"

"Captain Arbuthnot. Simon Arbuthnot."

The major's eyebrows rose. "Arbuthnot, eh? I know the fellow – or knew him, that is. Came across him a few times when I enjoyed my brief career in the City. Haven't seen him for years. Did very well for himself by all accounts. Became something of a tycoon."

"Really? You know I'm pretty ignorant about the City." Powell reached out for a bowl of nuts that the barman had just set in front of them. "I shouldn't speak ill of the dead, I suppose, but I have to say I found him to be rather a cold fish. We had very little conversation. He did say he had some land in the Midlands and interests in South America."

Watkinson gave his cousin a knowing look. "A very wealthy man. A lovely Georgian estate in Northamptonshire. A very substantial trading and industrial enterprise in Argentina, a finance house in the City and God knows what else. He married into the estate in Northampton. Bagged some young aristocrat filly, whose family goes back to the Domesday Book or thereabouts. Lady Caroline something. Pretty girl by all accounts."

Watkinson flicked a finger at the barman and raised two fingers to his lips. A large and ornate wooden box of cigarettes and cigars was produced. "Cheers, Faisal!" The major picked out a large cigar for himself while Powell took a cigarette. Watkinson trimmed his Corona and then, with a flourish, Faisal waved a flaming match in front of them and they lit up. The major took a long drag, blew a perfect circle of smoke in the air and continued. "Anyway, the poor girl died out of the blue within a year or two of the marriage. Some sort of fall, I believe – down the stairs or from a horse. She was the only child of the family and had inherited everything from her father when she was still a teenager. Anyway, Arbuthnot eventually got the lot."

"What was Arbuthnot's background before he married this girl?"

"Very ordinary. It's coming back to me now. His father was the fifth son of a fifth son of a moderately good family. I think the father was a minor businessman." The major screwed up his eyes in concentration. "Car dealer was it or machine engineer? Something like that. Anyway, Simon Arbuthnot started out as a junior stockbroker's clerk in the City but had begun a little financial business of his own when he met the girl. It was just after the war, which he'd somehow managed to avoid. Asthma or something." Watkinson put down his cigar and plunged his hand into the nut bowl. "Thank God they've got these back on the menu. For the past two weeks they only had olives. Can't abide olives. Ghastly things."

"Children?"

"One boy. Must be grown up now."

"What was Arbuthnot like when you knew him? As I said, I found him a bit cold. But I could see that he might be attractive to women."

"He was indeed a handsome fellow. Full of charm as well, if a bit fly. The wife was already dead when I first knew him. Put himself about quite a bit. A keen gambler. Not just on the tables. In business. With the opposite sex. There was a little mystery about how he did quite so well in business. Yes, he came into wealth through the wife but it was never really clear how he built up his South American business so quickly."

Powell started coughing. He had never been much of a smoker. His cousin passed him an ashtray and Powell stubbed out his cigarette.

"Steady on, old boy. Are you all right? I should pour some more drink down your neck if I were you."

"I'm all right thanks, Rollo. Obviously I need a little practice in dealing again with the finer things of life."

The two men were distracted by a flurry of activity at the doorway, which marked the arrival of General Wavell and a party of officers. Wavell led his group towards the restaurant but paused when he saw Watkinson and Powell rising to salute him. "Who's your friend, Major?"

"Lieutenant Powell, sir. A cousin of mine. A few days off the boat from Crete. Got out by the skin of his teeth."

Wavell, a tall, well-built man with a small, bristly moustache and a head of silvery hair, smiled warmly at Powell and extended a hand. Powell grasped it and smiled back at the imposing officer, the commander-in-chief of the British army Middle East command – although, according to growing barrack-room gossip, not for much longer. "A dreadful business, Lieutenant Powell, dreadful. No doubt you lost many good comrades?"

"I did, sir."

Wavell nodded gravely then patted Powell on the back. He glanced at the barman. "Give these two officers a round on me, please. Enjoy your recuperation, Lieutenant. I dare say you couldn't have a better companion for recuperation than Watkinson here, eh Major?" Chuckling, he turned and headed off to the restaurant.

The two men regained their seats. "Jolly decent of him to say hello. A fine fellow…" the major leaned closer to Powell "… if a little indecisive. Anyway, where were we?"

"The Arbuthnot mystery."

"Oh, yes. So Arbuthnot got a bundle from his wife but mostly in the form of property. There was some cash, of course, but the gossip was that it could not account for the rapid accumulation made by Arbuthnot in other areas. Within only a few years of his wife's death, he had the extremely valuable South American business and had set up a well financed bank."

"Did he sell any of the English properties to finance other investments?"

"Apparently not."

"Perhaps he borrowed against them?"

"Perhaps, though people said he had no need to."

"Maybe he was just a lucky investor?"

"Could be. Anyway, he can't enjoy it any more can he, poor fellow? I wonder how he ended up in uniform? Chap was around the same age as me but I'm a career officer. Whatever induced a rich man like him to sign up?"

"Patriotism?"

"We must presume so, my dear Edgar. Ah, here we are. Thank you, Faisal." The barman deposited Wavell's round in front of them.

"If I have anything more to drink without some food in my belly, Rollo, I shall be on the floor."

"Of course, dear boy. I should have realised. We'll get the drinks sent through to the restaurant. And that's enough of the Arbuthnots. Sorry for the chap but don't think he should hog all of our conversation. Come along. They do a very fine steak here."

As Powell followed his cousin out of the bar, he remembered, with a twinge of concern, the bloodstained envelope lying in his new army kitbag at the camp. Given all he had just learned about Arbuthnot, he couldn't help thinking it might contain something of great importance.

*   *   *

London

"Look, Olivier. Quite a sight, isn't it?" Commandant Auguste Angers stood tall in his stirrups as he pointed out the far distant dome of St Paul's. The bronzed roof of the cathedral was glistening in the sun during a brief break in the clouds.

The commandant and his colleague and deputy, Captain Olivier Rougemont, had enjoyed a morning's exhilarating ride in Richmond Park. The commandant was riding his favourite grey, Chloe, and Rougemont was on his boss's second string, a chestnut, Annette. Several sharp showers had failed to dampen their appreciation of the park and the great views of London laid out before them. The commandant, however, could not refrain from drawing an invidious comparison. "A wonderful ride, Olivier. I have to say, though, that this terrible English weather is getting on my nerves. Oh for a few hours on the Cap at this time of year, eh? Sunbathing by the sea, enjoying all the beautiful ladies, a glass of Dom Pérignon in one hand and a breast in the other."

"You forget, sir, that I have never been to the Cap d'Antibes nor, indeed, the South of France. I have been to Lyon but I don't think that counts."

"Of course Lyon doesn't count, Olivier. I forget sometimes that you are a Breton, imbued with all that strange Celtic puritanism and inhibition. Come, let's go back. The colonel wants to see me about something. Any news from the general? How go things in Syria?"

"I should have the latest report when we get back. It will be on your desk after the meeting."

Auguste Angers was a fine horseman. Unlike his deputy, he was riding bare-headed. The commandant was a strikingly attractive man of 35. He had lustrous, straw-coloured hair and despite the English climate, retained the residue of a Mediterranean suntan. Large, hazel eyes surmounted a narrow nose and a wide mouth, which always appeared to be on the brink of laughter. His deputy, by contrast, was short, dark and unprepossessing. An unsightly black mole sat on his left cheek and his features were too small for his large head. The hair currently constrained under his riding hat was wild, crinkly and difficult to groom. General de Gaulle was highly susceptible to Angers' charm but Rougemont irritated him, despite the fact that Rougemont was one of the brightest young officers attached to his army of the Free French.

"Come, Olivier, I'll race you. Loser picks up the tab at dinner tonight. Are you on? Good. *Allons-y!*" The rain began to fall again. They quickly reached a gallop and raced, shouting and laughing, all the way back to the stables.

*   *   *

"When on earth will summer arrive?" Detective Chief Inspector Frank Merlin wondered as he watched the steady patter of rain on the window. It had been a miserable May and the first few days of June had followed a similar pattern. He turned and looked back reluctantly into the room. Thinking about the weather was one way of shutting out of his mind the appalling bloody human mess sprawled out over the bed of this seedy hotel room in central London. The sight and smell was sickening – even to a hardened detective like him. Feeling the bile rising in his throat again, he hurried out into the dimly lit corridor. "Where are you, Sergeant? Is the doctor here yet?" Merlin went down the stairs at the end of the corridor to the hotel lobby, where he found Sergeant Bridges – a burly, ruddy-cheeked young man with an unruly mop of fair hair – interviewing the desk clerk.

"Not yet, sir."

"Mm. How are you getting on with Mr er…"

"Noakes, sir. Sylvester Noakes at your service, sir."

"Merlin. Detective Chief Inspector Merlin."

Sylvester Noakes was a small, balding man of indeterminate age. A few greasy strands of black hair strained to cover his large cranium. He wore a collarless white shirt, buttoned to the top, and a baggy green cardigan that had clearly seen better days.

"And what has Mr Noakes been able to tell us, Sergeant?"

"The gentleman has just been telling me…"

"If I may be so bold, Sergeant, as to begin again for your superior…" Noakes had a strangely mangled accent. He sounded like a Cockney who'd had a few partially successful elocution lessons. "As I was just saying to the Sergeant, a nice young man if I may say so, Chief Inspector. As I was saying, I came on duty today at midday, taking over from Miss Evanston. She is one of the junior receptionists; I am the senior." Noakes put his hand daintily to his mouth and coughed. "I asked if we had seen any business and she told me 'not much'. Just one room had been taken in the morning hours. A couple, she said. A young lady and a man. They had taken Room 14 on the first floor."

"In what name was the room booked, Mr Noakes?"

"Brown, sir. Mr and Mrs Brown."

"And did you yourself see this couple?"

"I caught a brief glimpse of the gentleman when he left the hotel later. The unfortunate lady, of course, I saw when I discovered her in the room." Noakes cast his eyes down respectfully.

"The man left alone?"

Noakes nodded.

"And about what time would that have been?"

Noakes looked across at the large oval clock on the facing wall. "I would estimate the time to be somewhere between one-thirty and two o'clock."

"Did you get a good look at him?" A door slammed somewhere and a draft blew through the reception area. Noakes pulled the cardigan tighter around his skinny body. "Alas no, Inspector. I was in the process of checking in another guest. I only caught a glance of him as he left. Appropriate to this dreadful summer weather, he was wearing a black mackintosh and a hat. He was normal height and weight, I should think."

"How do you know this was the gentleman from Room 14 if you hadn't checked him in?"

"Because prior to the arrival of the new guest I was checking in, the occupants of Room 14 were our only customers, so it seemed fair to assume…"

"Did the man return?"

"No."

"So the lady was left alone at this point?"

"Well, no, sir. By then there were two other gentlemen in the room."

"Two other gentlemen? You'd better tell us about them, Mr Noakes."

"Around an hour after I came on duty, the first gentleman arrived. A short, fat gentleman with black hair and a little goatee beard. Getting on a little. Rather bedraggled, to be honest. He was wearing a navy overcoat and carrying a large black bag."

Merlin closed his eyes. He hadn't slept very well the night before. The Blitz had been ruining everyone's sleep for months but the German bombers had been taking a break recently. It was something else that had kept him awake this time. On a case the previous year, Merlin had taken a bullet in the shoulder and, every so often, the old wound played up. He had tossed and turned most of the night in the spare bedroom, where he had gone to give his girlfriend a chance of some rest herself. His shoulder was fine now but the lack of sleep was beginning to take its effect. His eyes opened. "And what did this new fat fellow do?"

"He nodded at me. Said '14' and headed up the stairs."

"Had you ever seen him before?"

"No."

"What then?"

"Soon after at one-fifteen – I am sure of the time as I was listening to the radio then – at one-fifteen the second man arrived. Tall fellow. Dark-haired. I'm not sure if it was brown or black. As you can see, the lighting isn't that great in here. He was wearing a grey duffel coat. He asked whether a young lady had checked in earlier under the name of Brown. I told him 'yes' and directed him to Room 14. He immediately disappeared up the stairs."

"Did you get a good look at him?"

"Not really. He was also very well wrapped up. Collar up, scarf covering his mouth. All I could really tell was his height and his accent."

"What about his accent?"

"I think he was a foreigner of some sort. As was the other fellow. The fat bloke."

Merlin breathed out heavily in frustration at Noakes' apparent inability to relate his story in a straightforward fashion. "I see. Two foreign men. Any idea where from?"

"Sorry, sir. Not very good at accents."

"All right. What happened after the second man went to the room?"

"Well, within the next half hour or so, the lady's original companion came down, as we've already discussed, and disappeared. Another hour or so later the two other men, the fat one and the tall one, came down the stairs in a rush and hurried out the door. Another hour or so passed and I decided to check the room and enquire whether the young lady needed anything. There was no answer to my knock so I opened it with my pass key and discovered the poor young thing as... as you have seen her."

"Did you hear any noise from the room at all before the men left?"

"As you've seen, sir, the room is at the far end of a corridor on the first floor. No, I didn't hear anything."

"No screams?"

"No, sir."

"And you're sure you can't help us with the nationalities of the men?"

"We don't get much foreign trade here and I've sadly never been further out of London than Southend-on-Sea. I couldn't say which country. Continental, perhaps, if that helps, Chief Inspector."

"Not much but thank you, anyway, Mr Noakes. I'm afraid I'm going to have to ask you to return to the Yard with us to make a full statement. Perhaps you'll be able to fill out the descriptions a little more. It would be helpful if you could get word to Miss Evanston. We'll need her statement as well."

A harassed-looking bespectacled man hurried through the front door.

"There you are, Doc. Thanks for getting here so quickly. It's not a pretty sight, I'm afraid."

"When are they ever, Frank? When are they ever?"

*   *   *

Merlin fell heavily into the chair and ran his hands over his unusually tidy desktop. Bridges had clearly been at work. He threw his new brown hat at the coat rack behind him and, for once, it landed successfully on one of the branches. He hadn't expected to visit his office today, which had begun as a rare day off.

A dental appointment had been booked in the afternoon and the morning had been reserved for his invalid brother, whom Merlin hadn't seen for several weeks. At the neat terraced family home in Fulham, he had been pleased to find Charlie Merlin in much better shape than on his last visit. Since escaping from Dunkirk at the cost of a leg, Charlie had been mired in depression. Despite the loving care provided by his wife and son, there had been no improvement for months. Now, finally, there was a spark of life in his brother. Charlie's wife, Beatrice, told him the good news. "They've given him his job back, Frank. Martin's Bank. Say he can start at the beginning of July. What d'you think of that?"

Charlie had allowed a half-smile to grace his face as Merlin had hurried to slap his brother on the back. "Well done, Charlie!"

"Things may be looking up, Frank."

Beatrice was a wonderful cook, even with meagre resources, and Merlin had stayed for lunch to enjoy an excellent casserole concocted from bits of beef and mutton she had managed to scrape together.

He had then made the afternoon dental appointment in the small mews surgery near his flat, where Merlin had been pleased to discover that his teeth were in good shape and no work was required. It was just as he was leaving the surgery, intent on taking Sonia to the pub for a post-work drink, that the receptionist's telephone had rung. Sergeant Bridges had tracked him down.

"Sorry to bother you, sir. I remembered you said you were checking your teeth this afternoon. I'm afraid there's been a nasty incident. I thought you'd want to know. I'm at the Bedford Hotel in Newman Street just off Oxford Street. Are you happy to leave it to me or do you want to come?"

"What sort of nasty incident, Sergeant?"

"Young lady reported dead, sir. Very messy, apparently."

Merlin knew immediately that the pub would have to keep for another night. And so he had made his way to the hotel – and the poor girl they had found in Room 14.

Now back at the Yard, Merlin leaned back in his chair and hoisted his feet on to the desk. He reached into his pocket and found the packet of Fisherman's Friends he had bought in the small kiosk around the corner in Parliament Square. Few of his friends or colleagues appreciated his addiction to these strong menthol lozenges, but no-one yet, not even Sonia, had been able to wean him off them. He popped a couple in his mouth. As the menthol fumes passed upwards through his sinuses, he experienced the familiar feeling of his head being spring cleaned. He closed his eyes and thought briefly of his father. What would Javier Merino make of his policeman son now? Of his professional accomplishments, his father would be very proud. Of that Merlin had no doubt. Would he, however, have accepted Merlin's current domestic situation of living in unmarried bliss with Sonia, his beautiful partner? Probably, Merlin thought, although his mother… Anyway, here he now sat, Frank Merlin, a highly respected senior officer of Scotland Yard, born Francisco Merino to the said Javier, a wandering Spanish seaman, who had found love and modest fortune with Agnes Cutler, Cockney heiress to a Limehouse chandler's emporium.

Merlin swung his legs off the chair, stood up and went to hang his jacket beneath his hat. Turning back to his desk, he caught sight of himself in the new mirror Bridges had recently installed between the large map of London and the cuckoo clock, which was Merlin's souvenir of a Swiss case from before the war. The man he saw was tall and ramrod straight, with a full head of jet-black hair, except for the odd strand of grey just above the ears. A few minor lines and crinkles marked his face but they were nothing untoward for a man of 43. His large green eyes gazed back at him, above the long, thin nose and wide mouth. Suddenly, he pulled away with a snort of derision at this brief moment of untypical vanity and returned to his desk.

Sergeant Bridges was downstairs, interviewing the two hotel receptionists in an attempt to get better descriptions of the three men who had visited Room 14. The doctor's summary of his report had been brief and to the point. "Botched abortion, Merlin. Mother dead. Baby, a little boy, dead. A butchering. Appalling!"

This was, of course, not the first illegal abortion the Yard – and Merlin himself – had had to deal with. There had, in fact, been a spate of them in London over the past six months. In March, they had arrested a Dutch doctor, who had been very busy and very slapdash. Abortionists such as he were clearly in increasing demand since the war had fostered a more relaxed sexual environment. Most of the abortions took place in back-street hovels, where witnesses were few and far between. At least there were witnesses in this case, even if they weren't proving to be much use.

*   *   *

Reginald Tomlinson watched his young secretary's pert derrière disappear through the door. What he would give to be a young man again. A young man like the personable, young, sandy-haired specimen sitting on the other side of his desk.

"Did I get it right, sir?"

"Yes, Philip. Perfect. Well done. A good day's work."

Philip Arbuthnot looked suitably gratified. Tomlinson had asked him to draft a long and complex affidavit for use in a client's forthcoming divorce proceedings. The young man had been working as a clerk for the City law firm of Titmus, Travers and Tomlinson for four months. To his father's great surprise and anger, he had dropped out of Cambridge in October the previous year and devoted himself exclusively to enjoying a playboy's life in the capital for several weeks. His father had reacted by threatening the withdrawal of his son's very healthy allowance. The young Arbuthnot had eventually surrendered to his father's wishes and signed up for articles at the law firm his father used for the bulk of his business. Since the Arbuthnot file represented over half of the firm's revenue, it was a given that the boy would be taken on and given the greatest attention. The task of supervising Arbuthnot had fallen to Tomlinson. Although the young man was clearly bright, Tomlinson had already been able to gauge that it would be a struggle to make a lawyer of him. He was rich, good-looking and not interested in detail. However, for the moment at least, he was pretending to make an effort.

"Any news of your father?"

"None yet, I'm afraid."

Tomlinson toyed with the silver ashtray on his desk and tried to ignore the barrage of noises coming from the demolition site across the road. "I've said it before and I'll say it again,

I'll never understand why he signed up. A man of 45. What was he thinking? And with all his responsibilities."

"For king and country, Mr Tomlinson. He obviously wanted to do his bit. He always regretted that health problems prevented him from serving in the last war." Philip Arbuthnot adjusted his cuffs, which were fastened by a pair of large gold cufflinks. Tomlinson shrugged, reflecting not for the first time that the boy was always immaculately dressed in a Savile Row suit, Lobb's shoes and an expensive silk tie.

There was a moment's silence, which Arbuthnot felt obliged to fill. "Sorry I was late this morning, sir. A few personal matters to deal with."

Tomlinson pursed his lips. "Please, Philip, try and keep the hours. I have other clerks here and it is undermining to their morale if one of their number doesn't follow the rules, even if that person is the son of our biggest client. As Mr Titmus would say: 'It's not playing with a straight bat.'" In his younger days, Mr Titmus had played cricket for Surrey and was forever reminding his partners of this accomplishment.

Tomlinson assumed that Arbuthnot had spent another night on the town but, if he had, the young man looked remarkably fresh. He was as good-looking as his father had been when younger, although his features owed more to his fair mother than the more saturnine Arbuthnot senior. As tall as his father, he had light, copper-brown hair, which was slicked down with hair oil, a creamy freckled complexion, an easy smile and a neat little moustache in the style of Douglas Fairbanks. Handsome, well set up and blessed with easy charm. The solicitor could only envy him.

Tomlinson had also been an attractive young man in his day but now, in his 60th year, had most certainly run to seed. Overweight, stooped, balding and yoked for life to an equally unprepossessing wife, he had one consolation – he was very rich. He owed this to brains and hard work, leavened (as in most success stories) with a dose of luck. The luck was hooking up with Simon Arbuthnot, the prodigiously successful and active businessman who had generated huge fees for the firm. Tomlinson shuddered – now this man had, idiotically, enlisted in the army. He shuddered again.

"The presumption is that your father was on the island?"

"Last letter I got from him was in April. He was still in Greece. I understand that most of our forces transferred from the mainland to Crete shortly after. I've had no news since, other than what we read in the papers."

"You must be worried."

"The old man has always seemed indestructible to me. I'm sure he'll have found his way on to the boats."

"Let's hope so, Philip. Now run along to Mr Travers. I believe he's got some more drafting for you to get your teeth into."

*   *   *

Merlin was just about to go downstairs to see how Bridges was getting on with his interviews when he received the call from on high. His boss, Assistant Commissioner Gatehouse, had the room directly above his. According to Miss Stimpson, the AC's venerable secretary, Mr Gatehouse would appreciate a little chat, even though it was after seven o'clock. Merlin made his weary way up the stairs. He wasn't up to the usual spiky badinage with Miss Stimpson and ignored her welcoming smile as he entered the lion's den.

"Ah, Frank. Come in. Sorry to bother you at this late hour. Take a pew." The lion seemed intent on being charming for once. Merlin sat. The AC, a gaunt-looking man in his late 50s, was wearing his usual outfit of dark jacket, striped trousers, wing-collared shirt and sombre tie. "Everything all right with you, Frank?

Haven't seen you for a few days. Did that latest counterfeiting case get sorted out in the end?"

"Yes, sir. Inspector Johnson made the arrests."

"Johnson, yes. He's done very well, I must say. The bogus food and petrol coupon business must have taken quite a hit thanks to him."

"Plenty still out there to catch."

"Indeed." The AC fiddled idly with his wing-collar for a moment, then revealed his mouthful of mottled brown teeth in a wintry smile. "I'm afraid I'm going to have to relieve you of Johnson for a while, Frank."

Merlin sat up sharply. "Relieve me? That's going to be awkward. He's one of my best men."

"I know, I know, but it's out of my hands. I have received a request from the very highest authority to assign him to MI5 to help out with the Hess case."

"The Hess case? Why on earth do they want Johnson for that?"

The AC stood up and strode to the window. It was still raining and heavy dark clouds sat over the London County Council building opposite. "Bloody awful weather."

"Yes, sir."

The AC returned to his desk. "To be precise, the prime minister's office asked me if I could contribute our best officer to the ongoing investigation of Mr Hess's strange flight to this country. It is a few weeks now since his arrival but the authorities are apparently no closer to understanding why Hitler's deputy flew himself to Scotland and parachuted in to have tea and biscuits with the Duke of Hamilton. He says he wanted to discuss peace terms but that's hard to believe. Why on earth would he think he could discuss peace with Dougie Hamilton? A jolly good chap and everything but… well, I digress. Hess is currently being held in an MI5 safe house in Surrey."

"Surely the security services have sufficient manpower to deal with him themselves?"

"You would think so but I am not sure they are the ones making the request. I think it might be a case of the prime minister wanting a different perspective."

"If Mr Churchill is seeking to impose someone on MI5 against their will, I doubt Johnson will be able to get very far. And why Johnson in particular, sir?"

Gatehouse thrust his jaw out in irritation. "If you really want to know, Chief Inspector, the prime minister's office requested you for the job. As I formed the view, based on the very same judgment you just expressed, that this was likely to prove a wild goose chase and as I really can't do without you here, I decided that if I had to sacrifice one officer to such a likely waste of time, it would not be you. I volunteered Johnson as a credible alternative and, knowing his reputation, they reluctantly accepted the substitution."

Merlin sucked in his cheeks and looked up at the ceiling. "I understand, sir."

"You might say, thank you, Chief Inspector."

"I'll say thank you, sir, but life is going to be difficult without Johnson. And on top of that, we don't have Cole because you ordered him to be transferred away in light of… the situation. Cole was developing into a very useful asset."

The AC's face reddened. PC Tommy Cole had been transferred to Portsmouth in January because a relationship had developed between him and the AC's striking niece, WPC Claire Robinson, who was now established as part of Merlin's team. Cole was a bright but working-class boy, who was far from Gatehouse's idea of a suitable partner for the young lady.

Merlin ignored his boss's obvious discomfort. "Cole is a good lad and I miss him. Some months have passed. I understand Robinson is now walking out with a young barrister, sir. I would have thought it safe – if that's the right word – for Cole to return now."

The AC's high colour dimmed a little. "I'll give it some thought, Frank."

"Any idea how long I'll be without Johnson?"

"I think you should bank on at least a month."

"Any chance of a temporary replacement?"

"There may be some options in other departments. I'll look into it."

Gatehouse relaxed and the mottled teeth reappeared. "Care for a sherry, Frank?"

Despite his Hispanic origins, Merlin had never developed a taste for sherry. He realised, however, that it would be politic to accept the offer and glasses were poured.

"Did you see that the *Kaiser* died?"

"The *Kaiser*, sir?"

"Yes, *Kaiser* Wilhelm the Second of Germany, as was. The *Kaiser* of the Great War. His death has been reported in *The Times*."

"I can't say I knew he was alive. I thought he'd died some time in the 20s."

"No, no. He had a very nice and cushy retirement. After being obliged to abdicate, he was given a charming little estate in Holland. A place called Doorn. Spent his time gardening mostly, according to a friend of mine who was Dutch ambassador here before the war. He lived there very comfortably with his second wife."

"What would she be called, then? *Kaiserina? Kaiserea?*"

"You know, Frank, I have no idea. *Kaiser* is another word for emperor, really, so perhaps she was known as the Empress. Doted on the old bastard, apparently. The ambassador said there was a brief moment in the 30s when Hitler thought about bringing him back to Germany and reinstating him as monarch. In a figurehead capacity, of course, but that came to nought. No doubt the great *Führer* decided he didn't want anyone to dilute his national pre-eminence."

"Sickening to think that a man responsible for all those millions of pointless deaths in the Great War should pass his declining years in peace and comfort."

"Life isn't fair, Frank." The AC turned to look outside. "Ah, look, the rain has stopped." He finished his sherry. "I think I'll get off home to Mrs Gatehouse."

The AC went to get his raincoat from behind the door. "Don't worry, I'll get back to you on the subject of manpower tomorrow. Help yourself to another sherry if you like. Goodnight."

*   *   *

Colonel Bertrand Aubertin was a slim and elegant man of medium height. He had kindly eyes, a round, pink-cheeked face and would have passed for younger than his late 40s had it not been for his thick helmet of iron-grey hair. A career soldier, he had been stationed in north Africa when France had fallen to the Germans, and had made his way to London as a respected member of General de Gaulle's entourage. Within the Free French organisation, he had been given responsibility for liaison and coordination with the embryonic British military team planning clandestine operations in France and other parts of occupied Europe. This team had just been given a new name – the Special Operations Executive. Aubertin and his subordinates were based in a large old building in Dorset Square in Bloomsbury, while de Gaulle maintained a headquarters in Carlton Gardens near the Mall.

The colonel had returned to the office after a busy day in meetings, and this was his first opportunity to address the paperwork piled on his desk. He was tired and massaged his forehead as he sat down. Problems, problems. Aubertin's job was not easy and now he had a new problem to deal with. It was contained in the folder on the top of his pile. He had read it when first received the night before, and he had just read it again.

It had been compiled by Colonel Fillon, one of de Gaulle's closest aides. The British intelligence services had recently complained, over Aubertin's head, that they had sources alleging there was a leak within the Free French organisation. There were the early beginnings of a resistance movement in France and a small cell of French patriots had established radio contact with the Special Operations Executive. Somehow the existence of this cell had become known to the Nazis and the people in it had been liquidated. Suspicions of a leak had been communicated directly to the top. De Gaulle had given little credence to them but had asked Fillon to investigate. Now Fillon had been asked to join the general in Cairo, and the file had been passed to Aubertin, who, to his mind, should have been given the task in the first place.

The colonel closed his eyes for a moment then reached out to pick up the photograph that sat on a shelf to his right. It pictured his wife, Jeanette, in her prime in 1932. The scene was a charming restaurant overlooking the sea near the small hilltop town of Ramatuelle. They had been holidaying in the south of France and were celebrating his latest promotion. Jeanette was drinking a glass of champagne and directing her radiant smile at him, the photographer. He caught his breath. He hadn't seen his wife in 15 months. She was in Vichy France at their rambling house in the Auvergne. There had been thoughts of getting her to England but they had come to nothing. Her health had been poor in the years leading up to the war, she had had a minor stroke and Aubertin worried endlessly about whether she had access to the right medication. He only received the occasional letter from her and she never addressed the subject of her health. Jeanette had good neighbours and friends and they would look after her, or so he hoped.

He replaced the photograph with a sigh and skimmed through the file yet again. It was not quite clear what Fillon's methodology had been, but he had confined the investigation to three young officers, who had been privy to information concerning the resistance cell. There was nothing untoward about their seeing this information because they were on the distribution list that had emanated from Aubertin's own unit. The only reason for suspicion, as far as Aubertin could see from the file, was that the three officers were the three most recent arrivals in London. The covering letter with the file emphasised that, sceptical as the general was regarding the alleged leak, a proper investigation must be carried out.

Aubertin got up and called for his secretary, a cheerless, middle-aged Frenchwoman, who had taught French in an English boarding school for 15 years before offering her services to the Free French.

"A coffee, please, Madame." As he watched her thick tweed skirt disappear through the door, Aubertin fell back into his seat, looked up to the ceiling and began to consider how best to deal with this new problem.

CHAPTER 2
Friday 6 June

Cairo

Powell had not slept well. His bender with Watkinson the day before was partly, but not wholly, to blame. He had also been troubled by disturbingly vivid memories of his last days in Crete. He had been wide awake for a couple of hours when he heard the dawn call to prayer from the *muezzins* in the many mosques neighbouring the camp.

On his drunken return the night before, he had found a letter on the bed containing his new orders. 'Lieutenant Powell, you will present yourself at the Cairo RAF airfield at 1500 hours on Friday 6 June and return to England on leave until you are notified of your next posting'. Someone must have taken pity on him. Wavell perhaps? Or had Rollo managed to pull some strings? If he had, he'd made no mention of it. However it had been brought about, he was very grateful.

Powell sat up in bed and reached out for his new kitbag. After a quick rummage, he found the other letter. He was sorely tempted to open it. The story his cousin had told him about Simon Arbuthnot and his mysterious rise to power and riches was intriguing. He felt the envelope. It seemed like just one sheet of paper. If it were 'a matter of life and death', shouldn't he have a look so he could work out who to pass the message to?

Powell stiffened. No, no. It would be dishonourable to look at private correspondence. He examined Arbuthnot's dying scrawl for the umpteenth time. 'Si… So… Sa…' Another Simon? Simpson, Simone, son, solicitor, Sarah, Sally, sister, Saint? Powell sighed and put the letter back in the bag. His head started to throb. He would try to forget about it for now and seek advice on his return to London. He had a friend in the police: Frank Merlin would know the best course of action.

*   *   *

London

Eyes closed, Merlin reached out to the other side of the bed. It was empty. Then he heard the sound of a kettle whistling. He rolled his naked body off the bed, grabbed his dressing gown and padded down the corridor of his flat towards the kitchen. Merlin could hear the patter of rain outside but sunlight was streaming through the windows.

Sonia Sieczko stood by the cooker wearing the cream nightdress Merlin had bought her for Christmas, her perfectly rounded figure silhouetted against the window light. Her shining auburn hair swung in a graceful arc behind her as she turned round to greet Merlin. Smiling, she rose on her tiptoes to give him a peck on the cheek.

"Good morning, my darling. I have a surprise. I have eggs. Real eggs!"

"How on earth did you manage that?"

Sonia winked. "That is my secret, Frank."

Merlin guessed that Sonia's brother, an officer in one of the RAF's Polish squadrons, had managed to scrounge the eggs for her in Northolt. It wouldn't be the first time he'd brought her food from his flight base.

"I have three eggs. Two for you and one for me." Merlin demurred but to no avail. "No, sweetheart. You are a big man with a demanding and important job. I am someone with an unimportant – though often very irritating – job. You will have the two eggs. How would you like them? Poached, boiled, scrambled? I am going to boil mine." They settled on three boiled eggs.

Merlin sat at the kitchen table, mug of tea in hand, and watched as Sonia went about her business. She was a striking woman and he still couldn't believe his luck in having her. They had met on one of his cases at the beginning of 1940. Half-Jewish, half-Catholic, she had managed to get out of Poland just before the war. Penniless, she had been obliged to take whatever work she could. When Merlin first met her, she had been working in a seedy Soho nightclub. She had soon found something more respectable and become a sales girl in one of London's large department stores. Sonia Sieczko and Frank Merlin had hit it off pretty much straightaway and soon became lovers. Sonia had stayed in her own rented accommodation in Marylebone for a while but had finally agreed to move into Merlin's Chelsea flat six months ago. So far they had been very happy together.

"There you are, Frank. Two lightly boiled eggs, as you like them, and some toast. *Smacznego!*"

Merlin had been slowly picking up the odd word of Polish and he knew that this word meant 'enjoy'. He considered his first egg for a moment, looked circumspectly at Sonia, then tore some toast into strips and started dipping them into the yolk.

"There is no need to look so shifty, Frank. I know you loved your mother's little egg 'soldiers'. If you want to do it with me, there is no problem, my little baby boy." Merlin chuckled.

The breakfast disappeared rapidly. Merlin stared contentedly across at Sonia's beautiful face. A lock of auburn hair fell over her forehead. She carefully replaced it then looked up, her saucer-like blue eyes intent on him.

"Penny for them, Frank, as you English like to say."

"A cat may look at a queen, may he not?"

"Is that another one of your silly English phrases?" She stood and picked up their plates. "This queen is going to tidy up, get dressed and go to work."

"I may be a little late tonight. We have a new case and the AC told me I'd be without Peter Johnson for a while. He's been seconded elsewhere for a few weeks."

Sonia slid round the table and reached a hand up to his face. Her head came up to Merlin's shoulders. He leaned down to kiss her freckled cheek and then moved on to her full and inviting lips. They lingered for a moment before Sonia pulled away. "Let go or I'll be late for work. If you are going to be late tonight, let's try and make sure that we are home some time together this weekend. If you're not going to be here, I may go out for a drink with some of the girls after work. It is Friday, after all. There was some talk today about going for a drink at the Ritz."

"The Ritz, eh? Very posh. Of course, you go and enjoy yourself, darling." He leaned down to kiss her one more time.

*   *   *

"There you are, Auguste. Come in, please. Take a seat."

The commandant entered with his habitual ebullient air and did as he was bid.

"No riding this morning, my friend?"

"Rougemont was busy and I didn't feel inclined to go out on my own."

The colonel smiled. "You are a gregarious soul, aren't you, Commandant?"

Angers shrugged. "What can I say, Colonel? I like company."

"Indeed you do, especially female company, *n'est-ce pas*, my friend?"

The commandant returned a conspiratorial smile. "I do not believe I am alone in that." Aubertin leaned back and stretched his legs out under the desk. "As I hinted to you yesterday, Auguste, we have a new problem. I was hoping you might be able to help?"

"Of course."

Aubertin slid Fillon's file across the desk. "Please take a moment to read this."

Angers picked up the file. As he read, he made a variety of musing grunts. When he set the file back down, his attitude was dismissive. "Surely no-one really believes we have a spy? This must be British mischief-making."

"It may well be, Auguste, but the general has made it clear that we cannot afford to ignore the possibility, far-fetched as it may be. He requires me to follow up Fillon's work with vigour. I would like you to lead this effort on my behalf."

"You want me to investigate these officers?"

"I do."

Angers winked. "In a perfunctory fashion?"

"Please treat this as a serious commission, Auguste. You will report to me regularly and I shall review the exact status of what we are doing as we go along. If there is a guilty party, well…"

The commandant scratched his chin thoughtfully. "Do you know these men?"

"I know one of the men socially. He seems a good fellow and very trustworthy. Of the other two, one is a Jew whose family was German, I believe. The third is a young man whose father I knew some years ago. An arrogant young man, I'm told. He has connections among those in power in Vichy."

"Hmm. Interesting. Very well, I'll get on with it."

"This is a sensitive task, Commandant. Tact and delicacy will be required."

"I understand, Colonel. You can trust me."

"Excellent." The commandant got to his feet. "Good luck, Auguste."

*   *   *

"So, sir, I have the statements from the two hotel clerks," Bridges began. "There is a pretty full description of the gentleman with the bag from Mr Noakes. However, he is still pretty vague about the other two men – both well wrapped up, one of normal height in a mac, wearing a trilby, and the other taller, in a blue duffel coat and having some unspecified foreign accent.

"Miss Evanstone saw the man who arrived with the lady but not the other two. Her description of him is as limited as that of Noakes. The woman wears the thickest spectacle lenses I've ever seen so, even if she had seen more, I'm not sure how reliable that would have been. She says there was no conversation between the couple. The young lady just asked her for Room 14 and placed a £1 note on the desk. Again, a suggestion of an accent but Miss Evanstone couldn't say what."

Merlin considered his colleague. "The demeanour of the couple?"

"Pretty subdued, understandably. When the couple headed off to the room, Miss Evanstone thought she heard a sob or two from the girl." Bridges paused to consult his notebook. "Oh, yes. Going back to Noakes, he mentioned at the end that he had an idea there was something unusual about the tall man in the duffel coat – in addition to his being foreign – but he couldn't quite put his finger on what it was."

"Very helpful of him. You told him to call us if he did remember?"

"Of course."

"Well, I think our best line of attack is to try and identify the man with the bag. The abortionist, we presume."

Bridges pulled his chair closer to Merlin's desk. "I've already drawn up a list of the usual suspects."

Merlin sucked the last of his Fisherman's Friends. He'd have to get another packet at lunchtime.

"And by the usual suspects, you mean…?"

"All the illegal abortionists we know of operating in London over the past five years."

"With or without foreign accents?"

"I thought it best to make a comprehensive list, sir, regardless of nationality."

Bridges walked over to the small table in the corner where he worked when in his boss's office. Merlin's eyes followed him with a little concern. The young man had recently become a father. Merlin wondered whether this was the reason for his noticeable loss of weight. Before fatherhood, the sergeant's physique had been that of a rugby prop. Now he looked more like an outside half.

Merlin glanced at a photograph of himself in the Metropolitan Police football team 17 years before. Standing beside him was his good friend Jack Stewart, now a senior officer in the Auxiliary Fire Service. Good memories.

Bridges returned with the list. He could see the chief inspector's mind was elsewhere. "Sir?"

"Sorry, Sam, I was daydreaming. Baby keeping you up at night?"

Bridges' face lit up. "The lungs he's got on him. Bet he's going to be a sergeant-major like his grandpa."

"How much sleep did you lose last night?"

"A couple of hours, I should think. Iris does all the work, of course, but it's hard to go back to sleep once the boy's announced himself."

"Never had the problem, Sam."

Bridges winked at Merlin. "Not yet, sir."

"Hmm. Come on, let's get on with it. How many names have you got?"

"Ten, sir. Trouble is, five of them are inside. I got confirmation this morning that two of the other five died in the Blitz. Another two haven't been seen for a while and they might have copped it too. That leaves just the one we know for certain is alive and at liberty."

"And that is?"

"Denzil Thomas."

"Ah yes, Deadly Denzil. He's certainly got an accent, though I'm not sure Welsh counts as foreign. He's six foot four and thin as a rake, though. Nothing like our description. What's he up to these days?"

"He finished a stretch at the Scrubs last November. I spoke to Sergeant Reeves downstairs, who knows the man of old. He believes Denzil's trying to go straight. He's helping out as a medic at the Red Cross."

"Good for him." Merlin got his reading glasses out of a drawer in the desk. They had been a fixture in his life for several months and he had finally overcome his embarrassment at having to wear them. He examined the list.

"These two men who haven't been seen for a while, Ingram and Morris, I don't think I've ever come across them. Descriptions?"

"Ingram definitely doesn't fit the bill, sir. Tall and thin like Denzil. Morris, however, is a chubby fellow who might. Don't remember him having a beard, though."

"Maybe he fancied a change of look. Am I right in thinking Morris is not his real name?"

"You are, sir. I think he's originally Czech or Hungarian. Middle European at any rate. With a strong accent to match."

"Let's track him down, Sergeant. Put WPC Robinson on it. Has she finished giving evidence in that armed robbery case in the Bailey yet?"

"She has, sir."

"And you might visit a few hospitals. Start with Bart's and Thomas's. See if they've admitted any botched abortion victims recently. Check out any new gossip or intelligence they might have on the back-street trade. I would come with you but I need to collar Gatehouse. Inspector Johnson is being taken away from us for a while. He's being seconded to MI5's investigation of Hess."

"That's not good news."

"No. Anyway, the AC said he'd see if he could help us out somehow. I asked him if we could get Cole back."

"Bet that didn't go down well."

"No, but he did say he'd think about it. In any event, I want to see him again to press the issue. Is there anything else?"

"Oh, I almost forgot, sir. As you know, forensics didn't turn up anything of interest in the hotel room at first but one of the team, Johnnie Marsh – you know him, I think?"

"I do. Young and keen."

"Well, he decided to go back to the hotel for another look last night. He rang me to say he'd found something down a small crack in the floorboards by the bed."

"And?"

"It was a cigarette stub."

"Fingerprints?"

"No, too small for that but there was one interesting thing. He took it back to the lab and analysed the tobacco. Apparently he's developed something of an expertise at identifying cigarettes."

"What did he find?"

"It was the stub of a Gitanes cigarette. I know it's not much but…"

"Interesting, though just because it's a French cigarette it doesn't necessarily follow that the smoker was French."

"No, sir, but not many Englishmen smoke foreign cigarettes."

Merlin nodded. He had been a smoker himself once but had given it up a few years ago at the behest of his late wife. Before that, Jack Stewart had got him into the habit of smoking

Russian cigarettes for a while. Very expensive they were, too, he remembered with a shiver. "You're right, Sergeant. Tell Marsh good work. Now off you go and I'll catch up with you later."

As Bridges disappeared into the corridor, Merlin opened the bottom drawer of his desk and took out a framed photograph. It was a portrait of a pretty young woman. Poor dear Alice, his wife. Dead of leukaemia more than two years ago now. He used to keep the photograph on his bedside table at home, but it had seemed strange to keep it there after Sonia moved in. Not that Sonia had any problem with him holding on to his memories of Alice. She was nothing but sympathetic and understanding whenever he spoke of his wife. He stared at the photograph and wondered whether Alice would have approved of Sonia. She had a very generous nature. He felt she would.

∗   ∗   ∗

Le Poulet d'Or was a small bistro around the corner from the Free French office in Dorset Square. Formerly a long-established Italian restaurant called Gianni's, it had remodelled itself successfully to reflect the recent influx of French refugees and military personnel. The owner, Gianni, had renamed himself Jean, although none of his patrons were taken in by this transformation. The cuisine was rustic French and some items, like the *cassoulet* the two Frenchmen were enjoying for lunch today, were nearly as good as they could get at home.

"More wine, please, Jean." The proprietor disappeared behind his counter. "I wonder where he got hold of that Burgundy? Not bad at all."

"It is very pleasant, Commandant." Captain Rougemont had formed his view of the wine on the smallest of sips. He didn't like to drink at lunchtime.

"So, what do you think?"

Rougemont dabbed his lips carefully with a napkin. "If the colonel doesn't mind."

"I haven't told the colonel but why should he mind?"

"If you are sure, sir."

"You are our brightest officer, Captain. The colonel says I am to pursue this investigation diligently and sensitively. If I am to do that, I need your help."

"Very well, sir."

The commandant mopped up the remains of his *cassoulet* with a slice of bread. "And what about these three suspects? All recent recruits, I believe. I thought I didn't know any of them but I remember now that I have met Dumont briefly, but neither Meyer nor Beaulieu have crossed my path yet."

Rougemont watched as Angers' gaze shifted to the nearby table, where a pretty English girl was lunching with a bearded elderly man. She inclined her head in their direction and coquettishly returned the commandant's smile.

"Beaulieu is a new member of the general's personal office. A brilliant young man who arrived here, via the Middle East, in February. He has excellent connections. I understand one of those connections was a close relative of the general, hence…"

"Aubertin said he was connected with people in Vichy as well."

"Yes, I heard that, too. He worked under Darlan for a while, apparently. I understand the young man is not particularly popular. He is regarded as vain and distant."

The commandant laughed. "A cold fish, eh? Plenty of those around. Starting at the top. What about Dumont and Meyer?"

"Also relatively recent arrivals working under the general, though I believe in slightly less exalted stations than Beaulieu. I am on nodding terms with both. I shall make enquiries. I think, however, we should take a look at Beaulieu first."

"Because of the Darlan connection?"

"Yes. Perhaps I should invite him out for a drink? Take a close look at him. Would you like to come? Saturday night?"

"Yes. If he's not too stuck up to decline your invitation."

"Very well." Rougemont saw the commandant's eyes flicker again in the direction of the young Englishwoman. "A pretty girl, sir."

The commandant peered back at him. "Invite Beaulieu for drinks at the Ritz tomorrow at seven o'clock. Perhaps we'll go on for supper after." Angers pulled his chair back. "Now, Olivier, if you'll forgive me I think I might…"

"Say no more, sir. You go ahead. I'll sort out the bill."

The commandant sauntered over to the young lady's table to present his compliments. How Angers would deal with the problem of the elderly companion was not clear, but Rougemont was sure he would find a way.

*   *   *

Buenos Aires

Alexander Pulos had managed to put day-to-day business concerns to one side during his interesting and entertaining lunch in one of the Café Tortoni's private rooms. Along with several other leading lights of Argentinian commerce, he had been the guest of a group of senior army officers keen on gauging the business community's perspective on current events. He had been particularly impressed by one of the officers, a forceful colonel named Peron. The colonel had been outspoken about the weakness of the present government: President Roberto Ortiz was an invalid and had no business holding office, while his right-hand man, Vice-President Ramón Castillo, was a snake. Peron had just returned from a spell as a military attaché in Italy and was much enthused by the successes of Mussolini and Hitler. He did not spell it out but it was clear he thought Argentina would benefit from a similar dose of fascism. Pulos had been struck by the energy and confidence of the man. He resolved to keep an eye on him and maintain contact.

Pulos managed very substantial property, business and shipping interests in Argentina. It was naturally crucial that he keep his finger on the pulse of the nation. The last military coup had been more than 10 years before. The Uriburu junta had tried its own version of fascism for a couple of years until democracy had been restored in 1932. Pulos was not alone in thinking that another coup was in the wind and there was nothing in the lunch to suggest this idea was unrealistic. It would be important to have an ally like Peron if things went that way.

He decided to walk back to his office from the restaurant. Marco, his chauffeur and bodyguard, pulled up in the car but Pulos waved him away. It was only a 15-minute walk, the meal had been substantial and his short, increasingly portly body would benefit from the exercise. He continued to mull over the lunchtime conversation. Hector Martinez had been eloquent in his defence of the president and vice-president, but all those around the table were well aware that this was because he had them both in his pocket. Martinez had vast livestock, railway and oil interests and knew very well how to protect them from grasping politicians.

Pulos had kept his own counsel during the lunch. He had his own arrangements with politicians to protect the Argentinian business empire he and his partner now controlled, but those arrangements were not cast in iron. A few local problems had arisen recently. They were manageable with skill and concentration but Pulos felt that his senior partner's insane decision to enlist in the British army was not helpful.

As he strolled along the wide boulevard, Pulos thought back to the previous autumn and their arguments on his last trip to London. "Why, Simon? You are too old for this. Let the younger generation do their bit. What on earth do you think you can gain?

We have a huge business. It is going well but, as with any large enterprise, there are many problems. I cannot deal with them all on my own."

Simon Arbuthnot had mouthed some platitudes about doing his duty. "This is me you are talking to, Simon. You have never been much of a one for duty before. The only duty you have ever believed in is the duty to yourself and your self-enrichment. Since that duty has helped to enrich me, I am all for it, but duty to your country? Please. Give this little Greek boy a break. You owe nothing to your country. You have grabbed everything you have with no regard for your country's rules or laws. If Britain goes under, you have plenty in Argentina to keep you in clover."

All to no avail. Arbuthnot had given up arguing and had just adopted that supercilious smile of his. "If anything goes wrong, the boy will step up for me." Pulos had almost suffered an apoplectic fit. "The boy! That little wet-behind-the-ears playboy? You must be joking!" That irritating smile again. "He'll come good, Alex, mark my words."

And that had been the end of it. Within a few weeks of Pulos's return to South America, Simon Arbuthnot was an army officer in an English camp, and now he was on active service. A contact had run across him briefly in Athens, as the Germans chased the British army out of Greece, and now he knew from Reggie Tomlinson that Arbuthnot had been involved in the Cretan battle. He hoped to God he'd got out safely.

Leaving the Avenida de Mayo, Pulos cut through some side streets until he reached the Avenida Belgrano. His office was in a side street a few blocks away. He pulled his scarf tight. There had been a frost that morning and it had been unusually cold all day. Pulos loved his adopted home country with a passion. Cold or sweltering – he didn't mind the weather. This country had made him a wealthy man and he was grateful, even though an Englishman had been the principal mover in his success.

Of course, some corners had needed to be cut but that was always the case in business, was it not?

He arrived at the door of the small, elegant, 19th-century house that served as the headquarters of Enterprisas Simal. Pulos had never really liked the name, a confection based on the two partners' Christian names, but, as the junior partner, he had had to defer to Arbuthnot's wishes. Marco was already in his usual position in the corner of the lobby, behind the pretty young receptionist. Pulos walked up the one flight of stairs to his wood-panelled office suite. He had it all to himself this afternoon because his secretary had left early to visit a relative in hospital. Settling himself into an armchair in the corner of the room, he looked out of the window at the pine trees whispering in the breeze and lit himself a cigar. He had planned to ring Tomlinson in London to see if there was any further news of Arbuthnot. It would be well past office hours in London now but he had the lawyer's home number. He puffed away and decided to leave it. No doubt he'd be called if there were anything. He rose, cigar in mouth, and moved to the desk, where he noticed a new folder concerning that damned litigation. He took a long draw on his cigar then opened the file.

*   *   *

London

"May I come in, Frank?" The AC was standing at Merlin's door, looking very pleased with himself. Merlin wondered what was up. The AC didn't usually ask for permission to enter. Mostly he just barged in.

Merlin stood up. "Of course, sir." For once, late as it was, he was pleased to see the AC because he had been trying unsuccessfully to get hold of him all day. Gatehouse was not alone.

"May I introduce Detective Bernard Goldberg of the New York Police Department."

Merlin held out a hand to the stocky young man now standing on the AC's right. Detective Goldberg was an inch or two shorter than Merlin, with a closely cropped head of dark-brown hair and the crumpled face of a man who might recently have walked into a wall. A squashed, broken nose sat beneath a pair of intense brown eyes, the left of which was slightly higher than the right. The lower of Goldberg's thick lips jutted out beyond the upper. Despite its imperfections and imbalances, the face was arresting and strangely attractive. "Pleased to meet you, Chief Inspector. I've heard a great deal about you. A privilege, sir." Merlin shook hands and everyone sat down.

"I'd offer you some refreshment but all of my people are out on the job at present. We are a little stretched, as Mr Gatehouse may have told you, Detective."

The AC shifted uncomfortably in his chair. "Don't worry about refreshment, Frank. We just had something from Miss Stimpson."

Goldberg chuckled. "I came to this country last Friday. I've had more tea in the past week than in my entire life across the water, Chief Inspector. No need to worry about that."

Merlin nodded then looked expectantly at the AC, who was busy clearing his throat in his accustomed protracted way. Finally, he spoke. "Well, Frank, you are no doubt wondering what the detective is doing in London. Well, he has been sent over here for a few weeks as part of an Anglo-American policy of cooperation, encouraged at the highest level. The prime minister's office, to be precise. He arrived, as he said, a week ago. His aim is to see how our forces are coping with things under the current, rather difficult, circumstances."

The American smiled. "I love that British understatement, Mr Gatehouse. Your great capital city has been bombed to hell and back for month after month since last summer. For all that time you have been under clear threat of invasion and, while I guess things have quietened down a little over the past few weeks, that threat continues. London's criminals must be rubbing their hands at the opportunities presented by the destruction, by the blackout and by the huge disruption to the capital. And you say 'under the current, rather difficult, circumstances'. Great!"

The AC looked puzzled for a moment as he tried to work out whether he was being complimented or laughed at, resolving ultimately that it was the former. "Ah, yes, Detective. Ha! Ha! No doubt you will get used to our quaint British ways over the next few weeks. Anyway, Frank, the Detective is here to learn about our Scotland Yard policing ways."

Merlin stroked his chin. "It's very brave of you to put yourself at risk in this way, Detective. As you point out, London is a pretty dangerous place at the moment."

"It may be dangerous but so is late Saturday night in the Bronx. When they offered me the trip here, I have to say I didn't think twice. Some of my colleagues probably put that down to crass stupidity. Others might recall that one of my nicknames in the NYPD is the Lucky Jew."

"Let's hope you remain lucky, Detective."

The AC leaned forward. "Now, Frank, I am not just here with Detective Goldberg to pass the time of day. An idea came to me last night. A very good idea, if I may say so." The AC acknowledged his personal brilliance with a superior smile. "You were complaining because you are without Inspector Johnson for a few weeks. Goldberg here is keen to learn about our methods. What better way for him to do so than to step into Johnson's shoes for the rest of his stay? The Detective is highly experienced and is of a similar seniority and standing to the Inspector. How about that for an idea?"

Merlin looked thoughtfully across at the American. Goldberg appeared at first sight to be a decent fellow and no doubt he had good policing experience. Despite this, Merlin's immediate reaction was irritation – he would have preferred to discuss the pros and cons of his boss's proposal privately first. He felt he was being bounced into something.

Goldberg sensed Merlin's unease. "Hey, Chief Inspector. I understand that this has been sprung on you out of the blue and that you might have reservations. I sure as hell would if some English detective was put on me like this. I'll get out of your hair so that the two of you can discuss this together." Goldberg pushed back his chair and got to his feet. "Let me say, however, that if you do decide to give it a go, I would be deeply honoured. During the short time I've been here, I've heard your name mentioned several times and everything I've heard has been good. I'm sure I can learn plenty from you and, who knows, perhaps I can pass on one or two tricks of my own?" Goldberg turned to the door.

Merlin raised a hand. "Hang on, Detective. Don't be so hasty. I… I would be delighted to have you on our team for a few weeks." He nodded at the AC. "It's a good idea, sir. Thank you."

"Jolly good, Frank." The AC grinned happily and got to his feet. "Excellent! Well, I'd better get back to my office now. The home secretary is meant to be telephoning me shortly."

"There's one other thing, sir."

"Yes, Frank?"

"What about Cole?"

Gatehouse's grin evaporated and he grunted with annoyance. "All right, Chief Inspector. If you insist, you can have him back. But he'll be out on his ear if I hear any, of any… Well, you know of what." He hurried out, slamming the door behind him.

Goldberg shrugged. "A man of changeable moods, your boss."

"He is that, Detective. He is that."

*   *   *

"Darling Philip, I absolutely love this champagne. I could drink Krug all day and all night. Would you care to join me for the night part?"

Philip Arbuthnot leaned over to give Suzanne Edgar a peck on the cheek. "We'll see, Suzanne, we'll see." He sat down next to his other pretty friend, Janey Lumsden, and patted her thigh.

Suzanne sat down on Arbuthnot's other side. "Oh Philip, you tease. And don't make eyes at Janey like that! You promised me, you know. I shall never forgive you if you break your promise."

Suzanne was blonde and slim, and Janey buxom and brunette. Arbuthnot thought his mood favoured the plumper girl this evening. He was a lucky man. Charming, attractive to women and the son of a very wealthy man, he was in possession of a large and airy Mayfair apartment near Claridge's, where, as on most nights, he was entertaining friends.

There was a shout from outside. "Philip! Can you tell me where we are going on to after? I told Roddy I'd let him know. He's coming in on the train from Oxfordshire and said he'd telephone me from Paddington." Arbuthnot's friend, Rupert Vorster, was standing on the balcony, which overlooked Brook Street.

"Rupert, my old chap, do relax. I haven't really decided where we should go. Why don't you tell Roddy to come here? There are a few more bottles of bubbly to go yet and the night is young."

Vorster, a prematurely balding South African fellow-trainee at Tomlinson's firm, came back into the room, bottle of champagne in hand, and topped up everyone's drinks. "Girls seem a little frisky tonight. Planning to keep them both to yourself, are you?"

Vorster did not share Arbuthnot's degree of success with the opposite sex. A blond, strapping, athletic young man two years older than Arbuthnot, he would have been attractive had he not looked for most of the time as if he'd just been sucking a particularly sour lemon in his small, thin-lipped mouth. Like Arbuthnot, he had a wealthy father, in his case the owner of a mining company in Africa. Unlike Arbuthnot, he had no large allowance and could only afford a tiny flat in Battersea. For reasons unknown to Arbuthnot, Vorster had fallen out with his father in a big way. Vorster's father had also told him to get a job but, unlike Simon Arbuthnot, had provided no assistance. Vorster had ended up at Titmus, Travers and Tomlinson very much under his own steam. Arbuthnot had befriended him there and had appreciated Vorster showing him the ropes.

"Who knows, Rupert? We'll have to see, won't we, girls?"

There was a noise outside and Arbuthnot went to the balcony to watch with amusement as a policeman tried to arrest two drunken soldiers on the street below. When the drunks eventually broke away and scarpered down the street, he was on the point of returning to the drawing room when there was a buzz at the door. He stayed where he was as Janey answered and took delivery of something, which she brought straight out to him. It was a telegram. He took it from the girl and stared at it foolishly for a moment.

"Perhaps you've won the football pools or something, Philip? Not that you need to. I wonder, do they have the football pools now that there's hardly any football? My father…"

Arbuthnot tuned out Janey's prattle as he tore open the telegram. His heart lurched as he saw the first four words. 'The War Office regrets…' His hand began to shake. 'The War Office regrets to inform you of the death in action of Captain Simon Arbuthnot. Our deepest condolences, sincerely.'

"What's wrong, darling?" Janey reached out to him but he brushed her away. "Nothing. I'll tell you later. Please, go back in. I'll be with you in a second."

Janey pouted but did as she was asked. He read the telegram again. Father and son had not been so close in the past couple of years. He wished they'd got on better but they hadn't. Of course, as a boy he'd loved his father dearly and they'd enjoyed many happy times. His father had seemed like a god to him then. An indestructible god.

Arbuthnot looked down on the street as he finished his glass of champagne. He was shocked, sorry and saddened at the news, but he was also becoming increasingly conscious of another feeling he was reluctant to acknowledge. That feeling was relief. Relief that he would no longer have to live up to his father's high expectations or find excuses for his failings. Relief that he would no longer have to justify his heavy expenses or apologise for his overactive nightlife. Relief that, at last, he was an independent man and, indeed, as his father's sole heir, a very wealthy independent man. For the first time he could do exactly what he wanted. His hand steadied. He composed himself and went back into the drawing room. He managed to conjure a smile. "So, everyone, where shall we go tonight?"

*   *   *

The Red Lion pub was filled with the usual raucous Friday-night crowd. On their hemmed-in little table sat a pint of bitter for Merlin and a large whisky and water for his new colleague.

"Seems a pretty popular place, Chief Inspector?"

"Please, call me Frank."

"Sure, Frank. And I'm Bernie."

Merlin recognised a couple of MPs fighting their way through the crowd. The Houses of Parliament were only a stone's throw away and this was a regular watering hole for politicians.

"I don't like to repeat myself, Frank, but I'll say again – it was very good of you to take me on board. I could see that the AC was throwing you something of a fastball there."

"Fastball?"

"Sorry, baseball terminology. Guess there's a cricket equivalent but I don't know it."

"'Bouncer', I think, if I get your meaning correctly. Thanks." Merlin was parched and fell on his beer enthusiastically. It had been a tense day but, he reflected, when were his days ever without tension? The alcohol hit home and he relaxed a little. "That's better. So it's Bernie rather than Bernard?"

"I notice over here you say 'Bernard' with a short 'a'. In the States, it has a long 'a' as in 'Bernaaaard'. Either way, I'm not so fond of it. Bernie suits me better. I'm a Jew, as I said. From the Lower East Side. Father's a tailor. He's getting on now but he's still working away in his own little business. He still can't believe I'm a policeman. I love him dearly but he's a very meek and mild fellow. All those pogroms he lived through in Russia, I guess. Anyway, you could say I don't come from natural police stock. How about you?"

"Me? I'm from our East End. Something similar to your Lower East Side, I think. I am the son of an immigrant as well."

"Glad to hear we have something in common. Apart from being policemen that is." Goldberg took a sip of his whisky and made a face.

"Whisky all right?"

"Sure. Just takes a little getting used to. I'm a bourbon drinker. Never really drunk Scotch. Bourbon is what we common people drink, back home."

"Sorry, Bernie. I didn't really think when you said whisky. I'll get you another. I'm sure they have bourbon here." Merlin started to rise but Goldberg reached out a restraining arm. "No. No. Please, Frank. This is fine. It's a good one, I'm sure." He took another sip, this time without making a face. "I like it but I'll take it slowly, if you don't mind. So, son of an immigrant, you say?"

"I was born Francisco Merino. My father was a merchant seaman from Northern Spain, who wound up marrying an English girl here in London. My mother's father owned a chandlery in Limehouse, near the Port of London. My dad ended up running it with her. His name was Javier Merino but he got fed up with people getting his name wrong and changed it to Harry Merlin – he loved the stories of King Arthur and the Round Table. So we all – my mother, brother, sisters and me – became Merlins."

"It has a nice ring to it, Frank Merlin. Sounds rather heroic."

Merlin laughed. "You know, I think I'm going to like you, Bernie. You might be good for my ego. But how about you and your trip here? I know there were occasional exchanges of senior officers before the war. I was once offered a trip to Washington but had too much on my plate to take it up. However, I must say that it seems a little odd, if not downright mad, to send an officer to us in the middle of the Blitz."

"Luckily for me, the Blitz seems to have taken a holiday."

"Don't count on it. The planes could be back any day."

"Of course they could, I know.' He paused as a very drunk man squeezed awkwardly past their table. "To be honest, I think my colleagues in the NYPD came up with this idea so they could get shot of me for a while."

"Why would they do that?"

"Let's just say that I didn't see eye to eye with them on some of their policing methods – policing methods and their habit of turning a blind eye to certain criminal activities."

Merlin finished his pint and wiped the froth from his mouth. "I'm sorry to hear that, Bernie. We see a lot of Hollywood pictures where the police are portrayed as violent and corrupt. No doubt some are in real life. I won't pretend that we over here are whiter than white – there are British policemen like that too, though thankfully not in my section of Scotland Yard. It's not easy being the person who has to call out the rotten apples."

The two politicians Merlin had seen in the crowd earlier had now managed to find a nearby table, and were complaining to each other about Churchill and the leadership of the campaign in Crete. They were speaking very loudly and the two policemen couldn't help but listen in.

"Complete cock-up from start to finish," said the younger of the two men. "Churchill's losing his way. Picking the wrong generals. They are going to cock up north Africa as well."

"But what can we do, my friend? We can't replace him." The second man was a dour-looking fellow with a northern accent.

"Why the hell not? I knew the man would be a disaster when he came in last year. Halifax would have been the right choice."

"But Halifax was an appeaser."

"And what's so wrong with that? Since Churchill came in, half of London has been bombed to smithereens, our merchant shipping is being destroyed and we are making no meaningful progress anywhere. Perhaps appeasement would have been the right way forward."

The northerner shook his head mournfully. "What about Ethiopia? We did all right there."

"Against Mussolini's lot – I should think so!" They broke off their conversation as the younger man went off to get another round.

Merlin raised his eyes to the ceiling. The American looked confused. "I thought that Churchill was a hero to people in this country."

"Not to everyone, as you can see. To many, like myself, he is a man with acknowledged faults but who was right about Hitler throughout the 30s and is the best leader we have by a long way. To others, he was – and remains – an untrustworthy maverick who should never have been entrusted with the levers of power."

Goldberg drained the last of his whisky. "I guess it's the same in the States. Roosevelt has been a brilliant president but the man still has many enemies."

Merlin raised his glass. "Another?"

"My call." Goldberg picked up the empty glasses and ploughed his way through to the bar.

*   *   *

Sonia was opening the front door of the flat when Merlin got back at 11 o'clock. After their drink at the Red Lion, Merlin had taken Goldberg to a little Italian restaurant he knew in Soho. Then he'd hailed a taxi, dropped Goldberg off at his hotel near Regent's Park and headed home. "Had a good time, darling? Where'd you go?"

Sonia was clearly a little tipsy and she half-fell into the flat. Merlin reached his arm around her and led her to an armchair, into which she slumped with a giggle. "To the Ritz. The upstairs and the downstairs bars. Very nice. Very lively."

"What do you mean by lively?"

"Good-looking men and women, bad-looking men and women. Men hunting women, women hunting men, men hunting men, women hunting women."

"Goodness, Sonia, I don't know if I approve."

Sonia punched Merlin's leg feebly before reaching up to pull his face down to hers and kissing him passionately on the mouth. When he eventually managed to disengage himself, he walked over to the drinks cabinet. He peeked through the blackout curtains and saw the familiar sweep of the searchlights, moving back and forth over the city and river. He poured out a glass of brandy. "Nightcap, darling?"

"Sorry, Frank, but I'm too drunk." She looked up at him with an endearing, sloppy grin as he sat on the arm of her chair and stroked her cheek. Then a look of anxiety came over her face. "Frank, I have an admission to make. I accepted a drink from a man."

Merlin put on a stern look.

"No, Frank. It's not that bad. I went out with Ethel and Laura. There were some French officers in the upstairs bar. A couple of them came over to us and the other girls were very keen. They are single, as you know. Anyway, the Frenchmen offered us drinks and I do not like to be a – what's the word, I think it was used in some film we saw the other day? – a… a 'sourpuss', that's it. So they bought us all a drink."

Merlin laughed. "I'll bet these Frenchmen were keener on you than on your friends."

Sonia blushed. "Well, I must say, one of them was particularly dashing and keen but I made it quite clear that I was spoken for and he turned his attention to Laura. It was all very pleasant and civilised, but you know how champagne goes to my head."

"We are all entitled to let our hair down once in a while, darling. I've had a few drinks too. I think I'll give this brandy a miss. Come on, let's turn in."

"There seem to be quite a lot of Frenchmen around these days, Frank."

"Yes, there are, my dear. And Czechs, Canadians, Australians and New Zealanders. Not forgetting the Poles, of course." He winked as he lifted her to her feet.

CHAPTER 3

Saturday 7 June

London

The man's eyes opened slowly. Someone was knocking at the front door. Not loudly but there was definitely someone there. Running a hand over his beard, he turned on the bedside lamp. He looked at the clock. "*Merde!*" It was four in the morning. Through a gap in the curtains, he could see it was still pitch-black outside. Rain rattled hard against the window panes. His head pounded like the drums in the Soho jazz club where he'd spent most of the previous evening. He looked around the bedroom with bleary eyes. Thank God the girl had gone. There was little as tedious as stilted conversation with a prostitute the morning after.

A sudden panic struck him and he hurried from the bed to check his jacket, which was lying on the floor in a pile with the rest of his clothes. He reached inside and his heartbeat returned to normal. His wallet hadn't been removed and his money was still there. Then came another jolt of panic and he turned to check that his watch, the classic Jaeger-LeCoultre a happy client had given him many years ago – and that he'd managed somehow to keep from the pawnbroker's clutches – was still on his bedside table. It was, and he calmed down again. The knocking at the door continued. "All right, all right. *Attendez!* I'm getting dressed. Wait a moment."

He grabbed his dressing gown, put it on and tied the cord with some difficulty around his ample frame. For some reason, his fingers felt thick and unwieldy. Fingers that had once been the envy of his profession. He shuffled to the table where his wig lay. He set it in its place and headed to the hallway. "Who is it?"

"It's me. You know my voice, do you not?"

Surprise showed in the fat man's voice. "You. I… So at last you are prepared to see me. Why at this ungodly hour?"

"For heaven's sake, let me in. I can't talk to you from out here." The door was opened and the visitor entered, water dripping everywhere from his sodden raincoat.

"You resemble a drowned rat. Here, give me your coat and go into the living room. What a country! Rain, rain, rain."

The visitor remained where he was, staring grimly at his host.

"My dear fellow, you look like death warmed up. Whatever is wrong with you? Come through here. This place is something of a comedown from my apartment on the Ile St Louis but things could be worse. I could be dead or in a Nazi concentration camp. Come, let's sit down and talk."

The visitor's hand reached inside his coat. A gun appeared. The fat man gasped. "My dear fellow, what on earth are you thinking? There is no need for this. Put the gun away, I beg you. Let us have a drink and discuss things like gentlemen."

"Be quiet. Get in there."

The fat man did as he was told and shuffled, whimpering, into his bedroom, beads of perspiration running down into the double folds of his neck. The gunman followed, pushed the man roughly face down on the bed, sending his wig flying, then sat astride his trembling prey. A series of disgusting noises heralded the evacuation of the fat man's bowels. The gunman snorted with disgust as he reached for one of the pillows and jammed it over the fat man's head. He took a deep breath, held the gun to the pillow, then fired a shot. The body beneath him juddered.

He fired another shot, then another. The body became still. An owl hooted outside as the gunman pulled back the pillow and surveyed his handiwork.

*   *   *

The hotel maid arrived promptly with his breakfast tray at eight-fifteen as usual. He opened the door dressed in his favourite dark-blue dressing gown and matching pyjamas. "Come in, my dear Doris. How are you today? Not too harassed, I hope, by all the demanding hotel guests."

Charming as he was, there was something about Mr Sidney Fleming that Doris didn't quite care for. However, as an experienced employee of one of the finest hotels in London, she gave no hint of her reservations. She laughed pleasantly as she rolled in the trolley and set it beside the little window table in the sitting room of Fleming's large and opulent suite. It was one of the most expensive rooms in the Ritz and Sidney Fleming had been occupying it permanently since just after the war began.

Doris thought of what her friend and co-worker Florrie had often said. "How many banks did he rob to get his money, smarmy little twerp." One of her other friends, an East End maintenance man, said Fleming was a 'Cutty Sark', Cockney rhyming slang for loan shark, but Doris thought he was far too smooth for that. He had numerous meetings in his suite with men who appeared to be reputable businessmen. Fleming was clearly a successful financier or company director with plenty of money to spend. She knew in her bones, however, that there was something fishy about him.

"No, sir. Everything is tickety-boo."

"Excellent, my dear. What sort of kipper do we have this morning?" Fleming, a dapper little man with long, luxuriant, Dickensian sideburns – which Doris thought he must have grown to compensate for the shortage of hair on his head – lifted the silver cloche and purred with delight. "A particularly large specimen today. Wonderful. I didn't get much to eat last night and am ravenous." He stuffed a shilling into the maid's hand and sat down to eat. As Doris went out of the door, he called out: "Give my best to His Majesty when you see him. Tell him my idea worked and he should sell now."

His Majesty was King Zog of Albania, whom Fleming thought must be doing very well from his share tips, provided he was buying and selling when Fleming told him to. The monarch and his retinue had occupied most of a floor at the Ritz since early in the war, after Mussolini had had the bad manners to run him out of his country. A perfectly pleasant, affable chap with remarkably few airs and graces. Who'd have thought it, Fleming pondered as he finished his breakfast. He, a Bermondsey boy, mingling with royalty? He had his friend Simon Arbuthnot to thank for that.

He wiped his mouth and rose. The thought of Simon reminded him he had a call to make. He dialled and waited a long time for an answer but to no avail. "Another late night," he thought to himself. He would give the boy another hour before trying again.

*   *   *

"I just need to go in and see how Sam Bridges got on yesterday." Merlin was half-dressed while Sonia was sitting up in bed nursing a hangover and the cup of tea he had made for her. Luckily for her, she had the day off.

"We haven't had a free Saturday for ages, darling."

Merlin was fiddling with the knot on his tie. He hated a badly knotted tie. "I know. I'll try to get away at lunchtime. Why don't we go and see a show tonight?"

Sonia perked up. "That would be wonderful. What show?"

"How about Max Miller at the Palladium?"

Sonia squealed with excitement. Merlin found Sonia's love of English music-hall humour endearing but surprising. Most of the very English jokes and double entendres must surely pass her by but she laughed anyway. She would be glued to Tommy Handley's *It's That Man Again* radio show every week and had almost collapsed in hysterics at the latest Crazy Gang picture, in which Bud Flanagan and his pals discovered a secret training camp for Hitler impersonators in occupied France.

She had heard Max Miller on the radio and Merlin knew it was one of her keenest wishes to see him in the flesh. Bridges had told him earlier in the week that he had been given a couple of tickets to Miller's new sell-out show. Bridges wasn't able to use them because he and his wife didn't have a babysitter and, even if they could find one, Iris was too worn out by the baby to enjoy an evening out. Merlin hadn't said yes or no to the tickets but hoped he was not too late.

"I'll need to check that Sam still has the tickets. If he does, I think the show starts at six-forty-five."

"You've got me all excited now, Frank. My headache has suddenly gone!" Sonia stood and bounced on the bed, laughing. Her nightdress slipped a little, revealing one perfectly formed breast. Sonia caught Merlin's raised eyebrow. "I could be excited in other ways, Frank, if you were to hang around for a little." She knelt and put her arms around him. Merlin hugged her back for a moment before pulling away. "Why not save that for tonight after the show, darling?" Sonia pouted back at him as he put on his jacket and moved to the door. "I understand there's a new young singer called Vera Lynn in the show. Word is she's very good."

*   *   *

Bridges was happy to confirm that the theatre tickets were still available before he told Merlin about his unsuccessful tour of

London hospitals the previous day. "To cut a long story short, sir, none of the doctors or nurses I spoke to have seen any live victims of botched abortions in their wards for a while. Plenty of dead ones but…"

"None able to tell us anything. Any new gossip?"

"No, sir."

"Very well. Let's have a think. Meanwhile, I have a little news for you. The AC has seconded…" Merlin was interrupted by the telephone. It was WPC Robinson.

"Just got a call from Notting Hill police, sir. They've got a body in a flat, just off the Portobello Road. A man. Shot dead."

"We'll meet you downstairs by the car, Constable. Come on, Sergeant. Another body for us."

On the stairs, they found Goldberg on his way up and Robinson making her way down. Merlin made the introductions quickly and invited Goldberg to come along.

It was a short Saturday-morning drive to Notting Hill and Bridges was soon pulling the car up outside a small, blue-painted terraced house within shouting distance of Portobello Market. The house was on the southern side of the street, which appeared to have survived the Blitz largely intact. The northern terrace opposite had been less fortunate – only a few houses were still standing amidst crumbling ruins and bomb craters. A group of children was having a grand old time scampering over the debris. Bridges walked over to the youngsters.

"You boys and girls better take care. Any of those walls there could collapse right on top of you." The children paid attention for a moment, then took their cue from the obvious gang leader, a lanky and grimy boy of 14 or so, who sneered at Bridges before leading the children around a corner and out of view.

"Shouldn't these areas be cordoned off, Frank?"

"They should, Bernie. No doubt the ARP wardens or someone will get round to it but there are other priorities." Goldberg nodded and stood back, allowing Merlin and his officers to precede him into the house.

The house was divided into three small flats and the crime scene was on the second floor. On the first floor, Merlin found a constable from the local station being subjected to a tirade from a large, middle-aged woman in curlers. "It's a disgrace these foreigners coming in here with their filthy habits and filthy friends. I told Albert, when that man took that room a few weeks ago, he looked like a wrong 'un. Oily skin, garlic breath and a tatty wig. Wheezing and sweating all the time. Said he was a doctor. What sort of doctor I don't know. The people who came to see him all looked like wrong 'uns to me."

The woman paused to draw on a cigarette, the ash of which she had been sprinkling liberally on everyone and everything in her near vicinity. Merlin brushed his coat and acknowledged the constable's salute with a nod. The woman looked down her nose at Merlin before squeezing past and clattering down the stairs.

"Mrs Brampton. Landlord's wife. Has the place on the ground floor. The flat you want is up on the second floor, sir. Inspector Venables is there."

"Dear old Inspector Venables, eh? Thank you, Constable." Merlin led his team up the next flight of stairs. There was an open door on the next landing and he walked through it into a small hallway. On his left was a small sitting area and ahead of him was another open door, through which he could see a familiar hairless head bobbing up and down. A dreadful stench pervaded the flat.

"Good morning, Inspector Venables. Been transferred, have we?"

Venables welcomed Merlin with a wintry smile. He was a thin and ungainly fellow, whose over-large Adam's apple bounced around his neck as if it had a life of its own. "Merlin, how are you? Yes, they moved me over from Barnes a while ago. Shortage of experienced and first-rate officers in town. Nothing much happening in Barnes. Last serious incident was the one I helped you out with last January – that poor girl in the river."

Merlin couldn't remember the inspector being particularly helpful to him in the sad case of Joan Harris, but he let that pass. "Well, good to see you again, Hector. So what do we have here?"

Merlin looked at the corpulent body lying face down on the bed. Beside the shattered head lay a bloody pillow.

"Awful smell, eh? Poor fellow lost control of his bowels at some point. Well, it's pretty straightforward." Venables paused to shake out remnants of tobacco and dribble from his pipe before starting to reload it. Merlin remembered that this process took a while and took advantage of the hiatus to look around the room. There was a small desk by the window that looked out on to the street, a chest of drawers next to it, a bedside table and, on the other side of the bed, an oak wardrobe with a large suitcase resting on top of it.

Venables finally finished his pipe operation and pointed at the pillow. "Three shots in the head, through this. Pretty efficient job I'd say. No-one in the house admits to having heard any noise. The residents have got into the habit of leaving the downstairs front door on the latch so they can get out of the house quickly during air raids. The door to this flat was not forced so we presume the victim let his murderer in.

"The landlord, who lives downstairs, came calling for rent at around nine this morning. There was no answer, of course, but he could smell the stench through the letterbox. He had his key with him, came in and found our friend. He moved the pillows but claims to have touched nothing else and nor have we.

"The doctor and the forensic team are on their way. The landlord says the gentleman arrived in April. Introduced himself as a Mr White but the landlord thinks that wasn't his real name – it didn't matter because his money was good. Says he was obviously a foreigner of some sort. The landlord's wife – that awful woman downstairs – has been shouting that he was 'a filthy frog'. I haven't done anything apart from those interviews as I've been reminded by my sergeant that we are meant to call you fellows in the event of our encountering the violent death of an alien, so…"

"You did the right thing, Hector. Thank you for your patience. Ah, here are the forensic team. We'll let them get to work, shall we?"

A tedious hour and a half later, Merlin was finally given clearance by the forensic officers to start examining the victim's personal possessions. Venables and his officers had retreated to interview the neighbours and keep an eye on the large crowd that had gathered outside the house. The doctor had been and gone and estimated the time of death at somewhere between four and seven that morning. The body now lay on its back on the bed awaiting the mortuary van.

Merlin put on his gloves and checked that the rest of the team had done the same. They began their work. The dead man's clothes of the day before had been thrown down untidily on the floor. Apart from undergarments, socks, tie, shoes and a sweat-stained white shirt, there was a double-breasted pin-striped suit, which looked like it had seen better days. In the pockets of the suit Merlin found a comb, a leather wallet, a pair of *pince-nez* glasses, a small gold ring, a sheet of headed notepaper from the Ritz hotel with a telephone number on it, four £5 notes, three £1 notes, a half-crown and a threepenny bit.

Robinson's haul from the chest of drawers was a selection of shirts, socks and underclothes, an old photograph and an advertisement for a medical agency. Bridges went through the navy overcoat, a second suit and two pairs of trousers, which he and Merlin found in the wardrobe along with a pair of braces and two pairs of black shoes. He found more loose change, a railway ticket, the stub of a cinema ticket and an almost empty packet of Gitanes cigarettes.

When Merlin was satisfied that they had got everything out of the wardrobe, Goldberg lifted down the suitcase and put it on the floor. It jangled as he did so. The suitcase was locked but Goldberg easily picked its lock with a small pen-knife. It opened to reveal a black bag that contained a selection of medical and surgical instruments, pill boxes and medicine bottles.

Merlin looked back at the body on the bed and thought of the hotel clerk's description of the navy-coated, fat, bearded, foreign visitor to Room 14. He thought of the Gitanes cigarette stub found in the room and of the downstairs neighbour's description of the man as a 'filthy frog'.

"You know, Sergeant, I think fate has made recompense for your wasted legwork yesterday. I believe we have found our abortionist."

*   *   *

Philip Arbuthnot's eyes slowly cracked open. A thin ray of sunlight had forced its way through a small gap in the bedroom curtains and was illuminating the glass of water on his bedside table. He stretched out his arms and legs and realised that he was not alone. Which one was it? The working of his brain was inhibited by the fierce thudding in his head. He levered himself up and examined the back of his companion's head. Brunette. A short perm. Janey. He reached out and his hand encountered a slightly over-plump buttock. Definitely Janey. She muttered an endearment and reached out a hand in return, finding the inside of his leg to stroke. Arbuthnot twisted around to look at the clock on his bedside table. Past noon already. He remembered the telegram with a sudden jolt. His father. There were things to do. He removed Janey's wandering hand.

"Sorry, darling. Time to get up." He slid out of bed, went into the bathroom and ran himself a bath. It was on hungover mornings like this that he missed Clarke, his valet, who had signed up for service shortly after his father and who was now somewhere in north Africa. He'd decided not to replace Clarke because he had been facing his father's wrath about dropping out of Cambridge and the threatened withdrawal of his allowance. Although that had all blown over, he'd kept the status quo. As he lay back soaking in the bath, Arbuthnot again found it difficult to suppress the positive feelings about his father's death. He was free! He was rich! He could do what he liked. He could have a valet, a butler, a maid or two – pretty, of course – a driver, a fancy new car. Arbuthnot made a full list in his mind of the acquisitions he could make and the order in which he would make them. He was just evaluating the pros and cons of purchasing a boat at a time when the war precluded cruising down to the Riviera, when a naked Janey appeared, gave him a sly grin, then joined him in the bath. "Scrub my back please, Philip."

An hour later, Arbuthnot was dressed, in his study and waiting for Janey to appear. He had just telephoned Wheeler's of St James's to book a table for a late lunch. A few glasses of chablis would soon clear his thick head. "Hurry up, darling. I've booked a table for one-forty-five." There was a muffled reply from the bedroom. Arbuthnot picked up the telephone lead and toyed with it. There were people he should tell about his father's death. There were his grandmother and aunt up in Northampton. There was Tomlinson, of course. And his father's man of business, his *aide-de-camp* as he liked to call him, Sidney Fleming. A rather creepy individual, Philip had always thought, but his father had regarded him as invaluable.

As he lifted the receiver his companion appeared, looking rather striking in a bright blue outfit she'd left in the flat on a previous visit. He decided to postpone the sad task of informing family and friends of his father's passing. What would another day matter, after all? It wasn't as if there was a funeral to organise.

"Ready, for the fray, Janey darling? I could murder half a dozen oysters and some cold lobster."

*   *   *

Merlin was at his office window, watching a couple of river barges slowly making their way up the river against the current. The German bombers were still holding off. No raids at all, in London at least, since the middle of May. The Blitz was still going on, however, elsewhere in Britain. In the past week, bombs had fallen on Liverpool, Manchester and Hull among others.

Merlin wondered how his friend Jack Stewart was getting on. A senior officer in the Auxiliary Fire Service, Stewart had been out on the streets of London pretty much every night of the Blitz, from its early days in September 1940 until its recent tailing off. At the end of May he had been transferred north to share the benefit of his experience with the AFS in Liverpool and Manchester and to take overall command of several units. Merlin and Stewart had enjoyed a lively farewell night in the Surprise pub in Chelsea, their favourite local. Stewart had only been gone a couple of weeks but already Merlin missed him. He had been a rock when Merlin had lost his wife. Stewart was a working-class Scot with the intelligence and learning of an Oxbridge don. He always provided useful insight into Merlin's cases. Merlin wondered what he'd make of the latest two.

He went back to his desk, where Bridges and Goldberg were finishing off the tray of sandwiches Robinson had picked up at Tony's Café. She had skipped lunch herself, claiming to have no appetite. Not so surprising, Merlin had thought, as she was still a novice with dead bodies. She had gone to find out who now represented the French community in London so inquiries could be made about Mr White. They had found no evidence of his real identity in the flat.

Merlin had grabbed a couple of the sandwiches but hadn't got round to eating them yet. Spam was a new type of American processed meat that had just made its appearance in wartime London. It had been the advertised special at Tony's and Robinson had thought her colleagues might like to try it. Bridges and Goldberg – the latter was presumably already familiar with the product – had bolted theirs down but the luncheon meat looked distinctly unappetising to Merlin. He moved his plate to one side. Mumbling something about eating it later, he popped a Fisherman's Friend into his mouth and sipped at the now lukewarm cup of tea Bridges had made for him 10 minutes earlier.

"Venables just left a message downstairs with Sergeant Reeves to say he'd got nowhere with the neighbours. No-one saw anything. Not so surprising with an intruder that early in the morning but disappointing nevertheless. So let's now see what we have from the flat. Oh, and when will we be getting the fingerprint report on these items and on the rooms, Sergeant?"

"Monday, sir."

"Good. All right, put it all on the desk." Bridges emptied out the cardboard box into which he'd put everything. Merlin set the notes and coins to one side, then started sifting the rest.

"One comb, a few strands of hair thereon that appear to match the sparse real hair of the deceased. One phone number on Ritz notepaper. One brown wallet, which I shall now empty." He did so. "Two £5 notes and a 10-franc note in this small zipped side pocket." He put the money together with the rest. "A used train ticket." Merlin put on his reading glasses. "The destination is not clear – looks like there's a B or an L – can't make out the rest as it's not all there and what remains is wet and the ink has blurred. And here's another ticket, this time for a cinema show somewhere."

Goldberg looked at it closely. "It doesn't say which movie."

"No, tickets here don't, just the price, so I doubt it's going to help us much. What else have we? A plain gold band ring.

Some old-fashioned spectacles. Ah, yes, an old photograph. Hidden under our victim's underwear. Two young men, one dark, one fairer, the latter wearing some type of uniform. And two young ladies. The sun is shining and they appear to be standing in front of a pleasant country house." Merlin turned the photograph around for Bridges and Goldberg.

"Don't recognise the uniform, sir. I used to collect cards of military uniforms when I was a nipper but, no, don't know that one."

"There's a studio mark on the back – Studio Abel, Vichy. Not much use to us. It's not as if we can pop over to France on the boat train and find Mr Abel, is it?"

"We could show it to the French authorities here."

"We could, Sergeant. So we could."

"How about this, Frank?" Goldberg picked up the newspaper advertisement cutting that had been found in the dead Frenchman's chest of drawers.

"Now there, Detective, you have something that might be helpful. 'Cromwell Medical Agency, 213 Putney High Street. Medical vacancies and placement. Telephone Putney 9476'. Of all these items, this seems the easiest to follow up at the outset. We'll go through the other items again later. Sergeant, I believe a trip to balmy Putney awaits."

"It might be closed on a Saturday, sir."

"Still worth a shot, don't you think?"

"Yes, sir."

"Can I go too, Frank?"

"Of course, Bernie. I hope you don't mind but I'm going to leave it to you two. I made a promise for tonight that I have to keep."

*   *   *

Buckinghamshire

They were driving at the head of a convoy of four cars. The prime minister was never the earliest of risers and a meeting with newspaper editors had started late and gone on longer than anticipated so they had not got under way until the late afternoon. The cars had made their way out of west London, carefully edging around several nasty bomb craters near Shepherd's Bush, and were now almost halfway to their Oxfordshire destination. Instead of furiously dictating memos to his secretaries, as was his wont, Sir Winston Churchill had resolved to relax on this journey.

"When will we be there?" rumbled the distinctive voice from the back of the car.

"In about 50 minutes I should think, sir," replied the driver. "We'll be on the outskirts of Oxford in about 20."

Several wisps of cigar smoke undulated their way through the car. "Oh, Winston. Can't you leave off the cigar for just a while? We'll choke to death any minute."

Contritely, the PM stubbed out the seven-inch Romeo y Julieta in the ashtray positioned between him and his wife.

"Well done, Winston."

Moments later, he withdrew a green flask from inside his jacket and took a swig. "Drop of whisky, my dear?"

He took the sullen glare he received from his wife as a no and helped himself to another mouthful. Churchill stared out at the still sodden countryside and sighed. Crete had been a complete disaster. It wasn't poor Bernard Freyberg's fault. The New Zealander was a brilliant and brave soldier. He was a VC after all. His superiors had let him down. Bad tactics, bad strategy, poor leadership. Increasingly he was coming to the view that Wavell was not up to it.

Things weren't going particularly well in north Africa, either. After the successes earlier in the year against the Italians, things

seemed to have got bogged down in Libya. Having captured
Tobruk from the Italians once, the port was now being besieged
by Rommel and his *Afrika Korps*. Churchill had encouraged Wavell
and the others to be bold again but attempts at relief of Tobruk had
been ineffective. If things went the Germans' way in Libya, after the
calamities of Greece and Crete, it would be a huge hammer-blow
to the war effort. He leaned back in his seat and watched the damp
green countryside fly by. The cogs of his wonderfully creative and
flexible brain whirred. The minutes passed.

"Auchinleck."

"What, Winston?"

"General Claude Auchinleck. He might be the man."

"The man for what, dear?"

"For the Middle East Command, of course. I think Archie
Wavell is a busted flush. He's got one more chance with this
Operation Battleaxe and if that fails, well… Alan Brooke won't like
it, of course. Nor will most of the others but it'll have to be done."

Clementine Churchill put down the volume of Trollope she
was reading and gave her husband her full attention. "Remind
me again, Winston, what is Operation Battleaxe?"

"Another attempt to relieve Tobruk. Planned for a week or
so's time."

"I like Archie."

"I like him, too, but that's not the point. We need a fresh mind.
Auchinleck could be the man."

The car stopped at a traffic light. "Where the hell are we now,
Jock?"

"Kidlington, sir. Won't be long now."

They were headed for Ditchley Park, a beautiful country
estate belonging to the wealthy Anglo-American MP Ronald
Tree and his charming wife, Nancy. For Churchill, Ditchley Park
had become an attractive alternative weekend home to his own
estate at Chartwell and the PM's official residence at Chequers.

The security forces were unhappy about Chartwell's location to the south of London, where its exposed position in open country made it highly visible to German bombers returning from raids on the capital. There were other, similar, concerns about Chequers – especially, as Churchill put it, "When the moon is high."

Ronald Tree was happy to make Ditchley available to Churchill whenever he liked. The prime minister knew the place from before the war and had become increasingly fond of it. Tree had always made a point of peopling it with interesting and entertaining figures from the worlds of politics, diplomacy, society and the arts.

"Do we know who's going to be there this weekend, darling?"

"Brendan, no doubt, Winston. Clarissa said she thought she and Anthony would be able to get away. Mr Winant and others from the American Embassy, perhaps."

"What about that actor chap, Niven? He's a very entertaining fellow. A patriotic and brave man, too, to give up his Hollywood career and join the forces."

"As he should have, dear."

"Of course. Of course. As he should have, but there are plenty of British actors or artists staying in America and avoiding the war. Who was it we were talking about the other night? Oh yes, Wystan Auden. A fine poet but a shit of a man."

"Winston, please."

Churchill finished the remains of his flask and closed his eyes for a moment. Why had the Germans halted the Blitz? Had they just realised the pointlessness of it all – that the British people would never be ground down by the bombs, however many the *Luftwaffe* threw at them. No, the real story might be Russia. There was increasing intelligence of German military build-up and movements on the eastern borders of the Reich. Would Hitler really be mad enough to turn his forces against the Russian Bear? Of course, it would only serve Stalin right – after his craven treaty agreement with Germany the year before – if Hitler turned against him like the treacherous dog he was. A German attack on Russia would explain the suspension of the London Blitz – Hitler would need all the forces on land, sea and air he could muster. If this happened, how would the Russians fare against the Nazi *blitzkrieg*? There were many senior British officers in the general staff who doubted whether the Russians would be able to hold out for long. And what then?

Churchill was jolted out of these dark thoughts by the car's arrival at their destination. The gates opened and the convoy made its way up the elegant driveway. On his right Churchill saw the beautiful lake and the immaculate lawns that swept down from the delightful Georgian mansion. The estate's creator, the second Earl of Lichfield, and his architect, James Gibb, had done an excellent job.

The lead car pulled up to the entrance and the prime minister shuffled his ample posterior along the car seat to follow his wife out of the vehicle. He raised his hat as he greeted the welcoming party. "Ronald, my dear fellow, and Nancy. Thank you so much for deciding to put up with me and my gang yet again. Wonderful to be here. In the usual rooms are we? Any interesting company?"

*   *   *

London

Rougemont pulled up outside the general's Carlton Gardens headquarters in a taxi. When he had made the appointment over the telephone earlier in the day, Lieutenant Beaulieu had initially been cold and abrupt. After the captain had explained that he was a member of the intelligence and security committee in Dorset Square and observed, furthermore, that he was the lieutenant's superior, Beaulieu had thawed a little and agreed to meet.

Rougemont greeted the officer on duty at the reception desk. Around the walls hung paintings of French rural scenes, most of which the captain, a keen art lover, considered dull and undistinguished. From a large photograph over a doorway to the right, a serious-looking uniformed man with a small moustache stared down. The captain acknowledged the general with a tip of his hat.

The officer at the desk made a call and moments later a short young man in lieutenant's uniform appeared. "Captain Rougemont?" Beaulieu was a Breton, like Rougemont, and his wavy red hair bore more obvious witness to his Celtic ancestry than did Rougemont's mousy mop. Like the general, he affected a neat little moustache.

The men shook hands. "Pleased to make your acquaintance, Lieutenant. I am surprised we have not met before."

"Forgive me, sir, but I have had little opportunity to socialise. I have hardly left this building since my arrival. The general has plunged me into a maelstrom of work. With all that is happening in the Middle East, not to mention the machinations of the Vichy government in France and north Africa…" Beaulieu smiled regretfully before turning to lead Rougemont down a long corridor. At the end, the two men entered a small but airy room overlooking a neatly manicured garden.

"A pleasant office you have, Lieutenant."

Beaulieu gave a sniff of indifference. "It is convenient for the general's office, which is over there." He pointed over the corridor.

"I know, Lieutenant, I have had occasion to visit the general myself once or twice."

Beaulieu gave the captain a condescending smile. "Of course you have." The two men seated themselves on either side of Beaulieu's neatly ordered desk. "I would offer you some refreshment but the kitchen is apparently understaffed today."

"No matter, Lieutenant. I require nothing at the moment. The main point of my visit is to invite you to join Commandant Angers and myself tonight for drinks and perhaps some dinner. We had the Ritz in mind. The commandant and I like to make a point of getting to know our new recruits."

"I have been here several months, Captain."

"Of course you have. It has been an error on our part to have left things so long."

Beaulieu smiled then took a small pair of scissors out of his top pocket. He glanced in the wall mirror to his left and snipped a few hairs from his moustache. Rougemont looked on in amusement. "Forgive me, Captain. I cannot bear personal untidiness for a second. Anyway, thank you. Yes, I would be delighted to join you and the Commandant tonight. I have heard some of the officers talking about him – a boulevardier of the first rank, I understand. I have not managed to enjoy any London nightlife since getting here. I shall do my best to clear this desk in the few hours remaining so I can properly relax and enjoy myself tonight. Logically, the workload should be a little easier with the general travelling but it doesn't seem to be so."

"Where is he today?"

Beaulieu straightened. "Sir, you should know better than to ask me that."

"Goodness, Lieutenant. You must realise that I am fully aware that he is in the Middle East. I was just wondering in exactly which town, but no matter. I would not wish you to feel compromised in any way."

Beaulieu acknowledged the captain's sensitivity with the flick of an eyebrow.

"May I ask, Lieutenant, how you came to make your journey here earlier in the year? Assuming, of course, that information is not also confidential."

Beaulieu was oblivious to Rougemont's sarcasm. "It is no secret. I was at Admiral Darlan's side for several months after the capitulation. I was very close to him. He is a man torn, as are many of our countrymen. On the one hand there are the pragmatists – 'We are beaten, we cannot fight the Germans, we must reach the best compromise we can'. On the other there are, shall we call them the romantics? They devote themselves to what they see as the glory of France, the undying fire of our patriotism that dictates defiance to the last.

"We debated these things many times. I pride myself that the admiral took such a keen interest in me. Some called me his protégé. In any event, over the months his views hardened into that of a pragmatist while I…" he smiled and smoothed his moustache, "I could not help but come down on the romantic side. Clearly, at some point I would have to commit myself to the cause.

"Thus I needed a route out. In January I was in Tangier with the admiral. I made contact with some other naval officers, whom I had come to know were of a similar mind. We found a fishing boat and some amenable fishermen, for the right price of course, and made our way to Gibraltar on a clear and calm night and thence, via Lisbon, to London."

"Bravo, Lieutenant. A route similar to the ones many of us took. And was the admiral aware of your plan?"

"Certainly not. Had he been, I am sure he would have tried to stop me." Beaulieu looked in the direction of de Gaulle's office. "And, of course, as you know, the general here was aware of my abilities and was delighted to receive me into an important position by his side."

Rougemont nodded. "Thank you, Lieutenant. Well, I'll let you get on." As he got to his feet, he reflected it was little wonder this preening man had acquired enemies during his short time in England. The night ahead looked like being a long one. "Shall we say seven-thirty then, Lieutenant? At the Ritz Rivoli Bar. That's the upstairs one. The downstairs bar is probably a little rough-and-ready for a man of your obvious sensibilities."

"As you wish, Captain. I'll be there."

"I look forward to it." As Rougemont walked down the corridor, he could hear the sound of clipping scissors.

*   *   *

"You are later than I expected, Frank. I was getting worried."

"Sorry, darling. Something came up."

"Something is always coming up in your stupid job." Sonia seldom lost her temper but today her patience had been tried. It was gone five o'clock and they would have to hurry to make it to the Palladium in time for the opening curtain.

"I know, dear. What can I do?" A glimmer of a smile appeared on Sonia's face and she allowed herself to be pecked on the cheek.

Merlin had seen Bridges and Goldberg off on their trip to Putney and had been on his way home when he bumped into the AC on the main staircase of Scotland Yard. Gatehouse usually spent his weekends out of London, but was in town to take his wife to a piano recital at the Wigmore Hall. He'd left the tickets at the Yard, hence his visit. Merlin, having naturally told the AC about the murder in Notting Hill, was asked to attend the AC in his office to provide more detail. Gatehouse asked a lot of questions and Merlin was there for some time. As he was finally leaving, the AC had given him the bad news that Tommy Cole's return from Portsmouth was to be delayed for a fortnight or more. Cole was part of a team of officers investigating a naval espionage case and the local commanding officer refused to release him. Merlin had been pleased to learn that Cole was so prized in Portsmouth but this did little to dispel his frustration.

Sonia and Merlin found a taxi straightaway in Sloane Square but a burst water main on Oxford Street delayed their journey and they only made their seats with seconds to spare. Max Miller's latest show was called *Apple Sauce*. Merlin managed a quick flick through the theatre programme before the lights went down. The cover pictured Miller, the best-known comedian of the day, sporting his trademark Cheeky Chappie outfit and accompanied by a high-kicking chorus line. 'A laughter Blitz showered with stars' was promised. Other acts included Jack Stanford, the Dolinoffs, the Raya Sisters and Florence Desmond.

Sonia, tense with excitement, gripped Merlin's hand as the curtain rose. First up were the 24 Saucelets, a group of scantily-clad dancing girls. Then, to rapturous applause, Miller appeared with his stooges in a knockabout sketch about a television set. Tears of laughter rolled down Sonia's cheeks. The acts came and went. Vera Lynn appeared just before the interval and the pretty young singer immediately had the audience in the palm of her hand.

Merlin bought ice-creams during the interval and Sonia giggled as a large chunk of his ended in his lap. There was time to check the restaurant advertisements in the programme. The formal Hungaria restaurant in Lower Regent Street was promoted as 'The safe restaurant. Bomb proof – splinter proof – blast proof – gas proof and boredom proof. We care for your safety as well as your pleasure'. Or there was Oddenino's: 'Dancing in the restaurant from 8pm below 10 reinforced concrete floors to Tommy Rogan's Orchestra. Ample shelter accommodation'. Merlin's eyes finally fell on the Parisian skyline motif of the Montparnasse in Piccadilly Circus, which offered a cabaret as well as dancing and fine food. It had been a favourite haunt of his and Alice's. They had danced there in 1938. Their last dance. Somehow he felt Alice would approve of his stepping out again there with Sonia.

Merlin turned to admire Sonia's face, which was alive with anticipation. The house lights dimmed. The orchestra struck up. Work, as always, posed its many problems but in his personal life, he realised, Merlin was as happy as he had been for a long time.

CHAPTER 4

Sunday 8 June

Northamptonshire

As soon as Philip Arbuthnot woke, he knew he couldn't delay telling his aunt any longer. He got up and immediately sent two telegrams, one containing news of his father's death and a second warning of his impending arrival at around noon. For a moment, he thought of taking Janey or Suzanne with him but quickly discarded the idea. The open-top Morgan sports car was brought around from the garage by a porter and Arbuthnot was on the road by nine-thirty.

The journey usually took him two and a half hours. The rain held off and the sun managed a few brief appearances. The traffic was light and he made good time, pulling into the sweeping driveway of Sackville Hall just before noon. There was no-one about as he parked the car near the front door of the small, perfectly proportioned Queen Anne building that had been in his mother's family for more than 200 years. He was just about to lift the ancient bronze knocker when the door was opened abruptly to reveal Lucinda Cavendish, née Arbuthnot, his father's beloved only sister. "I thought I heard your noisy car. Come in, Philip. I got your telegrams. How are you coping, my dear boy?"

Lucinda Cavendish was a willowy woman with short, dark-brown, wavy hair, pale-blue eyes, a roman nose and a thin-lipped mouth. Her brother had often described her as a nicer-looking version of his friend, the novelist Virginia Woolf. Philip knew Woolf had been found drowned in a river in Sussex quite recently. He could never imagine his aunt coming to such an end. In terms of willpower and forcefulness of nature, she was the equal of her brother, Simon. Her motto was the same as the one he had heard attributed to Churchill: 'KBO – keep buggering on!' How Philip's father had been friends with Woolf was a mystery to his son, for a less literary man would have been hard to find.

"Well, you know, Aunt. Bit of a shock, of course."

"Not that much of a shock, was it, dear? We know things weren't going well in Crete. It's a blessing at least that he wasn't taken prisoner as I am sure that would have driven him mad." His aunt didn't look as if she had shed any tears that morning, although she had been very close to her brother. They had not had easy childhoods and had grown up to be tough. Recent events had further hardened Lucinda to adversity – the deaths in quick succession of her husband and her son a few years previously had been terrible blows. Her mother's stroke on the day war was declared was a further sad burden. And now, this, the loss of her brother.

"How is Grandma?"

"The same as usual. Doesn't know who or where she is most of the time. I told her about Simon but she stared at me blankly. I look at her and think that somewhere inside that little head of hers a part of her brain must be working but…" His aunt shrugged and led him into the large drawing room at the rear of the house. "I'll tell you one thing that is working though – her appetite! She's hungry all the time and eats like a horse. Not a pretty sight, I can tell you. You'll see for yourself at lunchtime."

They sat down together on an amply cushioned and intricately patterned settee, which faced a brightly blooming walled garden. A fire was burning. A maid appeared and was instructed to open the French windows. "It's too warm in here. Let us have a bit of air, Dawson. Sherry, Philip?" He nodded, another peremptory command was given and the maid scurried away.

"Is there a body?"

"I don't know. I suppose so."

"What I mean, Philip, is did the army manage to retrieve his body or is it behind enemy lines?"

"I don't know. I got a second telegram from the War Office yesterday but it added little to the first. 'We have received firm confirmation that your father, Captain Simon Arbuthnot, was killed in action in Crete in the last two days of the operation last month.'"

The sherries arrived on a silver tray. "Leave the decanter please, Dawson." A pleasant breeze from outside was now freshening the room.

"I presume that means his death was witnessed by a fellow officer."

"Or rank-and-file soldier."

"It would be good to find out the identity of that officer or soldier."

"Yes, Aunt."

"Meanwhile, it seems that we won't have a funeral to organise for now."

Philip shrugged as he finished his sherry. His aunt reached over to top up his glass. "We still have various legalities to deal with – and the business, of course. You've informed Tomlinson?"

"I, er…"

"Oh, Philip, that was the first thing you should have done."

"You know, it was the weekend. Thought it could wait until Monday."

Lucinda looked at her nephew and sighed. If only it was her beloved son, Robbie, who was sitting in Philip's place now. There was no doubt that Philip had a good brain but he was a dilettante. She doubted he had the judgment and drive to run his father's business empire. Robbie certainly had but he was sleeping forever now in the plot beside his father's in the village churchyard. "You will call him before we go in to lunch."

"What about Fleming?"

"Ask Tomlinson to tell that little weasel. He should know." She detested Fleming but Lucinda understood that men of his ilk had their uses and she had long accepted his elevated position in the scheme of things.

"Very well, Aunt."

"Oh my silly, darling brother." Lucinda set down her sherry glass and picked up a framed photograph of Simon Arbuthnot from a table next to her. "Such a good-looking boy. He must have been in his mid-20s here. Perhaps a year or two before you were born. If I remember correctly, this was taken before he went off to watch the tennis championships at Wimbledon. Here he is, decked out in his summer finery – boater, blazer, flannels. Now who was it he saw in the men's finals that year? He and I played a lot of tennis together, did you know that?"

"Yes, Aunt."

"I was quite good at the game, if I say so myself. Now who won it that year? He asked me to go with him but I had another engagement with Alfred." Alfred was Alfred Cavendish, her late husband, who had been an eminent barrister at the time of his sudden death in 1938. "Was it that Yank, Tilden – Bill Tilden – and an Australian, Patterson? Or was there a South African involved? The year after the war, I think it was '19 or '20. He had a lovely time with his friend Franzi. Some people were a little scandalised, of course."

"Scandalised?"

"Franzi was German. People felt it was a little off to be socialising with Germans so soon after the war."

"I think I heard my father and Fleming talking about Franzi once. Wasn't he…?"

Lucinda put the photograph back in its place and rose abruptly. "Enough of the past. We've enough to worry about with the present. Do you know we only just avoided having a platoon or a brigade, or whatever the appropriate military word is, of soldiers billeted on us? I had to…" A loud gong sounded from the hallway. "There's the luncheon bell. Go and make those phone calls while I find out where Mother is. It's roast pork, your favourite!"

CHAPTER 5

Monday 9 June

London

"Morning, everyone." Merlin surveyed the team that had gathered in his office at nine o'clock. Bridges looked worn out. Another baby-disturbed night, Merlin surmised. In contrast, Goldberg seemed to be bursting with vitality and raring to go while Robinson was also a picture of health, her cheeks pink, her eyes sparkling and her short strawberry-blonde hair glossy and immaculate. Merlin wondered for a second what would happen when Cole returned. Obviously the constable's new barrister friend, Rutherford, was a much better fit for her socially but Merlin felt a little for Cole. Office romances were never a good idea, especially in the police force, but the two youngsters had made an intriguing couple. Merlin tidied the papers on his desk and cleared his throat.

"To business, then. Two different cases, connected through Mr White. Five people involved. None yet identified. Let's go down the list:

"One – an unidentified woman, killed in a botched abortion, estimated age early 20s. Short, black hair, pretty face, slim, medium height. No person vaguely fitting her description yet reported missing in Greater London. WPC Robinson to contact forces outside London to see if there's a match. No moles, scars or other distinguishing physical features and no items of interest on the body or in her clothing so far as I am yet aware. Double-check on that with the medics please, Constable.

"Two – 'Mr White'. A short, fat, bearded, wig-wearing, Gitanes-smoking gentleman, reported to be French by one witness, shot in the head three times. Among his possessions a bag full of medical instruments. The appearance of the man closely matches the hotel clerks' description of our young lady's first visitor and this, when taken with the medical suitcase, is pretty incontrovertible evidence that this man is our abortionist. Such French authorities as exist in London have not yet been able to respond to Robinson's requests for assistance in identifying the man. We have work to do there. Sergeant Bridges and Detective Goldberg visited the Putney medical agency's office on Saturday but it was closed. Enquiries of neighbours revealed that the agency proprietor is thought to be French or Belgian. A repeat visit to the office will be made today. We also have that telephone number on Ritz notepaper to check."

"Not forgetting the cinema and railway tickets, sir."

"Not forgetting those items, Sergeant, no. Nor the old photograph.

"Three – the man who accompanied the young lady to the hotel, not clearly seen by the hotel receptionist but described not very helpfully as being of average height and wearing a trilby and a mac with the collar up. Last seen leaving the hotel soon after the arrival of the second male visitor.

"Four, the second male visitor, this one tall and dark-haired, wearing a grey duffel coat. Again mostly invisible to the clerks, apart from Noakes thinking he might have been a foreigner and that there was something else odd about him, which he can't remember."

"And number five, sir?"

"Number five, Sergeant, is the murderer of Mr White, who was professional enough to ensure he was unseen and unheard and left little evidence except for the bullet casing we found. When forensics get back to us later we should at least know what gun he used."

Goldberg raised a hand. "I have a question, Chief Inspector."

"Fire away, Detective."

"I was just wondering why your department was involved in investigating a back-street abortion in the first place? I understand your involvement now the case seems to be linked with another murder. But back in New York, an abortion gone wrong wouldn't normally command the attention of the homicide team."

"That's a fair question, Detective. Of course, we don't call ourselves 'the homicide team' but we are required to investigate the most serious crimes committed in the metropolitan area. A botched abortion would not normally be so categorised. Recently, however, there has been an epidemic of unlawful abortions. The authorities blame the war. With the Blitz, London is obviously a dangerous place and death could be round the corner at any moment. By the same token, military men on leave in town may shortly be returning to the dangers of the battlefield. It is clear that social behaviour has become freer in these circumstances, with one of the consequences being a large rise in unwanted pregnancies. And so London has become something of a boomtown for abortionists. My superiors have resolved to make this problem a matter of high priority. Accordingly, for the present, we are to investigate any such incidents."

"I understand, Frank. Sorry if the question was stupid."

"Not at all, Bernie." Merlin leaned back in his chair. "So, let's run over the job allocations for today. Constable, you carry on searching for the identity of the abortion victim. Also, can you please look into the Ritz notepaper telephone number. Bridges, you go out to Putney again. The office must be open on a Monday. Before you go, call forensics to find out where we are on the bullets. I am going to visit the Free French army headquarters, as that seems the closest thing there is to a French embassy in London, and I'd be grateful if you would accompany me, Detective Goldberg."

"A pleasure, Chief Inspector."

"You have the address, Constable?"

"The first I got was One Dorset Square. There is also another in Carlton Gardens. I'm not sure why there are two."

"We'll go to Dorset Square. No doubt we'll find out there."

*   *   *

Edgar Powell fell back into his seat with a gasp of relief. This train journey was the last leg of a very tedious three-day trip from Cairo. On the first leg, a rattling old RAF cargo plane had carried him and his fellow passengers to Khartoum. Then another cargo plane had taken him to Lagos in Nigeria. From there, a civilian flying boat had flown him via Sierra Leone, Gambia and the Canary Islands to Lisbon, where he had waited several hours before getting on a BOAC flight back to Britain. Disembarking exhausted that Sunday morning at Southampton airport, he was in desperate need of a bath and 12 hours' sleep. A taxi had driven him to the railway station, where he had had to wait an hour for the next London train.

Luckily he'd been able to find a seat in an empty first-class compartment. As the train slowly chugged out of the station, he lifted his legs on to the seat across from him. He was thirsty and remembered that he had a bottle of beer from the plane in his kitbag. Then he realised he didn't have a bottle-opener and the ticket inspector who appeared was not particularly helpful in getting one from the buffet. Powell was too tired to walk down the train, gave up on the beer and closed his eyes.

In Cairo, Powell had just had time to get a cable off to his wife to forewarn her of his arrival. According to the last letters that had got through to him, Celia was spending most of the time with her parents in the country so there was a good chance she had not been at the flat to receive it. They had last been together at Christmas before he shipped out to Greece. Unfortunately, they had parted on an argument. Her letters since had been friendly but distant. He wondered whether their reunion would be happy or uncomfortable. Powell chided himself for his anxieties. It would be happy, of course. He resolved to be optimistic. He was back home in England, he had in prospect a few days of leave with a beautiful woman – and he was alive! He would treat Celia to a nice dinner out if she were in town. Some good food, some good wine, perhaps some lovemaking. Then tomorrow, after a long lie-in, he would stroll over to Scotland Yard and consult his old friend Frank about that letter. The rhythmic motion of the train had its inevitable effect and he began to doze.

*   *   *

"I'm so dreadfully sorry, my boy."

Philip Arbuthnot, toying with his blue silk tie and not looking particularly grief-stricken, sat across the desk from Tomlinson. He shrugged his shoulders. "Sorry I'm late again. Went up to Sackville Hall to see my aunt and grandmother."

"No need to apologise, Philip. Of course you had to go and see your family. How did your grandmother take it?"

"She's not very well, as you know. Didn't really seem to take it in."

"I've not seen her since her stroke. Poor lady. If I know your aunt, though, I bet she took it like a brick. Always been a very plucky lady." Tomlinson leaned forward to press a button on his telephone. His pretty secretary appeared, casting a sweetly sympathetic look at Arbuthnot. "Sylvia, do you think you could find Mr Arbuthnot a black tie. I think you might find…"

"I know where to find your spare ties, sir. There are a couple of black ones." Sylvia departed with a swish of her behind. "I think you ought to suit up for appearance's sake, Philip. That suit will do for today but I'd wear a darker one tomorrow, if I were you. Meanwhile, the tie is a must."

Arbuthnot found Tomlinson's suggestion presumptuous but he didn't show his irritation, remembering that he would need to be on good terms with his father's solicitors while his succession to the Arbuthnot fortune was being formalised. "Very good, sir."

Tomlinson cleared his throat. "The firm naturally holds your father's last will and testament and most of the key papers relating to his business interests. Whatever we don't hold should be in the hands of Mr Sidney Fleming or your father's Argentinian partner, Alexander Pulos. If other papers are held elsewhere, I am not aware of them."

Tomlinson paused to remove two cigarettes from a silver box on his desk, one of which he offered to Arbuthnot. The two men lit up. "Philip, I'm not sure how much of his business affairs your father discussed with you?" Tomlinson disappeared momentarily behind a cloud of blue smoke.

"Very little." The young man's face clouded over. "It was a major bone of contention between us. I asked him many times to put me more in the picture. When he went off to fight, it seemed even more obvious that he should do so but he absolutely refused. My father just said: 'If I pop off, Philip, Mr Tomlinson will be able to inform you.' If I ever walked in on him chatting to Fleming or any of his other executives, he would clam up immediately and tell me to get lost."

Tomlinson tapped some cigarette ash into the ashtray and gave Arbuthnot an understanding look. "Your father was a very secretive man, Philip. He preferred to compartmentalise things so that his advisers and executives only knew parts of the picture, while he alone knew the whole. That was how I saw it, at least.

Perhaps his closest colleagues, Fleming and Pulos, were privy to the whole picture but I'd be surprised. In any event, the three of us should be able to piece everything together for you as you take the helm. Assuming, of course, that remained your father's testamentary intent."

A flash of concern passed over Arbuthnot's face. "What do you mean by 'assuming that was his testamentary intent'? Who else would inherit and take over the business? You drafted the will, didn't you?"

"Calm yourself please, Philip, calm yourself. I was being a little too lawyerly in my observations. Yes, our firm drafted the will and, yes, you are his heir. I was only reflecting my usual professional caution in case there might be some codicil of which I am not aware."

"Codicil? What codicil?" Despite his best efforts, Arbuthnot's impatience with Tomlinson was beginning to show.

"Philip, please, I am not aware of any codicil. Your father did like to tinker with his will every so often, but usually this was in matters such as how much to leave his chauffeur and the like. I am sorry if my poor choice of words alarmed you."

Arbuthnot took a couple of long draws on his cigarette and regained his equilibrium. Sylvia reappeared with a black tie, which he substituted uncomplainingly for his blue one.

Tomlinson sent Sylvia away again and stubbed out his cigarette. "And so, my dear boy, I shall speak this morning to Sidney Fleming and arrange a meeting so we can pool our knowledge of your father's affairs. Then I'll wire Mr Pulos in the Argentine."

"Can't we arrange a meeting of all the parties? A meeting that I can attend?"

"I think it would be easier at first if I attempt to collate the information for you. And of course, Mr Pulos is rather a long way away and it is not exactly easy or straightforward to travel from South America to Britain at the moment."

"He'll probably have to come here at some point or I'll need to go there, don't you think?"

Tomlinson frowned. "Just let me speak to Fleming. I'll see what he has to tell me, then I'll report back."

Arbuthnot got to his feet. "Just remember, sir. I'm not a little boy."

*   *   *

The Cromwell Medical Recruitment office was at the top of a steep flight of rickety stairs on the second floor of one of the terraced properties facing the Church of St Mary the Virgin in Putney. Putney Bridge and the River Thames were a stone's throw away. At street level, there was a sparsely stocked electrical goods shop through which Bridges had to walk to reach the stairs. By the time he got to the top, the sergeant was a little out of breath. Before the war he'd been an active sportsman and had prided himself on his fitness. Bridges was a thinner man now but not a fitter one. He was grateful to see that the office door was open and that his climb had not been in vain. He knocked.

"Come in." The voice belonged to a dumpy little woman with badly dyed blonde hair. Bridges flashed a warrant card and introduced himself. The woman gave him an anxious look before scurrying through the door behind her. Moments later, she reappeared with a smartly dressed little man sporting a crimson cravat.

"Henri Renard, proprietor of this modest establishment. Please come in."

Renard led Bridges into a surprisingly large room. Behind Renard's cluttered desk was a picture window through which the policeman could see the river, now sparkling in welcome sunshine.

"Be seated, Sergeant. How may I help you?"

Renard was a sharp-featured man in his 50s with a head of bouffant silvery hair.

"May I ask exactly what sort of business you run here, sir?" Bridges took out his notebook.

"As the name says, Sergeant, I recruit medical personnel. If there are hospital shortages or a medical practice needs support or requires temporary staff or, as you say, locums, I help out. My particular expertise is in the recruitment and placement of non-British doctors and nurses."

"How long have you been in business here?"

"For almost 15 years. I came here from France in the late 20s to further my medical studies. My mother was English and I preferred the prospect of practising here. After a few years as a doctor, a friend asked me to help him launch this business. We set up here and named the business in honour of Oliver Cromwell because we face the church over the road."

"Sir?"

"The Church of St Mary's is famous, Sergeant, for what they call the Putney Debates. You have heard of them, perhaps?"

History had never been one of Bridges' strong suits at school. He shook his head.

"They were important political debates that took place in 1647 during the English Civil War. Oliver Cromwell chaired these debates, hence…"

"Cromwell Medical Recruitment. I see. And is your partner still around?"

"Sadly no. He died of cancer in 1939." Renard leaned forward. "Excuse me, Sergeant, fascinating as this potted history of my company may be, could you tell me why you are here? I am a law-abiding individual running a legal and moderately successful little business. What is your interest in me?"

"I am investigating a murder, sir."

Renard reared back in surprise. "*Mon dieu!* Murder? And you think I have something to do with it?"

"We do not know who the victim is. We think you might be able to help us identify him. The murdered man went by the name of White. This was found among his belongings."

Renard put on a pair of half-moon spectacles and examined the newspaper advertisement Bridges set before him. "I see. Every so often, Sergeant, I place an advert in one of the London papers – this one I think was in *The Evening News*. Placed first in February and then in April." Renard put his spectacles away. "So you think your victim might have responded to the advertisement? The name White rings no bells. Do you have a photograph?"

They were interrupted by a cacophony of foghorns outside. Renard went to the window to see what was happening. Two large barges had just narrowly avoided collision. "These boats! Many of the barges are now being crewed by inexperienced youngsters because of the draft. The Navy has taken many of the expert navigators. Nearly every week there's a problem at the bridge. No disasters yet but it's only a matter of time." Renard returned to his desk. "Where were we?"

"You asked for a photograph, Mr Renard. Unfortunately, all we have is a head shot immediately after the murder. Very messy and not clear. We are expecting a better version later today."

"I see. Well, give me your description then."

"First of all, we think he was French."

"I see plenty of French medical people, Sergeant. There has naturally been an influx over the past year. People escaping the occupation or Vichy. And there was a sizeable group of French practitioners established here before the war.

"Mr White was a plump man. Five foot seven. Over 14 stone. He was partially bald and wore a brown wig. He had a small goatee beard and…"

"I know the man." Renard rose and crossed to a filing cabinet in the far corner of the room. After a brief rummage, he took out a thin folder and returned to his desk. He put on his spectacles again and opened the file.

"Your Mr White's real name is Armand de Metz. He came to see me in early May. He was seeking employment having arrived in this country from north Africa some time in February. Like many emigrés, he had a tragic tale. In the pre-war period he was one of the most eminent surgeons in Paris. The war brought the loss of his practice and his family. He was a Jew. He knew that he would be in trouble once the Germans arrived so took the precaution of arranging for his wife and children to take passage to the United States. The ship they were aboard was torpedoed by a German U-boat last autumn. There were no survivors.

"After the German invasion, he managed to make it from Paris to Vichy France with some of his wealth intact, but it became clear to him that it was only a matter of time before life would become impossible for Jews there as well as in occupied France. He managed to get to Algiers and thence to London. The money he'd managed to hang onto went in payment to those who facilitated his escape. He arrived here pretty much penniless." Renard looked up at Bridges. "Clearly his run of terrible bad luck did not end when he got here."

"Did you find him a job?"

"No."

"Why not? You say he was an eminent surgeon. Surely there would be work for a man like that?"

"He was a drunk, Sergeant. His hands were shaking. I could smell alcohol on his breath. It was apparent that the poor man's experiences had broken him. I could not trust him with any of my customers."

"So he left disappointed?"

Renard sighed. "He did indeed."

"Do you know how he was managing to survive?"

"I have no idea, Sergeant."

"Did you hear of him performing abortions?"

Reynard threw up his hands. "I most certainly did not."

Bridges put his notebook away. "Well, thank you very much for your help, sir. A sad story." The two men shook hands and Renard called for his secretary to escort Bridges out.

When he was certain that the policeman had gone, Renard picked up the telephone and dialled. After a short wait, he spoke. "It's me, Henri. There's something I think you should know."

*   *   *

Sidney Fleming returned to the Ritz from a country outing late on Monday morning. He had passed a most enjoyable Sunday at the Compleat Angler in Marlow and, on impulse, had stayed the night. Back at the Ritz, he found a small pile of messages in his room, the topmost being an invitation to a meeting – the prospect delighted him but he only had 10 minutes to get there.

Ignoring the other messages, he hurried to the suite on the third floor and, with only the slightest hint of trepidation, knocked on the door. A uniformed man appeared and bowed him into an opulently furnished drawing room. In an armchair in the far corner sat his host, a svelte, middle-aged man sporting a neat little moustache and wearing a brown tweed suit similar to the one Fleming himself was wearing. He was holding what looked like a whisky and soda in one hand and a cigarette in the other. Fleming had heard that the King was a prodigious smoker. The sound of a young child having a tantrum could be heard from one of the adjoining rooms.

As Fleming approached, he became aware of two other older men, one wearing a uniform and one in morning dress, talking at a nearby desk. His arrival brought an end to their discussion and the civilian walked over to make the introductions. "Mr Fleming, I presume? I am the King's cousin." He gave his name, which sounded to Fleming like a random collection of consonants. "I have the honour to be the prime minister of Albania." The gentleman made an abrupt bow. "Let me introduce you to His Majesty."

The prime minister oozed over to his sovereign, bowed and introduced Fleming, who followed suit and bowed deeply. The King pointed with his cigarette to a chair opposite and Fleming sat. The King redirected his cigarette to the prime minister, who grunted and moved back unhappily to his desk.

"I believe I have you to thank, Mr Fleming, for some astute stock tips you managed to get to me." The King spoke excellent English with only the faintest of accents.

"Yes, Your Majesty, assuming you bought and sold when I suggested?"

The King sipped his drink and signalled to another of his entourage for a second whisky to be brought. "I did indeed, Mr Fleming. I was advised against it," he glanced in the direction of the prime minister, "but I decided to have a little, how do you English say it, a little 'flutter'. I am obliged to you for the pleasing results."

"Only glad to be of service, Your Majesty. One neighbour helping another, so to speak."

"Ah, yes, neighbours. As it happens, Mr Fleming, we shall not be neighbours for much longer. I am moving to a place in the country, which should prove more congenial to my family and my government."

Fleming lifted the glass of whisky he had just received. "Sorry to hear that, but cheers sir, and good luck." The monarch raised his glass in response.

King Zog glanced towards his cousin again. "So, Mr Fleming, there sits my prime minister." A smile parted the monarch's thin lips. "But prime minister of what? This hotel room, that's all. My Albanian government-in-exile is not recognised by your British government, unlike those of Poland, Czechoslovakia, Holland and the others. I am ruler only of this room. It is enough to drive a man to drink." He finished off his whisky with a flourish.

"Ignominious as is our position here, Mr Fleming, it is made even worse by the knowledge that we have been ousted from our country by that obnoxious popinjay Mussolini and his pathetic army. He thinks he has revived the glory of Rome and its all-conquering armies but the abject level of Italy's current military capabilities has just been exposed by Wingate and his men in north Africa. If only we had possessed a tiger like Wingate to lead our army! Things would have been different then. Unfortunately, all we had were sheep." Fleming saw a door open behind the King and an elegant woman holding a toddler by the hand appeared and waved. "Yes, my dear, I'll be with you soon." The door closed.

"My wife, Queen Geraldine – half-American, you know – and my son, Prince Alexander, or Leka as we call him. The Queen is much happier now that we are to have the place in Surrey. I am a town man, myself. I will return here every so often and perhaps we may bump into each other again. In case we do not, I wanted to thank you in person for your help." He gave Fleming a sharp look. "I must ask, was there perhaps a hidden motive?"

"Not at all, sir. Once, many moons ago, I had some minor business dealings in Albania. Remembered my trips there with fondness. Heard you were here and thought it would be nice to do you a favour, for old time's sake."

"Ah, business dealings. And what, may I ask, is your business now?"

"I work with a chap called Simon Arbuthnot. We have interests here and overseas. I'm his oldest partner. I manage things in England."

"Yes, I have heard of him. Something in the City, is he not?"

"Yes, there is a bank, a trading house and operations in South America."

"South America? Some of my ministers wanted me to make my new home there but I wanted to stay as close as I could to my homeland." The King stubbed out his cigarette, snapped a finger and someone hurried over with two packs of Player's for him and Fleming. "Who looks after the South American interests?"

"We have a Greek manager out there."

The King laughed. "A Greek? I hope you know what you are doing. We have had our problems with the Greeks over the years and they with us. As I am sure you know, Albania has always had a large Greek presence in its population and vice versa. I suppose our relationship is a little like the English and the Scots – with us cast as a poorer version of the Scots. Many Albanians have made their fortunes in Greece." The King chuckled to himself. "I am reminded of that famous saying of your Dr Johnson, how does it go? 'The noblest prospect which a Scotsman ever sees is the high road that leads him to England.'"

Fleming clapped his hands in appreciation. "I see they gave you a fine British education in Albania."

"Indeed, Mr Fleming, indeed. No doubt the quotation could be adapted for Albanians and the high road to Greece." The door behind the King opened again and this time the toddler cried out to his father. "I am afraid we shall have to end our interesting discussion of Dr Johnson and other matters there, Mr Fleming. Let me just say that I hope your Greek fellow is a good man and that my petty prejudices prove unjustified." The monarch rose stiffly to his feet. "My back is plaguing me today, I am afraid. Thank you for coming. I wish you good day and good luck!"

King Zog disappeared through the door behind him and his entourage evaporated swiftly, leaving only the original uniformed man to let Fleming out.

The businessman entered his own room in a state of great satisfaction moments later. It was no mean achievement for Fleming, once a boy from the wrong side of the tracks, to mingle with royalty. Even if it was dispossessed, powerless royalty. It did occur to him that he might have missed a business trick. The King was obviously expecting him to ask a favour. Perhaps the monarch would have agreed to open an account at Sackville? He should have enquired. No matter. He had the contact and the entrée now. There was obviously money around, even if Zog's Albanian throne had been usurped. He decided to call room service for a bottle of champagne to savour in his suite before going down to the restaurant for lunch. Fleming made the call then picked up the rest of the pile of messages and sat at his desk. Most of the messages appeared to be from Tomlinson.

*   *   *

"So, Olivier, what did you think of Beaulieu?"

"An ass. I told you that on the night and I haven't changed my mind."

Commandant Angers was standing before his office mirror and attempting to flatten an unsightly crease in his collar with a hot, wet handkerchief. "Damn this thing. I'm going to find another laundry. The service of these places in England is very poor." He cursed, gave up on his collar and sat down in one of the armchairs by the window. "But a spy? The man is so self-obsessed I doubt he could ever find enough time for spying."

"The fact that Beaulieu appears to be an arrogant ass does not preclude it. Arrogance often goes hand in hand with success at espionage."

"I thought the typical spy liked to keep a low profile. Blend into the woodwork and so on."

"Not necessarily. What about Rudolph Stellman, whom we used before the war and, for all I know, is still being used? He had a pretty healthy opinion of himself that he wasn't loath to share. And what about English Fred? He was…"

"All right, all right." The commandant held up his hands. "You've made your point. I still don't think he's spying material. What's happened is that he's so full of himself because of his close connection with the general that he's got up everyone's noses, including some very high-up noses, and Fillon's suspicion is his payback."

"De Gaulle must think highly of him."

"De Gaulle? Ha! Another self-obsessive. The general is too busy hating Churchill or the British military or whoever for slights or imagined shifts to his *amour propre*. He doesn't take the time to get to know his people. His dislike of you bears witness to the poor quality of his people judgment."

Rougemont shrugged and picked up the newspaper he'd been reading before the commandant's late arrival. "No doubt the general is fuming somewhere over this headline." He held up the paper. 'BRITISH FORCES ENTER SYRIA AND LEBANON'.

Angers looked back in mock perplexity. "What's wrong with that headline?" Then both men burst out laughing. They knew de Gaulle would be furious at any report of operations against Syria and Lebanon that made no reference to the contribution of the contingent of Free French forces in the Allied army.

The commandant looked at the story. "I bet he'll be on the first plane to Damascus from Cairo or Brazzaville or wherever he is when Syria falls. Barging his way to the front of the victory parade."

"But, Commandant, back to Beaulieu. Surely it must concern us that he was very close to Darlan?"

"My dear Rougemont, I venture to say that very few of our fellow officers in London have not had any dealings with Darlan, Pétain or Laval over the years."

"I know but those would have been before the occupation. Beaulieu worked for Darlan under Vichy."

Angers crossed his legs and puffed out his cheeks. "But, Olivier, we must remember that the transition after defeat was not easy. Many people were placed awkwardly. And do we know exactly what he did for Darlan?" The commandant sniggered. "Perhaps he just cleaned his shoes!"

"You are not taking this seriously enough, sir."

"All right, all right." He got up and wandered over to his desk, where he sat in the new swivel chair he had just liberated from the office of a fellow officer, who had gone away with the general. "Perhaps we should put a tail on him? How about that Irish fellow? How about Devlin?"

"Harp, sir."

"Sorry, I forgot he has a code name. Anyway, he was useful to us in that Banstead case. You know where to find him?"

"I know the pub in Kilburn he frequents. He is a useful man. What instructions?"

"Follow Beaulieu and why not the other two? A day or two on each. See what, if anything, turns up."

"Money?"

"I'll leave that to you. Help yourself to my special kitty in the safe over there. You know the number." Angers swivelled round a couple of times in his chair. He laughed with a child's pleasure. "I love this chair! That idiot Le Clerc would be apoplectic if he knew I'd filched it." He swivelled again. "Off you go then. It's lunchtime. With luck De… Harp might be at his pub. Likes a drink, if I remember correctly."

On his way out, Rougemont bumped into a man standing in the reception area. As they exchanged apologies, he heard the man's colleague introduce himself to the receptionist, saying he was a police officer who wanted to speak to someone in authority about something important. The captain spent most

of his taxi journey to Kilburn wondering what that important
something might be.

*   *   *

Paris

The little boy was a fast runner – and needed to be. He stood
quietly in the queue at the butcher's shop on the corner of the
rue Mazarine until he heard the ruckus outside. The noise came
from his younger brother, François, who was the proud possessor
of a particularly ear-piercing scream. All in the shop, behind or
in front of the counter, turned to look out of the window to see
what was happening. Jules took his chance, squeezed through
the line of customers and crept behind the counter. The shop,
close as it was to the German Embassy, was one of the better
provisioned butchers in Paris at a time of growing scarcity. With
commendable efficiency, the boy swept as many pies and cuts
of meat as he could into his two sacks and crawled through the
customers' legs out to the street.

Once outside, he threw one bag to François, who hared off
towards the Luxembourg Garden, while Jules raced towards the
river. The boy ran along the embankment then over the Pont Royal
and into the Louvre Gardens. He slowed down a little, then cut
down the rue de Castiglione towards the Place Vendôme. He came
to a halt by the column in the centre of the square, sat down on a
step and began to recover his breath. Moments later, a group of
German soldiers walked by and stopped to admire the towering
monument to Napoleon. It was clearly time to move on but, just as
he got to his feet, he felt a hand on his shoulder. A voice spoke to him
in German-accented French. "Can I see what's in your bag, sonny?"

Jules turned to see a tall, solid man in German officer's uniform.
The boy felt a trickle of urine making its way down his leg despite

the fact that the officer was smiling pleasantly at him. He handed the sack to the officer. "Hmm. This seems rather a large amount of meat for a small boy like you. Or perhaps you have been sent on a shopping errand by your very rich mama and papa."

The officer turned and laughed to the occupants of an open-topped car parked a few yards away. Two soldiers sat in the front and an important-looking man with close-cut fair hair was seated in the back. This man said something in German to the officer holding Jules' bag, who nodded in response and turned back to the boy.

"You are unlucky and lucky. Unluckily for you, we saw what you did as we were driving past the butcher's. We saw you run off, then lost sight of you until we arrived in the square. You must be a very stupid boy to choose this square as a place to stop. Surely it would have been wiser to disappear into a back street closer to wherever you came from?" Jules' stomach began to make unpleasant noises.

"And yet you are lucky because my boss over there has had a tiresome day and doesn't want what remains of it ruined by any unpleasantness." The officer picked out a chicken pie from the boy's bag then threw the bag to the ground. "I wouldn't chance your luck again if I were you."

He started back to the car. Then, after a few paces, he turned, came back and picked up the bag. He rummaged through it, then looked at the boy. His face didn't look so kindly now. "No ham, no pork, no sausages. You're a Jew, aren't you?"

The urine now coursed down Jules' leg. He said nothing.

"Hmm. I was a bit slow there. I can usually smell a Jew at a hundred paces. I think perhaps you are not so lucky today, little boy." In one swift and smooth movement, the officer drew his revolver and shot the boy in the head. Jules fell to the ground and the officer kicked the twitching body a couple of times before heading for the car. The fair-haired man shook his head as the officer joined him in the back. "You just couldn't resist it, could you, Schmidt? Your little bit of fun. That sort of behaviour is not helpful, you know."

SS *Standartenführer* Fritz Schmidt looked at his boss with a smirk of amusement. "I'll put it about that the boy was a Jew terrorist who drew a gun on me and obviously had to be killed. Will that be all right, sir?"

The car continued across the square and came to a halt outside the Hôtel Ritz. The man in the back of the car was Heinrich Otto Abetz, who was indeed as important as he looked. Abetz, the plenipotentiary Nazi ruler of occupied France, was dubbed King Otto by celebrated French writer Louis-Ferdinand Céline, among others. Abetz thought of Céline, who had said he might join them later for dinner, and smiled wryly. He never thought he'd find someone who hated the Jews as much as his SS Chief Schmidt but Céline came pretty close.

Abetz led Schmidt through the swing doors of the Ritz. His day so far had indeed been one of extreme tedium and he was looking forward to some entertainment. The morning had been spent with senior Vichy civil servants, who were trying to finalise the details of the Protocols he had agreed in principle with Admiral Darlan in May. This was, of course, a complete waste of time because Abetz knew that the people back in Berlin didn't care whether or not the Protocols were finalised. Even if they were finalised, they would not be worth the paper they were written on as far as the *Führer* was concerned.

In the afternoon, there had been another long meeting, this time to discuss the first round-up of Parisian Jews, which had taken place the previous month. On 14 May, postcards had been sent to thousands of Jewish men aged between 18 and 40, asking them to present themselves at Paris police stations. More than 5,000 men had been arrested and despatched to detention camps at Pithiviers and Beaune-la-Rolande. The afternoon's meeting had focused on the organisation and condition of these camps. Unsurprisingly to Abetz, the state of the camps was very poor. One or two of his more enlightened civil servants and officers had argued for an improvement in conditions and rationing, but his finance people had balked at the expense and Abetz had certainly not wanted his many enemies back in Berlin to accuse him of being soft on Jews.

At the Ritz, a private room had been reserved for him and his party. Abetz found he was not the first to arrive – Céline had managed to get there earlier than promised. The call of free champagne was a powerful one. Throw in some caviar and a few potential rounds of Jew-baiting and it was clearly all too hard for Céline to resist. Also there already was the elfin Coco Chanel, the odd-looking writer Jean Cocteau and the ballet impresario Serge Lifar. The same band, more or less, with whom he had just passed an entertaining weekend at his Château de Chantilly.

Abetz's spirits rose as he anticipated a stimulating and enjoyable evening. He raised his hand in a restrained version of the Nazi salute to greet the party and took his place at the head of the table. Champagne was poured and Céline rose to propose the toast. "To King Otto and to France, the Kingdom of Otto!"

*   *   *

London

Merlin and Goldberg were driving back to the Yard from Dorset Square with the chief inspector at the wheel. Their meeting with the French had proved unproductive.

"Those guys really fancied themselves, huh, Frank?"

"Oh, I don't know. The colonel wasn't too bad."

"Maybe, but what about that commandant? Anjou, was that the name?"

Merlin beeped his horn. He hated driving in London. He had hated it before the war and it was worse now. Bridges normally did all the driving but as he'd gone to Putney, Merlin was stuck with the task. Traffic had backed up all along the Charing Cross Road. A passing pedestrian had mentioned a collapsed building. Merlin put the car into reverse and tried to cut down Shaftesbury Avenue but everyone else had had the same idea. He took his hands off the steering wheel and resigned himself to a wait.

"No, Angers – pronounced a bit like 'ballet'. I suppose he was a bit of a peacock."

"The only Frenchmen I come across in New York are the *maître d*'s in the best restaurants, where they always enjoy telling me I can't get a table. Reckon the commandant would be brilliant at that."

In Dorset Square, they had eventually been ushered into the office of Colonel Aubertin, who appeared to be the senior man in the building. The commandant had joined them a few minutes later, exuding superiority and boredom in equal measure. Merlin had told the officers about the murder of Mr White – the pseudonym of a Frenchman, it was thought – and their need to identify him. Merlin's physical description of White and the photograph of the corpse had been met with blank looks. At the mention of the business Mr White appeared to have been conducting, Aubertin and Angers had registered shock and disgust, reiterated their ignorance of the man's identity and made it absolutely clear that they could not help. As a minor concession to the policemen, the colonel had grudgingly promised to check whether any colleagues had come across someone fitting White's description.

The traffic began to move again and Goldberg looked out at the theatres lining Shaftesbury Avenue. "Guess I should try to see a show while I'm here. Any recommendations?"

"I went with a friend to see a revue on Saturday. Very funny but very English. It might not appeal to you."

Goldberg shrugged. "I've listened to some of your radio shows and you may be right. That Tommy Handley fellow, can't really understand a word he's saying. And everyone creases up when that lady says: 'Can I do you now, sir?' What the heck's all that about?"

Merlin laughed, thinking of Sonia. "Some foreigners get it. We don't seem to have any problem with your comedians. Have you listened to *Hi, Gang!*? That's got plenty of American humour in it and it's very popular here."

"Oh, yeah. Ben Lyon and his wife you mean? They're good." They turned into Whitehall and drove past Horse Guards Parade and Downing Street.

"One of the comics in *Hi, Gang!* is the son-in-law of our prime minister. I bet you didn't know that."

"You don't say!"

"Name of Vic Oliver. He's an Austrian, married to Churchill's daughter, Sarah."

"Now that is amazing. A vaudeville star and someone born in the same place as Hitler. I doubt Mr Roosevelt would allow anything like that."

Merlin drove through the gates of Scotland Yard and came to a halt. "Puts Churchill in quite a good light, I think. Does Roosevelt have any daughters?"

"One. Anne Roosevelt. She's a journalist."

"Interesting. Journalists aren't very highly regarded here. A lot of people in Britain might prefer their daughter to marry a foreign music-hall artist than a journalist."

"Really, Frank?"

"Really."

*   *   *

Buenos Aires

Alexander Pulos felt a little under the weather when he woke that morning. He looked in the mirror. His pointy little nose was unnaturally red and his face appeared pasty and sallow through heavy-lidded eyes. Pulos decided to take the day off. His young wife was still at their new chalet in Bariloche with friends. He had wondered why she wanted to go this early in June – the main ski season didn't start for another couple of weeks – but had said nothing. He didn't ask too many questions about her social arrangements in case she started to ask too many about his. He lay in bed dozing all morning and by one o'clock was feeling much better. He rang for his valet, Victor, who laid out his dressing gown and slippers then ran him a bath. Downstairs, Pulos ate a light lunch of cold meats and cheese then planted himself in the high-backed armchair that overlooked the immaculately manicured lawn of his spacious villa in Recoleta, one of Buenos Aires' most expensive *barrios*.

After another little doze in his chair, he called his secretary and asked her to come to the house. She began to tell him something but he stopped her. "Save it for when you get here, Paula." Pulos went upstairs to change out of his silk pyjamas and dressing gown and into his favourite baggy cream trousers, check shirt and tweed jacket, and was back in his chair when Victor let Paula in. The secretary was a little, sparrow-like woman of Italian extraction, who adored her boss with a passion. Pulos could see that she was agitated.

Paula drew up a chair beside him. She had with her a large file of papers from which she withdrew a telegram. "You had better look at this first, *señor*."

Pulos took it from her and scanned it. He suddenly felt a little faint. He had been half expecting bad news like this for some time but it was still a big shock. "Very sad, Paula. Very sad indeed. Mr Arbuthnot was a great man."

Pulos was someone who could switch off the worries of work relatively easily. The problems of Enterprisas Simal had not disturbed him at all during his morning of recuperation. Now, back in business mode, the wheels of his refreshed brain began running as normal. The death of his partner would create substantial new problems to add to those already existing. Chief among them would be those of control and leadership – the ownership of the company and its command structure would have to be resolved and this would be no easy matter. The pressing old problems concerning the origin of the company remained and Arbuthnot's death would not make them go away. The litigation would grind on, although thankfully the Argentinian courts were notoriously slow and corrupt and their opponents were weak.

The thing to remember, he thought, as Paula began to list the various pressing items at the office, is that change – even traumatic change like the sudden death of a major partner – also created opportunity. This could be an opportunity for Alexander Pulos. If he were to seize it, he would have to take on his English colleagues. There could be no room for sentiment. Arbuthnot had said that his son "would come good" in adversity. Pulos did not want that spoiled youth to have the chance to come good. As for Fleming, he was a smooth operator, whose ingenuity and quicksilver brain Pulos had eventually come to admire. And there would be other obstacles. There was much to consider.

"That will be all, Paula. We can deal with all that in the office tomorrow."

"But, *Señor* Pulos…"

"Don't worry, it can all wait 24 hours. You can leave the file. Now I need to mourn my friend. Off you go!"

Paula gave her boss an anxious look, advised him to retire early with a hot drink, then left.

Pulos asked Victor to mix him a Manhattan, lifted his feet on to the stool in front of him, closed his eyes and began to think.

He found it difficult to avoid the initial conclusion that it was he who was in the best of all positions – most of the physical assets of Enterprisas Simal were in South America. All except the merchant ships out at sea and the cash remitted to the Sackville Bank in London. Most of the profit-generating assets of the Sackville Group – the land, factories, mines and ranches – were all in Argentina or the neighbouring countries of Chile and Uruguay. He was the man in control of all these assets while all the other players were far away in war-torn Europe or, in the case of the litigation, the United States.

He tried to remember the English legal maxim that Arbuthnot used to quote frequently. "Ah yes," he muttered to himself. "Possession is nine-tenths of the law." He, Pulos, was in possession of the main physical assets of the business. However, if he were to take his opportunity to the full, there were other things he would have to possess. Tiresome as it was, he would have to make a journey. It was no easy thing to get from South America to Great Britain in June 1941 but he would have to find a way.

He picked up the file Paula had left with him. One of the papers inside was headed Enterprisas Simal Ship Movements. Listed within were the locations and planned weekly movements of the 32 merchant vessels owned by the company. He moved his finger down the list until it came to rest on the MV Montevideo, currently anchored in the Rio Plata and due to leave on Wednesday for Lisbon with a cargo of 6,500 tons of maize, wheat and flax. If he took passage on that ship, which he remembered had an extremely comfortable stateroom, then connected with an onward flight to London, he could get to England in just over a week, perhaps. Maybe longer. Too long.

No, he must get to Lisbon by air. He had done the journey that way several times before the war but there were not so many airline options now. He could fly to Rio, where he thought there were still connecting flights to Lisbon via Recife and Dakar. If the connections worked, he might be able to get to London in three or four days. Maybe less. It wouldn't be anything like as comfortable as the ship but time was of the essence.

He finished his cocktail. The telephone rang. An actress friend was having an impromptu party that night at a new nightclub in town. Did he want to go? He did. The Manhattan had blown away any lingering symptoms of the morning's bug. He would have an enjoyable time at the party and company would take his mind off poor Simon's death. It would not be a late evening, however: he wanted a good night's sleep. He usually found sleep to be a wise counsellor.

*   *   *

London

WPC Robinson was having a trying day. It was now after five o'clock and her search for the identity of the abortion victim had been unsuccessful. She had been in touch with forces in Bristol, Cardiff, Norwich, Birmingham, Leicester, Manchester, Liverpool, Leeds, Newcastle, Glasgow and Edinburgh, all to no avail.

Earlier in the day, her task appeared to have been made a little easier when she finally received the victim's post-mortem report. Contrary to initial information, the victim did have some useful distinguishing features. She had a small birthmark under her breast and there was a small defect in one of her toes. Unfortunately, while some of the regional forces had missing persons of the girl's approximate age and general appearance, none were noted as having these particular features. Some of the officers to whom she spoke had offered to contact their missing girls' relatives in case they had omitted to mention such details. Other officers, who shared the not uncommon provincial feelings of resentment towards their colleagues in 'the big smoke', were not so helpful.

Robinson consulted her list. She had one more regional force to contact – Northern Ireland. The name on her list was that of a Sergeant Callaghan. She rang, and after a long wait, the Belfast switchboard operator put her through. A female voice came on the line and introduced herself as Dorothy Callaghan. She had a bright and cheerful voice with an attractive Ulster lilt. "What can I do for you, Constable?"

"We have a deceased young lady here in London we are trying to identify, Sergeant. Approximate age 20 to 23, black hair cut short."

"As in a bob, do you mean?"

"Yes. Height five foot one, weight eight stone, one pound. Dark complexion, as if suntanned."

"Tanned, Constable? Sure we don't get much sun over here so you may be wasting your time."

Robinson laughed politely. "All her own teeth. Distinguishing marks, a small reddish-purple birthmark below the right breast and the top of the small toe on her left foot missing."

"I see. You do realise that we were bombed to hell and back in April and May, don't you? We've got a list of missing persons as long as your arm at the moment, with most of them being buried under rubble we haven't had time to shift yet."

"I appreciate, Sergeant, that every major city in Britain has major war-related problems. We've had plenty of our own here."

There was a pause on the line before the sergeant spoke again. "Of course you have, my dear. And I know you're only trying to do your job. How did she die?"

"A botched abortion."

"Ah, the poor lassie. All right, Constable. I'll have a look at our lists. Try to get back to you by tomorrow afternoon, is that all right?"

"Thank you very much, Sergeant." Robinson put down the receiver in a slightly better mood than when she'd picked it up.

She had one other thing to do before she could leave to prepare herself for the planned evening out with her new boyfriend, Anthony Rutherford, a young up-and-coming Middle Temple barrister. Rutherford had appeared on the scene after Constable Tommy Cole had been transferred out of London at the behest of her uncle. She had been furious with the AC but he had been adamant. "Leaving aside questions of whether the boy is appropriate for you, it is bad for morale and discipline for relationships to be carried on at work."

On reflection and despite herself, Robinson had found she agreed with the latter point. There had been a tearful parting with Cole and then, a couple of weeks later, she had been introduced to Rutherford at a dinner party. Robinson had felt guilty but by April they had become something of an item. Rutherford was good-looking in an old-fashioned sort of way. Afflicted with back problems, he had not been fit for military service – to his bitter disappointment – and to compensate had become an eager member of the Kensington Home Guard.

Tonight he had tickets for a production of Rossini's *La Cenerentola*. In truth, Robinson wasn't looking forward to it that much. Her cinema visits with Cole to see *Rebecca* and *Gone with the Wind* had been more to her taste than opera, but then again, Rutherford had agreed to take her to see the new Jimmy Cagney film at the weekend as a quid pro quo. And they were going to the opera with one of Rutherford's jolly barrister friends and his wife so it wouldn't be all bad.

Robinson picked up the Ritz notepaper they had found in Mr White's pocket. She had meant to get on with chasing this phone number earlier, but the missing person checks had taken the whole day. The number was KNI 4897. She had already discovered that the number was unlisted and had rung it a few times with no response. Now she would get on to the exchange and see what they could tell her.

⋆   ⋆   ⋆

"You're looking rather cheerful, Sergeant. Something to tell us?" Merlin set down his pen.

"Found the fellow, sir. A Mr Armand de Metz. I think that's how it's pronounced."

"Armand de Metz. An intriguing name. Sounds very *elegante* as my father would have said or 'posh' in straight English for you, Sam. I'm not sure what the New York equivalent is, Bernie?"

"Fancy, I guess. Sounds more German than French to me but what do I know, Sergeant?"

Merlin spent a moment rummaging in the drawers of his desk in search of a fresh packet of Fisherman's Friends. Unsuccessful, he looked up to find Goldberg offering him a stick of Wrigley's chewing gum.

"Don't mind if I do, Detective. Thanks."

Merlin chewed the gum contentedly as Bridges ran over the details of his meeting with Renard. When the sergeant had finished, Merlin wandered thoughtfully over to the window. Rain had fallen in intermittent showers for most of the day but it was dry now and bright sunlight was shining down on the busy river traffic. Merlin could see a section of the Houses of Parliament to his right. Last month, the Parliament buildings had been hit by a number of incendiary bombs. The Commons chamber had been completely destroyed and the roof of Westminster Hall set on fire. The damaged area was just out of sight but knowing it was there was bad enough. "So this fellow Metz must have been pretty well known in the right circles in Paris."

"Must have been, sir."

"It's surprising he couldn't find people to help him in London. One would have thought he would have found a few sympathetic friends or acquaintances among the French exile community."

"He was a Jew, Frank. Remember that Jews aren't so popular in France. There was that whole Dreyfus thing. Guy got dumped in the proverbial because he was a Jew."

"That was a long time ago, Bernie. Having said that, you wouldn't really have to go that far in this country to find anti-Semitism."

Goldberg laughed. "Nor in America. You'd just have to stand in my precinct office."

"All right, I think we can agree that there is anti-Semitism in all three countries. It still seems strange that a man of such stature could fall so quickly and so steeply without encountering a helping hand."

"There was a helping hand in the end. Someone must have helped him get regular abortion work."

Merlin returned to his desk. "Do we know that the work was regular, Bernie? Perhaps this was just a one-off? Perhaps a friend just asked him for a favour?"

"The man had to survive financially for several months. Abortion work might have helped him do so. If not that, what, sir?"

"Perhaps he did get someone to lend him money, Sergeant. Or maybe he performed a string of abortions. I'm not sure it matters. What does matter is the abortion we are investigating. I think the first thing we should do is revisit those French officers again now that we've got our victim's name. See if that prompts anything. Going back to our other case, any idea how Robinson has been getting on with the identification of our girl? Is she around?"

"She asked me if it was all right to go just before you got back, sir. Had a date with that barrister fellow. Said she'd made a lot of inquiries today but no hard facts as yet. I said it was all right. Opera tickets or something."

"Fine, Sam. We'll catch up with her in the morning. Fancy a drink, either of you?"

"Sorry, sir. Promised I'd get home to Iris as soon as I came off duty."

"Off you go then. Bernie?"

"Sorry again. Can't do tonight, Frank. I've been invited to a reception at the Embassy. Apparently there'll be a number of American notables there so I think I'd better not turn down the opportunity."

"Very well then. I'll be off home, too." Merlin put his jacket on. "Detective, why are you smirking at me?"

"As I understand it, you're not exactly going home to a lonely garret. I gather the young lady is a stunner."

Merlin shook his head. "I must remind my officers not to gossip."

CHAPTER 6

Tuesday 10 June

London

Merlin took the bus to work. He liked buses. He often caught the number 14 on the King's Road. There had always been a good deal of banter on the bus but it seemed to have increased since the Blitz. The bus was a good place to assess public morale. As he hopped off at Green Park and walked the rest of the way to the Yard, he considered today's bus chit-chat.

If he had to grade morale on the back of it, he'd say it was middling. Passengers were generally continuing to take comfort from the lull in the Blitz although there were plenty of doom merchants saying it was only a matter of time before the planes would return. The view on military developments was that things weren't looking great. The Cretan defeat had shaken many and there was disappointment at the recent lack of positive news coming out of north Africa. Against that, as one regular, an eternally optimistic post-office worker, had cheerily pointed out: "We sunk the Bismarck the other day, didn't we?" For some reason this morning, no-one had mentioned rationing, which was the usual main bugbear. There had been newspaper reports of further imminent restrictions on egg distribution, while jam, marmalade, treacle and syrup had recently been rationed for the first time, but the subject had not arisen today.

Just before he reached the Yard, Merlin decided to pop into Tony's Café in Parliament Square. Fortunately, Tony was somehow continuing to circumvent the shortages and Merlin's three slices of toast came with a generous helping of butter, marmalade and jam. Sonia had had to leave the flat very early that morning for a stock-taking exercise at Swan & Edgar and Merlin had missed out on his usual home breakfast. Tony's fare would be a more than adequate substitute.

Merlin watched the café owner as he bustled around the room. He had lost a lot of weight over the past year. Tony Martini had narrowly escaped being interned a year before when Italy had entered the war on Hitler's side. All Italians aged between 16 and 70, who had lived in Britain for less than 20 years, had been detained and sent to camps. Tony's parents had arrived from Naples with their young children in 1919 so the family was apparently exempt. However, the Home Office official who called him in for interview had found there to be some discrepancies in the old immigration paperwork and questioned the exact timing of the family's arrival in the country. In light of the uncertainty, the official had been minded to detain Tony and his father. Merlin had been asked to put in a word for his desperate friend, which, of course, he had been happy to do. His intervention had swung it and both men had retained their liberty. More trouble had arrived when a belated swell of anti-Italian prejudice had damaged custom in the autumn. This had eventually blown over and the café was thriving again, but Merlin could see that Tony had been changed by his experiences. He was not his old cheerful self and his reduced frame bore witness to a troubled mind.

"All well, Tony?"

"For now, Frank, for now. You know how it is." The café owner shrugged and moved off to take a new order. Merlin turned to his newspaper. A front-page report on the Middle East immediately caught his eye. An Allied army incorporating British, Australian,

Indian and Free French forces had invaded the Vichy-controlled countries of Syria and Lebanon on Sunday and had made good progress in their initial advances.

Merlin remembered reading something about Syria a few months back but he had not really taken in the fact that Syria and Lebanon, as parts of France's pre-war empire, were now under the control of the French puppet government in Vichy. He was surprised, when he thought about it, that the Syrian and Lebanese people hadn't taken advantage of events in France to take control of their own countries. The article explained that the invasion was principally launched in anticipation of the Vichy government's plan to make the countries available to the Germans as bases. His mind turned to the French officers at Dorset Square, his first port of call of the morning, and he wondered if the two men he had met were in any way involved with the planning of this operation.

Merlin polished off his meal and rose, leaving payment on the table. Tony had told him many times, after his help with the Home Office, that his drinks and meals were on the house but Merlin insisted on paying up. His help, he told Tony, had been for friendship, not for grub.

*   *   *

Robinson had thoroughly enjoyed her evening at the opera. Her only previous experience had been a performance of Wagner, to which the AC, an avid Wagnerian, had taken her a year before. It was a strange but admirable British characteristic, she had thought at the time, how little antagonism was directed against the great artistic creations of the enemy, even of Richard Wagner, the great idol of Hitler. There was no banning of the works of Bach, Brahms, Wagner or any great German musicians so far as she was aware. Robinson felt sure that great British artists were unlikely to be treated with such equanimity in the German Reich.

Brilliant as Wagner might be, however, she had found that he was not her cup of tea. She was delighted to find, therefore, on her second visit to the opera, that Rossini very much was. *La Cenerentola* was enchanting. She had not been bored for a second, as she had told Rutherford excitedly as they left the theatre. Afterwards the couple had dined with Rutherford's friends in Soho and then he had dropped her off at the small Pimlico bedsit into which she had moved in January. Standing outside the front door, buzzing with the excitement of the evening, she had allowed her suitor his first brief kiss.

This morning, she felt a little guilty as she thought of Tommy Cole, who had shared with her the small room down the corridor from the chief inspector, in which she now sat. Robinson quickly shrugged off the feeling as she picked up the pile of new regional missing persons reports on her desk and got to work. An hour later, she had ploughed through them all. None was positive.

She sighed before opening the note that had just arrived from the Knightsbridge telephone exchange. 'Re your enquiry as to telephone number KNI 4897, I would be grateful if you could come round in person to discuss. Please feel free to call in any time today. Yours Faithfully, Miss E Brinton'. She took down a book from one of the shelves behind her. It contained, among other things, the addresses of all the London telephone exchanges. The Knightsbridge exchange was in a street around the corner from Harrods. She could get there in 20 minutes.

*   *   *

New York

Anton Meyer woke early after another disturbed night in the small apartment off Washington Square he shared with his wife. He was finding sleep increasingly difficult these days. Meyer, a slight, dark young man with deep-set eyes, slid out of bed and went to the bathroom, where he splashed water on his face to the background accompaniment of his wife's gentle snoring. He wanted to get out before Ruth woke up. Last night there had been another argument. Although he worked somewhere he was downtrodden, overworked and unappreciated, it was often a relief to escape to the office these days.

Meyer brushed his teeth and shaved as quickly as he could. Ruth had stopped snoring but was still asleep, as far as he could tell. He dressed, picked up his briefcase and slipped through the front door. The office was on West 23rd Street, just around the corner from the Flatiron Building. It was not a long walk. He made good time and grabbed a coffee from a stall on the corner of Broadway and 23rd. As he drank, he watched a couple of tramps in Madison Square Park ease themselves out of their makeshift newspaper-and-rag bedding. He glanced at the old Swiss watch his father had given him long ago. It was just after seven o'clock and the building should now be open. As he entered, the Irish doorman greeted him cheerfully. "Hello there, Mr Meyer. Top of the morning to you."

"Same to you, Al." Meyer smiled. The doorman's jolly exchanges in the morning and evening were often the only friendly words he would hear all day.

The elevator took him to the sixth floor, where he entered the glass-plated doors of accountancy firm Liebman and Sachs. The frizzy-haired receptionist was not yet in position to give him her accustomed severe glare of welcome. Meyer made his way to the small box-room at the back of the office, next to the toilets, where he had been working since he joined the firm a year and a half before. Stacks of audit files lay piled high on his desk. The room had a small window that looked out on the small window of another office in an adjoining building. Occasionally he saw a pretty young girl working there but the hour was too early for her to appear just yet.

Meyer sat down and reached into one of the desk drawers. He took out the letter he had collected the day before from his box at the General Post Office Building opposite Penn Station. He had already read it many times. He took it out of its envelope and read it again. There was a decision to be made about the money. It was disappearing very rapidly and he was starting to think that Ruth might be right. From the outset she had said that he was on a fool's errand and they were wasting money that could have got them out of their cheap hovel in the Village and into a decent apartment. Shaking his head, he put the letter back in its envelope. He stared for a moment at the blue-and-white Buenos Aires postmark before he heard the sound of approaching footsteps and stuffed the letter back in the desk.

A dumpy middle-aged man with a pock-marked face came in with two thick files, which he dumped onto Meyer's overflowing in-tray. "Better get a move on, Meyer. Mr Sachs wants all this work done by tomorrow. Looks like you might be burning the midnight oil again."

"Very good, Mr Kramer."

Kramer turned on his heels and disappeared, leaving the smell of cheap aftershave to linger in the air.

*   *   *

London

"Pleased to meet you, Constable. Elizabeth Brinton. My office is over here." Robinson followed the surprisingly young Miss Brinton around the busy banks of switchboard equipment and attendant operators into a small room well insulated from the noise outside.

The two women seated themselves on either side of an oval desk. There was a strong smell of cigarettes and an open packet of

Player's lay between them. "I don't know how I'd get through this war without a cigarette." Miss Brinton lit up and smoke filtered out of her nostrils. "It's better than being a drunk, I suppose. Would you care for one? No? Very well. To business. Sorry to put you to the trouble of visiting me but I thought it best to tell you what I have to say in person. Managing an exchange can make one a little paranoid about security. One knows that there are many ways in which telephone security can be breached."

"Not at all, Miss Brinton, although I would have thought that lines to Scotland Yard were pretty safe."

"You might think that, Constable. You might think that, but…" Miss Brinton gave Robinson an enigmatic look.

"Is there a security concern here? I am trying to track down a number we found on a murder victim."

Her interviewee smiled coyly. Miss Brinton's face was an odd amalgam of features. Attractive eyes and nose but a strangely tilted and heavy-lipped mouth. "The number you gave me is unlisted."

"I know that, but, as a policewoman, I am entitled to know the line-holder's full details."

"I am afraid that's only partly the case in this instance. I can tell you that number is one of a few allocated to the security services. I can also tell you that if anyone enquires about such a number, I have standing instructions to notify the secret services. I have already told them of your enquiry. They got back to me a few hours later and told me to tell you what I have just said. They also asked me to tell you that it is possible they might get in touch with you to discuss your case – or they might not."

Robinson was taken aback. What on earth could a dead abortionist have had to do with the security services? "Can you tell me if this is a number used at offices of the security services, or perhaps at an agent's house or flat, or…"

"Of course I can't, Constable. I can tell you no more than I just have."

Miss Brinton's cigarette smoke now filled the room and Robinson found her eyes watering. She stood. "Well, thank you. I suppose I'll have to wait and see if I'm called."

"I suppose you will."

*   *   *

There was little enthusiasm at Dorset Square for another meeting with the police but an appointment was eventually agreed for the early afternoon. Over a mid-morning cup of tea, Merlin was having an interesting discussion with Goldberg about alternative British and American policing, when the telephone rang.

"Hello. Who's that? Say again? *Madre de Dios*, is that really you, Eddie? How the hell are you? You don't sound yourself."

"I'm very tired, Frank. But I'm alive, thank God."

"I heard you were in Crete. What was it like?"

"Awful. Bloody awful, as you can imagine. On top of that I've had an exhausting journey home. And then to cap… but never mind. That can wait. I'd love to see you for a chat and a drink. Any chance of doing that today?"

"I've got a meeting this afternoon. Why don't you come to the office around six o'clock? I should be able to get away then. How's Celia?"

"That's what I thought could wait but… she's leaving me, Frank."

"I'm very sorry, Eddie. What can I say?"

"Nothing, Frank. There is something I need to talk to you about. Nothing to do with Celia, a little advice I need. I'll tell you about it tonight. Look forward to seeing you later." The line went dead.

"Something wrong, Frank?"

"A friend of mine just got back home. Edgar Powell. Managed to get out of Crete alive. That's the good news. The bad news is that his wife just left him."

"Sorry to hear that." They could hear the sound of aircraft in the distance. "There's a lot of it about, I understand. Women letting down soldiers while they're in action, I mean. Heard a few stories like that at the Embassy last night. A close friend?"

"We were at the police academy together. He was from a reasonably well-off family. A good school and university education. There weren't so many around like that then – or now for that matter. Despite our different backgrounds we hit it off, played football together, shared a couple of postings. Then he met this girl, Celia, a bit of a snob who didn't really like the idea of being hitched to a policeman. Soon after they got married he packed it in. His family owned a large publishing company. Eddie had been determined to avoid working there but Celia nagged him and eventually he gave in and joined the family firm. We used to meet up as couples very occasionally, he and Celia and me and my… my late wife, Alice. He said he missed the force but he'd made his choice. He seemed happy enough with her then but now…" Merlin gazed through his open office window at the clouds banking up over the river. "Ever been married, Bernie?"

"Just the once, Frank. It didn't take and we only lasted about a year. Like Celia, Abbie wasn't so happy about being married to a policeman but not for snobbish reasons. She didn't like the hours or the danger. She would have been preferred a nine-to-five job of any kind for me. Luckily there were no children."

"Alice and I would have loved to have had kids. I suppose it's a good job that we didn't. If you haven't yet picked it up on the office grapevine, I was married to Alice for a few years. We were very happy but she contracted leukaemia and died a year or so before the war started." Merlin thoughtfully ran a finger over the Eiffel Tower paperweight on his desk. Alice had bought it for him on their last holiday together in Paris in the summer of 1938.

"But now you have someone else…"

"Yes, now I have Sonia, as you have learned on the Yard grapevine. Met her in a case at the beginning of last year. She's Polish. Also part-Jewish. Luckily the family got out of Poland just in time and made it here. Penniless, of course. She had to cut a few corners to survive but ended up with a decent salesgirl's job. Somehow or other she took to me and… so she's with me in Chelsea."

"Too soon for marriage?"

Merlin smiled awkwardly. "Maybe one day. She's a lovely girl. We'll see. And you, Bernie? Met any nice girls over here on your visit? I know you haven't had much time but we understand you Yanks are fast movers when it comes to the opposite sex."

"There were a few beauties at the party last night but none had eyes for this ugly cop. The prettiest girl I've seen in London so far, though, is your Constable Robinson. She's a real looker. I love that little beauty spot below her nose."

Merlin's eyebrows went up. "Please, Bernie, don't!" Merlin wagged a finger. "I've had quite enough trouble with office romances already. Hands off! She's spoken for, anyway. If you've got time to find anyone while you're here, make it anyone other than a policewoman – please!"

*   *   *

Cairo

Lieutenant June Mason watched with increasing concern as the tall, middle-aged man in French military uniform paced up and down the chequered marble floor of the anteroom over which she presided. She had told him several times that the commander-in-chief would see him as soon as his officers' planning meeting had finished. Mason had pointed out, in her very best schoolgirl French, that these meetings often went on for two or three hours and had suggested that her visitor return to his nearby hotel, where she would telephone him the instant the commander-in-chief became available.

This enquiry had been dismissed with an imperious glare. Despite the pacing, the heat and the inadequate circulation of the room's fans, the visitor's face displayed no hint of perspiration. The lieutenant herself could feel two lines of sweat trickling slowly down the back of her neck. She returned to her paperwork.

An hour later, the old English grandfather clock in the corner had just chimed twice when the large double doors opened and a troupe of English officers filed noisily out. The French officer stopped pacing and acknowledged with a curt nod one or two of the departing soldiers. Lieutenant Mason hurried through the doors and told her boss, Archibald Wavell, that he had a guest. Wavell, who was finishing one of the ham sandwiches left over from the officers' lunch, agreed with a sigh that the gentleman should be shown in forthwith.

The general greeted his guest in his serviceable French. "How are you, my friend? What can I do for you?" Wavell inclined his head to one of the chairs opposite him at the table. Charles de Gaulle seated himself carefully. "Care for a sandwich, Charles? They're very good. I understand you have been waiting some time so I would guess you haven't eaten."

De Gaulle declined with an abrupt shake of the head.

"You know it really would have been more sensible if you'd have rung Lieutenant Mason for an appointment. It would have saved you all this waiting around. You know what these planning meetings are like."

"Should I not have been invited to the planning meeting myself, General Wavell?"

"Archie, please Charles, call me Archie. No need to stand on ceremony here, old boy."

De Gaulle stared icily at his host and ran a long, bony finger over his moustache. "You do not think my point worth responding to, General Wavell? Why am I not invited to such meetings as a matter of course? Do I not represent the Free French army and, behind them, the true French nation? Are we not your close allies? Are we not fighting together at this very moment in Syria and the Lebanon?"

Wavell shifted uncomfortably in his seat, before rising to walk over to the window. He looked out at the square and watched a group of soldiers being marshalled together by a sergeant major for some task or other. He could hear the rapid drumming of de Gaulle's figures on the table behind him. This was not the first conversation of this sort he had had with Charles de Gaulle and no doubt would not be the last. Then again, he mused, perhaps he wouldn't be around to hear him much longer. Rumours of his possible recall from Cairo were rife.

This fellow Churchill, as his friend Field Marshal Alan Brooke often said, was like a runaway train. There was no doubting the man's particular genius, but his claims to superior ability in military strategic thinking were dubious. Wavell's long military experience had inculcated in him a healthy respect for caution and conservatism in military affairs. Churchill's political career bore witness to a preference for recklessness over caution. It was inevitable that the two men would clash eventually and in such a clash the civilian master could be the only winner.

However, the rumour mill was not always accurate and Archie Wavell had many friends in high places. He extracted a handkerchief from a jacket pocket and blew his nose loudly before returning to his seat. "Charles, we hold British military planning meetings for British officers. Then there are other military planning meetings coordinated with – and fully involving – our partners and allies such as your Free French. You, no doubt, have your own independent military planning meetings."

De Gaulle raised an eyebrow. "You know very well, General Wavell, that we are not in a position to plan and mount military operations ourselves. Such French-only meetings are accordingly pointless. I know that your supposedly all-British meetings include Australian officers. Why Australians and not French?"

Wavell picked up another sandwich. This one contained some sort of local speciality he had forgotten the name of. It looked like fish paste but smelt nothing like it. Surprisingly, it didn't taste too bad. He chewed it slowly and watched the muscles in de Gaulle's jaw twitch. Eventually he swallowed and replied. "No doubt, my friend, you meet with your officers to plan what you think is the best way forward militarily and then bring forward those agreed views for discussion in our broader Allied meetings. As regards the Australians, I need hardly remind you that Australia is part of the British Empire."

"You speak of empire, General. We too have an empire and our combined forces are now in action in part of that empire. To be more precise, on Sunday there were thrusts from north and south by the Allied forces into Syria and the Lebanon. Yesterday part of your dear Australian contingent was engaged in battle near the Litani River. And how do I have this information? I have it only from my men at the front. Have I been briefed by you, the commanding officer of the campaign? No! You have told me nothing. Why am I being kept in the dark? It is the same back in England. Churchill does his best to avoid telling me anything. You know it's true." De Gaulle's hunger finally got the better of him and he reached out for one of the two remaining hummus sandwiches.

Wavell and all the most senior British military commanders knew very well that Churchill was reluctant to pass on any meaningful military information to de Gaulle partly because of personal animosity and partly because MI5 kept on telling him that the Free French organisation in London was not secure.

Wavell looked wearily back at de Gaulle, knowing that whatever he said would not placate the man. "I am sorry if you are put out by any apparent failings in the communication of military developments to you and your colleagues. I shall consult London about the appropriate protocols for liaison with you. Now, if you will excuse me, General." He got to his feet.

De Gaulle also rose, his face reddening. "I learned a new English phrase the other day from one of the American diplomats here – soft-soaping. Do I have that right? It is a useful phrase, I think. London will no doubt assist you in soft-soaping me but please know this…" de Gaulle moved around the table and stood within inches of Wavell.

"The military progress of our joint forces is one thing and no doubt my people will continue to keep me in the picture one way or other. The outcome of our activities is another matter. If our forces regain Syria and Lebanon from the French imposter government in Vichy, then these colonies of our French empire must revert to me." He drummed his chest with both hands. "I, as the only legitimate French leader, shall take control of these colonies and I shall determine what is to be done with them. I, Charles de Gaulle, not you, Archibald Wavell, nor Mr Winston Spencer Churchill." The Frenchman turned on his heels and strode out of the room.

Wavell walked slowly over to his desk and picked up the telephone. "Lieutenant, please bring me a couple of aspirin and a large scotch."

*   *   *

London

"Dear old Simon, I remember that time we spent down in Greece and Albania in the 20s." Sidney Fleming had gone misty-eyed as he swirled the Courvoisier cognac around in its balloon glass. "I can't say much for the girls in Albania, but there were some very fine specimens in Athens. One night…"

"Sidney, please! This is not appropriate." Tomlinson nodded meaningfully at the third member of their lunch party.

"Oh, yes. Sorry, Philip. You don't want to hear all that. Anyway, we had great fun down there." Fleming paused to straighten his trademark spotted bow-tie. "Also made quite a bit of money in the end, although we had a few tricky moments. It was then that your father met Pulos. Unprepossessing individual I found him at the time but your father saw something in him and so it turned out."

"Turned out how?" Philip Arbuthnot asked as he sipped his glass of dessert wine. He had eaten shellfish and was feeling a little queasy. He hoped he hadn't consumed a dodgy oyster. A friend of his had died from one not so long ago but surely Claridge's oysters would be all right?

"Well, he's been an excellent representative for us in South America, hasn't he? Kept everything ticking over marvellously."

"I understood from my father that Pulos was more than a representative. He said he'd given Pulos some equity." Arbuthnot sipped some more wine. It seemed to be settling his stomach.

Fleming relit the large cigar that had just fizzled out on him and took a puff. "Yes, he has a minority interest in Enterprisas Simal, as I do in the bank holding company. I won't claim to know all the ins and outs of your father's dealings with Pulos in South America but no doubt," he looked across quizzically at Tomlinson, "everything will come out in the wash." He waved his empty brandy glass at a waiter. "I do claim, however, to know pretty much all there is to know about your father's British affairs and you'll be glad to hear that, despite the war, the businesses are in fine fettle. The merchant bank, the commodity trading house, the investing arms – all are in excellent health."

"My father used to tell me that all those businesses required a very hands-on approach. Are you the hands-on person, Mr Fleming?"

Fleming waited for the waiter to refill his brandy glass and depart. "I have been, Philip, but now I delegate. Delegation is the key, as I learned very well from your father. I have some very good men overseeing the businesses in the City. All have been with us for several years, all are diligent, trustworthy and well remunerated. I keep in close touch with them, of course, as did your father until last year."

Tomlinson nodded. "Your father, Philip, always expressed his regard for Sidney and the London management team in the highest terms." An uncomfortable silence fell on the table, which the lawyer eventually broke, wringing his hands nervously. "I hope you don't think it's inappropriate, Philip, to interrupt these reminiscences of your father with a little business?"

"Not at all. Thought that was what we were here for."

"We need to review the specific legalities relating to the consequences of Mr Arbuthnot's death for his family and his ongoing business."

Fleming, who was by now a little drunk, punched Tomlinson's shoulder impatiently. "For God's, sake Reggie, can't you speak English rather than that dreadful legalese? What you mean is that we need to discuss what is to happen to the business now that Simon's gone. Let's cut straight to the quick. He always told me that in the event of any accident befalling him, the reins would pass to me."

Arbuthnot went very pale and almost choked on his wine. "What do you mean?" He turned to the solicitor. "I am the heir, aren't I, sir?"

"You were always intended as such, Philip, but…" The solicitor, who in contrast to Fleming had been abstemious during the meal, began to regret that he didn't have a drink to hand.

"I am afraid that we might have a little problem." He paused to smooth down the tablecloth in front of him. "We appear to be missing some information."

"What information?" Fleming enquired loudly.

"Last autumn you may recall that I had a small operation and was out of the office for a few weeks."

"Hernia, wasn't it?"

"Yes, Sidney. Rather unpleasant. In any event, this absence coincided with the last few weeks Simon Arbuthnot spent in England before he was posted abroad." Tomlinson looked across uncomfortably at his companions.

"Yesterday, as soon as I got into the office, I asked my secretary to bring in Simon's personal files. She could not find them in my filing cabinet, but she did find a note where they should have been, saying they had been temporarily removed to Mr Titmus's office. Now you know that Mr Titmus only does a two-day week for us now and he wasn't in yesterday.

"In Mr Titmus's absence, my secretary enquired of Miss Evans, who looks after Mr Titmus, about the files. She was told that Simon had turned up one day at the office unannounced. Having been informed at reception that I was away, he had asked to see another partner. Mr Titmus was in the office, so he saw him. Apparently your father asked for his personal files. My own secretary had taken a few days' holiday herself when I was away but she had shared my safe combination with Miss Evans. Miss Evans opened the safe, found the files and took them to Mr Titmus."

"So, what the hell happened then?" Fleming had set down his brandy and his cigar and was beginning to feel his blood pressure rising.

"I managed to get hold of Leslie Titmus yesterday afternoon after he got off the golf course. I naturally remonstrated with him for not telling me about this when I returned from my operation but, as is his way, he blithely rejected my complaints.

His father founded the firm, Philip, as you know, and as the majority partner, Leslie, is not an easy person to call to account."

"For Christ's sake, Reggie, get to the point before Philip and I die of suspense."

"The fact is that Simon asked Titmus to leave him alone with the probate section of his files, which was in its own separate box. He did as he was requested without asking why. He was always a little frightened of your father, Philip, as he was the firm's most important client. When he returned half an hour later, he found your father had gone. The probate file was sitting on his desk. He opened it and found it empty, save for a letter which Arbuthnot had asked one of Titmus's clerks to witness. He then gave it to his secretary and forgot all about it."

Philip Arbuthnot's lips were parched. He licked them ineffectively. "What did the letter say?"

"That Simon Arbuthnot thereby revoked all previous wills and codicils and would be preparing a new will that would be forwarded to me shortly."

"Needless to say…"

"Yes, needless to say, Sidney, I have received no such copy."

Arbuthnot looked confused for a moment but then his eyes brightened. "Hang on. If he has revoked the will you drafted for him and nothing else turns up then he died intestate and everything naturally comes to me anyway, doesn't it? So what's the problem?"

"If your father died intestate, you are of course correct, Philip. You are, so far as we are aware, Mr Arbuthnot's only child and…"

"What on earth do you mean 'so far as we are aware?'"

"Forgive me, Philip. I am regrettably prone to overcautious lawyerly language. If you are, as we can reasonably assume, your father's closest living descendant, you inherit as a matter of course in the absence of a will. However, we cannot pretend ignorance of what your father's letter says. Somewhere there is, or may be, a new will that we should attempt to find, or which someone may shortly send to us. I would be very surprised if any new will differs in its main provisions from the one we drafted before."

"Which said what?"

"I can't reveal that, Sidney."

"Why the hell not?"

"Well, it is clearly irrelevant now, anyway. Either we have a new will, or an intestacy, we shall have to see." Tomlinson paused to clear his throat rather noisily, then resumed. "I am afraid that there is another problem. There were further items of importance contained in the probate box."

"What items?"

"Very important documents relating to parts of your father's business, Philip." Tomlinson looked hard at Fleming. "They have gone missing too."

Fleming's face was blank for a moment before a look of anxious comprehension spread over it. "My God, not...!" His hand came down heavily on the table, knocking his empty brandy glass to the floor. "Oh, Christ!"

*   *   *

It was agent Conor Devlin's first day on the job. Devlin, or Harp, as the French wanted to call him, was in Carlton House Terrace, 60 yards or so along from the cul de sac of Carlton Gardens, where the Free French had their main headquarters. De Gaulle had ensured that his people were lodged in an attractive house in a beautiful London street. Unlike the other navvies, he'd worked with on building sites in his youth, Devlin had taken a keen interest in the end product of their backbreaking work and had spent many hours in public libraries reading about the great architects and their works. The supremely elegant Carlton House Terrace had been designed by the Regency genius John Nash and

Devlin had thought on his arrival that if he had to hang around somewhere for several hours, there were worse places.

He had been in position since trailing Lieutenant Beaulieu to work from his Soho digs that morning. Rougemont had asked Devlin to make Beaulieu his priority on this, the first day of surveillance, and had given him Beaulieu's address and description. Details for Meyer and Dumont were to follow. So far there had been nothing for him to see. He checked his watch. It was nearly three o'clock and he was thirsty. A pint of Guinness would go down a treat but he was standing in one of the only parts of London lacking a pub within yards. The nearest place was at least 10 minutes' walk away and that was too far to risk. He liked his drink but placed professionalism over personal needs.

His caution was justified when, a minute later, Beaulieu walked out on to the pavement. He was accompanied by two other French officers, one tallish and walking with a cane, the second a swarthy, shorter fellow. The men set off immediately down the road towards the Duke of York Steps and Devlin followed at a discreet distance. A group of workmen and ARP wardens were sorting out a pile of sandbags at the bottom of the steps. The officers stepped around the obstruction, crossed the Mall and a few yards on turned into St James's Park, where they headed towards the lake.

The three officers finally came to a halt beyond the water and sat down on a bench overlooking a children's playground. Devlin observed them for a while from a clump of plane trees on the other side of the lake. The Frenchmen lit cigarettes and chatted. After about 10 minutes, a man in a pinstriped suit appeared from somewhere, hailed the officers and joined them. Space was made for him on the bench. Devlin realised that if he was to hear anything of the men's conversation, he'd have to get closer.

One of Devlin's useful attributes in performing covert work for Rougemont was that he spoke fluent French while looking nothing like a Frenchman. He was not a tall man but was broad-shouldered and solidly built. With a head of thick, reddish-brown hair and a lined and weatherbeaten face, Devlin had the rugged and battered look of the middleweight boxer he had once been. He was also a former labourer, artist's model and driver.

In Paris, where he had spent several years in the 1930s, he had graduated from sleeping on the streets to sharing the beds of numerous Frenchwomen, both young and mature, who had found him, to his surprise, strangely attractive. He had somehow ended up moving in interesting circles. He had sparred with boxing champion Marcel Cerdan, posed for wild Spanish painter Pablo Picasso and drunk wine with his fellow countrymen, Samuel Beckett and James Joyce. After his return to London in 1939, Devlin found a more mundane social circle, although he still occasionally encountered the odd bohemian, such as the verbose Welsh poet he drank with occasionally in Fitzrovia. This was probably a reflection of the dull way he now made his living. In partnership with an old friend, Devlin was running a small detective agency specialising in matrimonial affairs, which provided him with a modest but congenial living. Assignments like this from Rougemont were a welcome bonus.

Seeking a better vantage point, Devlin edged carefully from one tree clump to another until he reached the playground. He sat down on a swing and opened the copy of *The Times* he had already read from cover to cover that day. A pretty woman pushing a pram entered and sat down on the other side of the playground. With the racket the ducks and geese were making, he was still too far away to hear what the Frenchmen were saying. Devlin moved closer by joining the lady on her bench. Here he found he could hear snatches of conversation. There was no way he could get any closer without attracting attention.

The woman on the bench turned and gave him a nervous glance. Devlin smiled back in a way he hoped reassured her that he posed no kind of threat. His eyes then bored into the newspaper as he concentrated on the conversation behind him. He heard some discussion about the war in the Middle East. Someone, he presumed the visitor, occasionally spoke in English. He heard the words 'Damascus', 'Beirut', 'de Gaulle' and 'Cairo', before the conversation was temporarily halted by the noise of a low-flying RAF aircraft.

The baby in the pram was woken by the plane and loudly made everyone aware of its existence. The aeroplane disappeared, the bawling stopped and Devlin could hear the officers' voices again. He heard mention of 'New York', 'Vichy', 'money' and 'stock exchange' in quick succession. Then there was a conversational lull during which the woman with the pram chose to depart. When he had bade her good day and she had gone, the men were talking again but in lower tones and Devlin could make out less. Then the officers and their friend got to their feet and shook hands. The pinstriped man walked off towards Birdcage Walk, while the officers headed back in the direction of Carlton Gardens.

Devlin, who had no idea whether the encounter he had witnessed had any bearing at all on Rougemont's investigation, thought briefly of following the civilian but decided it was wiser to stick with Beaulieu and made his way back to Carlton House Terrace.

*   *   *

Commandant Angers was feeling very pleased with himself. Rougemont had gone to Aldershot on a military errand and Angers had lunched alone in the little local bistro. To his delight, the same young English beauty who had been at the restaurant the previous Friday was there again, this time accompanied by a girlfriend. Flirtatious words had been exchanged, a few glasses of wine shared, and telephone numbers exchanged. The girls were in showbusiness, appearing in the chorus of a popular revue on Leicester Square. He would call them tomorrow. If he could persuade him, he'd get Rougemont to make up a foursome later in the week. Angers' colleague was too intellectual and reserved – a little sex would be good for him. The commandant, now back in his office, glass of port in hand, was just wondering how he was going to persuade Rougemont when the two detectives were ushered into his room.

Angers rose, a little unsteadily, to his feet. "Bonjour, *Messieurs*. I'm afraid the colonel was called out urgently so you'll have to make do with me. Please be seated."

Merlin could see straightaway that the man was the worse for drink.

"Glass of port, gentlemen?"

Merlin pursed his lips. "A little early in the day for us, sir. Thank you."

"Of course, Chief Inspector, you are on duty. I should have realised. Well, to what do I owe this repeated pleasure? As the colonel told you yesterday, we know nothing of this 'Mr White' fellow you were enquiring about. Is there something new?"

"There is. We have learned the man's real identity."

"Goodness! That's quick work, Chief Inspector. Who was he?"

"A Mr Armand de Metz. According to our information, he was a well known surgeon in Paris before the war."

Merlin thought he caught a flicker of recognition on Angers' face. "Ah, yes, I…"

"You know the name, Commandant?"

Jumbled fragments of thought passed through Angers' slightly addled post-lunch brain. De Metz. Rougemont. The colonel. Carlton Gardens. He couldn't remember what had been said. His mind was blank. In such circumstances, wasn't denial always the best policy?

"No. I mean, yes. No. Sorry, yes, I think I recognise the name."

"How?"

The commandant hummed and hawed for a moment before recovering his confident air. "Why, in the context of his being a famous surgeon, of course."

"Did you… did you know the guy, sir?"

"I did not, Mr Goldberg. The name, however, seems familiar. Perhaps my doctor in Paris mentioned him, or I read his name in the newspaper, perhaps in the medical section, perhaps in the social columns. I cannot remember." Angers ran a hand through his fine mane of hair. "I am very sorry if an eminent French medical practitioner has suffered such an ignominious end but what can I say? There are many people dying sad deaths all over Europe, and doubtless there will be many more before this war is over."

"Yes, sir. I have to say that I'd find it surprising if a man like de Metz had never come to the notice of anyone in the French exile community in London."

"Well, I can't speak for the French exile community but only for myself, Chief Inspector. I never came across the gentleman."

"Mr de Metz had clearly fallen on hard times, Commandant. It would have been natural for him to approach other Frenchmen for help."

The commandant shrugged. "De Metz… De Metz… Was he a Jew?"

Angers' eyes flicked to Goldberg then back to Merlin.

"Yes, I believe he was." Angers gave a knowing nod. "It's a fact that Jews are not generally popular with the French military. I myself have no such prejudices, but…"

"You're saying that Mr de Metz would have believed he wouldn't be welcome so he didn't bother?"

"Exactly so, Chief Inspector. Exactly so."

Goldberg's antipathy towards the commandant was clear in his face. "I wouldn't have thought a man as desperate as he would have been deterred from speaking to you guys by the prospect of a little old-fashioned anti-Semitism."

"What more can I say, Detective? I am just speculating. As I said, I did not know the fellow."

Merlin had spotted lies from cleverer dissemblers than Angers and he knew he was being lied to now. He didn't see how, however, he could press the issue further. The commandant was a senior officer of an Allied military force. He didn't want to cause a diplomatic incident. Not this early in the investigation at least. He had experience of such things in the recent past. He got to his feet. "So, Commandant, I trust we can still look forward to hearing the results of the colonel's enquiries among your colleagues? You have the significant added benefit of a name now. Also I know that there is another Free French outpost in Carlton Gardens. We propose to pursue further direct enquiries there."

Angers looked doubtful. "There is no need for you to go to Carlton Gardens, Chief Inspector. Trust me. We shall contact everyone both here and there about the dead man. Then we'll be in touch. There will probably be a similar answer but please, leave it to me."

Their meeting over, the policemen waited for a taxi in Dorset Square. Merlin hadn't been able to face driving through the West End again.

"The guy's lying."

"You bet he is, Bernie. The question is, is he lying because he's just too lazy or too cussed or does he have a particular reason to do so?"

"He was obviously half cut. Pity we didn't get to see someone else."

"You noticed he wasn't keen for us to go to Carlton Gardens?"

"Sure, but we're not going to go by what he says, are we? Let's go there now."

"We'll go tomorrow morning. I've got to be back at the Yard to see my friend back from Crete."

A black cab pulled up and they climbed in. "All right, Frank. I'm meeting someone tonight too in a couple of hours. For a drink. Someone I met last night at the Embassy. An American journalist. Name of Murrow."

"Ed Murrow. I'm impressed. He's highly regarded here. Well connected too, I should think. You might ask him what he knows about the French in London. Perhaps he'll be able to pass on something useful."

*   *   *

WPC Robinson hoped when the telephone rang that it might be the kindly police officer from Belfast with whom she had exchanged missed calls throughout the day. The caller, however, was a man and he didn't sound particularly kindly.

"I understand you have been making some enquiries, Robinson."

Disconcerted by the man's surly tone, Robinson remained silent.

"I understand you got hold of one of our special numbers."

Robinson suddenly realised MI5 was on the line. She found her voice. "Yes, we found a telephone number on the body of a man. A murder victim."

There was a pause before the reply. "Name of the man?"

"Armand de Metz. A surgeon and a refugee from occupied France. Do you know him?"

"It is not for you to ask me questions, young lady. Please tell me clearly and succinctly what happened to Mr de Metz and when."

Robinson did as she was told and summarised the facts known about de Metz's death.

"I see. Anything else of interest you might care to tell me?"

"It appears that de Metz was earning a living in London as a back-street abortionist."

"I see…" There was another pause. "Well, thank you, Constable. I'll have a chat with my colleagues and may get back to you."

"Why did Mr de Metz have your unlisted telephone number?"

"As I said, Constable, it is for me to ask the questions. If we decide to release any information to you, it will be after careful consultation at this end."

"And your name, sir?"

"Let's say Smith for the moment, shall we? Pip, pip." The line went dead.

Robinson was still mulling over this uncomfortable conversation when the telephone rang again. This time, thankfully, it was the officer from Belfast.

"Sergeant Callaghan. How are you?"

"Bright and breezy, Constable, just like the weather today. I have something for you. A colleague and I trawled through our missing person files but to no avail. However, I was having a snack by chance with a friend who works in another department here. It's the one that has responsibility for Republican violence."

"Do you mean Republican as in the IRA?"

"I do. We were just chatting about the cases we were working on when I mentioned your young woman. My friend – well, to be honest, he's more than a friend, he's my fiancé – was interested so I gave him the details. Your description, the birthmark, the missing toe and so on."

"And?"

"He has a woman on his files who matches the description exactly. Her name is, or was, Bridget Healy, 22, from County Wexford. It must be your girl."

Robinson hurriedly grabbed her notebook and pencil. "How did she end up on his files?"

"She was a suspected IRA activist. Her brother, Finian, is an IRA leader known to have committed various acts of violence against private individuals and against the authorities here in

Northern Ireland. It is suspected that he involved his sister in some of those activities. Last November a bomb went off at a police station and she was found outside in the street with concussion. She was taken to hospital, hence our knowledge of her distinguishing features. Nothing could be pinned on her but our boys were keeping her under surveillance when she suddenly disappeared at the turn of the year. It was assumed she had gone to America or England."

"Can you please send me a copy of the file, Sergeant?"

"Of course, my dear. I'll get it over to you on the next packet-boat. You should have it by tomorrow night."

"I'm very grateful."

"Not at all, Constable. Just doing my job."

"Good luck with your fiancé."

"Oh, he's got a bit of a temper on him but he's a good boy at heart. He should do me fine."

*   *   *

Edgar Powell had left a message for Merlin suggesting they change their arrangement and meet in a pub instead of at the Yard. Merlin telephoned and they fixed to meet at six-thirty in the Surprise, which was convenient for both of them because Powell also had a flat in Chelsea.

Merlin had spent many happy hours at the Surprise with Jack Stewart but hadn't been in there since his friend had been posted north a few weeks before. Arriving a little early, he found a cosy corner table for two. The bar was crowded. London publicans were having a good war. Their pubs had been doing a roaring trade most nights, even with the Blitz at its peak. The prospect of sudden, violent death significantly boosted the average Londoner's desire for alcohol. Merlin liked a drink as much as the next man but there had been times when he knew he liked it too much.

He had gone a little overboard after Alice's death. Stewart had been a great emotional support but they had gone on far too many benders together. Things had eventually settled down around the time Sonia came on the scene, but Merlin realised that Stewart's absence made restraint easier, ungenerous as that thought was to his good friend.

"All right, Inspector? Like a butcher's?" One of the regulars, known to all as Peabody Pete, offered Merlin his copy of *The Evening News*. "Nothing in it as usual." Pete was the sort of person who would say there was 'nothing' in the paper even if the front page was reporting that Martians had landed on the Old Kent Road. Always immaculately dressed in a three-piece suit and regimental tie, he was a retired draughtsman who lived in a tiny flat on one of the nearby Peabody estates.

Merlin took the paper with a nod of thanks and had a 'butcher's'. He loved Cockney rhyming slang. 'Butcher's' was short for 'butcher's hook', which meant 'look'. 'Apples and pairs' – stairs. 'Trouble and strife' – wife. 'Adam and Eve' – believe. Pete had the full vocabulary and used it constantly to the bemusement of some of the Surprise's more refined clientele. The news of the day was the expected Parliamentary debate on the management of the war. The prime minister was expected to have a difficult time but Merlin was confident that Churchill would be able to handle it. His belief in the prime minister remained strong and he remained convinced that no other man could lead Britain safely through the morass.

"Frank Merlin! How the bloody hell are you?"

Merlin stood to embrace his old friend. "Fine, Eddie. How the bloody hell are you?" Both men stepped back a pace to take each other in. Merlin tried to hide how shocked he was by Powell's appearance. The man he knew had been well built with chubby cheeks and a bit of a paunch. The Powell he saw now was drawn, gaunt and seemed to have shrunk an inch or two. The bushy brown hair Merlin remembered had thinned considerably and Powell's skin was cruelly sunburned.

"You had a rough time, then?"

"I know. I look bloody awful, don't I? It was pretty rough but, what the heck, I got out. Many didn't so I've got to be grateful for that. You are looking well! I could murder a pint and I see your glass is empty – get you another?"

When Powell returned to the table with the drinks he collapsed on the bench and immediately gulped his beer thirstily. "Ah – that's good! I used to dream of London Pride in my Cretan foxholes." He wiped the froth from his lips.

"I was very sorry to hear about Celia."

"Celia? A disaster waiting to happen. We weren't getting on at all well when I went off to the army. Arguments about the usual things – the job, money, the family (hers and mine). And Celia's not the sort of girl to wait quietly at home for the return of her warrior husband. No darning socks and running soup kitchens on bombsites for her. Nor is she the sort to curl up on her own in bed with a good book either.

"I hoped otherwise but I guess it was inevitable that she'd find some fellow to fill in for me while I was away. The biggest surprise is that she has allowed herself to get attached to someone. As I think you know, Frank, a wallet beats where her heart should be. Whatever my shortcomings, I am a wealthy man. She appears to have given up on me despite that, which is, as I say, surprising."

"Who is the man?"

"A penniless charmer apparently."

"Have you seen her?"

"No. When I got back to the flat in Flood Street there was no sign of her. Just a letter on the desk spelling out the unsavoury facts from her viewpoint: I'm a cold, uncaring and, of course, absent, husband. She's fallen madly in love with someone who understands her. Best for both parties if we call it a day. Would appreciate a cheque for £100 to tide her over. And, oh yes, she added an afterthought: 'Glad you made it out of Crete.'

"I had managed to send her a cable from Cairo saying I was on my way home. That gave her the time to clear out as many valuables from the flat as she could." Powell stared off into the distance for a moment. "Well, there it is. Probably for the best. No point moping, just move on."

Merlin felt his sympathetic nod was a little inadequate but couldn't think of anything else to do or say. He raised his glass and clinked it with Powell's. The conversation moved on. Merlin asked about Powell's adventures in Greece and Crete, and Powell asked Merlin about his work at the Yard. Another round was bought and Merlin disclosed his new relationship with Sonia.

"Delighted to hear that, Frank. You deserve some happiness after the terrible… what happened to Alice. Sorry, perhaps I shouldn't mention her…"

"Not to worry, Eddie. I don't mind talking about Alice. We had a happy time then a very sad one. I'll never forget her, of course, but life goes on."

"Quite. Life goes on." The two men stared thoughtfully into their half-full beer glasses.

"I would be grateful for a little advice, Frank. Nothing to do with Celia."

"Of course, Eddie."

"It concerns something that happened in Crete. You remember I mentioned my brigade captain, the one who was shot down when we were only a few miles from the evacuation point at Sphakia."

"Yes, poor chap."

"His name was Simon Arbuthnot. A wealthy businessman with interests in the City and abroad. He…"

Peabody Pete interrupted them to request the return of his newspaper. "Sorry, Inspector. Need to do the crossword. Only way I can get to Bo-Peep." Merlin thanked Pete and handed the paper over. Powell gave Pete a strange look as he left.

Merlin laughed. "Sleep, Eddie. Bo-Peep means sleep. You need to brush up on your rhyming slang. Anyway, you were saying, Simon Arbuthnot. The name sounds familiar."

"A well known City figure apparently. So, as I told you, we were raked by German *Stuka* guns on open ground. I was lucky but Arbuthnot and the other soldier with us were not. Arbuthnot wasn't killed outright. He was conscious and asked me to remove a sealed letter from his jacket pocket. The envelope was unaddressed. He tried to give me some instructions about the letter but was fading fast. He managed to convey that the letter was important and that it should get to someone but not whom. When he became unable to speak, he made a sign that he wanted a pencil and I gave him one.

"He managed to write a little. 'Give to my' is clear and then there's a word clearly beginning with the letter S. After that it becomes a scrawl, which is open to interpretation. Of course, I promised I would try and get the letter to its intended destination but I'm in a bit of a quandary about what that destination is. Clearly I have to get it to someone. Arbuthnot was an influential man and the letter might be very important."

"What do you know about Arbuthnot's family?"

"I've been able to do a little research today. There's a mother still living, a son, Philip, who is an only child, and a sister called Lucinda. The family has an estate in Northamptonshire. The son works in London and presumably lives here."

"Have you got the letter with you?"

"No. I've put it in the safe in my flat. I was worried I might lose it walking around London."

"Perhaps you could bring it into the Yard tomorrow? I'd be happy to have a look at it and help you decide what to do. I'll be out for some of the day. Say five o'clock?"

"Thanks, Frank. That's very good of you. You know, I'm absolutely famished. Do you think we could get hold of a pie or something here?"

CHAPTER 7
Wednesday 11 June

London

Robinson had just told Merlin the helpful news from Belfast. For the first time in what seemed like weeks, the office was bathed in bright sunlight and Merlin was feeling positive. "Good work, Constable. Ah, here are the others. Good morning, Sergeant, Detective. Take a pew. Robinson here has identified our dead girl. She was a suspected Republican fugitive from Ireland, name of Bridget Healy, last seen in Belfast when was it, Constable?"

"December, sir.

"Bridget Healy disappeared from official view in Northern Ireland at the end of 1940. Let's make the assumption that she came to London in January. According to the medical report, she had been carrying the baby for three months when she died so she had conceived it in March. Perhaps she had a boyfriend in Ireland who came with her? Perhaps the boyfriend was already in England and she joined him? Or perhaps she only met the father of her child in London, although that is pretty fast work."

"It doesn't take long to make a baby, Frank."

"No, it doesn't, Bernie. So she's pregnant. She or her lover or both don't want the baby. Someone makes an introduction to hard-up French doctor Armand de Metz. He undertakes the abortion in the Bedford Hotel. The abortion is botched and Miss

Healy dies. Three men are seen with Miss Healy or going to the hotel room. Two excluding de Metz. The hotel staff have been in again but their descriptions of these two men haven't improved. All we have still is that the taller of the men might be foreign."

A passing police car's alarm rang loudly outside. Merlin waited until the noise faded away before resuming. "So we know what we know about de Metz. The officer we saw yesterday at Dorset Square still maintained ignorance of de Metz although Detective Goldberg and I are both convinced he was lying for some reason."

"You bet he was."

"Now, Constable Robinson did come up with some interesting new information about de Metz yesterday. That telephone number we found in his flat was an MI5 number. De Metz was a contact of our domestic security agency. An MI5 officer gave Robinson a friendly call yesterday."

"Not that friendly, sir."

"Well, he did say he might call back, didn't he?"

"Possibly. After he'd talked to his colleagues."

Merlin briefly recalled his various tiresome run-ins with MI5 and MI6 over the years. He felt a twinge of anger. "Well, we aren't going to sit on our hands while we wait for those buggers to condescend to help us. I'll see whether the AC can pull a few strings to get them to move." He turned to Robinson. "Very well done again, Constable." Robinson blushed. "See what else you can find out about Miss Healy. Friends, relatives and so on."

"I should be getting her complete file from Belfast later today."

"Good. Sergeant, where are we on the various forensic matters?"

"As reported yesterday, we found one shell casement in de Metz's flat. The killer must have picked up the other two but missed this one, which had fallen behind the back of the bed. Unfortunately, they are having a reorganisation in the forensics lab and the shell has temporarily gone missing. They're trying to find it."

"That's damnably careless and inefficient of them."

"Yes, sir. I've made my feelings known. They are confident it will turn up. As regards fingerprints, none were found other than those of de Metz."

"What about those tickets?"

"The cinema ticket matches those issued at one of the local cinemas in Notting Hill. I asked the young bobby we saw, Constable Phillips, to investigate and he found an usher who recognised de Metz from the Constable's description. He remembers him watching a cowboy film last Wednesday. He was alone."

"That doesn't help us much. What about the railway ticket?"

"I am working on it, sir. As you recall, the train destination began with BL. There are quite a few British railway stations beginning with BL, ranging from Blackpool to Bloxwich to Blaenau Ffestiniog."

"Excellent Welsh pronunciation, Sergeant." Merlin had been on a case that had taken him to Blaenau Ffestiniog years before when he'd been a young sergeant. He had met a pretty local girl, who had given him a crash course in the Welsh language. For some reason he'd retained quite clearly all the things she'd taught him, not just those pertaining to her native tongue.

"What about stations in and around London?"

"Of course, I'm going to focus on those first. There's Blackfriars and Blackheath. A little further away going north there's Bloxwich, Blake Street and Bletchley. Then…"

"All right, Sergeant. Well done. Keep up the good work. Right. Now, I'm off to see the AC. Wait here, please, Bernie, and as soon as I'm done we'll head off to Carlton Gardens."

*   *   *

Rougemont sat back in the warm Holborn sun and enjoyed watching the world go by as the shoe-shine boy went to work on his boots. Two attractive brunettes passed by, chattering cheerfully as they entered the Tube station. Had the commandant been there, no doubt he'd have been off swiftly in close pursuit.

The captain closed his eyes and tried to imagine he was having his shoes cleaned at his favourite spot on the Champs Elysées. He wondered, as he frequently did, how everyone was bearing up under the German occupation. His sources told him that the German governor of Paris, Abetz, was trying to go easy on the population.

Many Parisians would be taking it all in their stride, of course. Girls would be fluttering their eyelashes at the handsome German officers in their smart uniforms. Barmen and waiters would be relishing the generous tips of the newcomers. Many of the fancier shops would be profiting from the new kind of tourist trade. Life would be particularly good for those Frenchmen who shared a similar world view to that of the Nazis. For others, provided they kept their mouths shut, life would be all right. But then there were the Jews. Life would definitely not be all right for them.

He opened his eyes to see another pair of pretty young girls entering the station. The commandant would certainly have enjoyed himself here today. The commandant. He sighed. Angers worried him. Rougemont had received a drunken telephone call from him last night. The policemen had been at Dorset Square, quizzing Angers about the French surgeon. The commandant had mentioned his jolly lunch so no doubt he was already tipsy when he'd seen them. He could be a bit of a liability, his boss.

The shoe-shine boy, a scrawny little Cockney in his teens, set down his brushes and looked up at his client expectantly. Rougemont complimented the boy on his work, paid what was due plus a generous tip, and got to his feet. "*À bientôt, mon ami.*"

He cut through the traffic on Kingsway and headed down a side street at the end of which lay his destination. It was after

10 o'clock and the morning rush in the grimy little café had passed. There were only three customers, one of whom was his man.

Rougemont nodded a greeting to Devlin, who asked the waiter for another coffee. The Frenchman grimaced as he settled himself in his chair. "I would have preferred a cup of tea. The coffee in this country is not fit for pigswill."

Devlin laughed and drained his cup. "Well, I suppose this pigswill is good enough for an Irishman like me."

When the waiter returned with the coffee, Rougemont gave it a quick glance then pushed it to one side. He lit a cigarette and switched to French. "And so to business, Mr Harp. What have you to tell me? How did you get on with Beaulieu?"

"A man of distinctive appearance, as you said. With all that red hair he could be an Irishman. Do you have photographs of the other two you promised me?"

"I have them here in my pocket. But first tell me about Beaulieu."

"Early days yet. The young gentleman is a solitary beast. Works hard or, at least, he spent most of the day in the office. No evidence yet of his being a nightbird. Bedded down, on his own, before 10 o'clock after dining alone at a little place in Soho. His only break from routine was a walk with two other officers in St James's Park, where they met up briefly with another young man. Not a military man. I didn't catch any names, unfortunately."

"Descriptions?"

Devlin lit himself a Gauloise.

"Still smoking the French cigarettes, I see."

"Got hooked on them in Paris."

"Ah, yes. During your Bohemian period. Do you miss that life?"

"I do but I don't think I'd like to return to it under the current regime."

"No, indeed. You should write up your experiences, though."

"Someone's already written it, or something close. Fellow called Orwell. Well, Blair – that's his real name."

"I forget what an erudite man you are. So, the other two officers… Describe them and I'll see if I can identify them."

"Same uniforms as Beaulieu as far as I could see. One of them was tall, six foot or thereabouts. They were all wearing their caps, their *kepis* or whatever you call them. Well, this one had dark hair underneath. Brown, I think. I couldn't really make out his features but he had a cane."

"Interesting. One of your other targets, Dumont, occasionally uses a cane, I understand. And the other officer?"

"He was shorter. Five foot nine or 10. Dark. Very slim. The hair under his cap was black. That's really as much as I could see."

Rougemont took out the two photographs he had in his pocket. "This them?"

"Could very well be." Devlin gave both photographs a careful look. "I can't say I'm 100 per cent sure but, yes, this could be a picture of the man with the cane and the other could be the shorter one."

"Dumont and Meyer. The other suspects. If it were them, I wasn't aware the three officers under suspicion were all friends, but I'm not sure it means anything. Officers of the same rank working in the same office – would be surprising if they didn't have some sort of relationship, wouldn't it? What about the other chap? The civilian."

"Maybe five foot 11. Wearing a pinstriped suit. Solid looking. Fair hair, a middle parting. Balding slightly. Clean shaven. They were all clean shaven except Beaulieu. I may be wrong as I was at some distance but this man seemed a little nervous. He was looking about him quite frequently. The others seemed more at ease."

"English?"

"He looked English. So far as I could tell they were speaking a mixture of English and French. I'm not sure if he spoke any of the French."

Rougemont blew a neat smoke ring into the air. "And what did you hear of their conversation?"

"Thanks to the ducks, a low-flying plane and a bawling baby, not much."

"That's a pity. You heard nothing at all?"

"I heard mention of various places in the Middle East – Damascus, Beirut, Cairo. I heard mention of New York, Vichy, de Gaulle and the stock exchange. And I also heard a few other odd words that probably aren't relevant – mines, Ritz, poker, surgeon."

A flicker of surprise registered on the captain's face. "Surgeon? Are you sure you heard that correctly?"

Devlin nodded. "As you know, I speak pretty good French. *Chirurgien*'s the word, isn't it?"

"Yes." Rougemont abruptly stubbed out his cigarette and gazed thoughtfully at his untouched cup of coffee. "Anything else?"

"No. Their conversation lasted no more than a quarter of an hour or so. Afterwards the officers returned to Carlton Gardens and their friend disappeared up Birdcage Walk."

Rougemont turned his thoughtful gaze on Devlin. He reached again into his jacket. "For your trouble, Mr Harp. Your usual rate, as agreed. Thank you."

Devlin pocketed the envelope and the photographs. "Do you want me to keep on Beaulieu for the moment?"

"I think it would be wise to spread yourself a little and keep an eye on all three."

"Obviously, if I'm trying to cover the three, things may fall through the gaps."

"I heard that Beaulieu has a day or two's leave this week. Seeing some friend in Oxford."

"Legitimate?"

"So I'm told. I have a contact in the university. His friend is a respected academic. My contact can let me know if he turns up there. If he does, you have more scope to observe the other two."

"Very well. If you're sure."

"I'm not sure about anything. To be honest, I'm not really sure if Colonel Aubertin really wants a proper investigation. It is strange that he chose to give the job to the commandant, even though it has ultimately been devolved to me. Anyway, I've got you and I know you'll do the best you can in imperfect circumstances."

Devlin eased himself out of his chair.

"Friday, Mr Harp. Same time, same place. I'll pay your next instalment then."

Devlin nodded, flicked Rougemont a casual salute and left. The captain stayed behind for a few minutes. He wondered about the three officers. If there were really something to Colonel Fillon's suspicions, perhaps they were all involved together? Who was the other man they met?

Then again, the snippets of conversation Devlin had caught did not seem particularly suspicious. The major French military activity at present was in the Middle East, while de Gaulle and Vichy were perennial subjects of gossip for the Free French officers. New York? He had learned that one of the officers, Meyer, had connections there. The stock exchange? Shares continued to be traded despite the war. No reason for soldiers not to take some interest in the markets. No, the only thing he'd heard that disturbed him was the reference to a surgeon. Surely that could only be de Metz? But no. He was sure Devlin must have misheard.

*　　*　　*

"Come in, Frank. I've been meaning to talk to you. I was wondering how you and this Goldberg fellow were getting on." The AC was enjoying his elevenses – a pot of tea and a plate of McVitie's digestive biscuits. He had one of these staple British delicacies in his mouth and seemed oblivious to the spray of crumbs being ejected as he spoke. Merlin edged his chair back a few inches.

"He's a very pleasant chap, sir. A *buen chico* as my father would say."

The AC frowned. He didn't care to be reminded of Merlin's Hispanic origins. "Mmm. Good." Gatehouse pushed the biscuit plate across his desk but Merlin shook his head. "Has he been of any use?"

"I really can't say that yet, sir, but I believe he will be. It takes time to settle into what, after all, is an alien world to him."

"Yes. Well… Never been to New York myself but no doubt it's very different to London and the fellow looks like he can handle himself if you get into any sticky corners. Might be useful then?"

"I've no doubt, sir."

"Very good." The AC fiddled with the stud in his wing collar then. "What else do you have for me?"

"In our inquiries into the murder of Mr de Metz, we have learned that the security services are aware of the gentleman and may have had some dealings with him."

"May have had some dealings? What does that mean?"

"We don't know yet. De Metz possessed a telephone number that Robinson was following up. It turned out to be an MI5 number. She received a call from an MI5 officer acknowledging this, but he wouldn't give any more information. He said he'd talk to his colleagues and get back to her in due course if they felt there was anything they could tell us."

The AC paused as he attempted to dislodge a chunk of digestive from a gap in his teeth. Mission accomplished, he looked across thoughtfully at Merlin. "I thought this man was just a back-street abortionist. What the devil was he doing with MI5?"

"That is the question. It's possible it could put an entirely different complexion on the case. We need to hear back from MI5 as soon as possible. As you well know, we don't have a very good track record with these people. I myself have one reliable contact there but I know he'd prefer me to go through the proper channels. I was wondering if you could put in a word to whoever oversees those channels to help expedite matters."

The AC turned towards the window, which, like that in Merlin's office directly below, looked out on the London County Council building opposite and Westminster Bridge to the right. The gun emplacements on the top of the LCC building had been idle for more than three weeks now. "Strange, isn't it, Frank? We'd all got so used to the bombing that it now seems unnatural not to have the planes coming in every night."

"It does, sir. My next-door neighbour says the Germans are just taking a break before launching an even greater barrage than the one on 10 May. Says he's heard there's some type of new bomb the Germans have developed that will knock us for six."

"Fiddle-faddle, Frank. I hope you told him to desist from such defeatist claptrap."

"I did, sir."

"The story in Whitehall is that the bombing has stopped because Hitler needs his planes elsewhere. Perhaps to push out eastwards."

"Against Russia, you mean?"

"Hitler is mad enough to do anything." The AC straightened up. "Anything! Now back to your Frenchman and MI5. I think we are entitled to take the view that we have greatly assisted MI5 by lending them Inspector Johnson for the Hess case."

"I thought the prime minister imposed Johnson on them?"

"That may be one interpretation, but I would prefer to claim that we have deprived ourselves of one of our best men to help them out. As far as I'm concerned, a favour given deserves a favour in return. I'll get on to the home secretary this morning."

The AC paused a moment. "No, what am I thinking? I won't bother with the home secretary. He doesn't have much clout. I'll go directly to the new chap who's taken over at MI5. Petrie. David

Petrie is the man. Now, my brother George was telling me at the weekend that Petrie was a colleague of his in the Indian police before the war. They were good friends, he said. For once, my brother can be of use to me. I'm sure I'll be able to get Petrie in line. Leave it with me, Frank. Of course, you'll let me know if an officer from MI5 does follow through and contact you?"

"Of course, sir." Merlin got to his feet. "There's one other thing. A friend of mine recently returned safely from Crete. He is the custodian of a letter from a fellow officer, who died in the retreat. Doesn't quite know what to do with the letter and has asked my advice. I think I know what to tell him, but just wanted to run it by you."

"What's the name of the dead officer?"

"Simon Arbuthnot."

"Goodness, I know that name. Big chap in the City. Went shooting with him a couple of times just before the war. Sorry to hear he's dead. What's the problem with the letter?"

"Let me explain."

*   *   *

New York

Anton Meyer's wife had gone to New Jersey to stay with her sister for a couple of days. For the first time in a while, his day hadn't ended in an argument and he'd been able to enjoy a good night's sleep. It was 10 in the morning and Meyer had already dealt efficiently with most of the files on his desk. He had taken a moment to congratulate himself on this when Maurice Kramer appeared at his door. "Daydreaming again, Meyer?" Kramer's beady eyes glared meanly at him.

"I just finished all of this, Mr Kramer." He pointed to the pile of files in his out tray.

"Big deal, Meyer." Kramer disappeared behind the door and reappeared with a large cardboard box containing several more files. "Here's more for you. Have fun. And oh…" He reached into his trouser pocket. "This just came for you. Whoever this fellow Rodriguez is, I'd be grateful if you'd tell him not to send you personal cables at the office. If Mr Liebman were to hear about it, he'd go nuts. You're lucky he's out on the golf course today." Kramer slapped the telegram down on the desk and departed with a snort of disapproval.

Meyer read: 'PULOS LEFT FOR ENGLAND STOP SOURCE IN OFFICE SAYS SOME BIG PROBLEM STOP PROCEEDINGS ADJOURNED AGAIN STOP PLEASE SEND FUNDS AS PER LETTER STOP YOURS RODRIGUEZ'.

Meyer looked out of the window and saw the pretty young girl opposite settling at her desk. This was a sight that normally raised his spirits but not today. Not only was the case in Argentina still stalled but he would have to fork out another 2,000 dollars. There were 15,000 dollars remaining of his 25,000-dollar lottery win. The 10,000 already spent on the litigation so far had advanced his case very little. Ruth and he could still do a lot with 15,000 but it stuck in his craw to think of Pulos and his partners getting away with everything.

Meyer looked again at the cable. He had told Rodriguez before not to send communications to the firm – it just gave Kramer something else to hold over him. It must be something pretty serious, though, for Pulos to travel to England given the state Europe was in. He wasn't sure how one went about getting from Buenos Aires to London these days.

He picked up a pencil and started sketching. The young Anton Meyer had wanted to be an artist. His father had seen his talent and encouraged his son in the belief that all would be done to enable him to pursue his dream. Then everything had changed. His dreams of making a creative living had gone forever.

Meyer still drew for fun, though, and the little sketch he now dashed off caught his brother Felix to perfection. The crooked smile, the eyes permanently crinkled with laughter, the small button nose and cleft chin.

He ought to telephone his brother and tell him about Pulos. Perhaps Felix could find out what was up. He would refuse, of course. His brother was in Ruth's camp when it came to Anton's legal adventures. "Let it alone, Anton. Our parents are dead. What was is no more. There is a life to be lived and greater battles to be fought. It is more important to defeat Hitler and his Nazis than to pursue personal vendettas. Yes, we were betrayed by those men but we can't do anything about it. Your legal proceedings will get you nowhere. Ruth is right, she is a good girl and you can be very happy with her. Concentrate on that, just as I am going to concentrate on the war."

Felix had a point, of course, but Anton just couldn't let it go. He kept seeing the look on his father's face as he died, slowly and painfully, in that dirty Parisian attic in the rue Berthe in Montmartre. There still lingered a flicker of hope that something could be done. Anton Meyer was desperate to keep that flicker alive.

The door opened and Kramer reappeared. He didn't say a word but stared hard at the new box of files. Meyer sharpened his pencil in the machine attached to the side of his desk and picked up the audit file of Weinberg and Co, a ball-bearing company in Jersey City.

As Kramer slid away, Meyer resolved to call Felix the following morning before work. Ruth would still be away and he would be able to discuss things with his brother without her interrupting. At least now there was something specific he could ask his brother to do, assuming he was still in London. He had read something in *The New York Times* about Free French forces being sent to Syria but he was sure that Felix would have let him know if he was being posted overseas.

It would be good to know the reason for Pulos's trip and Meyer would try to get his brother to investigate. He would book a call for six on Thursday morning – 11 his brother's time – and he would send a cable during today's lunch break to prepare his brother for the call.

Relieved to have worked out his little plan, Meyer picked up the new file and looked at Weinberg and Co's draft trial balance sheet. Sharpened pencil in hand, he went to work.

*   *   *

London

Carlton Gardens was only a 25-minute walk from the Yard and Merlin felt the need for some exercise. Goldberg was more than happy to make the journey on foot and, as a bonus, received a running historical commentary from Merlin as they crossed Parliament Square, walked down Birdcage Walk, passed Horse Guards Parade and the Admiralty, and went over the Mall.

Merlin loved history almost as much as he loved poetry and was particularly knowledgeable about London. As they reached the Duke of York Steps, he was just explaining how the Mall had originally been a playing field for the game of pall mall, an early version of croquet, when Goldberg interrupted. "Sorry, Frank. That's all fascinating but I just wanted to say that I had an uncle who died somewhere around here. He was a military scientist for you guys. Got run over by a hit-and-run driver. They found the man who…"

Merlin stopped abruptly. "Emmanuel Goldberg?"

"Yes. Poor old guy. You remember the case, Frank?"

"Of course, Bernie. I investigated it. Why didn't you say before?"

"I… I don't know. The sergeant told me it was one of your cases. I guess I was going to mention it sometime and that sometime turns out to be now. Where did it happen exactly?"

Merlin pointed back in the direction from which they'd come. "I told you the road we turned off to come past Horse Guards Parade was called Birdcage Walk."

"Yes. Where you said James I had kept his aviary?"

"Right. Well, if we'd carried on 150 or 200 yards further down that road towards Buckingham Palace, that was where your uncle was hit."

Goldberg nodded. "Perhaps when we're going back we can make a short diversion."

"Of course, if you like. And if you want to talk about the case any time…"

Merlin led Goldberg up the Duke of York Steps and into Carlton House Terrace. He halted briefly outside number nine. "This used to be the German Embassy before the war. Ribbentrop's little citadel." Workmen were doing something to the front door. "I've no idea what it's used for now."

At the end of the road there was Carlton Gardens. General de Gaulle's Free French Headquarters was Number Three. A French flag flapped gently above them in the light breeze.

"Ed Murrow told me a few stories about de Gaulle last night."

"He did?"

"The general's not a very popular man in some quarters. Roosevelt detests him and he's never met him. Murrow said that's entirely due to Churchill's influence. The PM finds de Gaulle a real handful. Murrow has himself interviewed de Gaulle and found him a little prickly. Always looking out for examples of English deceit and – what was that word Murrow used? – oh yeah, perfidy. English perfidy. De Gaulle doesn't trust you guys, and I guess you guys don't trust him."

"It was ever thus between the English and French. Let's hope the Frenchmen here go against type. By the way, I got a note from the AC enlightening me about the exact set-up of the Free French in London. This building houses the overall headquarters of the

Free French forces and their commander, de Gaulle. It is also the headquarters of something called the French National Committee, the closest thing to a French government-in-exile, also headed by de Gaulle. The place in Dorset Square is the HQ of the French operational section of the SOE. That's the outfit set up by our security services to infiltrate agents into France among other things."

"I would guess from what you say, Frank, that there would be some British officers working in Dorset Square."

"That would seem logical. But come on. Let's see what this lot have to say."

They walked through the door into an elegant foyer. On the right at the back, a young officer manned a desk. He appeared to be engaged in a heated telephone conversation. Merlin and Bridges waited patiently until the officer angrily slammed the phone down. Merlin explained who they were and asked if they could speak to someone in authority.

The officer replied tetchily: "The general is not here, if that's who you mean by authority."

Merlin smiled. "No, we do not wish to trouble the general. A competent officer involved in the administration of this place will do." The Frenchman took Merlin's card, then disappeared through a door behind him. He was away for some time before returning to lead them back through the door and down a long corridor. They were shown into a small windowless office, a partitioned space in a larger room, as could be deduced from the background hum of murmuring French voices and typewriters.

A serious-looking dark young man rose to greet them. He had closely cut black hair, uneven teeth and intense blue eyes. "Gentlemen, a pleasure. I am Lieutenant Felix Meyer. I understand from Villeneuve here that you have a few questions for us. I would be happy to assist you in any way I can."

Merlin introduced himself and Goldberg as the detectives took their seats at Meyer's cramped desk. "We are here pursuing an investigation into the death of one of your countrymen." Merlin proceeded to tell Meyer about Armand de Metz, the botched abortion, his murder and their so far unsuccessful inquiries at Dorset Square. Meyer listened patiently, scribbling the odd note on a small pad in front of him.

When Merlin had finished, Meyer set down his pencil and nodded. "Why yes, indeed, Chief Inspector. We are aware of this gentleman. I am surprised that my colleagues in Dorset Square could not help you as there was much gossip among our officers about Monsieur de Metz. You will appreciate, of course, that information is a precious commodity in wartime. Some of my colleagues are a little resentful of the limited information provided to us by our British military counterparts. Perhaps this feeling soured the meeting with my Dorset Square colleagues. Then again, perhaps I am wrong, and the gossip about de Metz never reached them. In any event, I am happy to tell you what we know."

"Thank you, Lieutenant."

"*Monsieur* de Metz was indeed, as you say, an eminent man in Paris before the war, who lost his position, possessions and family in short order after the Germans arrived, then managed to escape to London. He came here several times. Initially he was just seeking financial help as a penniless Frenchman in exile. Unfortunately for him, we are not set up to act as some sort of welfare service here, Chief Inspector, so money was out of the question. I understand that *Monsieur* de Metz was pointed in the direction of some medical recruitment agencies by one of my colleagues – Lieutenant Dumont or Lieutenant Beaulieu, I think it was. He went on his way.

"This did not lead to anything and he returned here a few times more. He became something of a pest, hovering around this building and the pubs and cafés we frequent. I don't know if he did the same at Dorset Square. At some point he began to claim that he had important security information he needed to discuss.

I saw him and suggested it would be more appropriate for him to speak to an officer at Dorset Square about such matters. For some reason, he was not keen to do that. He produced an old photograph that he used to wave around as some sort of unexplained element of the information he wanted to impart. He spoke to a number of us about this. Little credence was placed in him. We thought it was just another creative way of trying to extract money."

"Did he give you any idea of the nature of the information he claimed to have?"

"All he would say is that there were unknown links between Vichy and London. He could tell us all if we put him on a retainer as some sort of informer or spy. You may not know, Chief Inspector, but we are approached frequently by people with spurious stories suggesting shady dealings between our officers in London and our countrymen in France. It is a simple fact that everyone here has family, friends or business contacts who remain in Vichy France or the occupied zone. If we investigated all these stories, we would never have time to get on with fighting the Nazis."

Goldberg frowned across at Meyer. "Was there really no-one in the French community here who could vouch for de Metz? I mean, the guy was a medical bigwig in Paris. Surely there were émigrés here who knew him and could help?"

"Perhaps there were, Detective. The last I heard of him, he appeared to have come into some money."

"As I said earlier, Lieutenant, he was performing back-street abortions just before he died."

Meyer shrugged. "The man was obviously desperate."

Goldberg shifted in his chair. "Was one of the reasons he couldn't get help here because he was a Jew?"

"There are no doubt some anti-Semites here, Detective." Meyer paused. "But not everyone. I myself am a Jew. I don't think his Jewishness had anything to do with it. He couldn't get help

because, as I said earlier, we do not operate as a welfare agency."
Meyer pushed his chair back and stood up. "Now I'm sorry,
gentlemen. My duties call and I doubt I can tell you any more."

"Thank you, Lieutenant. You have my card. If anything further
occurs to you, please do not hesitate to call. It's also possible we
may wish to speak to some of your fellow officers."

"Of course, Chief Inspector."

*   *   *

Rupert Vorster went regularly to a small gymnasium off Liverpool
Street to do physical jerks or box a few rounds with one of the
trainers. Pinson's Gymnasium was run by former Regimental
Sergeant Major Charlie Burns, with the help of a couple of old
military colleagues. Vorster had caught an early-morning train
from Cambridge, where he had been on a legal assignment for
Titmus, Travers and Tomlinson the previous night, and decided
to sneak in a session at the gym before going to the office.

He had some clean kit in his locker, changed and went in
search of Burns. The sergeant, a wiry Scot who, despite his
60 years, packed a considerable punch, agreed to spar a few rounds
with him. Vorster usually managed to hold his own with Burns
but today he took quite a pounding. Afterwards, the sergeant put
an arm around his shoulder. "What's up, Mr Vorster? You weren't
yourself today – made it easy for me. Something on your mind?"

Vorster took off his gloves. "You were the better man on the
day, Burnsie. That's all."

The sergeant threw Vorster a towel. "Och no! Something's
bothering you, I can tell. I think you might have had a few
drams last night but there's something else, isn't there? Woman
trouble, is it?"

Vorster sat down on a bench and wiped the sweat and blood
from his forehead. "Let's just put it down to a late night and

leave it at that, eh, Sergeant?" Burns smiled wryly at him before disappearing into the locker room.

From where he was sitting, Vorster could see into the weights room. He recognised one of the men there as Roger Forbes, a senior manager at Sackville, the banking firm owned by his friend Philip's father. Although he was feeling a little tired and battered, he resolved to be sociable. It always paid to keep up with City contacts. He was fed up with training for the law on a pittance and it would be a kick in the pants for his father if he managed to find himself a good job at a bank or broking firm.

"Rupert, you Boer dog, how are you?" Forbes set down the barbell he had been lifting. "Haven't seen you since that party at Harry's. Quite a do, wasn't it?"

Vorster remembered a rather boring evening at the Kensington home of one of his father's business protégés. It had not been a completely wasted night though because he had found a couple of takers for his friend Peregrine Beecham's late-night entertainments.

"Yes, great. How are you, Roger? How's business?"

Forbes frowned and stroked his chin.

"Surely you've heard the news?"

"News? What news?"

"Haven't you seen Philip?"

"We had drinks last Friday but I haven't spoken to him since. I had to go out of town on business. What's happened?"

"His father died. Killed in the Cretan retreat. We found out yesterday. Announced it last night and naturally there's been a lot of concern in the markets. Fleming – you know him, don't you? Sidney Fleming, formerly deputy chairman and Arbuthnot's right-hand man? – Fleming has assumed the chairmanship and has stated his intention to strengthen the board with two or three experienced City figures. Confirmed the businesses are in good shape, strong management still in position, no-one's irreplaceable and so on. An announcement to that effect went out an hour or so ago and has calmed things down."

Vorster was shocked. He thought for a moment before speaking. "I must get in touch with Philip. I'd better get off to the office."

"Fleming told me that Philip was taking leave from work. You'd be better off calling him at home."

"I'll do that."

"How's the soliciting going, Rupert? Never quite saw that as your kind of thing."

"It's not, Roger. But my father…"

"Ah yes. Your father. Getting you prepared for the family company, eh?"

"Well, actually…"

"Sorry, Rupert. I'd better get on. I'm giving myself another 15 minutes before I go back. Shouldn't really be here at all with what's going on. Let's meet for a drink after work one day."

"Sure. I'll call you soon." Vorster turned and hurried to the locker room. As he showered, it occurred to him that there might be some way in which Arbuthnot's death could be exploited to his advantage. Not a very nice thought, but there it was. The question was… how?

*   *   *

Vichy

Laval had arranged the interview for four-thirty. This was, in his experience, the best time to see the marshal, who was usually at his most alert after a post-prandial nap. In the morning, when one might expect him to be at his most alert, it seemed to take a while for the cogs in his brain to gear up. Then, just when they were beginning to move smoothly, lunchtime came along to slow them down again. The afternoon doze, however, usually restored him to his best. Not that the best was that sharp, Laval mused, as he waited in the anteroom to the marshal's suite. Henri Philippe Benoni Omer Joseph Pétain had been born on 24 April 1856, just a month after the end of the Crimean War. Napoleon's nephew, Napoleon III, had already led the Second Empire for four years. Pétain was 85 years old. No-one's brain was that great at 85.

As he checked his watch for the third time, the marshal's office doors opened. The young lieutenant who served as the marshal's principal aide beckoned Laval in. Pétain was seated at his desk. A little redness around the eyes bore witness to his recent nap but otherwise he looked good. He was stroking his bushy white moustache while reading some papers. He looked up. "Pierre, there you are! Take a seat, dear boy. Jean, bring up that comfortable chair by the window for my friend. You will forgive an old man for not rising to greet you, I hope?"

"Of course, Marshal, of course, and thank you for seeing me at such short notice." Laval lowered himself into the chair and applied a handkerchief to his perspiring forehead.

"Yes, it is a warm day, isn't it? I'm sorry, I don't seem to feel the heat as I should. I am not sure if that is a benefit of old age or a disadvantage. Jean, open the balcony doors, will you? Let us have some fresh air for my friend." Jean did as he was told and Laval immediately felt the relief of the light breeze from outside. The marshal waved a finger at his aide and the young lieutenant disappeared behind another door. "Well, Pierre, what news do you bring?"

"I doubt I have any news that you don't already have, Marshal. I presume the admiral keeps you fully posted?"

The marshal chuckled. "Of course, Admiral Darlan keeps me up to date. However, Pierre, you have your own sources, your own network. No doubt there is interesting information there to which the admiral is not privy. You would not withhold this from me out of any feeling of resentment, I hope?"

Laval chuckled in turn. "Resentment? Me? You know me better than that, I trust, Marshal?"

Both men smiled thoughtfully for a while, contemplating the fact that Laval did indeed have strong grounds for resentment towards the marshal. Until December, Laval had held Darlan's position as, effectively, prime minister of the Vichy state. However, the marshal had taken fright at Laval's closeness to the Germans and, egged on by Laval's many enemies, had sacked him, replacing him eventually with Darlan.

The marshal broke the silence first. "The admiral tells me that all is going well in his negotiation regarding the implementation of the Paris protocols."

"Does he now? My sources tell me there are some difficulties."

The marshal turned to the window. A bird was singing outside and had distracted him for a moment. "What a sweet sound. An ortolan, I believe. A lovely little bird."

"Especially on a dinner plate."

The marshal threw back his head and laughed. "You are a barbarian, my friend, although I must admit that I have myself partaken. Delicious, I agree. You were talking about difficulties?"

"According to my sources, yes."

"And your sources would perhaps include *Herr* Abetz in Paris?"

"Yes, Marshal. To put it bluntly, the Germans are questioning whether the admiral has his heart in the matter."

"And why are they doing that?"

"Because Darlan is quibbling excessively about various details. He has expressed concerns about the agreed provision of conscript labour, about the requirements concerning Jews, about…"

"What about the Jews?"

Laval pursed his lips. Pétain liked to profess ignorance of the stream of oppressive anti-Jewish laws and regulations his government had introduced. French Jews were now excluded from all commercial and industrial jobs, from the civil service, the army and the press. Draft statutes and regulations for the effective prohibition of Jewish businesses, for the exclusion of Jewish students and for the prohibition of Jewish lawyers and doctors were awaiting imminent passage through the Vichy legislature. And Pétain was asking him innocently about the Jews? Laval decided to ignore the question.

"Suffice to say, Marshal, the Germans are troubled. It is, in my view, unwise to trouble them. They have made a number of very meaningful concessions to us. I don't need to repeat them, do I, sir?"

The marshal grunted with irritation. "Yes, yes, of course. The occupation costs have been reduced by a quarter, the prisoners of war are being returned and so on. I know."

"And at the same time some of the things we agreed to give them are proving worthless."

"What do you mean?"

"Well, for example, our offer to give the Germans military access to our territory in Syria and Lebanon is likely, as it stands, to prove of no value."

The marshal reached out to a file on his desk. "I have just been reading the latest report from General Dentz. Yes, the British have launched operations but the general is confident of rebuffing them. He has seven infantry battalions at his disposal, including some crack Foreign Legion regiments. He has another 11 special infantry battalions, including horse and motorised cavalry. On top of all that, he has air strength of nearly 300 aircraft. He's a good man, Dentz. I am sure with the substantial forces to hand he'll be able to do his job. A successful job."

"I understand he has already lost a battle. At somewhere called Litani in the Lebanon."

The marshal took a paper from the file and flourished it at Laval. "I already have a report on that. You say a battle? It was a minor skirmish over a small river crossing. Nothing of importance. Really, Pierre, I would not have expected such defeatism from you."

Laval shrugged. "It will be no easy thing to keep the British out."

"Hah! The British. And what sort of shape do you think they are in? They had to scuttle with their tails between their legs from Dunkirk last year, since when they have been bombed to hell and back by the *Luftwaffe*. They have been able to achieve nothing in north Africa, except for beating the Italians, which is hardly something to crow over."

Laval gave the Marshal a weary look. "You have always underestimated the British, I think, Marshal. Of course, it is not just the British in Syria. There are Australians. There are also a couple of what are called Free French brigades. Those brigades have some Foreign Legion soldiers too."

The marshal banged his hand down so hard on the desk that the young lieutenant poked his head through the door to check that everything was all right. The marshal waved him away, looking so angry that Laval thought he might break the habit of a profoundly conventional and conservative lifetime and curse. Instead he spat out the words 'Free French' as if they were swear words. "By what right does that treacherous young man de Gaulle allocate this description to himself and his ragged band of followers?"

"By right of the fact that he lives in England and can do what he wants."

"For the moment, Pierre, for the moment." The marshal sat quietly for a moment, recovering his equilibrium. "And what do your sources tell you about him?"

"That he is in Cairo at the moment, trying unsuccessfully to get himself into the confidence of the British Middle East Command."

"Is he involved with the military planning in Syria and Lebanon?"

"Apparently not, much to his disgust. Churchill doesn't trust him and so inevitably neither does Wavell."

The marshal tugged at the right corner of his moustache. "We must be grateful for small mercies. And what of London – while the cat is away are the mice at play?"

"No doubt, being Frenchmen, the officers will enjoy intriguing against each other."

The marshal gave Laval a pained smile. "Must you always have such a low opinion of your fellow countrymen, Pierre?"

Laval opened his arms wide with a look of injured innocence.

"Hmm. And what of British counter-intelligence, Pierre? Have they flown over any more agents? I know you have some man or men well placed to advise you on these matters."

"I have no fresh information on that, sir. I would expect to hear more shortly."

The marshal turned to look out of the window again. The birdsong had stopped but one of the military bands had started up in the square. Pétain paused to listen to a few bars. "I think that is a march by the American Sousa – rousing, isn't it?"

Laval, who had no ear for music, nodded.

"De Gaulle was one of my protégés. You know that, don't you, Pierre?"

"Yes, sir." Laval raised his eyes to the ceiling, where a fan revolved slowly and creakily. He had heard the marshal on the subject many, many times since de Gaulle had risen to prominence as the leader of the French opposition in exile. "But to return to what I was saying, Marshal."

"And what was that?"

"You must do whatever you can to keep in good relations with the Germans. Keep an eye on Darlan as he is rubbing them up the wrong way. If necessary, replace him."

"Replace him? Replace him with whom, Pierre?"

Laval smirked mischievously and rose to his feet. "I must now say *adieu*. I am, as always, at your disposal and at the disposal of my beloved France."

*   *   *

London

The Bridget Healy file had just arrived from Belfast. It was a slim one. Bridget Mary Healy had been born on 3 February 1919 in the village of Adamstown in County Wexford in the south east of the Irish republic. Her father, James, was a farm labourer and her mother, Annie, a seamstress. She was the youngest of three, with a brother, Finian, 25, and a sister, Patricia, 24. There was a paragraph on Finian's involvement with the IRA and the terms of a possible prosecution of him for trafficking firearms into Northern Ireland. There was nothing on the sister.

The report included a summary of general police suspicions regarding Bridget's involvement in Finian's illegal activities and specific suspicions regarding the bombing incident that led to her hospitalisation. There was a note about Bridget's disappearance from Belfast at the end of 1940 beneath which someone had scrawled in pencil 'New York? London?' A couple of her addresses in Belfast were listed.

The typed report ended halfway down the second page but there were a number of pencilled telephone numbers beneath. The legible ones were Belfast numbers with ticks against them, by which Robinson understood the local police had checked them out. However, at the very bottom of the page was a number that someone had partially crossed out. There was no tick against it. She held the paper up against the small window and tried unsuccessfully to decipher the number. There wasn't enough light and she couldn't use the ceiling lightbulb because it was broken. She picked up the file and walked over to Merlin's office, where she found Bridges at his table, engrossed in a book.

"I just need to look at this in the light, if you don't mind, Sergeant?"

"Go ahead."

"Good book?"

"Railway timetables, Constable." He nodded at the several thick volumes in front of him. "Don't ask. I think I'm going blind."

Robinson went over to the window and turned the sheet of paper to and fro in the daylight. She was disappointed. "Still no luck. Have you got a rubber, sir?"

Bridges reached into a drawer. "Here." He threw the eraser sharply to Robinson, who caught it with aplomb. "Well caught! Played some cricket, have you?"

"Rounders."

"Oh, well, pretty similar. I've always found it strange that rounders is so popular in America."

"They call it baseball there, Sergeant."

"So they do." Bridges returned to his railway timetables.

Robinson set the sheet of paper down on Merlin's desk and started trying to remove the crossings out without eliminating the underlying numbers. After a few minutes of delicate rubbing and tweaking, she felt she was getting somewhere. She raised the paper to the window light again. A number was emerging. She felt a little thrill of excitement before reminding herself that the number might be a complete irrelevance. She walked over to Bridges.

"Sorry to bother you again, sir. Do you think this is a D or a B?" Bridges looked hard at Robinson's piece of paper.

"I think it's a B. Definitely a B."

"And what do you think the whole number is?"

Bridges held the paper closer. "BEL, I think, then 5468 – or is it 5443? No, definitely 5468. BEL5468 – that's a London telephone number, of course. BEL for Belgravia."

"So it is." Robinson felt a buzz of excitement again.

"Whose number is it?"

"I don't know, Sergeant. It's written at the end of Bridget Healy's file. It could be nothing but…"

"Better ring it and find out if it's nothing or something, hadn't you? I'm sure Mr Merlin wouldn't object to your using his phone."

*   *   *

"So, sir, you said you wanted to explain something important to me?"

"Yes, Philip. And, by the way, I think we needn't bother with the 'sir' any more. As your father is now gone you are my firm's largest client, so I think it would be more in order for you to call me Reginald or rather Reggie, as my friends do."

"Very well… Reggie."

They were seated at a small corner table in the bar of Tomlinson's club, White's, in St James's Street. Tomlinson had just completed a strained lunch at the club with his fellow partners. The principal subject of discussion had naturally been Simon Arbuthnot. Tomlinson had upbraided Leslie Titmus over 'the obvious cock-up' regarding Arbuthnot's will. Titmus had not taken kindly to this criticism. For once, their other partner, Arthur Travers, had been of some use and had calmed Titmus down. The partners had reached the unsurprising conclusion that Tomlinson should do all he could to find Arbuthnot's new will. The will, however, was not Tomlinson's main worry. It was the other problem that really concerned him and which he now wanted to discuss with Philip Arbuthnot.

"It was very good of you to respond so quickly to my telephone call, Philip."

"Not at all, sir… sorry, Reggie. It was only a matter of 10 minutes to get here. Much easier than if you'd wanted to see me at the office."

"Indeed. Well, I have just had a meeting here with my partners. We all agreed that the sorting out of your father's estate is the firm's number-one priority. The new will devised by your father will either turn up – with you, no doubt, as the principal beneficiary – or it won't and you will be the principal beneficiary through intestacy. The former would be preferable but either way you'll be all right."

"And what happens while I wait for you to sort all this out?"

"You take your rightful place at the helm of your father's business empire, of course, although I trust that as you are learning the ropes you will allow the counsel of my firm and your father's principal associate, Sidney Fleming, to guide you."

The young man smiled nervously. "Mr Fleming seemed to have different ideas at lunch yesterday."

"I think we need to act with sensitivity. I shall take it upon myself to broker a sensible plan of action with Fleming and the other important players. Fleming has taken the chair of the business at the request of the other directors for the present and this should be respected. The fact remains, however, that he is only a minor shareholder. You are, or will be when we have sorted out the technicalities, the majority shareholder. It will all be in your hands to do with as you will."

A sliver of sunlight caught the glass ashtray on their table and made it sparkle. Arbuthnot raised a hand to shield his eyes. "What about this fellow Pulos? He holds an important position in the Sackville Group. Won't he want a say in what happens?"

"Fleming says Mr Pulos may huff and puff a little but assures me that he can be managed."

"But if Fleming decides, as the Yanks say, not to play ball…?"

"Philip, trust me. You will be the majority shareholder and everyone will eventually fall into line. If they don't we shall find replacements."

"Very well. If you say so. What was this other important matter you wanted to talk to me about?"

Tomlinson drank some water before speaking. "Philip, as you know, when your father came to our office he removed all the papers in the testamentary box file."

"Yes, of course, as you said. He took the will and just left that short letter saying he would be replacing it."

"Yes. Well, as I mentioned yesterday without going into detail, there were other documents in that box. Not just the will. He took those too and they are important."

"What are these documents?"

"Do you know what a bearer share is, Philip?

"Can't say that I do. That law study programme you've got me on hasn't got to company law and stocks and shares yet."

Tomlinson smiled nervously. "In this country, securities holdings in corporations are normally held in the form of share certificates, issued to the holder by the corporation and registered in the company's books."

"Yes, I do know that."

"Most other countries have a similar system but, in some jurisdictions, there is an alternative or variation on this means of ownership. Instead of having their names registered in the company books, shareholders may hold their securities in the form of bearer shares."

"Which are?"

"As the name implies, the shares are owned by the bearer. There is no registration process. Possession of the shares is all that is required to confer the full benefits of ownership."

"And why are you telling me this?"

"There were bearer shares in your father's file. He took them when he removed the will."

"And what did these bearer shares represent?"

"Argentina is a jurisdiction where bearer shares are not uncommon. Your father's bearer shares represented his holding in the South American enterprise, Enterprisas Simal."

"So that is…" Arbuthnot started to make a calculation in his head but Tomlinson beat him to it.

"Approximately 75 per cent of your father's total business empire."

"Christ!"

"We obviously need to find them."

"But why on earth did he remove them?

"I have no idea. One of the first things your father did years ago when he retained our firm was to deposit those shares with us for safekeeping. Initially they were kept separately and securely in my office. Then, when we prepared your father's first will, he suggested we keep everything together in the same file. So we did."

Arbuthnot looked down and fiddled distractedly with the knot of his tie. "I'd better go and make a thorough search of the office in my father's flat. I've been putting it off as I know it will be depressing. But now needs must. I'll go there right now. I have his safe combination and his housekeeper has his desk keys. I'll bet the certificates are somewhere there."

"Do you want me to come and help? It's possible the new will could be there as well."

"No. No, thanks. I'd rather do it myself. There'll be a lot of personal stuff. I'll go right now."

"Of course, Philip. Let me know how you get on." Tomlinson watched the young man walk off purposefully. Simon Arbuthnot had often told him that, despite appearances to the contrary, the boy had some steel in him. Perhaps his father would be proved right?

*   *   *

Felix Meyer lifted his cup, closed his eyes and happily breathed in the aroma of grade A French coffee. Good coffee was like gold dust in London but somehow Three Carlton Gardens still had a plentiful supply. Next to the coffee cup on his desk sat a small, framed drawing of a black-haired youth. It was one of his brother's better likenesses of him. Felix smiled as he looked at the initials his brother had signed with a flourish under the gap in the face's cleft chin.

Meyer finished his drink and reached into one of the desk drawers. He took out the note he had made of the telephone conversation earlier with Anton. His poor, obsessed brother. How many times had he told him that it was best to forget the past and get on with life in the present? Anton was lucky enough to be well away from the war in New York. He had a pretty and loving young wife and had won the lottery. The lotto winnings would have set up the young couple nicely. They could have moved out to Long Island or Connecticut, bought themselves a little suburban house and started the family Ruth so fervently desired. Instead they were living in a dingy Manhattan apartment while, as Ruth had explained in her many desperate letters, the lotto money was being steadily frittered away on unnecessary legal fees and she was being turned into a demented shrew by Anton's compulsive determination to set ancient wrongs to right.

Meyer read over his notes. Anton wanted Felix to find out if the general manager of Enterprisas Simal, Alexander Pulos, was in London and, if so, why? Despite his better judgment, he felt obliged to help. He loved his brother even if he were mad. And this was just a question of information. He knew Sackville Bank was the affiliate of Enterprisas Simal in London. Presumably someone there would be able to provide the required answers. How to find that someone? He had a contact who worked in the City. A friend for whom he had done some favours. Rupert Vorster. Perhaps he knew someone at Sackville?

Then again, if he got the information about Pulos, would that be enough for his brother? Would some sort of action be required? If Pulos was in London, would Anton want him to meet or do something to the man? That might not be so congenial. The lieutenant shrugged his shoulders and sat up in his chair. He resolved to speculate no further. He would have a word with

Vorster and see if he could help. He would pass what he learned to his brother, who could deal with it as he saw fit. That was all he would do. Felix Meyer had enough on his plate without having to worry about settling old scores, big as those scores might be.

*   *   *

WPC Robinson pressed the bell of the elegant end-of-terrace house just off Eaton Square. A young maid opened the door and invited her into a large marbled hallway. The telephone number BEL5468 on the Healy file had been unlisted but she now knew it belonged to this house. She had called the number an hour earlier, given her name and told the man who responded that she had urgent police business to discuss. Shortly after, a woman had come on the line and asked her the nature of that business. The constable had simply replied: "Bridget Healy." There had been a moment's silence before the woman, who had an authoritative voice with the hint of an Irish accent, told her to come to 14 Belgrave Place at two-thirty. She terminated the call before Robinson had a chance to ask her name.

Robinson waited on an uncomfortable antique chair by the door. She was not kept there for long. The clatter of high heels on the marble staircase to Robinson's left announced the arrival of a striking and expensively dressed young woman. Her hostess had high cheekbones, sparkling green eyes, a warm, full-lipped mouth and a long mane of chestnut hair. She wore a dazzling diamond-and-sapphire necklace with matching earrings. She looked like a film star and Robinson felt distinctly dowdy by comparison.

"Constable Robinson?"

"Yes, ma'am. Pleased to meet you, Miss…"

"Mrs Lafontaine. Patricia Lafontaine. Please follow me." Mrs Lafontaine led Robinson through double doors into a large drawing room, decorated in warm pastel shades of blue and yellow. As she walked ahead, Mrs Lafontaine's coppery brown tresses swung in almost perfect equilibrium behind her.

"Please be seated," said the hostess as they reached two armchairs, furnished in eggshell-blue fabric and positioned either side of a small marble table. The room was filled with beautiful antiques and works of art and two Siamese cats lounged by a fireplace to their right.

Mrs Lafontaine came straight to the point. "You mentioned Bridget Healy on the telephone. What have you to tell me of her?"

"She is dead, I'm afraid."

Initially Mrs Lafontaine's face registered no emotion but, after a moment's silence, her mouth turned down and a large tear rolled from one eye, leaving a trail on her heavily powdered cheek.

"I'm sorry. She was…"

"My sister. My poor deluded sister. How did she die?"

"She was pregnant. There was an attempted abortion. Mother and child died."

Mrs Lafontaine nodded and raised a finger to wipe away the teardrop.

"A back-street abortion, was it?"

Robinson nodded. "In a West End hotel, just off Oxford Street. We found her last Thursday. Three men were observed at the scene. One was the abortionist. We have identified him but not the other two. The abortionist is now himself dead."

Patricia Lafontaine looked away. "She was always stupid, just like my idiot brother. I knew she'd end up in a bad way." She reached into a black box on a table to her right and withdrew a cigarette.

"May I ask you when you last saw your sister?"

Mrs Lafontaine lit her cigarette with an expensive-looking lighter. "About two months ago. I can't remember the exact date. She came over from Ireland in January. Penniless, of course. Turned up on my doorstep looking for a bed and a contribution.

Despite my better instincts, I let her in and allowed her to stay here for a while."

"How long was she here?"

"She came in early January and left at the end of March."

"Why did she leave?"

"I had pretty much had enough of her by then but I suppose the main reason she left is that she found somewhere else to stay."

Robinson turned a page in her notebook. "And where was that?"

Mrs Lafontaine uncrossed her long legs and reached out to drop ash into a nearby ashtray. "She never told me. Look, Constable, let me be completely candid. As you can probably tell, I didn't really like my sister. I put her up out of a misconceived feeling of family loyalty. I let her have a spare room in the servants' quarters, gave her a back-door key and £5 a week spending money as well as all the food and drink she wanted. I encouraged her to get a job but she made no effort to do so, as far as I am aware.

"I saw as little of her as I could but my staff kept me posted on her comings and goings. According to them, during the first weeks of her stay she was out frequently during the day and infrequently at night. Gradually her daytime outings decreased and her nocturnal ones increased. Latterly, when she went out in the evening she seldom returned. I dined with her once or twice just before she disappeared. She drank a lot but remained tight-lipped about what she was getting up to. However, from a few passing remarks she made – and the fact that she seemed to have acquired some new items of jewellery – I deduced that she had found herself a man."

"Did you find out who that was?"

"No."

"Did she say anything that might give us a clue?"

Mrs Lafontaine closed her eyes in concentration for a moment. "She did mention going to the Ritz bar. Which one, I'm not sure.

Said she'd been there a few times and liked it. The Ritz is the only place she mentioned."

"Any hints about what she got up to in the daytime?"

"None. Got together with some of her Republican friends is my guess. For all I know my idiot brother might be over here, stirring up trouble. I assume from the fact that you have tracked me down that you know all about our family?"

"If you mean do we know of your sister's and brother's suspected involvement with the IRA, the answer is yes."

"Suspected, my foot!" Mrs Lafontaine snorted a mirthless laugh.

"Did Mr Lafontaine ever have conversations with your sister?"

"There is no Mr Lafontaine, Constable. I am a widow."

"I'm sorry to hear that."

"You needn't be. He lived to be 82. He had a long and enjoyable life. His wealth provided him with many beautiful and desirable things, right up until his swift and painless end. I was one of those beautiful and desirable things."

She registered Robinson's look of surprise. "You don't move from a two-room shack in County Wexford with only a bucket to do your business in to somewhere like this…" she waved a hand at their opulent surroundings "without making some sacrifices. I sacrificed myself in marriage to an ancient French businessman. There are greater sacrifices, I can assure you. Marcel was spectacularly rich, charming, intelligent and attentive. Of course, as a man in his late 70s there were downsides but, all in all, it was a bargain worth making. Look at me now. He disowned his only son, had no other living relatives and left it all to me."

"What was your husband's business?"

Mrs Lafontaine extinguished her half-smoked cigarette. "He was an arms dealer. The 30s were, of course, pretty good for arms dealers. He sold to all and sundry, including the fellow with the moustache in Berlin." She smiled wryly. "I assure you he never did anything illegal. All licensed and above board. My husband had the very best of contacts. He dined with the likes of Mr Chamberlain and Mr Baldwin."

"Back to your sister. Did she leave any of her belongings here when she moved out?"

"I don't think so. You are welcome to look at her room if you want."

"Do you have a photograph of Bridget?"

Mrs Lafontaine thought for a moment before she rose and walked over to a large bureau at the other end of the room. She looked in several drawers before finding what she was looking for and returning to her chair.

"This is the best I can do. Bridget is on the left." The black-and-white photograph she held showed two pretty and cheerful young girls in Trafalgar Square with the base of Nelson's Column and fluttering pigeons in the background. Bridget was darker than her sister, with almost Latin looks. Her hair was cut short. Like her sister she was very pretty but in a different way.

"She came to visit me once before in London, a few years ago, just after I arrived here. I was 18, she was 16. She was different then, before Finian got his claws into her. I was in digs in Lambeth and she stayed with me for a week in the summer. We had a laugh." Suddenly, Mrs Lafontaine's eyes began to fill. She put both hands to her mouth but couldn't prevent a couple of strangled sobs escaping. She bent over and began to weep. Robinson hurried over to her but was waved away. After an awkward minute or two, Mrs Lafontaine got up and ran out of the room.

Robinson remained in her chair for a few minutes, not knowing quite what to do. Then a man appeared at the door. "I am Simms the butler. Mrs Lafontaine has asked me to show you her sister's room, miss. If you'd care to follow me."

*   *   *

"Bletchley, sir."

"Bletchley? What about Bletchley?" Merlin raised his eyes from a turgid paper on new police security procedures the AC had insisted he read.

"Bletchley is where de Metz went. The railway ticket, sir."

"Are you sure? How did you work it out?"

"You remember we had half a ticket." Bridges put the ticket on the desk. "We have the letters B and L, the rest having disappeared with the other half of the ticket. We also have the train time – 11.23 – and then we have the colour of the ticket, which is red."

"Yes."

"Different railway companies use different colours for their tickets. There are a few railway companies that use red tickets but obviously we can eliminate those that don't. Taking stations within an 80-mile radius of London that begin with BL and that are served by railway companies that issue red tickets, there are three results. However, if you add the 11.23 departure time, there is only one."

"Bletchley."

"Yes, sir."

"Well done. So what do we know about Bletchley?"

"Small Buckinghamshire market town about 50 miles from London. A busy railway junction. Pleasant place."

"Sounds like you've been there."

"As soon as I worked out that Bletchley was the place we were looking for, I got a taxi to St Pancras and caught a train. The journey takes about an hour. I interviewed the station manager and a couple of clerks, had a quick look round then caught a return train."

"Very resourceful, Sergeant. Get anything useful?"

"A positive identification of de Metz. I described him to the younger of the clerks, a Mr Whitby. He remembered someone of that description coming to his booth and asking for directions to Bletchley Park. Said the man had a foreign accent. A few hours later, he saw him waiting for the return train to London. Whitby observed that there had been quite a few foreigners travelling to Bletchley in recent months."

"What is Bletchley Park?"

"According to Whitby, it's a large Victorian house not far from the station. It's not a private residence and no-one knows for certain who occupies it. The gossip in the town is that it houses some branch of the civil service."

"A place of safety out of town for some London department?"

"Very possibly, sir."

"I wonder what de Metz wanted there?"

Merlin's cuckoo clock came to life and announced that it was five o'clock. "Goodness, is that the time? Eddie Powell will be here any second." There was a tap on the door and there he was. Bridges nodded to the visitor before slipping out of the room.

"Sit down please, Eddie. Cup of tea? Or perhaps something stronger?" Merlin pointed to the bottle of J&B whisky on the shelf beneath the clock.

"No thanks, Frank. I shan't stay long as after this I've got to go and speak to Celia. I'd better have a clear head for that."

"She's reappeared then?"

"Yes, wanting money, of course. But let's not talk about her. Is that a young me I see in that picture?"

"It is." On the wall behind Merlin was a photograph of the 1924 Metropolitan Police football team. Merlin walked over to the black-and-white print and pointed out a dark-haired young man at the back on the right. "That's me." He pointed to a curly-haired man three places along. "And that's you."

Powell laughed. "You've aged a lot better than me, Frank. That would be the year after we left the Police Academy, wouldn't it?"

"Yes. A year or so before you left the force."

Powell gave a regretful shake of the head. "If we could only turn back time and make our decisions again. I liked being a policeman. It was just Celia…"

Merlin nodded sympathetically. "Have you got the letter?"

Powell produced a blood-spattered white envelope. Merlin picked it up and felt its weight. "Quite light. One sheet?"

"Feels like it."

Merlin reached into one of his desk drawers and found his reading glasses. He studied the inscription on the envelope carefully before setting it down. "As you said. 'Give to my s…' The pencil mark falls away abruptly after the S and could be any letter. So you have to decide who the S is. The first candidate must be the son you mentioned. Philip, wasn't it?'

"Yes."

"Then there was a sister."

"Lucinda."

"Candidate two. Did he have a secretary?

"He did have one for many years, someone close very close to him, but she died two years ago. There was no specific replacement, I was told."

"And then there must be a solicitor?"

"Reginald Tomlinson of Titmus, Travers and Tomlinson. A well respected City firm."

"No doubt." Merlin removed his spectacles and rubbed his eyes. "Sweetheart?"

"He didn't strike me as the sort of man to address a letter to a 'sweetheart'. It's possible but not likely, I think."

"Well, let's just say you have three prime candidates – son, sister, solicitor. For what it's worth, I discussed the matter briefly with my boss, the assistant commissioner. I don't think you ever knew Edward Gatehouse, did you?"

" No. After my time. What did he say?"

"Exactly what would you'd expect from a seasoned bureaucrat. He said you should give the letter to Arbuthnot's solicitor. It's possible the family members might have conflicting interests. If the letter went to the sister when it was meant to go to the son, the son's interests might be compromised in some way contrary to Arbuthnot's wishes. And vice versa. You have to take a pretty cynical view of human nature to contemplate that but lawyers have to deal with such possibilities all the time, I suppose.

"The AC said it was reasonable to presume the solicitor would be independent and fair and would wish to ensure that his client's wishes were fulfilled, even if it turned out that the solicitor himself were not the intended recipient."

"Of course, that is the most obvious answer, Frank, but there was something about the intense way he looked at me. Something that suggested the letter was more than just a routine letter for his solicitor."

"The man was dying, Eddie. Chances are his intensity was more to do with that, don't you think?"

Powell nodded, picked up the letter and got to his feet. "You are right, of course. I'll make an appointment with the lawyer and hand the letter over and that will be an end to it. Thank you for the advice. I don't know why I allowed myself to get into quite such a dither."

"You had a hellish time in Crete, Eddie, and on top of that you returned home to find yourself with nasty personal problems. No surprise if you found yourself a little off-kilter. Just remember I'm here if you want to talk to someone. Come round to the flat one night to meet Sonia. She could cook for us or we could go out together for a bite to eat."

"That would be lovely. Thanks, Frank. You are too kind. Just let me sort this and Celia out and I'll telephone you in a few days."

After the door closed, Merlin found himself eyeing the bottle of J&B again. It had been a long day. He poured himself a glass.

*   *   *

"Thank you, Brightwell. Very illuminating. I'd be grateful if you could keep all this to yourself at the moment while I consider the appropriate action."

"Very good, sir."

Sidney Fleming watched the towering, beetle-browed figure of the bank's finance director disappear through the thick, oak-panelled doors of his new office. He turned to admire the Canaletto masterpiece of London *en fête*, which hung above the large, 18th-century marble fireplace. Fleming had wasted little time in appropriating Simon Arbuthnot's grand office. He always thought the neighbouring office, which Arbuthnot allocated him, rather small and cramped. That was why he had conducted much of his business at the Ritz.

Fleming had had little time today to relax and appreciate his spacious new accommodation. He had spent the morning rummaging anxiously through the desk drawers and filing cabinets in the chairman's office for the missing bearer bonds. To no avail. The more he thought about the missing bonds, the queasier he felt. Now his afternoon meeting with George Brightwell had given further cause for queasiness. He got up from the huge desk and wandered over to the drinks cabinet by the window. The Tower of London loomed in the distance as he poured himself a large brandy and replayed Brightwell's revelations in his mind.

"I'm afraid that I have discovered a number of worrying exposures for the bank, Mr Fleming."

"Exposures? What do you mean?"

"There were a number of account files that Mr Arbuthnot insisted on keeping to himself."

"Did he now? What of them?"

"Well, after hearing of his sad demise, I arranged for one of my clerks to retrieve those files."

"Where were they?"

"In his desk."

"I rather wish you'd waited, Brightwell. As the man now in charge I would have appreciated going through Mr Arbuthnot's desk first."

Brightwell steepled his long bony hands before him. "I am very sorry, Mr Fleming. I should have thought but my lack of access to those files has been worrying me intensely ever since Mr Arbuthnot's departure for the army last year. I have had to assume the status quo ante with regard to them for all my quarterly reports."

"And you didn't think to search for those files earlier?"

"How could I, sir? While Mr Arbuthnot was, to my knowledge, alive, I was bound in honour by his instructions to leave them in his possession."

"And what was in these files?"

"Details of some of the private client funds we manage."

"And?

Fleming watched a small drop of sweat trickle into Brightwell's collar. "It appears that Mr Arbuthnot had taken control of those funds."

"What's the problem with that?"

"We are looking at quite substantial sums."

"How much?"

"£2m."

"So, Simon took under his control – from the fund management department under Forbes, I presume – a substantial portion of the client monies we manage. That is not necessarily so odd. One of the ways he and I built up this company was by attracting client funds and by investing them successfully. He was, of course, a very successful investor, whether on the stock market or in financing projects and ventures. Otherwise we would not be sitting here. Perhaps he decided he wanted to have a bit of investing fun again and get his hands dirty."

"He certainly got his hands dirty."

"What does that mean."

"The £2m has shrunk substantially."

"To what?"

"To just under £500,000."

"Good God! I don't believe it!"

"That is what the records show. There is a reference to some bad market investments but there are also substantial unusual transfers and withdrawals."

"What do you mean, withdrawals?"

"Mr Arbuthnot seems to have transferred substantial sums directly to overseas banks."

"What's wrong with that? He was probably playing some currency game."

"I have established that the funds so transferred are no longer in the accounts to which they were sent."

"Are you suggesting, Mr Brightwell, that Mr Arbuthnot was stealing from his own bank?"

Brightwell's thick eyebrows danced a little jig. "I am afraid that's what it looks like, Mr Fleming. And there is worse."

"Worse. What could be worse?"

"It seems that a similar operation has been going on in the banking department."

"Explain."

"A number of substantial corporate loans were approved directly by Mr Arbuthnot without being submitted to the Bank Loan Committee."

"So?"

"It appears that these borrowing entities are mostly fictitious."

For once, Fleming found himself at a loss for words. He allowed Brightwell to run on in greater detail but stopped listening. Eventually, he halted the finance director's flow. "That's enough for now. In summary, would you say the bank is in some difficulty?"

"I would say that is a rather mild way of putting it, Mr Fleming. We have several important clients whose accounts have effectively been pilfered and, on top of that, we have a pending liquidity crisis. There are a number of significant interbank loans that fall due next month. Then…"

"Very well. Perhaps you'd be so kind as to give me some time to think. We can discuss this again tomorrow morning."

And so Brightwell had left Fleming alone with his thoughts, the most prominent of which was that old cliché about leopards never changing their spots. Simon Arbuthnot had been a chancer all his life. Fleming returned to the desk and, swirling the Courvoisier around in his glass, remembered the first time he had met Arbuthnot.

It had been the summer of 1919. Arbuthnot called himself a junior clerk but, in fact, he was little more than an errand boy at one of the City's less prominent stock-jobbing firms. Fleming had been an equally lowly employee of a small stockbroking company and was enjoying an after-work drink with a couple of friends in the Jampot (as the Jamaica Wine Room, in an alley just off Cornhill, was known to City workers).

Fleming saw a dark, handsome young man playing cards with three men in a corner. Suddenly one of the men had jumped to his feet and shouted: "You're a bloody cheat! Give me my money back, you swine! I'll have your guts for garters." The young man, who appeared to be the person so addressed, was laughing his head off. One of the barmen walked over to the group and asked them to pack in their game and get lost. The aggrieved man was in no mood to budge and had to be removed forcibly by the barman and a colleague. The laughing young man gathered up his apparently substantial winnings and walked out into the alleyway. The two other card-players melted away.

When Fleming left the pub a few minutes later, he encountered the young man destined to be his lifelong business partner sitting calmly on a stone step. Simon Arbuthnot winked as he took a long draw on his cigarette. "Rum old do in there, eh?"

"What did you do to upset the man?"

Arbuthnot blew smoke through his nostrils. "Fellow's a poor loser, what can I say?"

"Did you cheat him?"

"Cheat? An interesting word that, isn't it? No, I don't think I cheated him. I took advantage of the knowledge I had, which he was not aware I had. It's easy to win at cards when you know the other fellow's hand."

"And how did you know his hand?"

"Ah." Arbuthnot expelled another cloud of smoke. "That would be telling, wouldn't it?" He smiled enigmatically at Fleming. "It's a bit like the stock market, really."

"How do you mean?"

"Let's take a clever chap, who makes a killing in the market. Just as I might know in a card game something another player doesn't – like the fact I've worked out what cards he's holding – so chances are the clever chap in the market also knows something that the fellow on the other side of the bargain doesn't. Some good or bad results about to be reported, new contracts won or lost, a top manager about to jump ship, a large amount of stock about to be dumped, etc."

Fleming leaned against the railing beside the step. "That's a rather cynical view, isn't it? What about investors who have carefully assessed the prospects in a business market and then back their educated judgment?"

"If they are any good, they are taking advantage of the superior market knowledge they have acquired. They know something that the chap on the other side of the bargain doesn't. It's the same thing, don't you see?" Fleming couldn't help laughing and his companion joined in with his idiosyncratic giggle.

"Arbuthnot's the name, making it rich is my game." He reached out a hand and grasped Fleming's firmly.

"Sidney Fleming."

"One of THE Flemings?"

"No such luck. My father owns a shoe shop in Bermondsey, not a merchant banking empire."

"What a pity! Notwithstanding, if you are bright and ambitious I think you and I could be friends. Look." He produced a bunch of notes from his jacket pocket and waved them in Fleming's face. "I'm quite flush at the moment. Let's go up west and have some fun. What do you say?"

And so it had started. Within months, the two men had left their clerking jobs and started a small 'investment company' as they called it. Arbuthnot raised most of the initial capital through his card-sharking skills. They traded stocks and shares, commodities, government bonds. Whatever could be traded. Fleming developed a valuable expertise in specialist financial stocks and in overseas trading and commodity companies.

However, from the outset, there was never any doubt about who would be the boss. Arbuthnot would have been the leader even if Fleming had raised the capital. He had charisma, brains and pluck. Fleming, though no shrinking violet, was happy to be the number two and he felt lucky to have fallen in with Arbuthnot. Soon, a one-room office in Moorgate had expanded into a more comfortable suite of rooms in Finsbury Square, overseen by a shrewd and sharp secretary called Vera.

Within a few years, their business had become comfortably profitable but Arbuthnot was not content and wanted to take on more exciting projects. That was how they had ended up doing business in Albania.

In the middle of a God-forsaken part of that God-forsaken country there was a copper mine. Using the contacts they had made in the City, they raised £20,000 to develop the mine. Arbuthnot charmed the local bandit chiefs and government officials and paid the necessary substantial bribes. Work began but within the year it became apparent to Arbuthnot and Fleming that the mine was a dud.

Arbuthnot got local accountants to produce figures, which showed that all but £1,000 of the investor funds had been spent. This sum was returned to the investors. In fact, a total of just under £5,000 had been spent. The balance of £14,000 was retained and eventually found its way into the balance sheet of their London business. Fleming had initially been kept in the dark about the accounting sleight-of-hand and had argued with his partner when he found out. He'd had two choices. Do the honourable thing, blow the whistle and be ruined. Or stick with his partner and weather the storm.

He had capitulated. Arbuthnot was a persuasive man. "Don't worry, Sidney. We'll make this money grow and we'll get the investors their money back plus a good return with the other deals this money will fund." Of course, the investors were irate and Arbuthnot's reputation took some buffeting but such was his charm that few considered the possibility of fraud. Those that did simply participated no more in their deals. Arbuthnot had little difficulty replacing them.

Fleming refilled his brandy glass. And Simon had been right. The investors who stuck with them did very well for several years. There were further rolls of the dice. Simon had met his wealthy wife soon after their financial partnership began. He wasn't able to access her funds at the outset but by the time the Wall Street Crash knocked them back, his wife was dead and he had found a way to break up the trusts in which those funds had been tied up. So that money came into the investment pot.

In 1931 Arbuthnot and Fleming had founded Sackville Bank. After the crash, and with Arbuthnot's slightly racy reputation, it was no easy thing for them to get the bank off the ground. But a few years later, Arbuthnot had pulled off his master stroke and after that there had been no stopping them.

Arbuthnot had been charismatic, bright and brave. He had also been a massive risk taker and had taken many shortcuts. Now it looked like the man had returned to his old ways in the months before his death. Why? Fleming finished his brandy. He closed his eyes and thought he could hear that charming giggle again. He addressed Arbuthnot's spirit out loud. "Everything was such a laugh to you, Simon. This, however, is not funny. What sort of a catastrophic mess have you left us in?"

CHAPTER 8

Thursday 12 June

London

Pulos pulled back the silk curtains and collapsed exhausted on to the four-poster bed. In the hallway of his Ritz suite, Marco was tipping the porters and sorting out the luggage. Pulos had originally intended for his bodyguard to have a separate room but, after some thought, had booked a big enough suite to accommodate them both. There were two small bedrooms on the other side of the drawing room, one for Marco and one for the luggage.

Marco was a useful man to have close to hand if things got dangerous, as well they might on this trip. He had been with Pulos for several years and had always done efficiently what was asked of him, however unpleasant the task might be. Recently, Pulos had wondered whether he shouldn't have sent Marco at the outset to deal in his own direct fashion with the Meyer problem in New York. It still might have to be dealt with that way.

In the end, he had travelled from Argentina by air. He had left with Marco on the Monday evening. There had been stops in Rio, the Azores and then in Lisbon. There had been three aircraft and all had been noisy and uncomfortable. Sleep on the planes had been almost impossible and on the final leg he had acquired an earache. Once Marco had unpacked, Pulos would send him out to a pharmacy to get some ear drops.

His watch was still on Argentina time. It was eight in the morning in Buenos Aires so one o'clock in London. A greater time difference than usual because, as his secretary had advised him, wartime Britain was now operating something called Double British Summer Time to extend the evening light. Despite his exhaustion, Pulos knew he should really crack on. Much might have happened since he left Buenos Aires. He had cabled Sackville from Lisbon to notify the bank of his impending arrival. Perhaps it would have been better to turn up unannounced? Be that as it may, he was here now. He leaned back on the soft pillows. He'd be more effective after a nap, though.

He yawned then called out. Marco hurried into the room. "I'm going to lie down for an hour. Then we'll get started. I have a few small errands I'd like you to run. I'd also like you to arrange for the hotel to lay on a permanent car. I don't want to rely on taxis."

"You wish me to drive, *Señor* Pulos?"

"No, no. This is your first time in London. I think that is too much to ask of you, especially as the place is such a terrible mess." Pulos had been shocked by the destruction and wreckage they had seen on their way from the airport to the hotel. "No, ask them to get us a nice car with a good local driver."

"Yes, *señor*."

Pulos gave Marco further instructions regarding ear drops and buying newspapers. Marco would have no problems because he spoke perfect English. Pulos had arranged lessons for him a couple of years back and he had proved an excellent student. Pulos had kept Marco's linguistic talent a secret from Simon Arbuthnot and his English colleagues. Accordingly, Pulos had learned many interesting things from Marco's stints as chauffeur or guide.

After Marco had departed on his errands, Pulos undressed and got under the bedcovers. He was soon asleep.

*   *   *

Merlin, refreshed by a particularly good night's sleep, stood by the open window of his office enjoying the view of the river and the warmth of a sun already quite high in a cloudless blue sky. He turned at the sound of the door opening and saw his team file in. Back at his desk, he acknowledged everyone with a smile, and looked down at the notes he'd made earlier.

"We are making some progress. Thanks to more good work by Robinson, we now know that, from early January, Bridget Healy stayed for several weeks in the Belgravia house of her wealthy older sister, Patricia Lafontaine. Mrs Lafontaine is, for what it's worth, the widow of a major arms dealer. We know little about Healy's activities in London during this time. About the only thing we do know is that she wasn't in the house much. She eventually moved out at the end of March and her sister suspected she had found a man to look after her."

"The father of her child?"

"A reasonable presumption, Sergeant. What else do we know, Constable?"

"Bridget never told anyone in the house where she was going except once when she mentioned the Ritz bar. As it happens, when I searched her room, I found one of those sticks people use to stir their cocktails. Sorry, I've forgotten what they're called."

"A swizzle stick."

"Thank you, Detective. Well, I found a corroborative swizzle stick in her room."

Merlin looked back at his notes. "So, the Ritz bar. Worth following up. So, just to be clear about the timeline, Bridget Healy left her sister's at the end of March and we found her dead at the Bedford Hotel on Thursday 5 June. According to the medical report, the aborted child had been conceived three months before at the beginning of March, three or four weeks before she left her sister.

"Moving on to de Metz, we had a better meeting with a French officer at Carlton Gardens and now have more background on him. This officer had met de Metz, who had made several visits to the Free French HQ, seeking financial help. When such help was not forthcoming, he started making claims that he possessed important and thus financially valuable security information. His claims on this weren't believed. We also know that the train ticket we found was to Bletchley in Buckinghamshire. De Metz went there and enquired about a place called Bletchley Park, which is rumoured to be some sort of government installation." Merlin steepled his hands in front of him. "Have I missed anything?"

Robinson raised her hand. "I spoke to Mrs Lafontaine's staff just to confirm what she had said. Everyone was there except the chauffeur. One of the maids made a point of telling me that Miss Healy made good use of her sister's cars and the chauffeur."

"Better go back and speak to him, Constable."

"Sir."

"Go with her, Sergeant. Then both of you go on to the Ritz. See if anyone recognises Healy from that photograph her sister gave us."

"Very good, sir." Bridges and Robinson disappeared.

Merlin leaned back and swung his feet on to the desk. "We could really do with that briefing from MI5 now, Bernie. The AC is following up, but…"

"I have to say that whoever killed de Metz did a pretty professional job."

"You mean professional as in an MI5- or MI6-style killing?"

"The only professional murderers I've dealt with are the mob. I've seen plenty of their handiwork. I presume your spies are as proficient."

"Hmm. Now that's an interesting subject. The mob. You can tell me more over a drink one night."

"Sure. And we can also talk about how gorgeous the constable is."

"Bernie, I've already warned you on that score."

"I said 'talk', Frank." Goldberg laughed. "Just talk!"

*   *   *

Bridges drew up to the traffic lights on Buckingham Palace Road. They were minutes away from Mrs Lafontaine's house. A lorry pulled up beside them and the man in the passenger seat shouted down at Robinson. "All right, darling? You look lovely in that uniform. Fancy meeting up later?"

Robinson quickly rolled up the car window. As Bridges drove off, they could hear him shouting something about frigidity.

"I suppose that happens quite a lot?"

"Unfortunately it does, Sergeant. You get used to it."

"So my Iris used to say. Don't think it's happened to her for a while though. She's carrying a few extra pounds after the baby."

"I'm sure she's as attractive as ever, Sergeant. Men are bound to be more restrained towards women pushing prams."

"Of course."

"Surely you're happy she can walk down the street unmolested?"

"I am, but I'm not sure she is. When women have babies they worry about losing their looks. I think Iris wouldn't mind an occasional wolf-whistle."

Robinson laughed. "I don't mind if I never heard one again." They passed Victoria Station then turned right into the warren of streets backing on to Eaton Square. "It's that one, Sergeant." Bridges pulled up outside 14 Belgrave Place and they got out. The butler answered the door.

"Madam is out, I'm afraid."

"That's all right, chum, we're here to see her chauffeur. The constable here missed him yesterday. We'd like a quick word for the sake of completeness. Is he in?"

"Wilson lives above the garage. This way." Simms led Bridges and Robinson into a cobbled alleyway at the side of the house. The garage was at the far end and they could hear a loud banging from behind its closed green doors.

"Sounds like he's in. I'll leave you to it, if I may." Simms disappeared down the alley and Bridges waited for an interruption in the banging before knocking sharply on the small door that was cut into the larger garage doors.

The man who opened the door was dirty-faced and wearing oil-splattered blue overalls. He was perspiring and several strands of light-brown hair hung down untidily in front of his eyes.

"We're from the police, sir."

Wilson took a step back. "Oh. Hello. I suppose I should have been expecting you after what I heard from the people in the house yesterday." He extended a hand but then swiftly withdrew it. "Sorry. Just been under the Roller. Oily hands. Please come in."

There were two cars in the garage and room for one more. There was the Rolls-Royce on which Wilson was working and alongside it a foreign-looking, open-topped sports car. Wilson saw Bridges looking at the sports car with an appreciative eye. "Alfa Romeo. 1930 model, 12 cylinders. My late boss brought it with him from Paris before the war. There's a Bugatti as well. It's having a major refit at the moment. Taking forever as, of course, it's well nigh impossible to get the parts." Wilson indicated a small table behind the Rolls-Royce. "Hang on a sec and I'll rustle up some seating." He disappeared behind a partition and returned with three chairs. They sat down and Bridges made the introductions.

Wilson wiped his face with a rag then combed his hair. "Sorry. Rude, I know, but I must look a bit of a mess."

Now that he'd cleaned up, Robinson could see that Wilson was a pleasant-looking young man. He resembled the film actor Leslie Howard, who had been so wonderful in *Gone With the Wind*, which she had seen with Cole the previous year. That evening wasn't so long ago but strangely it now seemed like a lifetime. Much had happened since.

"So how can I help you, officers? I hope I haven't done anything wrong?"

Bridges moved his chair a little closer to the table. "No, sir. We just need to have a word about Bridget Healy."

"Poor Bridget."

Wilson was well spoken. Unusually well spoken for a chauffeur, Robinson thought.

"As you must know now, Miss Healy was found dead in a hotel a week ago after a botched abortion. We are investigating her death and accordingly trying to find out as much as we can about her, her friends and, of course, the father of her child."

"Have you identified him yet? The father, I mean."

"No, we haven't."

Wilson looked away for a moment. "I liked Bridget. She was very intelligent and had a good sense of humour. Of course, if she got on to the subject of Irish nationalism and English oppression of the Irish she could bore the pants off you, but thankfully, more often than not, we talked about other things."

"You and she talked a lot?"

"Yes, we did, Sergeant. She was a down-to-earth girl from the Irish sticks. She had no problem conversing with a lowly chauffeur."

"If you don't mind my saying, Mr Wilson, you don't sound like you come from a lowly background?"

"I had a decent education, Constable, if that's what you mean. Clifton College. My father had a good job and my parents tried to do the best for me. The thing is, I was always obsessed with cars. I raced them for a while. Then I overstretched myself financially, fell out with my parents, fell on hard times. I was desperate for a job. This one came up and I ate humble pie and took it. No regrets, either. I get to work on and drive these lovely vehicles and Mrs Lafontaine, as was her husband before, is a good boss."

"Would you describe yourself and Bridget as friends?"

"In a way, I suppose. She didn't really have any friends in London when she arrived. Her brother met up with her once or twice. A bit of a maniac from what she told me. She didn't see much of her sister so she was a bit lonely. I used to take her on drives out of London. Madam told me to do whatever her sister asked, so I did."

"And did your relationship progress beyond friendship, Mr Wilson?"

Wilson laughed. "You mean, was I the father of her child, Constable? No, I wasn't. She was a pretty girl and I wouldn't have minded taking things a little further but no. There wasn't much of a chance as within a few weeks of her arrival she had a boyfriend. I don't know who and I don't know where they met but she let slip one day as we were returning from a sightseeing trip to Windsor that she was keen on someone.

"I got the impression that whoever it was wasn't short of a bob or two. I'm not particularly observant but even I couldn't help noticing that she started wearing some fine jewellery. I didn't think her sister was the kind to lend her jewellery to anyone and I didn't think Bridget was the type to borrow or steal it. Ergo, as one of my old teachers used to say, a man must have given it to her."

"When exactly do you think this man appeared on the scene?"

"As I said, Sergeant, within a month or so of her coming here. She arrived in early January. She must have met him in early February."

"And she left at the end of March?"

"Yes. Told me she was moving on to bigger and better things."

"But she gave you no indication of where or with whom she was going?"

"None, Sergeant."

"Did you see her again after the end of March?"

Wilson nodded. "I bumped into her in the street. Near Piccadilly Circus. Some time in late April or maybe early May. She seemed a little preoccupied but otherwise fit and healthy. I couldn't have told that she was pregnant, if she was by then. We had a quick little chat about nothing in particular and then went our separate ways."

"And you have absolutely no idea who the man might be?"

"No."

"Nor of where she might have met him?"

"No, Constable. She did boast a few times that she'd been to some nice places but the only one I remember her mentioning by name was the Ritz. She liked the Ritz."

"You never drove her on any of her evening assignations?"

"No, Sergeant. I would have but she never asked. I presume she walked or took buses or taxis. It's not really far from here to the West End."

The officers asked a few more questions about Bridget Healy's friends, activities and demeanour in London, to which Wilson had no useful answers. Eventually, Bridges nodded to Robinson and they got to their feet. Bridges handed over a card. "Thank you, sir. Please let us know if you think of anything else that might be helpful."

"Will do, Sergeant."

*   *   *

Edgar Powell's head was pounding. After what had proved a very distressing meeting with his wife the night before, he had poured himself a whisky. Then another. And another. After an hour of moping and drinking in the flat, he had taken himself off to Soho. Walking up Brewer Street, he'd seen a seedy nightclub where he'd been taken by some fellow officers before they'd shipped out to Greece. He had gone in and allowed himself to be relieved of a large amount of money in return for a few bottles of dire champagne and some uninspiring female company. It had been past one when he had managed to rouse himself to escape the girls' clutches and go home. The only good thing about the evening was that when he got to bed, he slept like a log.

Powell crawled out of bed, removed the uniform in which he had slept and drew himself a bath. He had always derived great pleasure from luxuriating in a piping hot tub. He soaked for half an hour then picked up his watch and realised with a start that it would soon be midday. After a coffee and some of the stale biscuits, which appeared to be the only food present in the flat, he felt almost human.

Returning to his bedroom, he noted with a grunt of satisfaction that Celia had had the decency not to remove the entire contents of his wardrobe. She had mentioned the previous night that her lover was of similar height and build to Powell and she hoped he didn't mind but she'd 'borrowed' a few suits, trousers and other items for her new beau's use. No doubt Powell would never see them again but he was pleased that his favourite old navy suit had not been 'borrowed'. He realised it would need taking in, but, with a tight belt on the trousers, it would do for today.

He found a clean white shirt and a favourite red tie. Dressed, Powell picked up his sweaty, crumpled uniform and stuffed it into a small canvas bag. Just before he went out, he made a telephone call.

There was a dry cleaner's shop nearby on Flood Street, where he dropped his laundry before heading off towards the King's Road. Just before he got there, a taxi pulled up and he gave an address in the City. His telephone call had been to the office of Titmus, Travers and Tomlinson. Powell had told a secretary that he required an urgent meeting with the partner responsible for Simon Arbuthnot's affairs. Informed that the partner in question was tied up all afternoon, he had said he was on his way, regardless. He knew the lawyer would make time for him when he learned what Powell possessed.

*   *   *

"Andreas, my dear fellow. How are you?"

Andreas Koutrakos almost jumped out of his skin as he heard the familiar voice. He had just left the Ritz switchboard office and was on his way to lunch in the employees' canteen. He had a dog-eared copy of Rousseau's *Confessions* hanging out of his jacket pocket and was looking forward to half an hour's company with his favourite philosopher.

Pulos saw the book and grimaced. "Still reading that old claptrap, are you, Andreas? A lovely man, Rousseau. The great philanthropist who treated his women abominably and abandoned all his children." Pulos put a hand on Koutrakos's shoulder. "I wouldn't place too much faith in that old charlatan's philosophy, my friend. And how are your good friends, Marx and Engels, these days? Still keeping you happy?" Pulos didn't wait for an answer to this question. "A word if I may, Andreas. I'd like you to come up to my room."

Koutrakos, a small, wiry man of middle years with neatly combed salt-and-pepper hair and a permanent five o'clock shadow, shook his head. "Sorry, Alexander… I mean Mr Pulos. Operators are not allowed in hotel rooms."

Pulos smiled, revealing the creamy-white dentures installed by the best dentist in Buenos Aires 12 months earlier. "Nonsense, Andreas, if there is any difficulty I shall simply say I wished to say hello to an old friend and fellow countryman. For that is what we are, is it not, old friends and fellow countrymen?"

Koutrakos sighed and shrugged in resignation. He turned and followed Pulos along the service corridor, out into the lobby and into the main hotel lift. Pulos had first met Koutrakos in the 20s when they were both young Athenians on the make in their own different ways. Pulos had been a small-scale wheeler dealer operating a variety of business scams, some legitimate, some not. Koutrakos had been a firebrand union leader in Piraeus, whom Pulos had met when he was trying to sell protection to shop owners in the port area. After various skirmishes the men had developed a grudging respect for each other.

Later, when Pulos was moving up in the world with Arbuthnot, Koutrakos was getting into difficulties with the Venizelos government because of his strong Marxist beliefs and support of Communist Russia. It became clear that Koutrakos would have to quit the country and Pulos helped him to do so, using some of Arbuthnot's contacts. A job at the Ritz was arranged and Koutrakos had been able to hold it down for over a decade now.

Over the years Pulos had used Koutrakos for odd jobs on the side when he came to London. The initial warm feelings of gratitude Koutrakos had felt towards Pulos and Arbuthnot had disappeared over the years and been replaced by resentment. Promises to bring his family to London had been broken and his wife had found another man. His job at the Ritz was not particularly well paid and, even with the bonuses he got for Pulos's odd jobs, Koutrakos had to live a frugal life.

On Pulos's last trip to London, Koutrakos had finally allowed his resentment to come to the surface. He had refused to do what he was asked. The jobs were relatively minor and less unsavoury than most – one to follow a man one night in the West End, another to pretend to be Pulos in a meeting for reasons that were never explained. In any event, he had refused and Marco had been let loose on him. Koutrakos's face had not been harmed but his body had taken a pummelling and he had ached for days. He had also been reminded that a word in the right place about his Marxist proclivities might not be helpful to his continued residence in Britain. He might not agree with the political system there but now he didn't want to live anywhere else.

And so Koutrakos came to Pulos's suite and sat under Marco's menacing glare, grimly awaiting instructions on a task he knew he would have to carry out. He just hoped it wouldn't involve violence, he was getting too old for that.

"Give him a drink, Marco. I have a bottle of ouzo just for you, Andreas."

"I shouldn't drink. I have to be on duty again shortly."

"One glass won't do any harm. Go on, Marco, pour it. Yes, you add the water just like that. That's it. Take it, Andreas." Pulos sent Marco off to his own room then poured and mixed his own ouzo.

"*Yamas*, Andreas." He clinked his glass against his old friend's and they drank. Pulos switched from the English they had been using until now to their native tongue. "I must say, Andreas, your English has come on a treat. And your accent! My God, one might almost think you went to Oxford or Cambridge. No doubt this is why they have moved you on to the switchboard."

Koutrakos made no reply.

"Come on, cheer up. You would think I was going to ask you to kill someone." Koutrakos's hand trembled and a little ouzo spilled on to the carpet. Pulos roared with laughter. "Is this really the brave man of the left I met all those years ago in Piraeus? Get a grip, man. I only have a very small request. There is no blood involved."

"What is it you want of me?"

"It is a stroke of fortune that you now work on the switchboard. All I want is for you to listen in to someone's telephone conversation."

"I'll lose my job if anyone finds out."

"No-one will find out if you are careful and I tell you what. There'll be some real money in it for you if you do the job well. What do you think?"

Koutrakos looked down and finished his ouzo. Perhaps his taste buds had changed over the years but he hadn't enjoyed it. His wife had always said it tasted like shoe polish and now he felt inclined to agree with her. "All right, Alexander, if you insist. Who am I to listen to?"

*   *   *

Felix Meyer sat back on the bench, eyes closed, and enjoyed the warm midday sun. The small public park in Finsbury Circus was full of office workers enjoying their lunchtime sandwiches. He watched as two pretty young women laid out a blanket on the grass opposite the bench where he sat. One of the women knelt down and Meyer saw that the seams of the nylon stockings she appeared to be wearing were, in reality, lines drawn on her bare legs. Nylons were in short supply and Meyer was smiling in appreciation of the girl's ingenuity when Rupert Vorster sat down beside him.

"Felix, *bonjour. Tout va bien?*"

"*Très bien*, Rupert."

Vorster blinked and smoothed his trousers. "That's pretty much the limit of my French, as you know."

"Of course, Rupert. We'll speak in English as usual. How goes the stock market?"

"Fair to middling, last I heard. Some interesting things bubbling away. But you said on the telephone that you had a small favour to ask."

"It's nothing to do with the market or stock tips. You mentioned the other day that you worked with a chap called Philip Arbuthnot?"

Vorster looked down with pleasure at his gleaming black shoes. He had spent some time that morning giving them a good polish. One of the few things he shared with his father was a distaste for dirty shoes. "Yes, I know Philip. He's a good friend."

"There's a Greek fellow who works for Philip's father in Argentina. His name is Alexander Pulos. My brother in New York has had some… some dealings with Pulos."

"I've heard the name mentioned once or twice by Philip. What dealings?"

"Oh, just commercial matters. I… I'm not exactly sure what. The thing is my brother needs to contact Pulos. Apparently he was told that he had left Argentina and gone abroad on a trip. He wasn't told where but suspects Pulos may be on his way to London. He asked me to find out if his suspicion was correct. I was hoping you might be able to help me and, if he is here, get details of where he's staying."

"You want to meet him?"

"No. Just find out where he is and let my brother know."

"So he can get in touch with him?"

"Yes."

Vorster felt his jacket for cigarettes before remembering he'd left them in the office. Meyer offered him one of his Gitanes. "Thanks, Felix. I love these. They are very hard to find."

"I'll get hold of some for you, if you like."

"Very decent of you." Vorster lit up and took a moment to savour the taste. "Back to Pulos. I wouldn't be surprised at all if he's on his way to England. You see, Philip just heard that his father was killed in Crete. Obviously that is an event of great importance for the Arbuthnot business."

Meyer's eyes widened. "Simon Arbuthnot is dead?"

"Yes. Died in the Cretan retreat. Philip doesn't have the exact details."

Felix Meyer knew his brother couldn't be aware of this development. He lit his own cigarette and looked off thoughtfully to the little refreshment hut in the centre of the park, where he could see the girl with the homemade stockings buying drinks.

"Is that it then, Felix? Find out if Pulos is here and where he's staying?"

"That's it."

"I'll call you later. Or better still, let's have a drink. Perhaps your colleagues would like to come. There's a chance I might have some useful inside information from South Africa. A good mining stock." Meyer distractedly smiled his agreement and Vorster patted the lieutenant's shoulder before striding off to the park exit on London Wall. Meyer remained on the bench for a while, thinking hard. Arbuthnot's death might create a real opportunity for Anton to make headway with his cause. And if it did, shouldn't he, Felix, forget his antipathy and get more involved?

*   *   *

Paris

François Bouchard, or John Webster as he was known to his colleagues in the Special Operations Executive, squirmed in agony on the small bunk bed in his cell in the basement of 84 Avenue Foch, the SS headquarters in Paris. The last of his fingernails had been extracted an hour or so ago, soon after the water torture had been halted. So far he had told them nothing but he didn't think he could hold out for another session. Once he had revealed what he knew they would probably kill him anyway, but that would be a release.

Bouchard was one of the first Allied agents to be parachuted into occupied France. Born and bred in the well-to-do Parisian suburb of Neuilly, he had followed his father into the wine trade after wasting (as his father claimed) or enjoying (as he saw it) three years at the Sorbonne. At the outbreak of the war, he had been running the London branch of his father's business in a shop just off St James's Street. Bouchard was distraught at the invasion of his country and, as a proud Frenchman, was keen to do his bit however that might be possible.

A chance encounter with a Free French officer in a bomb shelter had led him to a meeting at 1 Dorset Square and his recruitment soon after as an agent. His training had been carried out by British and French officers at various locations in and outside London. By March, the officer with principal responsibility for him, a Captain Morrison, had decided that Bouchard was ready for the field and a mission had been agreed. He was to be parachuted into countryside 60 miles or so to the west of Paris, carrying with him radio equipment to be passed to members of the embryonic French Resistance, along with some small arms and plastic explosives. Once he had successfully accomplished this, he was to remain in France for an as yet undetermined period and perform other tasks to assist the Resistance.

The aircraft had left Biggin Hill on a rainy night a week before. 'Or was it two weeks?' he wondered as the wrenching pain in his hands subsided for a moment. A week, a month, a day, a year… Seconds, minutes, hours all seemed as one in the pain-wracked blur of his consciousness. Whenever it was, they had been waiting for him. As soon as he hit the ground, the Germans were on him. There must have been seven or eight of them. They cut the parachute away then something hard and heavy had connected with his skull. When he'd come to, Bouchard found himself trussed and gagged in the back of a moving lorry.

He was in a tiny cell with one high, barred window through which a little sunlight found its way. From the hum of people and traffic outside, the smells, the cries of the newspaper vendors and the squawking of the birds, he knew he was in Paris but in which arrondissement he could not tell. Bouchard closed his eyes and imagined he was dining at his father's favourite table in Maxim's. *Escargots à la Bourguignonne* followed by duck breasts in cherry-port sauce. His favourite. He had almost succeeded in conjuring up the delicious flavours when he heard feet outside the cell door. The grille in the door slid open and the captive felt eyes on him. Bolts were unlocked and two men entered.

"Get up, Bouchard." The first man was tall and immaculately turned out in the uniform of an SS *Standartenführer*.

Bouchard groaned.

"Get up, I say, or would you prefer I get Lieutenant Braun in here with his little electric toy to get you going?"

Bouchard rose.

"I can't stand the smell in here. We'll find somewhere a little more pleasant to chat. It's a lovely day. Why don't we have a little walk in the garden? Get him something to put on his feet, Weber."

Private Weber, a short, fat man with a large red birthmark in the middle of his forehead, clicked his heels and replied enthusiastically. "*Jawohl, Standartenführer* Schmidt!"

"For God's sake, Weber, I am not deaf, although I soon will be if you shout at me like that."

Weber scurried out of sight to return seconds later with a pair of filthy canvas slippers.

"Put them on."

Shortly after, Fritz Schmidt and François Bouchard were sitting on a small wooden bench under the shade of an old horse-chestnut tree. Weber hovered beside an ornamental pond 20 yards away.

Schmidt turned to look Bouchard in the face. "You are not looking your best, *Monsieur*. You were quite a nice-looking young fellow before you fell into our hands. I am sure you had few problems with the girls but now…"

Bouchard squinted back at Schmidt, who had the sun directly behind him. He shrugged and said nothing.

"It will no doubt disappoint you to know that the information for which my officers have been pressing you, so far unsuccessfully, has come to us in any event. Thus your terrible pain and suffering have been for nothing." Bouchard struggled to take in what Schmidt was saying. The only thing that really registered with him was the high quality of Schmidt's spoken French.

"Your identity, for example? François Bouchard. Wine dealer. Son of Hercule Bouchard of Neuilly. We have made his acquaintance, by the way. A remarkably healthy and fit old man. Or at least he was until we gave him a few lessons in the ways of the SS."

Bouchard was able to register this and immediately felt as if Schmidt had kicked him hard in the privates. Unrealistically or not, he had never thought that what he was doing would rebound on his father or his family.

"Is he dead?" he croaked.

"Dead. Goodness no. Do you take us for barbarians? No, we are just entertaining him, so to speak. For the moment, anyway."

"What other…?" Bouchard's lips and throat were so dry he could barely speak.

"Private. Get him some water, please." Weber disappeared into the house.

"Charming garden, isn't it? I do so love Paris. How does that Josephine Baker song go? Something about having two lovers, one Paris and the other France. You love Paris and you love your country, do you not, François? Unfortunately for you, so do we Germans. As we take our rightful place in the world, other countries have to take theirs. France has acknowledged the superiority of the Reich and nothing can be allowed to undermine this satisfactory state of affairs... Ah, here is your drink. Help him, Weber."

Bouchard's hands were bound so Weber wrenched the prisoner's head back and poured the water into his mouth. The water must have gone down Bouchard's throat the wrong way and a violent coughing fit erupted. As he waited patiently for this to pass, Schmidt reached down to remove some specks of mud from his boots. The Frenchman's coughing eventually subsided.

"So, *Monsieur* Bouchard, we also learned the names of your contacts in France. We have some of them now, together with the comrades of yours we took at the landing site. Of those, several have not managed to be as stoic as you under interrogation, I'm afraid. We have at least six more people to pick up, of whom a couple are apparently rather attractive young ladies. There will be more, of course." He laughed. "So you and your Resistance cell are completely blown, my friend." Schmidt patted Bouchard on the head. "Would you like to know how we found out about you?"

Bouchard couldn't stop picturing his father's face. Had they beaten him up? Had they tortured him as they had his son? If so, what for? He could tell them nothing. Schmidt patted his head again. "Wakey, wakey, François. Did you hear my question?"

"No… No… What?"

"Shall I tell you how you were betrayed?"

"If you must."

"Yes please, sir."

"Yes… please… sir."

"One of your own countrymen betrayed you. A Frenchman in London. An officer. He works for Vichy and passed on news of your visit to someone there, who was then good enough to pass the information on to us. We didn't have the complete picture. We had your alias, John Webster, and a few other details. We were able to get the rest through good police work by the *Sûreté* here – more Frenchmen – and hard work by the *Gestapo* and ourselves. The *Sûreté* were able to identify you through an old photograph. An impressive filing system they have. Apparently you got into some minor trouble on a drunken night out in your student years. A small fine but they kept your picture. Impressive, eh?"

Bouchard slumped back in the chair. He was almost beyond caring.

"You may wonder why I am revealing this to you. If you managed by any chance to escape, the information that Vichy has a spy in London would be very damaging indeed."

Bouchard turned away from the SS chief, who slapped his leg in irritation. "Oh, *Monsieur*! You are making this very boring with your lack of interest. Very well, the reason why I am revealing this sensitive information to you is that you will not be escaping. In fact…" Schmidt suddenly reached inside his jacket, withdrew his pistol and shot Bouchard in the centre of his forehead. The Frenchman's body slid to the ground. Schmidt paused to flick a few small pieces of grey brain matter from his tunic before bending down to whisper in the dead man's ear. "The reason I am telling you this, *Monsieur* Bouchard, is that you no longer exist."

*   *   *

London

Sidney Fleming had not slept well. Worry about the newly disclosed financial problems at the bank, the missing will and shares had ruined his night. He had finally managed to nod off at five in the morning and, when he woke a couple of hours later, found he had a heavy cold. Fleming knew he was desperately needed in the office but stayed where he was. He dozed on and off for a few more hours, vaguely conscious of the phone ringing and the door being knocked.

When he finally got up he found four messages pushed under the door. Three were typed and said the same thing: 'Mr Alexander Pulos wishes to inform Mr Fleming of his arrival from overseas and would be grateful for a meeting at Mr Fleming's earliest convenience'. The fourth was handwritten. 'For Christ's sake, Sidney, answer the damned phone. I have travelled halfway around the world to be here!'

Fleming did not need long to decide that he was not in the mood to see the Greek. He was about to ring the front desk switchboard and ask them to tell Pulos he was ill and could not see him at the moment when the telephone rang again. He sighed and picked up the receiver in trepidation, expecting to hear Pulos at the other end of the line. "Yes?"

"Fleming? Tomlinson here. Have you a moment?"

Fleming answered with a sneeze.

"Bless you."

Fleming sneezed again.

"Are you all right, Sidney?"

"I've got a stinking cold and a sore throat. Not at my best. Can't it wait, Reggie?"

"I'm sorry but I think you'll want to hear this straightaway."

Fleming sighed and slumped into his chair. "Very well then. Fire away."

"I was just visited by an army officer. Lieutenant Edgar Powell recently returned from Crete. Do I have your attention, Sidney?"

Fleming sat up instantly. "You do. Did he…?"

"He was with Arbuthnot at the end. He, Arbuthnot and another soldier were on the retreat, trying to get to Sphakia, where our ships were waiting to evacuate troops to Egypt. They were crossing open ground when they were attacked by two German aeroplanes. Powell was the only survivor."

An extremely fat pigeon landed on the hotel window ledge and looked inquisitively through the glass. Fleming closed his eyes and tried to imagine his partner's final moments.

"Sidney, are you there? Sidney?"

"Yes, sorry. I was just…" The pigeon flew off. "Did the lieutenant say it was quick? Was he in much pain?"

"It was quick. There was pain but not for long. But look, Sidney, this wasn't just a thoughtful visit by someone who was with a man when he died. Powell has something of Simon's. Something that might be very important."

"What?"

"Simon gave him a letter. Insisted with his dying breath that Powell deliver it."

"To whom?"

"That's the point. Arbuthnot tried to write down the name of the addressee when he could no longer speak but couldn't complete it. Powell didn't think it was right to open it but he'd like to fulfil his promise and give it to the right person."

"So no-one has seen the contents of the letter?"

"No."

"And who does Powell think is the right person to give it to?"

"Powell says Simon only managed to get the first letter down clearly. An S."

"Did he show you the letter?"

"No. He didn't have it with him. He just wanted my advice as Arbuthnot's lawyer."

"Well, I hope the advice you gave him was to give it to you. Solicitor begins with an S, doesn't it?"

"Of course I pointed that out. He said that a police friend of his had advised him likewise."

The mention of the police made Fleming uncomfortable. "And so?"

"He said he knew Arbuthnot had a son and a sister. He had decided that the letter should go either to me, Philip or Lucinda. I assured him that if it were handed to me, I would immediately pass on its contents to them."

"Any problem with that?"

"He said what if it turned out that the contents of the envelope were to be kept secret from one or other of them?"

"All the more reason to give it to you."

"As I advised him. He said he'd think about what I said. Emphasised that he wanted to do the correct and honourable thing in fulfilling a dying man's last wish."

Fleming reflected that Powell sounded like one of those typical stuck-up 'play up and play the game' Englishmen he'd always detested. 'Correct and honourable' for Christ's sake! He was only delivering a bloody letter. "So how was it left?"

"He's going to sleep on it. He'll decide tomorrow morning but said he was inclined to give it to me."

"Good. What's in the letter do you think?"

"With luck, something about the missing will and bearer shares."

"I hope you're right." Fleming wondered if there might also be something about the shenanigans Brightwell had uncovered. If so, it would be best if he saw the letter first. Best for other reasons too. And S also stood for Sidney, didn't it?

"Where does Powell live?"

"He gave me an address in Flood Street – 44 Rossetti Garden Mansions. Why?"

"Oh, just wondering. Presumably that's where the letter is."

"Presumably."

"Well thank you, Reggie, for putting me in the picture so promptly. Please keep me posted."

"Of course, Sidney, and I wish you…"

"Do you know that Pulos is in town?"

"Yes. He telephoned the office. I haven't called him back yet. Going to do it now."

"Tell him I've got the flu, will you? And that I'll call him as soon as I'm feeling better."

"Very well, Sidney." As he put the telephone down, Fleming thought he heard an odd clicking noise. However, preoccupied as he was with considering how he might get first sight of Simon's letter, he gave it little thought.

*   *   *

Sonia had lit candles, which flickered in the gentle breeze filtering in from the open window behind the blackout curtain. She and Merlin normally ate in the kitchen but she'd wanted to make this dinner a special occasion. So she had opened up the antique mahogany table, which Frank had inherited from his parents and that was normally folded away in the corner of the drawing room.

Their two guests could not have been more different. On Sonia's right sat her brother, Jan Sieczko, resplendent in his RAF pilot's uniform and on his first visit in weeks. On her left was Bernie Goldberg, wearing a double-breasted charcoal suit and a rather loud green tie. Merlin had reluctantly given in to Sonia and put on his best suit, a blue-grey number he had last worn at Bridges' wedding. Sonia was wearing her favourite frock, a white cocktail dress that hugged her shapely figure tightly. Goldberg was finding it difficult to keep his eyes off her.

Sieczko was darker in complexion than his sister but the resemblance was close. His hair was a similar reddish-brown to hers, he had her warm eyes and engaging smile. Merlin noticed that his moustache had become much bushier since he'd last seen him. Jan was a good-looking young man, who had taken advantage of the admiration of the RAF Northolt canteen girls to secure a large leg of mutton for Sonia to cook. She had turned the joint into a delicious stew, which had been thoroughly enjoyed by everyone. Cheese and biscuits had followed and Merlin was just polishing off a piece of Stilton when he noticed the wine glasses needed refreshing.

"More wine?" They were drinking some vintage rioja from an old case Merlin had found in his mother's basement after she died. Sonia held a hand over her glass but the men were all ready for more. "I think Bernie would love to hear a little about your squadron, Jan."

"I certainly would, Frank, if that's all right with Jan."

Sieczko waited until Merlin had refilled his glass then looked at Goldberg. "It's called the Kosciuszko Squadron. A bit of a mouthful, I know. Tadeusz Kosciuszko was a Polish engineer and soldier, who fought with your General Washington against the British in the War of Independence. Then he fought against the Russians who, like the Germans, are always keen to deprive Poland of its independence. A great hero and so a good name for a fighter squadron."

"And this is a squadron of Polish pilots but it's part of the RAF?"

"Yes. I and most of my fellow officers fought against the Germans as part of the Polish Air Force at the outbreak of the war. After Poland's defeat, we managed to make our way here and the RAF welcomed us. We have a few British officers, all very fine fellows, in the squadron. And we carry on fighting Germans."

Sonia beamed with pride. "Jan is too modest to say himself, Bernie, but his pilots have – how do you say it? – the biggest hits in the air so far."

Merlin twirled his wine glass in the light of the candle in front of him. The blackout curtain flapped away briefly from the window. He saw that the summer dusk had finally given way to darkness. "What Sonia is trying to say is that Jan's squadron has so far shot down more German aircraft than any other squadron in the RAF. Isn't that so, Jan?"

Sieczko shrugged his shoulders and grinned awkwardly. "Everyone is doing their best but all pilots are very competitive and, yes, we do keep count. So far the squadron is doing well. At the moment, of course, the skies above London are quiet so no-one is adding to their tallies here for now."

"But I thought you were flying further afield?"

"Yes, Sonia, but we shouldn't talk about that."

"Oh, is it a secret? Sorry, Jan, but I don't think Mr Goldberg is a spy."

Sieczko shifted uncomfortably in his chair. "Forgive me, Bernie. Our British officers keep warning us to be careful. 'Careless talk costs lives' is the phrase we hear all the time."

"Don't worry, Jan. Quite right too. I've seen the posters." Goldberg laughed. "I like the one where an attractive broad – er, sorry, Sonia – an attractive lady is sitting surrounded by British officers with the punchline 'Keep mum she's not so dumb!' But your reserve is quite understandable. Is it permissible to say how many German planes your squadron has downed so far?"

"Yes. The last number was around 170."

"Of which your own hits were…?"

"Maybe 16 or 17."

"Wow, Jan. That's quite something."

"Thank you, Bernie. But enough of me, please. Come, Frank, tell us what you are up to."

Merlin wiped his lips with a napkin. "We have an illegal abortion case where a poor young girl died, and we have the murder of the man who performed the abortion."

"Perhaps the procurer of the abortion and the murderer of the abortionist are one and the same man?"

"That is very possible, Jan."

"Were these people English?"

"No. The girl was Irish and the abortionist was a French Jew down on his luck."

Sieczko nodded. "One of many."

Sonia reached over to pat her brother's hand. "We must count ourselves very lucky, mustn't we, Jan? We are half Jewish, Bernie."

"And I'm all Jewish."

"You grew up in New York?"

"Yes. Classic Jewish immigrant upbringing. Parents escaped from Russian pogroms at the turn of the century. Got to Ellis Island, then the tenements of the Lower East Side. My father was, sorry, is a tailor. Still working hard in his 70s."

"He prospered?"

"Did OK, Jan. He has three shops now, two of which are run by my other two brothers, and he runs the third, though my sister and her husband help him with that."

"Are you the only one of his children who did not follow him into the business?"

"I have another sister, who is a nurse. Otherwise yes. My father still can't get over the fact that I'm a policeman. It's not something he thinks Jews are made for."

Sieczko finished his glass. "Probably has bad memories of authority from the Russian days. Do you find any prejudice among your colleagues?"

Sonia rose and started collecting up the dishes. Merlin rose to help her but she pushed him back in his chair. "As well as the meat, Jan brought us some decent coffee from the base. I'll go and make some." She disappeared into the kitchen.

"You asked about prejudice, Jan. Yes, of course there is. But what was Poland like before the war?"

"Very bad, but compared with what is happening there now…"

"Have you any knowledge of present conditions? The country is split, right? The Germans have the west and the Russians the east?"

Sieczko sighed. "Yes, that is right, Bernie. One of our pilots is a recent recruit. He only got out of Poland six months ago. He was in Warsaw, which the Germans control. They have corralled all the Jews into a walled-off ghetto in the centre of the city. Conditions are disgusting. There is limited food. Militias rule the ghetto with much cruelty under the control of the Nazis. There are terrible, terrible stories. The old, women, children are…" Sieczko put a hand to his eyes. "I'm sorry. Please, gentlemen. Let us not ruin our lovely evening with talk of this."

Goldberg reached out to touch the pilot's shoulder. "I'm sorry. I shouldn't have asked. It's a stupid question. We know the Nazis are animals."

Sonia arrived with the coffee and looked with concern at her brother. "What's all this then?"

Sieczko looked up at her and forced a smile. "Nothing, my beautiful sister. Just a little chat about our poor homeland. I got upset for a moment but now we are changing the subject. What shall we talk about now, Frank?"

Merlin was helping Sonia set the cups out on the table. "I was wondering, Jan. Have you had any dealings with Free French pilots?"

"I have met a few. I have drunk with a man called Jean Dubois. A good fellow."

"What does he think of his fellow Free French in London?"

"Said he didn't have much time for the army and navy officers. Unlike him, they were not involved in military action and, as far as he could see, quite a few of them did nothing more than play politics or have a good time. He didn't have much time either for the chap in charge, what's his name, de Gaulle? A man with a baton up his arse. That was his description."

"A nice turn of phrase, your French friend, I'm sure, Jan."

Sieczko reached out to embrace his sister. "Forgive me, Sonia. I have obviously been around pilots for too long."

"Brandy, anyone?"

The evening ended at eleven. Goldberg went off in search of a taxi, while Sieczko, declining the offer of the couch, hurried off to catch the last Tube. When Merlin and Sonia were washing up, she asked about Bridget Healy. "I'm afraid I am a little naïve about these things. How exactly did this man de Metz go about his business? The abortion, I mean."

Merlin dropped his tea towel in surprise. "I can't answer that, Sonia. If you really want to know you'll have to ask one of your girlfriends. Suffice to say it is cruel and disgusting."

"Sorry, Frank. I have just been feeling sorry for that girl. I was just hoping what happened to her wouldn't have been too painful."

"I can't say, darling. With luck the drugs he gave her would…"

"All right, Frank. Let's get to bed. I just… to have the chance of producing a beautiful baby and then to kill it. I just can't understand."

Merlin leaned over to kiss her on the forehead. "It was a lovely dinner party, darling. Thank you."

CHAPTER 9
Friday 13 June

London

Pulos rose from his bed at seven. Although it was still the middle of the night in Argentina, he managed to get through to his secretary and some senior executives to hear their latest reports. An outbreak of foot-and-mouth disease had hit a farm neighbouring one of the company's largest cattle ranches in the south of the country. A planned railwaymen's strike was about to get under way in Córdoba and an accident at one of the company's copper mines had killed a couple of workers. All matters of concern but very much routine problems for a big company such as Enterprisas Simal.

Just after eight-thirty, as he was enjoying his breakfast of poached egg on toast, there was a knock at the door. "Get that will you, Marco?"

Andreas Koutrakos appeared in the doorway.

"Andreas, my friend. Come in. *Kalimera*. How are you?"

Koutrakos's lips parted into a thin smile as he sat down at the table.

"A piece of toast, Andreas? A spot of coffee? No? Very well then. I presume this is not purely a friendly visit. What do you have for me?"

Koutrakos fidgeted nervously. "I heard something yesterday."

"Yesterday? And it has taken you this long to come and see me?"

Koutrakos smoothed his hair with a shaking hand. "The call was yesterday afternoon and I was on duty until midnight. I came at the first opportunity."

"If the information is of interest, I wouldn't have minded being woken up but no matter. What did you hear?"

"Fleming received a call from a Mr Tomlinson. A Mr Reggie Tomlinson."

"Yes, yes, I know him. What did they discuss?"

Koutrakos told Pulos about the conversation that had passed between the two men. When he'd finished, he couldn't help but cast a longing look at the jug of orange juice on the breakfast table.

"Help yourself, Andreas. Go on. You could do with the vitamin C."

Koutrakos poured himself a glass and gulped it down.

"You have done well, my friend. What was that address again – 44 Rossetti Garden Mansions, wasn't it? In Flood Street. A nice part of town as I recall. Very well. Marco! Money please." Marco produced Pulos's wallet. Pulos took out a note and waved it in front of Koutrakos. "There you are – £5. Don't spend it all at once. Off you go then and, if you hear anything else…"

Koutrakos wiped his orange-stained lips, nodded and hurried out of the room.

Pulos's coffee had gone cold but he finished it anyway. He looked thoughtfully out of the window then called out. "Come here, Marco. I think I have a job for you."

*   *   *

"Mind if I trouble you for a second, Colonel?"

Colonel Aubertin was at his desk, sipping a morning coffee and reading a letter from his wife when Gordon Vane-Stewart appeared at the door.

"Not at all, Major. Please come in."

The major sat down. His manner was mild and self-effacing. The real man, as the colonel well knew, was quite different. Gordon Vane-Stewart was a man of ambition, courage and an iron will. He was one of the driving forces behind the Special Operations Executive. The SOE had been formed almost a year before at Winston Churchill's initiative. The organisation had resulted from the amalgamation of separate departments operated by the Foreign Office, MI6 and the War Office. Its brief was to conduct espionage, sabotage and reconnaissance in occupied Europe and to assist local resistance operations.

Aubertin and his colleagues had often laughed about the British predilection for nicknames. In the case of the SOE, two nicknames were already current – the Baker Street Irregulars (referencing the location of its headquarters) and Churchill's Toyshop, reflecting the keen interest the prime minister took in its activities. The exact hierarchy of the SOE had never been made clear to Aubertin but he knew that Vane-Stewart was very senior. More to the point, he was his principal liaison with the organisation. A section of the SOE had a part-time office in Dorset Square and Vane-Stewart was in charge of this section.

Vane-Stewart noticed the letter that Aubertin was putting away bore a Gibraltar stamp. "All well, Colonel?"

"Yes, Major. A letter from Jeanette, my wife. It somehow got through to me via north Africa and Gibraltar. She is at our house in the Auvergne – or was when she wrote it four weeks ago."

"I spent some happy times in France before the war. Mostly in the south. We used to rent a house in a place called Grimaud."

"I know it well. We also used to holiday around there."

"How does your wife fare in the current difficult circumstances?"

"It is hard to tell as, by necessity, the letter is bland and guarded. One has to assume that the post is not secure in Vichy. She is not well so, naturally, I worry but she says nothing of her health."

"Difficult for you. Have you tried to get her out?"

"Before things got really bad, yes. But she wanted to stay to protect the house. It has been in her family for several generations. We have no children and…"

"The house is her child? Say no more, Colonel. I understand. We have a family seat in Sussex going back to James I. We would no doubt have similar issues." The major drew his chair closer to the desk. "I'm afraid I have some rather unpleasant news."

The colonel straightened in his seat. "Oh?"

"We appear to have lost an agent."

"I'm sorry." The colonel removed his reading glasses.

"Reliable sources have informed us that the French agent John Webster, real name François Bouchard, has been arrested by the Germans and is being interrogated at the SS headquarters in Paris."

"Where was he arrested?"

"It appears the Germans were waiting for him when he landed. They also caught the waiting Resistance reception party, who are no doubt also in custody. Presuming they are not already dead." Vane-Stewart stroked the sandy-coloured moustache that nestled under his formidable nose.

"So they knew he was coming and they knew where and when."

The major cleared his throat. "It is hard to believe they stumbled upon him by accident in the middle of a very isolated part of rural northern France. I suppose they might somehow have been able to track the aircraft."

"Perhaps."

"More likely they got the information from London."

"A leak."

"The word leak implies the information might have got out by chance. Unwise gossip or the like. I'm afraid we need another word here, Colonel, a stronger word."

"And what word would that be?"

"Treachery. Someone here – and by here I mean either in this building, in our office in Baker Street or in your other offices in London – has intentionally passed this information to the Germans directly or via the Vichy French and a brave man has been lost." The major leaned back and stretched out the gammy leg he had acquired at Dunkirk. "The question is, Colonel, what are we going to do about it?"

*   *   *

The telephone rang as Merlin came into his office with Bridges and Robinson. "Chief Inspector Merlin?" a drawling voice enquired.

"This is Merlin."

"I am Mr White. I spoke recently to your Constable Robinson." Merlin's eyebrows rose. "Oh. Yes."

"We'd like to have a little chat. I gather you know one of my colleagues. I won't mention his name on the line. Let's call him Mr Black. I've arranged for you to meet him for lunch today at the Reform Club. Be there at one o'clock sharp."

Merlin was allowed no time for reply. He put down the receiver. "Your friend Mr White from MI5 has finally got back to us, Constable."

"Is he going to meet you, sir?"

"Not him. Someone else. I think I know who." If it were that person, Merlin was cheered to think he would at least get a straight story. "I'm lunching with him." He turned to Bridges, who was opening a window. "So, Sergeant, Constable. How did you get on yesterday? I'm sorry, by the way, that I wasn't here on your return yesterday afternoon. The AC dragged me off to a tedious meeting at the Home Office about police liaison with the Home Guard, which I could have done without."

Bridges ran over what Peter Wilson had told them. When he'd finished, Merlin leaned back and swung a leg up on the desk. "So the fellow was friends with Bridget Healy but denies anything stronger than friendship. Confirms there was someone seeing her, someone who could afford to take her to nice places, but has no idea who. Did you get any sense at all that he might not be telling the truth?"

"My gut feel is that he was a straight shooter. Well educated sort of fellow. Not your average chauffeur. I think the constable agrees." Robinson nodded.

"All right. Now tell me about your visit to the Ritz."

"Well, we hit gold straightaway with a barman we spoke to in the upstairs bar. He recognised Bridget from her photograph and said he'd seen her in the bar several times, always with a crowd of people."

"Any names?"

"No."

"Civilians or military? Men or women?"

"A mixed bunch mostly."

"And the military men, what nationality?"

"Some British, some Canadian, some French, some he wasn't sure."

"Would he recognise any of them?"

"He said he'd try if we went to the bar in the evening and any turned up. Said, if he remembered correctly, the lady and her crowd were usually latecomers, arriving after ten."

"Well, it seems we'll have to endure an evening in the Ritz. Tonight, I think. Friday night is my delight. I'll have a think about what numbers we go in."

*   *   *

The same café. The same time of day. The only difference this time was that Rougemont had not troubled to get himself a shoe-shine. As before, there were only two other customers when the captain joined his spy.

"Nice day."

"Some improvement. What do you have for me?"

"A couple of things. The British police visited Carlton Gardens yesterday."

"Did they?"

"I don't know who they met."

"Don't worry, I can find out." The captain added some sugar to his tea. Normally he took it without but this morning he felt the need for something sweet. Probably something to do with the plentiful cheap champagne he had drunk with the commandant the night before. He had unwisely agreed to accompany Angers on a double date with his two English showgirls. After watching the girls in their revue, they had all gone on to a club in Soho. He had not taken to the girl Angers had allocated to him and had drunk too much in compensation. That was the first and last time he'd do that for the commandant. "What else?"

"I can give you the identity of the civilian your officers met in the park."

"Yes?"

"A fellow called Vorster. Rupert Vorster. He was the man who met with Beaulieu, Dumont and Meyer."

"And who is Vorster? How did you identify him?"

"Beaulieu is away, as you know, so…"

"I checked out his story by the way. He turned up at Oxford as planned. The fellow Beaulieu's been visiting is whiter than white."

"Very well. So the two other officers I'm tailing met up with Vorster again, this time for drinks in a St James's pub. Another customer called out Vorster's name. It was noisy but I could hear Vorster's response. He has a South African accent – I shared digs with someone from Cape Town once and recognised it. I didn't hear anything of particular interest. They seemed to be talking about mining companies and the stock market mostly. After a while, they all moved on to the Ritz. I followed but wasn't really dressed for the place. I stood outside until 11 o'clock then called it a day. I did see one other thing, by way of coincidence."

"Yes?"

"I saw your boss go into the Ritz as I was leaving."

"Angers?"

"No, the colonel."

"Aubertin?"

"You've never introduced me but I've seen him with you and Angers from afar. Yes, Aubertin."

"Well, he likes to enjoy himself as much as the next man."

"Perhaps he was meeting up with the other two?"

Rougemont frowned. Could that be possible? Would there really be anything wrong with that, if he did?

"Or perhaps he has decided to do a little investigating of his own?"

"Perhaps, Mr Harp, but probably meeting up with another friend, I should think. Anything else?"

Devlin shook his head. "I followed the two men in alternating blocks of four or five hours. Most of the time they were both at the office. Meyer went out somewhere around lunchtime yesterday but my time was allotted to Dumont then. Then there was the meeting with Vorster. Nothing else of note except that Dumont appears to have a girlfriend, who visited him in his digs on Wednesday night."

"Hmm. Very well, let's keep it up with the three of them for a few more days. You needn't worry about Meyer for the rest of the morning as I'm going out riding with him. Maybe I'll learn something more. You don't mind working the weekend, I suppose?"

"Not as long as I get a weekend rate, Captain."

*   *   *

"Felix, is that you? It's Rupert here. I've found your Greek for you."

Meyer had just returned to his office when the phone rang. He had enjoyed his ride with Rougemont in Hyde Park. He was a reasonably accomplished, if rusty, horseman. The captain's purpose in inviting him did not seem, in retrospect, to be purely social. In between pleasantries and military gossip, Rougemont had interrogated him on several subjects. He had asked about Meyer's own background, about what he knew of Beaulieu and Dumont, about Vorster, whose name he somehow knew, and had been particularly inquisitive when Meyer said he had spoken to the police on their visit to Carlton Gardens. He had been open in his answers on all these matters, saving his family background. The story of his family's decline and the events precipitating it were still, he believed, a secret to his fellow officers and he intended to keep it that way.

"Thank you, Rupert." Meyer looked out at the sunlit back garden, where two blackbirds were noisily squabbling over a worm. "Where is he, then?"

"He's at the Ritz hotel. Got in from Argentina yesterday. Word is, according to Philip Arbuthnot and others, that the main players in the Arbuthnot business empire will be meeting in London to discuss the ramifications of Simon's death and the management succession. Despite his lack of experience, Philip wants the top job. He says it's his due. However, he thinks there may be some difficulties to overcome but wasn't forthcoming as to what those might be.

"Pulos runs the South American part of the business. It's natural that he should participate in the management discussions although Philip was surprised that he had risked the journey. Anyway, I don't have Pulos's room number at the Ritz but it may interest you to know that the new chairman of Sackville Bank, Sidney Fleming, lives permanently in a suite there. Now is there anything else I can do for you?"

"No. I'm very grateful, Rupert. Thank you." Meyer put the receiver down and sat pensively at his desk. He would try to get hold of his brother later and pass on his news. Would that be all he should do? Or should he venture a meeting? In the changed circumstances, perhaps there was something to be gained from a face-to-face encounter with Pulos, or maybe even Fleming. He would see what Anton said. Meanwhile, there was work to be done. He had the latest cables from Syria and Lebanon to review and analyse. He also had a new summary of the proposed Special Operations Executive operations. He pulled his in-tray towards him, removed the top file and began to read.

*   *   *

Philip Arbuthnot had spent Wednesday afternoon and much of Thursday carrying out a thorough search of his father's flat with the help of Mavis, the live-in housekeeper, who had all the necessary keys and combinations. He had not found what he was looking for. The new will and bearer certificates remained lost.

The study safe had been empty, save for a photograph of his father as a young man in tennis kit with his arm around the shoulder of a pretty young dark-haired woman. His father's desk had contained little more than routine bills and useless bric-a-brac. There had been, though, a mildly intriguing sheet of paper with a pencilled list of numbers and two initials. Philip had recognised his father's hand and, before pocketing the note, had wondered briefly who or what PB was. Now, on Friday morning, as he sat in his kitchen waiting for the kettle to boil, he began studying it again.

Apart from Mavis, he hadn't seen anyone since his lunch with Tomlinson on Wednesday. The girls had been ringing incessantly but he hadn't been in the mood. He'd chatted with Rupert a couple of times but had declined his suggestion of a drink. It had taken a few days but the true emotional impact of his father's death had at last hit home. His initial shameful feelings of relief had given way to others more natural on the death of a loved one.

Despite the recent strains in their relationship, Philip fully recognised that father and son had dearly loved one another. They had probably been closest and got on best during Philip's mid-teens, a time when fathers and sons often rub each other up the wrong way. Philip remembered a fishing trip to Scotland, when his normally unemotional father had seemed on the brink of confiding something of momentous impact to his son.

"I have some things to tell you, my boy. To tell you and no-one else," his father had said as he cast a line on one of the best salmon fishing stands in Scotland. "I'd like to relieve my conscience and you're the only one I can… I just hope you won't lose respect for…" The words had tailed off and, although Philip had waited expectantly over dinner that night for them to be followed up, nothing more had been said.

There had also been jolly trips to rugby matches, the pictures, to Wimbledon for the tennis and more. However, father and son had seen little of each other in the past couple of years and, while searching the flat, Philip had realised with a shock that he had very little idea of what his father had done with himself during that period. There had been many women in his life after his mother had died but Philip had the impression that his father's interest in the opposite sex had waned in recent years. Mavis had told him that she wasn't aware of a girlfriend since a year before the war had begun. She did say that his father was never home much in the evenings and she often heard him coming in very late.

Who had he been with and what had he been doing? Fleming and Tomlinson had also remarked how little they had seen of him, in the office or out, in the months before he signed up. They had told Philip that he appeared to have been similarly reclusive with his wider circle of friends. It was a mystery.

The kettle came to the boil and he made his tea. He returned to his chair and his father's note. He ran his eyes over the sheet again.

14123

12917

16421 PB

9856

13876

17182

What on earth were these numbers? To what did they refer? Perhaps he should ask his aunt.

*   *   *

Tomlinson was bemoaning to himself the loss of his Saturday morning golf game when Rupert Vorster appeared before him with some papers to sign. He gave them a cursory look then penned his signature with a flourish. "There are some more to come, aren't there, Vorster? When will I get those?"

"Later today, sir. Thank you."

Tomlinson's secretary Sylvia popped her head through the door to tell him that Sidney Fleming was on the line.

"All right. Oh, and Sylvia, can you pop out and get me some sandwiches for lunch? Any flavour will do as long as it's not corned beef. Thanks. Put Fleming through, then. That will be all, Vorster."

Vorster backed out of the room as Tomlinson picked up the phone.

"Sidney, hello. What can I do for you?"

"Have you heard from Powell?"

"Yes, he called earlier to say he's busy with family commitments today but he's happy to meet me here at 10.30 tomorrow to give me the letter. He's buggered up my morning. I was in a foursome at the club."

"Well, this is just a little more important than golf, Reggie. It could give us the solution to some big problems. Perhaps Powell, contrary to what he said, has opened the letter and knows what's in it. Perhaps he's now the one who knows where the will and the certificates are."

"I very much doubt it, Sidney. He seems the honourable sort to me. However, I share your optimism. I very much hope the letter will direct us to the will and the bearer shares. That, in the circumstances, is what I would expect a final letter from Simon to me to address. But we must now wait until tomorrow morning to find out."

Outside Tomlinson's door, where Vorster had taken advantage of the secretary's temporary absence to listen in to this conversation, the sound of approaching steps could be heard on the stairs. He couldn't risk staying longer and hurried away. Vorster was smiling, however, because he felt he'd heard what he needed to. Now he'd have to decide what to do with what he'd learned.

Back in the office, the conversation continued. "I finally saw Pulos today, Reggie."

"How was he?"

"A pain in the arse as usual. I'm going to convene a meeting at the bank tomorrow at noon. I'd like you there. Hopefully, you'll have Simon's letter by then. I'm not asking Philip. I think it might be best for just the three of us to meet at first."

Fleming could hear Tomlinson's deep sigh at the other end of the line. "Very well. My Saturday is pretty much ruined anyway. By the way, Philip rang me this morning. He's searched his father's stuff for the will and shares. No luck. He did, however, find an odd scrap of paper. Some figures and initials. PB mean anything to you?"

There was a brief silence before Fleming replied. "Does Philip still have the list or has he given it to you?"

"He has it at his flat."

"I think I'd better pay him a visit tomorrow morning before our meeting."

*   *   *

It was Merlin's first time in the Reform Club but he could see instantly it was cast in a similar mould to the various other London gentlemen's clubs he had been obliged to visit before in the course of his duties. He had never been able to understand the attraction of these gloomy places, where upper-class, middle-aged and elderly men hid themselves away behind rustling newspapers or dozed in dark rooms full of heavy leather armchairs splattered with cigar ash and drink stains.

On leaving his taxi by the club entrance, Merlin had paused to survey the hole in the ground next door, which had once been the Junior Carlton Club. The *Luftwaffe* had obliterated it with a direct hit at the height of the Blitz the previous October. He had been entertained there only a month before its destruction by the eminent pathologist Sir Bernard Spilsbury. Investigating the murder of one of Sieczko's fellow pilots, he had discussed causes of death with the man who had convicted the infamous Dr Crippen with his forensic evidence. Merlin had heard recently that Spilsbury had not borne the death of one of his sons in the Blitz well and had become a bit of a recluse. He was sorry because he liked and respected the man.

His lunch companion was awaiting him in the lobby. Harold Swanton was a former police colleague of Merlin's. When Merlin had been a young sergeant in 1934, Swanton had held his current rank and he had worked under Swanton for a year. The two men had got on well. Merlin had learned a good deal from Swanton or 'Sparky' as he had been known behind his back (owing to his keen interest and proficiency in electrical engineering and radio technology). It was this particular expertise that had attracted the attentions first of the Special Branch, where he had moved in 1936, and then of MI5, which had recruited him just before the outbreak of war.

Everything about Swanton was big. A large-boned man in his mid-50s, his head was covered with a thick brush of greying brown hair. He had wide grey eyes, a prominent square chin and a bulbous nose. At six foot five he towered even over Merlin. The only small thing about him was the little moustache that took up a modest amount of space on his upper lip. He lumbered over to Merlin and shook his hand firmly. "Frank, my boy. How are you? It's been too long."

Merlin realised with a jolt that they had last met at Alice's funeral. Swanton looked just as he had in the Brompton Cemetery on that miserable day. Perhaps there were a few more flecks of grey in his moustache, perhaps a few more lines beneath those intelligent eyes.

"You don't look a day older, Harold. What are they feeding you over there in St James's?"

"They give us a special diet." Swanton lowered his voice to a whisper. "Spy food. There's this place called Porton Down. Most people in the know think it's working on chemical weapons but in fact it's making superfood for us. Not for those bastards at MI6, of course! They can poison them at will." He shook with laughter. "Oh dear, there I go again. Letting my prejudices run away with me. Come on, Frank, this way. I've got a small private dining room organised. I believe rabbit is on the menu."

Merlin followed his old colleague out of the lobby and into the Coffee Room, which Swanton explained was the traditional name for the club restaurant, on through a door, down a corridor and finally into a small, wood-panelled room looking out on to an attractive garden. A dining table in the centre was laid for two. Swanton moved to a drinks cabinet at the side of the room and reached for the Bombay gin.

"Gin and tonic, Frank?"

"I shouldn't really, Harold."

Swanton poured two stiff ones and shrugged. "Inter-service liaison meeting, Frank. Alcohol permitted, nay required, in such circumstances." Merlin took the proffered glass.

"Chin-chin." They touched glasses and drank. Merlin grimaced.

"Too weak for you, Chief Inspector Merlin. Shall I top it up?"

Merlin put a hand over the glass and laughed. "No thanks, Harold. The opposite, as you well know." The two men stood by the window and watched as a gardener mowed the lawn. A side-window was open and they savoured the fragrance of newly mown grass.

"It's still possible, isn't it, Frank, to appreciate the joys of nature, despite all the terrible things that are going on and the dreadful danger in which our nation finds itself?"

"Life goes on. Bees make honey. Spiders spin webs. Grass grows. Hitler can't stop that."

Swanton moved back to the drinks table and rang a small bell. "Let's get on and order the grub. Then we can discuss what we're here to discuss."

The two men sat down. The choice was rabbit or sausages. Rumours were rife about the dreadful things going into sausages as the food shortages worsened. Although he suspected that the Reform Club's sausages would have proper ingredients, Merlin plumped for the rabbit, as did Swanton.

"Glad to hear your personal life's looking up, Frank. It was all so tragic about poor Alice."

Merlin was taken aback and showed it.

"Oh yes, we keep a close eye on our most valued police officers, Chief Inspector. One of our jobs. Ensuring that the home front is protected and that all its key defenders are fit, healthy and uncompromised. Don't worry, we haven't got someone following you about. We just keep an eye open."

"I'm not sure I like the sound of that, Harold."

"Look, there are a hell of a lot of new foreigners milling around in the country and in London in particular. We are as vigilant as we have to be. You hook up with one of those foreigners. It doesn't require much effort to check out that she's a decent sort with no unfortunate friends, contacts or beliefs. Sonia seems a very nice lady. A beauty by all accounts, with a heroic brother as well. You're a lucky man, Frank, as you deserve to be."

Merlin smiled awkwardly and took a gulp of his drink.

"Apologies by the way for our Mr White. I'm sure he spoke rudely to your people. He's a bit up himself, I'm afraid. I'm going to have to take him in hand. Ah, I see you're getting low already, Frank." Swanton took their glasses to the cabinet for replenishment.

When Swanton returned, Merlin leaned forward over the table. "Let's talk about business, shall we, Harold, before I collapse from alcoholic poisoning or from embarrassment at MI5 knowing all about my private life."

Swanton patted Merlin's hand. "All right, Frank. Armand de Metz. You are investigating him on suspicion of his being an abortionist."

An elderly waiter appeared with a basket of bread and a jug of water and took their orders. Merlin waited until he had disappeared. "We know he performed the abortion in question. A young Irish girl died."

"Very sad. Shortly after this fatal abortion, de Metz was shot dead?"

"He was."

"We at the service know nothing about the abortion or the shooting. What we do know is that de Metz attempted to contact someone at a government facility outside London."

Merlin nodded. "We are aware that he travelled to Bletchley."

"I see, but you're probably not aware that Bletchley is a highly sensitive location. I'm afraid I can't go into any detail. To be honest, I don't even know what really goes on there myself. All I can say is that it is extremely hush-hush and we are on notice to be on the highest of alerts concerning breaches of security there." Swanton paused and poured himself a glass of water. "So de Metz's visit was reported to us."

"Did he get in?"

"He did not. It turns out that he has a relative working there. One of his sisters married an Englishman. Their only son became a mathematics don at Cambridge and is working in some capacity at Bletchley."

"Mathematics don?"

"As I say, we don't know what goes on there."

"De Metz was in a bad way. He was broke. Perhaps he just wanted to touch one of his few surviving relatives for a tenner? Did he try and contact his sister and brother-in-law as well?"

"That would not have been possible. They and their only daughter perished in the Blitz. Their house in Wandsworth was blown to smithereens last November."

"Had he any other relatives in England?"

"Not so far as we are aware."

"So de Metz hears that his nephew, possibly his only surviving relative, is working at Bletchley and tries to get to see him?"

"But fails and is reported to us."

The elderly waiter returned with their lunch. Merlin was pleasantly surprised to see the meat and veg came in large helpings and were swimming in gravy. He loved rabbit gravy.

"Looks good, doesn't it? Tuck in, Frank."

Merlin did as he was told. The rabbit was delicious. "So what happened next?"

"We pulled him in. He was in a pretty sorry state, as you say. Dishevelled. Stinking of booze. We found it very hard to believe that, as he told us, he was a leading surgeon in Paris before the war. However, we investigated and we found he was telling the truth. The reasons he gave for trying to see his nephew were as you surmised."

"Where did you take him?"

"Round the corner to our place in St James's at first. Then while we were checking his story out, we took him to Blenheim."

Merlin knew that MI5 had been based in Wormwood Scrubs at the beginning of the war but, after the prison had been bombed in September 1940, some operations had been moved to the Duke of Marlborough's glorious palace at Blenheim, near Oxford. They had also retained a London office in St James's Street, around the corner from the Reform Club. No doubt there were other locations he wasn't aware of.

"We eventually decided he was completely legitimate. However, during the interrogation, he began hinting that he might have some important information of interest to us in another quarter. Something relative to security in de Gaulle's London outfit."

"And did he?"

"I think I can tell you that there are indeed security concerns about the Free French in London, but my colleagues who were handling the questioning didn't think de Metz had any knowledge of such things. They took the view that he was so enjoying his new surroundings in Blenheim that he wanted to prolong the experience. The talk about having information was just a way of stringing out his stay and perhaps getting himself some money from us. They sent him packing. They gave him a number to call just in case. That's what you found."

"On Ritz notepaper?"

"Some of our chaps have expensive tastes." Swanton ate the last slice of his rabbit then mopped up his gravy with some bread. "Sorry, Frank. I'm a working-class boy like you. Lovely gravy!"

Merlin followed suit. "You can take the boy out of the East End, but you can't take the East End out of the boy, eh, Harold?"

Swanton wiped his mouth with the back of his hand and gave a contented sigh. "So he was put on a train back to London and that's the last we saw of him."

Merlin drank a glass of water. The spirits he had consumed had already given him a slight headache, as was usually the case if he drank at lunchtime. "So I can cross your lot off my list of potential murderers?"

Swanton drank the last of his gin and tonic, leaned back in his chair and massaged his stomach. "Certainly, but I can't answer for other services. Who knows? Perhaps MI6 or the SOE had dealings with him. Perhaps he did know something? I was told de Metz's interesting parting words to my officers. You'll forgive my pronunciation, Frank: *Il y a un armée de viperes autour du general.*"

"You'll have to help me there, Harold. My French is a little rusty."

"Something like: 'The general is surrounded by an army of snakes'. I presume the general is de Gaulle."

*   *   *

Colonel Aubertin and his two colleagues sat on a park bench in the private garden of Dorset Square. They were sheltered from the hot, early-afternoon sun by the thick canopy of beech foliage overhead.

Rougemont sat between his two superiors, pleased that for once the commandant appeared to have had an abstemious lunch. "Major Vane-Stewart was telling me the other day that this was once the site of the first important cricket ground in London, established by the same Thomas Lord who later built the famous ground that bears his name, a few miles to the north of us in St John's Wood. There is a plaque recording this fact in that shed over there. In the middle of the square."

"Cricket." Angers spat out the words with disgust. "A stupid game played by idiots. Only the English could invent such a boring game."

Rougemont smiled tolerantly at the commandant. "You may not like cricket, sir, but the English have invented other rather good games – football, rugby, tennis, for example. They do seem to have a knack of inventing sports."

"Didn't we invent tennis?"

"I think the English invented it in its modern form, didn't they, Colonel?

"I think one could have an argument about tennis but I take your point, Captain. Badminton, billiards, hockey as well – they have a knack for it, no doubt. I watched a few cricket matches myself on trips over here before the war. I found it incomprehensible but soothing." The colonel looked around. The garden was almost deserted. The only people in sight were some toddlers and their nannies, who were picnicking at the far end. He stretched his long legs out in front of him.

"But to more serious matters, gentlemen. Vane-Stewart came to see me this morning. He gave me some disturbing news." The colonel related what the major had told him about the arrest of the SOE agent in France.

"So there must have indeed been a spy, Colonel?"

"It seems so, yes, Captain. It's just as likely in my view that he's in the SOE but there is no doubt the pressure is on us to pursue our inquiries vigorously. On that score, I was wondering whether you have got any further with your investigation of Beaulieu and the others?"

"Would Beaulieu have known about Bouchard?"

"As you know, Captain, the joint SOE operations with us are documented. There is a limited distribution of such documentation but the general is, of course, on the list. The officers in his private office are cleared to see whatever he sees."

"I see. So that would include Dumont and Meyer also, wouldn't it?"

A flush of pink came to the colonel's cheeks. "It would."

"But as you say, sir, who is to say that there isn't a leak from within SOE itself or MI6 for that matter?"

"Who indeed, Auguste? However, we have been entrusted with the task of checking our own people. I have been hoping all along that our own investigation would prove fruitless but with this new development..."

The three men paused for a moment with their thoughts. The toddlers had finished their picnic and were being shepherded through one of the garden gates.

"So, Captain, the Commandant tells me you have that Irishman carrying out surveillance. Has he seen anything of import?"

"Not really, sir. No suspicious activity. He has learned that the three men are friends or at least good acquaintances."

"I am particularly interested in Beaulieu."

"From my own experience, it is clear the man thinks a lot of himself."

The commandant snorted. "He is an insufferable prig!"

"Insufferable prig or no, there is no evidence he is a spy."

Colonel Aubertin rose awkwardly to his feet. "I'm afraid my back is playing me up again today. Please excuse me." He walked off 20 yards or so then returned and resumed his seat. "And the other two?"

"Meyer seems like a nice enough fellow, Colonel. He has a Jewish background. I don't know the exact circumstances but his family managed to get out of Germany in the 30s."

"I've said it before but shouldn't his German background cause us concern?" Angers' eyes were following the last and prettiest of the nannies to leave the park as he spoke.

"A persecuted Jewish German? I doubt it, sir. He is a little unforthcoming about his past but I understand he was very thoroughly vetted when he entered the service a few years ago. If there were anything untoward, I am sure our people would have discovered it."

"You say that, Captain, but my God, it is easy to make a mistake."

Aubertin brushed a fly off his trousers. "Auguste tells me the men have been getting together with some South African fellow. Anything in that?"

"No, but we'll be keeping an eye out, sir."

"There are many Nazi sympathisers in South Africa, Captain."

"So there are, Colonel. This man seems quite respectable. A lawyer of some sort."

"Hmm. You are keeping the surveillance going over the weekend?"

Rougemont nodded.

"Anything else?"

"Meyer was interviewed about de Metz by those policemen. He told them he had met de Metz and heard his wild claims."

"We know nothing of the man, do we, Auguste? Except that he was a drunk and a liar. I'm sure Meyer will have told him this and now, hopefully, the police will pursue more promising lines of inquiry elsewhere."

"Yes, Colonel."

"Now, will you please excuse us, Captain. I just need a quick word with the Commandant."

Rougemont rose, saluted and walked briskly away towards the park gate.

"I believe, Auguste, that we shall be in difficulties if we don't produce a culprit in short order. I am sure that SOE are not going to come up with a culprit of their own and we are in danger of being cut out of the picture on their activities."

"Yes, Colonel."

"We'd be better off finding someone. Even if the evidence is not overwhelming, circumstantial might be enough. Do you get my drift?"

The commandant edged closer to the colonel. "I think I do."

"As to the best candidate, I think you know my choice?"

"Beaulieu?"

"Yes. Dumont is a good stick and a bright boy. We have just heard Rougemont's good impression of Meyer. Also, you know I have a bit of a soft spot for Jews so I would prefer it if Meyer is in the clear."

"Beaulieu has some powerful friends, sir. The general for one."

"Yes, but he is far away from London at present, as are all the others. If he returns to find that a member of his private office has disgraced himself and been dealt with, he'll get over it. He has greater things to occupy him."

"And if we find real evidence that one of the others is guilty?"

The colonel got slowly to his feet. "Well, unlikely as it is, that would be another thing. But if that happened you would keep everything to yourself and do nothing before first discussing the situation with me."

"Colonel."

"And Auguste…"

"Yes, sir."

"I was surprised and disappointed that you had recruited Rougemont and Devlin to the investigation without consulting me but there is no use crying over spilt milk. All I ask is that you keep them both under a tight leash. And I want to bring this to a conclusion, one way or another, within the week. If I haven't yet made myself clear, tell the Irishman to concentrate alone on Beaulieu for the next few days. I am convinced something will turn up."

The colonel glanced up at the sky, where he saw a plane emerging from behind a small fluffy cloud. "There's a Spitfire going somewhere. Not another aircraft in sight. Strange how quickly we have become accustomed to the empty skies again."

*   *   *

Peregrine Beecham set down the book he was reading and briefly closed his eyes. He was feeling relaxed and rested. He had passed a most enjoyable Friday so far. On this day, as usual, his head had hit the pillow at just after five in the morning. Capable of surviving on a minimum of sleep, he had dozed for three and a half hours before rising. Beecham washed, dressed and drank coffee on the balcony of his Arlington Street penthouse, appreciating as always the fine view of Green Park. The front page of his newspaper had reminded him that it was a Friday the thirteenth. Unlucky for some, no doubt, including inevitably several of his customers. It would not be unlucky for him, though. For Peregrine Beecham was a winner.

At nine-thirty, he'd walked the short distance to Pall Mall and the Royal Automobile Club, where he had swum his regular 100 lengths, followed by an hour in the steam room. Beecham had discussed the current state of the war and other matters with two other regular Turkish bathers. The older of the men, a tough and craggy Scottish Lord, who had resisted his wife's entreaties to withdraw to the safety of the glens for the duration of the war, had joined with Beecham in commending the committee's work in putting the club back in order after the recent bomb damage. Later in the changing room, Beecham had politely declined the invitation of the other bather, an infamously promiscuous homosexual theatre critic, to join him that evening in Manchester for a pre-London performance of Noël Coward's new play, *Blithe Spirit*.

When his companions had left and he found himself alone, Beecham had taken the time to admire himself in the large mirror opposite the lockers. He could quite see, of course, what had attracted the critic. His slightly unconventional rough good looks had often been compared by ladies of his acquaintance to those of Rex Harrison. He had once met the notoriously rude actor at a Café Royal party. Harrison had made a sneering comment about the likeness. Something about Madame Tussaud's having knocked off an inferior copy of the original. In a different place Beecham would have decked him but he'd let it pass.

After his morning at the RAC, Beecham had returned to his apartment to review the business paperwork of the previous night. This was the work of a half-hour and was something he enjoyed. He was a meticulous man, as he had to be in his business, and kept his records in small, neat handwriting in leather-bound notebooks.

At noon, on hearing the chimes of the fine 18th-century grandfather clock in his hallway, Beecham had left the apartment again. He walked along Piccadilly, through Leicester Square and into Trafalgar Square. His destination was the National Gallery, where he regularly made time to listen to one of Myra Hess's daily piano concerts. Chopin and Schubert were at the heart of this day's programme and Beecham had thrilled to Hess's delicate playing of Schubert's *Impromptus*. After the concert, Beecham had enjoyed a meat pie at the Lyons' Corner House in the Strand before making his way home.

Now, in the late afternoon, he sat in his favourite armchair, preparing himself for the evening's work. The book in his lap was an Agatha Christie novel he had picked up in Hatchards the day before: *Evil Under the Sun*, the brand new Poirot story. He liked Hercule Poirot but was aware that the Belgian detective would be unlikely to return the compliment. Poirot would not like Beecham one little bit. For Peregrine Beecham was a criminal. An elegant, suave and intelligent one but a criminal nevertheless. Like Poirot, he was also a work of fiction. His own creation. His real name was not Peregrine Beecham and he had come a long way from his true origins. He savoured the thought as he began to read. To his irritation, one page on, there was a knock at the door.

"Yes, Miller, what the hell is it? Can't you see I'm enjoying a little peace?"

"Sorry, sir, but it's that South African bloke on the blower. Says it's really urgent."

"Tell him to call back later." Beecham put the book down and shook his head. His interest had been piqued. "No, keep him on the line. I'll be there now."

*   *   *

After he'd telephoned Tomlinson to arrange their Saturday morning meeting, Powell spent Friday morning at the office of an old school friend, who also happened to be his solicitor. The subject of divorce was discussed at length and Powell found it a relief to have a practical discussion about what it would entail.

At two o'clock he caught a train to Cholsey, where he visited his parents at the Elizabethan farmhouse where they now spent most of their time. It was depressing to learn that his mother's relief at his safe return from Crete was an emotion far less heartfelt than her feelings of distaste and disgust at his pending divorce. His father said little, as usual, and his parents' half-hearted invitation to him to spend the night was declined without complaint. He got back to Marylebone Station after seven o'clock and stopped in the buffet for a snack that would suffice as his dinner.

Powell got home very tired just before eight and decided to have another leisurely bath. He went into the bathroom and set the taps running slowly so that he had time to make himself a cup of tea. As he passed through the living room on his way to the kitchen, he suddenly felt dizzy and fell into the nearest chair. A tear started trickling down his cheek. That Celia! Damned Celia! He'd never have believed his wife's departure would affect him so much.

In Greece and Crete he'd given very little thought to her. Every week, up until the battle, he'd written her a short letter not so different from the perfunctory ones he'd sent his parents from boarding school. He wasn't allowed to say anything about where he was or what his division was doing. The limited subjects had been the weather, the food and his fellow officers. But at heart, Powell now realised his feelings for her were much stronger than he'd thought.

He suddenly became aware of the running taps. The bath must be close to overflowing. He stood up, found that the dizziness had passed and got back to the bathroom just in time. He decided to forget about the tea and just get in the water. He stepped in, immersed his body, lay back and closed his eyes.

He really must get a grip, he told himself. There were plenty more fish in the sea and he and Celia had never really been right for each other. They had different outlooks on life. He was just taking things so badly because he was in a fragile state after his Cretan experiences. He would enjoy a good soak, followed by a good night's sleep. In the morning Powell would deliver his letter and he would be free of that burden. Then perhaps he'd ring Wentworth and book himself a round of golf. That would get his mind off things and clear the cobwebs. He was just reaching for the soap and wondering where his golf clubs were when he heard the doorbell ringing and some muffled words on the speaking tube.

"Damn it!" He thought for a moment of staying where he was but then, with a grunt, hauled himself out of the bath and grabbed a towel. His flat was on the ground floor. He ignored the speaking tube, which was ancient and didn't work very well, and poked his head out of his front door. He could see the shape of a man through the stained glass of the street entrance. He looked like he was carrying something.

"Who is it?"

"Delivery for Mr Powell."

"I haven't ordered anything but… oh, well. Better see what you have." Powell pulled the towel tighter around him and tiptoed over the linoleum of the lobby floor to let the man in.

*   *   *

Merlin's cuckoo clock sounded the 10th hour. Bridges was due back now. As soon as he arrived, they would head off on their evening outing. Goldberg was going to the Ritz too but it had been agreed that he would arrive on his own and operate independently. For once, Robinson had been happy to miss out.

Merlin had managed a quick trip home for supper with Sonia. She'd said she wasn't feeling well but had waved away his concern. "It's only a little tummy bug. Off you go to work, although I must say it's a strange type of work that takes you to the Ritz bar." Sergeant Bridges had also nipped home to Battersea to see Iris and kiss the baby goodnight.

It had been a glorious early summer's day, so welcome after the terrible weather of recent weeks. There was nothing quite like an English summer's day, Merlin thought, though to be fair he'd never seen any other type of summer's day. His father had often waxed lyrical about Spanish summer nights. Perhaps one day he would get to see one for himself. When the war was over he ought to go and visit his Spanish relatives with Sonia. He had his father's extended family to see but, most importantly, there was his sister, Mary.

She had gone on a holiday to Spain almost 10 years before and had met and fallen in love with her second cousin, Jorge. They married and Mary had become Maria. There were now three children and they ran a café in a small village outside Corunna. They had survived the traumatic years of the Civil War and were happy as far as Merlin knew. There hadn't been a letter for a while. Spain was a neutral country but everyone knew that Franco was backing Hitler and Mussolini. Perhaps he'd banned mail to England? In the last letter he'd received, nearly a year before, Mary had been begging him to get out of England and join her in Spain. She had claimed to be living in the safest part of the country – Galicia was Franco's homeland. Merlin had never considered going but he realised that if he had, he'd never have met Sonia. What tricks fate played and how easily lives could take completely different paths.

There were a couple of new folders in his in-tray. He decided to leave them until tomorrow. He thought of Edgar Powell and wondered what he'd done with his letter. Powell had left him his telephone number and Merlin rummaged through the desk in search of it. He was unsuccessful but on opening the address book on his desk found the number there from years before. He rang but there was no answer. It was Friday night after all. With luck, Powell was out enjoying himself and putting that woman Celia behind him.

Bridges finally appeared at the door. "There you are, Sam! Ten minutes late. Couldn't break yourself away from the family, eh? I see that Iris has togged you out quite well. Is that your Sunday suit?"

"It is, sir. Sorry, but our household doesn't quite run to black tie."

"Neither does mine." Merlin was in the work suit he'd been wearing all day. "Come on then. Might as well walk it. It won't take long."

"You did make clear to Goldberg that he was to go to the upstairs bar, not the downstairs one?"

"Yes, I'm pretty sure I made it clear."

"It's just that the downstairs place is a…"

Merlin nodded knowingly. "I understand, Sergeant. Sonia went there by mistake the other night. It's mostly for people who like their own sex, isn't it?"

"Yes, sir. It's known as the Pink Sink, apparently."

"Is it indeed? Charming. Well, let's hope Goldberg follows his instructions correctly. Now, *vamos*."

*   *   *

A haze of smoke floated over the chattering clientele of the bar. Bridges led Merlin through the melée towards the counter. When they arrived, Merlin turned and looked for Goldberg, whom he soon happily spotted in a far corner of the room, chatting to a sultry-looking brunette. It was clear that Goldberg had seen him too.

Merlin leaned back against the bar and surveyed the room. A good half of the customers were in uniform. British service uniforms predominated but there was a fair mix of others. He recognised Canadian, Polish and Czech insignia. There were also a few Free French officers sporting the uniforms with which he was now familiar. Some of the civilians were in black tie or evening dress but there were others, like him, who were less glamorously attired. There appeared to be a roughly even split of men and women.

Bridges managed to find his barman but the hubbub at the counter made proper conversation impossible. The man found the policemen a reasonably secluded table in a corner of the room and promised to join them there as soon as he was free. This turned out to be 15 minutes later.

The barman was a short and plump Scotsman with heavily oiled black hair. He shifted nervously in his seat. "I can't stay here for long. The manager will have my guts for garters if he sees me taking a break."

"Don't worry, Mr…"

"Laurie. Michael Laurie. I've only had this job since November. I'm hoping to keep it."

"We only need a minute or two of your time. If there is any difficulty with your manager, we'll have a word."

Laurie shook his head unhappily. "My boss won't enjoy the fact that you policemen are here at all. So let's get on."

"Sergeant Bridges says that earlier today you recognised someone in a photograph he showed you. A young lady called Bridget Healy."

"I did."

"We'd just like to know if you can recognise among tonight's customers anyone who mixed here with Miss Healy."

"I'll need a proper look. Give me a moment." Laurie stood up and walked off into the crowd. Ten minutes later he returned with a satisfied smile on his face. "There's two of her friends over there near the entrance. You see that fellow in a French uniform? The one laughing his head off?"

Merlin found the tall French officer Laurie meant. He was obviously having a very jolly time in the company of a fair-haired, non-military man.

"I do."

"Seen him and his friend with that young lady several times. I remember the Frenchman because he's a good tipper. I remember the other fellow because he's not. He's an Australian or something. Some kind of colonial."

"Anyone else, Mr Laurie?"

"No, just those two."

Merlin thanked the barman and released him back to his job.

"Get all that, Bernie?" Merlin spoke without looking behind him to where Goldberg had been loitering.

"Yup."

"We could either be heavy-handed and take the men back to the Yard for questioning, or we could be more subtle. Why don't you wander over and see if you can get into conversation with them? I'm afraid that after all my years in the service, I have the taint of the Yard about me and Sam does too. You are different. A foreigner in a strange land, like them. Might open up to someone like you. Are you game?"

"Leave it to me." Goldberg grabbed the bourbon and soda he had deposited on a nearby shelf and sauntered over to the two men.

PART 2

Chapter 10

Saturday 14 June

London

Before going to bed on Friday night, Sonia had drunk a mug of Ovaltine, a soothing English night-time drink she had recently discovered, and had slept straight through, undisturbed by Merlin's late return. When she awoke at just after eight, whatever bug she had was gone and she felt good. Merlin was still fast asleep, his mouth making those little putt-putt noises she found so endearing. She let him sleep on – she had a chore to do.

Sonia's parents had managed to escape from Poland soon after her and were now living with relatives in Manchester. Her mother's last letter was due a reply. Sonia went to the desk in the drawing room and picked up one of Frank's pens. The main subject of her mother's latest letter had been how her father, a respected engineer back in Poland, was still struggling to find work in England and was becoming ill with frustration. His specialism was aerodynamics and he had been trying to get a job in the aircraft industry but people were loath to take on a foreigner in such a crucial and sensitive war industry.

Sonia and her brother had discussed this several times. They found it ironic that their father, desperate to use his specialised skills to help the war effort, was having such difficulties as a foreigner, while his equally foreign son had been welcomed with open arms by the RAF. There had to be some way that Jan's impressive war service record could boost their father's work prospects but they hadn't been able to devise it yet.

There was little more Sonia could do than write a letter encouraging hope. Once she had finished it, and addressed and stamped the envelope, she made some tea and toast and took a tray into the bedroom.

Merlin's eyes cracked open as he heard the door close. "And to what do I owe this luxury?" He levered himself upright and smiled at Sonia.

"You owe it to being the most wonderful man in the world." She leaned across and kissed him on the lips.

"Feeling better today, are we?"

"Much better, thank you, darling. Let's go for a walk in the park after breakfast. I've got the morning off. It looks like it's going to be a lovely day."

"I'll have to go into the Yard at some point but, yes, a walk in the park would be good."

Merlin drank his tea and ate his toast. He put on the casual brown trousers and matching shirt that Sonia had bought him in a recent sale at Swan & Edgar and which he hadn't yet worn. They were just going out of the door when the telephone rang.

Merlin looked apologetically at Sonia. "I'd better take it."

"Sergeant. You got home all right then? Did you…? What…? Oh my God. How…? All right, I'll be with you shortly. I'm only a few minutes away. The poor man." Merlin put down the receiver.

"Frank, you've gone quite white. What on earth…?"

*   *   *

Edgar Powell's eyes stared up blankly at Merlin. His body lay naked and inert in the scummy bath water, more like a waxwork than a dead human being. Merlin sighed, wishing that, for dignity's sake, his friend's body could be taken out of the water and covered up. The correct procedure had to be observed, however. Nothing must be touched and what might be a crime scene had to be preserved. "So, is this exactly how you found your husband, Mrs Powell?"

Celia Powell's baby face was streaked with mascara stains. The tears had stopped flowing for the moment but she couldn't bring herself to respond. Merlin turned to Mr Herbert, the porter of Powell's apartment block, who was standing next to Bridges at the bathroom door. "She came to get me straightaway, Chief Inspector. I tried to calm her down, then headed over here. I used to be in the military police years ago, so I know the score. I made sure she didn't disturb the scene when we came in."

Herbert looked every inch a former soldier. He reminded Merlin of Bridges' father-in-law, an ex-regimental sergeant major.

"Well done, Mr Herbert. Are you in permanent residence here?"

"I have a room at the back of the flats opposite, which I also look after. I'd just got back there this morning when Mrs Powell came to get me. My mother is unwell and I went to see her yesterday morning and ended up staying the night."

"So you can't tell us anything much about what might have happened?"

"Sorry, sir. No."

"Do you know whether Mrs Powell might have disturbed the scene before she came to find you?"

"I didn't ask her that, sir. She'll have to tell you herself. If she can."

Merlin turned his attention back to Edgar's wife. She shuddered and choked back more tears before removing the handkerchief she was holding to her mouth. She had the sort of pale-porcelain, baby-doll looks that seemed to appeal to many Englishmen but did nothing for Merlin. She shook her head. "I didn't touch anything. Except him." She spoke in a soft high register. As Merlin knew from Eddie Powell, the sweet little girl looks and manner disguised a selfish, hard and predatory woman.

"I tried to speak to him on the telephone yesterday. He and I had decided to go our separate ways. We had discussed some of the practicalities but there were a few items we had not yet covered. I wanted to come over and discuss them. I couldn't get through to him so decided to come over in person this morning."

Merlin asked Herbert to man the front door while he escorted Mrs Powell into the drawing room. Celia seated herself on a wicker armchair. Merlin and Bridges remained standing. He had met Celia a few times with Eddie a long time ago but she gave no sign of recognition. She muffled more sobs in her handkerchief then took a deep breath. "I came in. I still have a key, of course, but the door was unlocked."

Merlin had already noticed that no damage appeared to have been done to the door or its lock.

"I entered. As you can see, the place is a mess. There was an empty cardboard box by the door for some reason and ornaments, lamps, papers, everything all over the place. I called out. There was no reply. I went… I went into the bedroom. More mess but no sign of Edgar. Then I went into the bathroom. For a moment I thought he was sleeping. He sometimes does… did that, you know. In the bath, I mean. I shook him. No response. I looked at his face more closely. Then I realised… I realised that he was…" More tears flowed until she pulled herself together again. "I'm sorry, I'm being silly. It's not as if we loved each other any more."

Merlin looked her in the face as he recalled his recent conversations with Powell. "We were friends, you know, your husband and I."

"Oh yes, Merlin. I thought the name was familiar. You were pals when he was wasting his time in the police, weren't you? You've kept your looks, I must say. I'm afraid Edgar wasn't ageing so well." She opened her handbag and found her compact.

"God, I look a real mess." She applied some powder and lipstick and pouted into the mirror. "A little better." A weak smile parted her lips and she sat up in her chair.

"I believe Eddie had a safe in the flat, Mrs Powell?"

"Call me Celia, please. Frank was your first name, wasn't it?"

"I think, in the circumstances, we'd better keep things formal, Mrs Powell."

A flicker of annoyance crossed her face. "As you wish. A safe? Yes, there is a safe. It's quite well hidden. Edgar couldn't see the point of putting it behind a picture like everyone else seems to do. Come with me." She rose and led the way to the bedroom. Celia Powell pointed to an old oak chest by the window. The lid was open and the chest was empty. "We kept our linen in there." The linen was now on the floor with the other bedroom debris. "Look under it."

Merlin nodded to Bridges. The chest, even empty of its contents, was heavy and Bridges grunted as he shifted it. There was an old rug underneath, which Bridges removed to expose the bare floorboards. The policemen searched hard but couldn't spot anything like an opening.

"Edgar was clever at this sort of thing. You have to stand on two separate boards at a distance from each other, to make the right one pop up." She pointed out the boards and Bridges duly stood on them. A floorboard sprang up into the air. Merlin bent over to look into the hole that had now appeared. He could see a small, black, metallic door with a dial on the front.

"Clever."

"Very clever, Sergeant. Seems untampered with. What exactly did your husband keep in there, Mrs Powell?"

"My jewels. A few personal mementoes of his and some personal documentation."

Merlin went to sit on the bed and tried to think. Clearly the place had been turned over. Someone had been searching for something. Had they found it? If the something was in the safe, then apparently not. Had Powell been forcibly drowned by the person or persons searching?

"Seems like someone wanted something from your husband. Given the mess the place is in, they wanted it very much. If Eddie wouldn't tell them where it was, it would be very surprising if they didn't use violence to try and loosen his tongue. Violence like holding his head under water for long periods of time. That's how it seems to me, Sergeant."

"And they kept going until eventually they went too far. Seems a fair theory, sir."

"Did your husband have any enemies, Mrs Powell?"

"Edgar? No, of course not."

Merlin got up from the bed. "We'll need to see what's in the safe. If there is valuable jewellery in there…."

"There isn't. I removed all of my jewellery the other day."

"Ah. But still someone might have known about the jewellery. They wouldn't necessarily know you took it out. Is it worth a lot?"

"There are some nice pieces. Edgar was generous with presents. They are worth several hundred pounds."

"I presume you have the combination?"

"Of course. Here it is." She produced a piece of paper from her handbag. "I should have it in my head but I have a terrible memory for figures." As Merlin looked at the numbers there was a commotion at the door. The medics and the forensic team had arrived.

Merlin guided Celia out of the flat and into the lobby area by the front door. "Best if we let these chaps get on with their job, Mrs Powell. Are you all right to get home on your own? Is there anyone we can call or perhaps Mr Herbert could accompany you?"

Celia shook her head. She cast a quick glance back towards the flat and stifled another sob. "I would be grateful if you could hail me a taxi, Mr Herbert." She looked strangely at Merlin and seemed as if she was about to say something before she turned abruptly on her heels and followed Herbert out on to Flood Street.

"We'd better get out of everyone's way too, Sergeant. But before we go, let's get that safe open. The combination is 673429. Ask one of the chaps to dust it for prints first."

*   *   *

Fleming arrived just as Philip Arbuthnot, casually attired in cricket sweater and slacks, was finishing his breakfast. The young man ushered his guest into the drawing room, sat him down and poured him a cup of coffee. "Are you feeling all right, Mr Fleming?" There was a small red welt running across the left side of Fleming's forehead, and he was looking very pale. On the few occasions he had met Fleming, Arbuthnot had been impressed by the man's air of healthy vigour. This morning he looked neither healthy nor vigorous.

"I had a bit of a bug, Philip. I'm over it now but I suppose with that and all the worry about your father's affairs, I'm looking a little drained."

"Looks like you've taken a bit of a bash to the head."

Fleming put his hand to his forehead. "Oh that. Yes, I managed to walk into one of my wardrobe doors, idiot that I am." He paused to check the damage in a nearby mirror. "And so, dear boy, how are you bearing up?"

Arbuthnot joined Fleming on the settee. "Not so bad but I'm very worried, of course. I still can't understand what the old man was playing at. Fiddling with his will, removing those important certificates from Tomlinson's custody then disappearing into the army when there was no need for him to do so. If anyone in the family should be pulling on uniform, it's me."

Fleming sat up. "Goodness, Philip. I hope you haven't been called up?"

"No. It's only a matter of time, though, isn't it?"

Fleming looked at the young man solemnly. "A little bit of advice, Philip. Don't be in too much of a hurry to take the King's shilling. You have important family responsibilities. If your papers do arrive, give them to me. I have a few strings I can pull."

"I can't do that. If, as Kitchener said last time round, my country needs me, then so be it."

"Don't be foolish, Philip. There are plenty of other mugs to do the dying." His eyes brightened. "Come to think of it, how about a posting to Argentina? That will get you well away from the prospect of soldiering."

"That assumes we'll have an Argentinian business to be posted to. If someone else gets hold of the certificates…"

"Don't say that, Philip. They'll turn up somewhere in Simon's effects, mark my words. I think…" The sound of raised voices in the street interrupted him. An unexploded bomb, which had been found in the ruins of a pub opposite, had been disarmed by the UXB people the day before and the site was now clear for demolition. The working party were congregating noisily outside.

Fleming moved closer to Arbuthnot. "Look, Philip. I'm very sorry to disturb you on a Saturday morning but there is something we need to discuss."

"We certainly need to talk about the business. I really need to get up to speed on that."

"All in good time, dear boy. All in good time. That's not what I wanted to talk about this morning."

"What, then?"

It was warm in the flat and Fleming had begun to perspire. He removed his jacket. "If you don't mind, Philip, I think I must still be running a bit of a temperature. Now then. I wanted to see you because I think it's very important that we try to get to the bottom of what your father was up to just before he went off to war."

"I don't think I can help you much with that. I've been through my father's papers. Routine sort of stuff. No wills or certificates, as you know. Nothing of interest really."

"Reggie mentioned that you found a list?"

"A list?"

"A list with numbers."

"Oh, that. Now where did I put it? Oh, yes. It's over there on the bureau." He went to get it. "I also found this old photograph." He handed both to Fleming and sat down again. "My first thought was that the numbers might be share certificate numbers but don't they tend to run in sequence? My father gave me some shares in Anglo-Iranian Petroleum as a birthday present a few years ago. Not the most exciting present for a teenage boy but… anyway I got several certificates for the few thousand shares I received and I remember that they were all numbered in sequence."

"No, they're not share certificate numbers, Philip."

"Do you know what they are then?"

Fleming continued to study the list in silence.

"And PB? Is that a person, do you think? Or a place? Or initials signifying something boring like 'personal bank'? I suppose they could be deposits at banks. And what about the photograph? I found it in his safe. Strange place for it, I thought."

"I think I know what the numbers signify, Philip. And I have an idea who PB is. As to the photograph…" Fleming looked again at the beautiful young face and sighed. "The lady is someone your father and I knew a long time ago. A long, long time ago. The wife of a friend who fell on hard times. I think your father and she had a bit of a thing going for a while. Then something came between them. She is dead now."

*   *   *

"I'm so sorry, Frank. That's terrible."

"It's tragic, Bernie. To survive everything Eddie went through in Crete and then to get home and die such a squalid death." Merlin shook his head. He was finding it difficult to take in.

"Seems the guy used up all his luck."

Merlin looked away towards the window and the bright sky outside. "You know, Bernie, I saw scores of corpses in the trenches in the last war, some of whom were good mates, and plenty in this job. Then I've had family bereavements. My father and mother, of course, although there wasn't much of my father left to see."

Merlin saw Goldberg's puzzled look. "Sorry, you don't know what I'm talking about, do you? My father had the distinction of being one of the few British casualties of Zeppelin bombing in the last war. He was blown to kingdom come so there were only bits and pieces to bury. Thankfully, my mother died painlessly in the comfort of her own bed. Then there was my wife…" Merlin shuddered. "However, this is the first time I've had to look at the murdered body of a man who was a good friend to me in normal civilian life."

Goldberg perched himself on the edge of Merlin's desk. "I've seen a couple. Of friends, I mean. Both fellow officers killed in the line of duty. Good men."

Bridges came in with a tray of tea. He poured three mugs and the men sat quietly drinking for a while. Goldberg eventually broke the silence. "Do you think they managed to find what they were looking for, Sergeant?"

"Not likely, sir. Everything was topsy-turvy in the flat. Papers, books, ornaments all over the place. The chief inspector and I think the murderer overplayed his hand with poor Mr Powell and killed him by accident. A little too much pressure, a little too long under the water. He or they mucked up."

"How do you think the murderer got in?"

"There's a speaking tube at the front door that connects with the flats. Also a bell. Someone rings the bell and speaks in the tube. Whatever they said was enough for Powell to let them in. There was an empty box by the door. We think the murderer might have said he had a delivery and had the box with him for credibility's sake. Powell let him in either on his word or on sight of the box through the door. Something like that. Or, of course, he just knew him."

"And do you have any idea of what it was they were looking for?"

Merlin reached into his jacket. "Eddie had a safe that his murderers didn't discover. We found this inside." Merlin laid a bloodstained envelope down on the desk. The words on the front read: 'Give to my s…'

*   *   *

Felix Meyer had dreamed of his parents again that night. He often did. He liked to dream about them. Thus they lived on.

Like many of his fellow French officers, he lived in Soho. His landlady, a Welsh widow called Mrs Evans, was a cheerful and straightforward woman. He had found it strange at first when she addressed him as 'Mr Elephant'. However, all was explained after a few days, when a fellow resident explained that he was actually being addressed as 'Mr Frog' in Mrs Evans' native language, *llyffant* being Welsh for 'frog'. Meyer had decided not to take offence. He had been called many worse things in his life and Mrs Evans always seemed very friendly to him.

Mrs Evans was already up and about when Meyer had gone downstairs in the morning. He had declined the offer of breakfast, the landlady had wished Mr Elephant a good day and he'd headed off for Carlton Gardens.

As always, Meyer enjoyed the walk. It was a bright morning with a slight chill. He went down Shaftesbury Avenue into Piccadilly Circus. He looked up at the big advertising sign asserting that

'GUINNESS IS GOOD FOR YOU' and the hands on the large clock above showing it was coming up to seven. He had tasted Guinness, a heavy dark brew that was not to his taste, but not yet the hot Bovril drink that was advertised alongside.

There was little traffic. A milk cart rumbled past Swan & Edgar, its driver appearing half asleep. The famous Eros statue had been covered up to protect it from bomb damage. A couple of hungover servicemen sat on the steps beneath the boarding while two heavily made-up women stood a few yards off, trying to attract the men's attention for their last work of a long night.

Meyer cut down Lower Regent Street, turned right at Pall Mall and then walked up to Carlton House Terrace. The night duty officer at the Free French HQ, a cheerful Provençal, was manning the lobby desk.

"Any news, Coriot?"

"*Bonjour*, Meyer. Yes, our people in Cairo wired that there has been an engagement in the Lebanon between the Australians and Vichy. Somewhere on the way to Beirut. No news on our boys."

Meyer nodded and headed for his office. He had a report to write and paperwork to clear. He settled down and made good progress for a couple of hours but then found it increasingly hard to concentrate. A strong coffee induced little improvement. He couldn't stop thinking about the man Pulos.

When he'd spoken to his brother the day before, Anton had discouraged him from attempting to meet Pulos; his brother had felt that such a meeting might somehow prove prejudicial to the lawsuit. However, Felix felt he could not ignore the man's presence in London. The more he thought about it, the more he felt he should try and see him.

Meyer had his own opportunity now to confront a grotesque injustice. He realised that Simon Arbuthnot and the others had been living in London all along and could have been confronted at any time. Pulos, however, was the principal defendant to his brother's action in Argentina. He was the man running the businesses. It felt different, somehow. Pulos's arrival in London had galvanised Meyer and changed his perspective. He took a deep breath. He would go and see the man. Nothing might come of it but he had to try. Meyer looked at the clock. It was 10.30. He tidied up his papers, got up and made his way to the front door. He set off for the Ritz.

Behind Meyer, Devlin followed at his usual discreet distance.

*   *   *

"I've been asked to present myself at the US Embassy in an hour's time, Frank."

"That sounds a little formal. Everything all right?"

"As far as I'm aware. I just thought that now you are obviously very busy with this new Powell case, shall I give you my report on last night another time?"

The still unopened Arbuthnot letter was on the desk and Merlin's hand was resting on it. He slid it back and forth a few times before answering. "Sorry. That had gone completely out of my head. Tell me now, Bernie, please. Edgar Powell's death doesn't diminish the importance of our investigation into Bridget Healy's. What happened? The Sergeant and I saw you leave with those other two and then we saw you and one of the men go into that block of flats. We waited for a while then threw in the towel. Who were they?"

"The Free French guy is called Dumont, Georges Dumont. Got here at the end of last year via north Africa. Quite softly spoken but a man with strong views. He's a great fan of de Gaulle. Not such a great fan of the British. Said some rather rude things about Churchill. Very scathing about the people in Vichy, too. Not completely dour though. Likes to tell jokes.

"The other fellow is called Rupert Vorster. A South African, not an Australian. A lawyer in the City. Also claims to be a whizz at investing. Gave me a few share tips and said I could subscribe to his informal investor service for a modest £1 a week."

"And what did they have to say about the girl?"

"I told them I was a diplomat travelling back and forth to the States. Mentioned that on a recent trip I visited the Ritz and met a charming Irish girl called Bridget. I described her and asked if they knew her."

"And?"

"They said they did know some Irish girls but she wasn't one of them. Later in the evening, however, when more alcohol had been drunk, I'm sure I overheard one of them – Dumont, I think – let slip the name Bridget. I couldn't hear the context but I definitely heard the name and one other word."

"What word was that?"

"Pregnant."

"Hmm."

"I didn't get much else out of them but I'd say we definitely need to follow up."

"Of course. We'll pull them in. However, given poor Eddie's murder and our limited manpower, I don't think we can take that on today. What about the place you went to after the bar?"

"Now that was very interesting, although I'm not sure it has anything to do with our case. Vorster made the running on that. Said there was somewhere exciting I had to go. I thought Dumont was up for it as well so but he ducked out at the last minute. There's a swish penthouse on the top floor of the block where they run high-roller card games. And when I say high-rollers, I mean high-rollers. There was a lot of money floating around.

"I think Vorster is somehow connected to the operation. He seemed very pally with the main man, a smooth-looking fellow in a cravat. I got the impression Vorster was some sort of finder. You know, a guy who hangs around places like the Ritz looking for wealthy types who might fancy a round with Lady Luck."

"You're saying he picked you for a high-roller?"

"Funny as it seems, yes. People over here seem to think all Yanks are flush."

Merlin couldn't help smiling. "So how did you live up to your new status?"

"As a high-roller? I didn't. I watched. Said I'd like to see how things ran, then maybe return another night when I had some cash on me. They offered me credit but I declined."

Merlin was pensive. "Well, as you say, Bernie, very interesting but I think we've got enough on our plate at present without taking on illegal gambling dens. Not our patch either. It's for vice, not us."

"Of course, Frank."

"You say there was one 'main man' as you put it?"

"Yes, there were a few house operators around but it was clear who was in charge."

"Did you get his name?"

"I heard someone call him Mr Beecham."

"Means nothing to me. Well, you'd better get off to your meeting. Hope it goes well. We'll go after Dumont and Vorster tomorrow or more likely Monday. Dumont will presumably be at Carlton Gardens or Dorset Square but where can we find Vorster?"

Goldberg passed a business card to Merlin. It read: 'Rupert Vorster. Titmus, Travers and Tomlinson. Solicitors'. Merlin frowned. "Titmus, Travers and Tomlinson – now, where have I heard that name before?"

* * *

Vichy

Laval set down his coffee cup, smoothed his moustache and straightened his tie before picking up the receiver. "Otto, what a pleasure. How are you? To what do I owe this honour?"

Abetz returned Laval's pleasantries in his perfect French. Laval was always impressed by Abetz's command of the French language. All the top Nazis he'd met in France were fluent but Abetz was the most impressive. His accent was also the best of any non-Frenchman he had ever met. He had to remind himself every so often that he was speaking to a German rather than one of his countrymen.

"I'm glad to hear the sun is shining in Paris, Otto. Here also. This is the best time of the year in France. I have just been for a post-prandial walk in the Parc des Sources with my secretaries. Most enjoyable. You should visit us down here one day."

Abetz chuckled down the line. "One day, perhaps, though I doubt the marshal would be very happy to see me in his seat of power. And speaking of power, how are you getting on, my friend? Can I look forward to hearing of your reappointment to the Cabinet soon? You know we would much prefer to see you back in post. If you would like us to exert a little pressure…?"

"No, no, Otto. As I have told you before, that would only play into the hands of my enemies, who already believe I am too close to you. Thank you, but please do nothing. I think the apples will fall my way in due course. Darlan does not have his heart in the job and the marshal…"

"Is past it."

"Increasingly so, I'm afraid."

The line crackled. "This connection is secure, isn't it, Pierre?"

"Absolutely. I have it checked out every week."

"It might be better to do it every day. In any event, I look forward to your successful reinstatement in the near future. We would…"

The strident opening chords of a French military march filled the room as the teatime concert began in the park. Laval laid down the receiver for a moment and went to close the window.

"Sorry about that, Otto. The band is a little over-enthusiastic sometimes. Now, how can I help you?"

"I am just calling to say thank you. Your man in London helped us to capture a British agent parachuted into France last week."

"Did he? That is excellent news." Laval was aware of information passed from London about an agent named Webster but had heard nothing more.

"I say British agent but the man was a Frenchman. His name was François Bouchard, from a family of Parisian wine merchants. Moved to England before the war."

Laval realised with a shock that he knew the man's father and had bought many cases of wine from him.

"Are you there, Pierre?"

"Yes, Otto. I am here. What has happened to *Monsieur* Bouchard?"

"He was interrogated and shot, of course. As were a good number of his Resistance accomplices – with more to come. I wanted to commend you and your men in Vichy and in England on this effort."

Laval nodded his head slowly. He was a pragmatist, committed to ensuring that French interests, compromised as they might be, were defended to the hilt. If that required, as he believed it did, a close Franco-German working partnership, then so be it. The opponents of Germany were the opponents of France in the current circumstances. If those opponents were French, their deaths must be in the best interests of Vichy. Nevertheless, events like this were hard to stomach. "I am most happy that our network has been of assistance to you, Otto. I only hope we can be of further help."

"Oh you can, Pierre. You can. Just let your fellow in London point us in the direction of more François Bouchards. *Adieu*, my friend and *heil* Hitler!"

Laval picked up his cup and drank the rest of his now cold coffee. He winced. The drink, as did the conversation, left a sour taste in his mouth.

*   *   *

London

Arbuthnot's letter still lay unopened in front of him. Merlin allowed himself another Fisherman's Friend before reaching down to the bottom drawer of the desk. He withdrew his father's letter opener. It was a beautiful object and he paused to admire its striking colours and swirling curves. His father had claimed it was a true antique, a dagger made in Toledo some time in the 1500s. Merlin had doubted this and used to put it down as one of the tall stories his father was prone to telling. Now he wasn't so sure. Whatever its origins, it was a good letter opener.

"Shall we, Sergeant?"

Bridges nodded and Merlin carefully slit the envelope open. Inside he found a sheet of cream letter paper embossed in red with Arbuthnot's name and London address. Across the middle of the paper was written in ink a sequence of numbers and one letter: 23918174933232382228492331313383X. Merlin read them out to Bridges.

"Is that all of it, sir?"

"Yes. Looks like some sort of code."

Bridges moved around to Merlin's side of the desk. The two men stared hard at the characters in search of inspiration and might have carried on doing so for some time had they not been disturbed by Robinson's arrival.

Merlin looked up. "Constable."

"Sir. I was having lunch at my uncle's house when I heard him talking to someone on the telephone about a murder."

"I guess that someone would have been me."

"He told me who the victim was. I'm terribly sorry, sir. I decided to come in as soon as I heard."

"That's very good of you, Constable. However, I understood from the AC that you were taking your young man, the barrister, round for lunch. I don't want your coming here to spoil…"

"You needn't worry about them, sir. He and my parents are all getting on famously. I would much rather be here trying to help."

"Very well, if you're sure. Take a look at this. You've got a good brain. Bridges and I can't make hide nor hair of it."

Robinson pondered the sequence for a while then eased herself back in her chair. "I think it's much too long to be a safe combination, sir. If it is a code of some sort, I should mention that my brother is something of an expert in such things."

"Would that be the brother who helped us on the Kilinski case? The Spanish history don?"

"No. This is my other brother, Robert. He was studying for a PhD in applied mathematics at Oxford when the war broke out. One of his areas of interest is the analysis of codes."

"Goodness, Constable. What a clever family you have. Is he in London?"

"Yes, sir."

"In the forces?"

"No, he's still in civvy street. He's working for a government statistical department, or so he says."

Merlin raised an eyebrow. "In the secret… no, I'd better not ask. Well, Constable, if you could get him in here to help us, that would be much appreciated."

"I'll ask him. By the way, sir, I never heard how your MI5 lunch went."

"Sorry, Constable. You weren't here when I briefed the others. Let me tell you now. After that, if you're sure the AC doesn't want you back, I'd be grateful if you could help Bridges out with his door-to-doors of poor Eddie's neighbours in Chelsea."

"Pleasure, sir."

*   *   *

Devlin watched as Meyer hovered indecisively outside the main entrance to the Ritz hotel. Finally he went in and Devlin followed. Meyer went up to the front desk and Devlin heard him ask the clerk for a Mr Pulos.

"I'm afraid we can't give you the number, sir, but if you'd like to give me your name, I'll call up and see if Mr Pulos will see you."

Meyer shook his head and backed away from the desk. He turned, walked through the lobby and found himself a seat at one of the tables where, later in the day, the famous Ritz afternoon tea would be served. Devlin watched Meyer order a coffee then did the same at a table a distance away. For the next half hour, Devlin watched as Meyer kept the passing hotel traffic under close observation.

This was Devlin's second visit to the Ritz in the space of 12 hours. He had been in the bar the night before observing Dumont and Vorster drink together. He had watched as the pair were joined by a dark-haired, foreign-looking fellow and he'd followed the three men later when they left and walked down Arlington Street before trailing Dumont home. Something about the apartment building he'd seen Vorster and the stranger enter had been niggling Devlin ever since. The Irishman was sure he'd heard someone tell him about something fishy going on in there. It would come to him eventually, Devlin thought, as he watched an increasingly impatient Meyer order a second cup of coffee.

It was just after 11.30 when, finally, a uniformed bell boy appeared, holding a large card bearing the name Mr Alexander Pulos. Two men were talking quite heatedly together in a corner of the lobby not far from Meyer, and Devlin saw the shorter and older of the men break off the conversation and walk over to speak to the bell boy. A message was handed over and the bell boy disappeared. As the man Devlin now presumed to be Pulos rejoined his companion and headed for the door, Meyer put some money on the table and followed. Devlin did likewise.

*   *   *

Before the war, Bert Perkins had worked as a mechanic in the Clerkenwell garage where Simon Arbuthnot's many cars had been serviced and maintained. Arbuthnot had enjoyed his cars. He had owned a string of Bentleys, Rolls-Royces, Hispano-Suizas and other high-performance vehicles. Perkins' particular favourite was the blue SS100, a beautiful machine with the leaping Jaguar mascot on its stylish bonnet. Perkins had been the chief mechanic for all of the Arbuthnot cars and enjoyed a friendly relationship with their owner. When, despite the substantial revenue from Arbuthnot's custom, the garage company had gone bust in 1938, Arbuthnot had helped Perkins out by getting him a job as a security-man-cum-night-watchman at Sackville Bank.

Perkins, a spare, wiry little man, had received a good salary from the garage and, as a bachelor with no family, should have had enough savings at 60 to live comfortably in retirement. He had a serious gambling habit, however, and there were no savings. The Sackville job as a night watchman was for him a lifesaver and he was deeply grateful to Arbuthnot. The hours were anti-social but he had no social life to speak of. He worked four out of five nights during the week and a good part of the weekend. Arbuthnot often got him out to his country house to tinker with the cars he kept there. Some people found Arbuthnot cold and distant but not Perkins. Perhaps, Perkins thought, Arbuthnot's warmth towards him reflected one gambler's sympathy for another.

Perkins had been one of the last to learn of his employer's death. He hadn't seen the notice posted on the employees' noticeboard in the basement and his hours gave him little opportunity to chat to other bank workers. Perkins' reading glasses were broken so he did not read the news in the paper either. It was only on the Thursday that he heard a couple of late-working secretaries gossiping about it as they loitered in the lobby before leaving the building.

"Old Edie in accounts, who worked for him from quite early on, said he was a real good-looker when he started out."

"Well, he isn't that bad-looking now."

"You mean 'wasn't' that bad-looking, I think. Fact is, it was hard to tell if he still had his looks as he always looked so miserable when I saw him."

"Well, all I can say is rest in peace, Simon Arbuthnot – but let's hope your son is just as successful and our jobs stay safe."

Perkins had been shocked and upset by the news and, later that night, had opened a half bottle of Bell's whisky, which he kept in an old sock in his locker, and drank to his boss.

Two days later, Perkins was at his post in the bank. He alternated Saturdays and Sundays with the other security man. This weekend he had Saturday. People seldom worked the weekend at the bank so he was surprised to see Sidney Fleming at the door just after noon. Perkins let him in and the chairman disappeared, preoccupied, into the lift. Moments later, the Argentinian gentleman, whom Perkins had seen occasionally at Simon Arbuthnot's house, arrived with another man, followed by the portly fellow Perkins knew to be Arbuthnot's solicitor. "Something is up," Perkins muttered to himself. "Something is definitely up."

*   *   *

Colonel Aubertin was also to be found at his place of work this Saturday lunchtime. A folder sat on the desk before him. It was headed 'Top Secret' in both English and French. Vane-Stewart had left it with him after their meeting on Friday. The folder was tied in red ribbon and Aubertin felt a little tremor of excitement in his fingers as he began to untie it. The knot was very tight and he had to pick at it for a while before it yielded. 'Damn the English and their stupid red ribbons,' he thought.

Aubertin had passed a restless night worrying. He was concerned that Angers might not be up to the job assigned to him. It was proving to be a task requiring considerable finesse. He didn't think the commandant had much finesse. Rougemont was intelligent and capable of managing delicate affairs but he was not biddable like Angers, who would do anything the colonel asked of him. Then there was this Devlin fellow. It had definitely been a mistake to involve him.

He was worrying too about the general. Before de Gaulle's departure for the Middle East, he had called in Aubertin and warned that he was not happy with several of the colonel's subordinates at Dorset Square and told him he might have to arrange for their replacement. "A shake-up," the general had said. A shake-up would be awkward from the colonel's point of view.

Then there was his wife to worry about. Was she well? Was she safe? He loved her dearly. This love, however, did not prevent him from enjoying the freedom of his London life to the full. Aubertin was a man in the prime of life and he knew his wife would understand his need for physical release – as she had in the past. He picked up his photograph of her and kissed it. Then he set to work and opened the folder. The first page was blank. The second was headed 'Ops – June/July' and there followed a list of dates. The heading on the third page was '21 June – Operation Purple' and he read on with interest.

*   *   *

"I'd prefer it, Alexander, if you kept your trained gorilla outside."

Marco, the gorilla in question, glared at Sidney Fleming but obeyed the wave of Pulos's hand and left Fleming's office. As he did so, Tomlinson pulled Fleming to one side and whispered: "Powell didn't turn up."

Fleming's shoulders slumped. "Shit."

"I hope you two gentlemen aren't keeping any important secrets from me. That wouldn't be very friendly, would it?"

Tomlinson shook his head. "Not at all, Alexander. I was just talking about a mutual friend."

The three men settled themselves around the elegant Chippendale table in front of Simon Arbuthnot's old desk.

Reggie Tomlinson raised a finger. "I would just like to say that I hope this meeting is not going to be too lengthy. My wife reminded me this morning that we have friends coming for bridge and dinner and she will be on the warpath if I'm not back home at a reasonable time. I have had to cancel one engagement already today. I would prefer not to have to cancel another."

Fleming reddened. "There are matters of the utmost importance to discuss, Reggie. Matters of greater import than a bloody game of bridge or golf. Life and death matters. Simon has left us in a bloody awful mess. No, I can't guarantee you'll get back at a reasonable time but let's just see how we go."

Tomlinson gave a petulant shake of the head before subsiding back into his chair.

Pulos poured himself a glass of water. "May I enquire as to what exactly you are referring when you use the words 'bloody awful mess'. Do you mean the missing share certificates, the missing will, the question of succession management, the business of Sackville or what?"

Fleming examined Pulos's pale and weary face. He noticed a small scar on his chin that hadn't been there the day before. "Get any sleep last night, Alexander?"

"Unfortunately no. The time difference is not easy to overcome."

"You look a bit rough. Didn't fall out with Marco, did you?"

"If you'd made the journey I've just made, you'd look rough, Sidney. And while we're on the subject, you don't look so wonderful yourself."

"A touch of flu, as you know. Now I suggest we get on and you'll understand what I mean by 'bloody mess.'" Fleming opened a notepad on which he had scribbled some aides-memoires. "I do not have a pleasant tale to tell. Last week I heard some very disturbing news. When I came into the office after we had heard about Simon, George Brightwell asked to see me. He informed me that there was a problem relating to an account. More specifically, an account where we have client funds under management. For some time before he undertook his military adventure, Simon had taken a particular interest in this account. To put it more bluntly, he assumed personal management of the account and thereafter removed it from the oversight of Brightwell and his team."

"Why would he do that?"

"We shall get to that, Reggie. Now, not only did he keep this account's activities secret but, when he went away, Simon specifically warned Brightwell to keep away from it. He left it in charge of one of his old hands, Paul Lawson, who provided the accounts department with no updates on the account other than to confirm all was as it was when last audited, so Brightwell accounted accordingly."

"And what is wrong with that? Simon was the boss." Pulos rapped the table to emphasise his point. "He chose to take control of one of the bank's investment accounts. Perhaps he had some great investment ideas that he wanted to try out. Simon was always buzzing with innovative ideas, was he not? Then, when he went away, he put Lawson in charge of the account. Paul has been with us since almost the beginning. A loyal, reliable man."

"Not so loyal or reliable any more, Alexander. Lawson has, as they say in the colloquial, done a runner. He hasn't been seen since Simon's death was announced. Furthermore, once

Brightwell was at last able to get into the account, he discovered, completely contrary to Lawson's summaries, a very substantial deficit. There were numerous unexplained transfers out of the account. Brightwell is of the opinion that most of the companies named as recipients of these transfers are bogus. The unavoidable conclusion he has reached is that Simon was siphoning off client funds for his own purposes."

Pulos snorted. "Oh come now, Sidney. Please forgive my relaxed Greek attitude but the fact is that Simon was the boss. If he did use company funds for his own purposes, so what? No doubt if the clients wanted their money back, Simon would find a way. We all know he was the most creative of men."

Fleming flushed. "The fact is that those funds are missing and Simon is in no position to wave a magic wand and replace them. Besides, on top of that, Brightwell has identified other major discrepancies in the lending department where Simon got involved. There is a big hole."

Tomlinson scratched his head. "How much are we talking here exactly?"

"Around £2m."

Pulos whistled and Tomlinson looked astonished.

"If the Bank of England finds out about this, we shall be in serious trouble. While business as a whole has been steady, for various reasons cash flow has been poor. We haven't at present got the funds elsewhere in the bank to cover this deficiency. The only solution I can think of is to arrange a remittance of that amount from the overseas arm of our business. The ball is thus in your court, Alexander."

Pulos bridled. "I'm sorry but that will be quite impossible, Sidney. Apart from anything else, there are the Argentinian exchange control restrictions."

"You have always been able to get around those before. And Brightwell has told me that while he has not received the up-to-date figures he requested from you, his most recent information put your cash balances at approximately $21m."

"That would have been some six months ago, Sidney. Those balances have been significantly reduced since."

"How so?"

"Investment, my dear fellow. My mandate from Simon has always been to expand, particularly since avenues for growth in Europe have been closed off to the business here. New land has been acquired, ships, rolling stock. He sent an investment programme to me before he went abroad."

Fleming gave Pulos a look of disgust. "This has always been the trouble with your side of the operation, Alexander. A nice closed shop between you and Simon, with little or no information being conveyed to your other colleagues. We shall be managing things differently from now on. Meanwhile, I need to know quickly how much you can send us. I cannot believe for a moment that all of that cash has been spent. Besides, you must have substantial unutilised bank lines."

Pulos's eyes flitted shiftily back and forth between Fleming and Tomlinson. "I shall speak to Buenos Aires on Monday. Before I do that, however…" a sly smile split his lips, "should we not first talk about the ownership of Enterprisas Simal? Is that not in question in the absence of the bearer certificates?"

"As you well know, the shares are the subject of a declaration of trust by Simon in favour of Sackville. Sackville owns the company."

"Except for my 10 per cent, Sidney, which, by the way, is also missing as Simon insisted on keeping all the certificates together. And, anyway, Simon is dead. There is no will and we don't know where the shares are. The owner of the shares is whoever has them in his possession. In the circumstances, as the managing director of Simal, I think I would be bound to take legal advice before I could transfer any funds away from the company. Do you not think so, Reggie?"

Tomlinson opened and shut his mouth like a floundering fish a few times before offering his opinion. "Well, these are very unusual circumstances. Perhaps we need to consult counsel?"

Fleming banged a hand on the table. "Don't play these games with me, Pulos, or you'll have cause to regret it." Fleming and Pulos exchanged venomous looks and a tense silence settled on the table. It was Tomlinson who eventually broke it.

"Gentlemen, please, calm yourselves. I am sure we can work this all out sensibly if we remain calm. Sidney, surely you must have some idea of what Simon was using this money for? Was there some new business project he wanted to keep temporarily secret from the board?"

"Would that were the case. However, I do have an idea of the use to which Simon put the money."

"Yes, Sidney?"

"I think the money was used to fund Simon's gambling debts."

"But these are huge amounts!"

"So they are, but, as you know, Reggie, Simon never did anything in half measures. Some of us can well remember the young Simon's love of gambling. After a while, he had enough sense to pack it in but I fear at some point recently the habit returned. He became very reclusive in the year or two before he joined up. For most of '39 and '40, I saw little of him in the office or out. I think he kept himself aloof so he could pursue his gambling habit without us knowing."

"And how are you so sure about this?" Pulos produced a bright-blue silk handkerchief with which he mopped his forehead.

"I had my suspicions but they were confirmed by Philip this morning. You mentioned a list, Reggie, which Philip found in Simon's flat. It contained a column of numbers. Long numbers. There were also two initials – PB. There is a dangerous chap called Peregrine Beecham, who runs a high-stakes private gambling den. I think the list records some of Simon's gambling debts to Beecham."

Pulos shrugged his shoulders. "Who is to say that it wasn't a list of his winnings from this man?"

"I think that the circumstances favour my interpretation. I suggest…" Fleming was suddenly interrupted by loud voices outside. There were sounds of a scuffle and then the door burst open. A young man in uniform fell through, one arm held by Marco, the other by Fred Perkins.

"Who on earth is this, Perkins?"

"Sorry, Mr Fleming. This man came to the door and enquired about Mr Pulos here. I told him the gentleman was on the premises but in a meeting with you. Said he could wait in the lobby. I was just asking his name when he pushed past me and ran up the stairs. I chased him but I'm afraid he was too quick for me."

Fleming examined the intruder carefully. "You are an officer of some sort. I take it you'll behave like a gentleman if you are released?"

The man nodded.

"Check him for weapons, Marco. Good. He's clean? Very well. You may release him. Sit down and tell us what this is all about, Mr…?"

"Lieutenant Meyer. Felix Meyer."

Fleming paled at the sound of the name. The past came flooding back to him. He waved a hand at Perkins and Marco. "Please leave us."

*   *   *

Sonia was a calm, unflappable sort of woman. Merlin had seldom seen her flustered. Understandably, she had got into a bit of a state when Jan had been shot up in his Hurricane during the Battle of Britain the previous September. That aside, she had maintained an air of admirable serenity for someone living in a city under frequent bombardment. Tonight, however, all serenity was gone.

Sonia was extremely flustered. She was going out for dinner with Merlin's boss and his wife.

The invitation had come at short notice. Merlin received the AC's call late in the afternoon. There was a dinner reservation for four at Quaglino's. The AC and his wife were to dine with his sister and brother-in-law but their guests had belatedly pulled out. Would Merlin and his young lady like to make up the party? The AC and his wife would so much like to meet Sonia. Merlin could hardly refuse, although after the day's tragic events he was not in much of a mood for socialising.

They were in a taxi on the way to the restaurant in Mayfair. "Please, Sonia, relax. Gatehouse is a dry old stick but he's not all that bad. I bet he'll be bowled over. You look wonderful!"

Sonia was wearing the same white cocktail dress she had worn at dinner on Thursday night. Having only had time to give it a quick iron, she was worried about not looking smart enough. She checked her face in her compact mirror for the umpteenth time and made some more lipstick adjustments. "It is not so much your boss I am worrying about, it is his wife. Does she know that we are living together unmarried? What if she disapproves and shows it?" Sonia shook her head, dislodging a curl that she hastened to replace. "What am I saying? She is bound to disapprove. She is an upper-class English lady. What else is she likely to think?"

Merlin smiled. "I didn't realise you were so conventional."

"What does conventional mean? Ah, yes, I think I know. The French would say *bourgeois*, yes? I am no *bourgeoise*, Frank, as you know, but I fear the condemnation of such a person, especially if that person is your boss's wife."

"For what it's worth, darling, I have never discussed you in any detail with the AC. If they know anything, it is only through office gossip, which we can always dismiss as such. And, anyway, if they had any problem with our living arrangements, they wouldn't have invited us out, would they? Now let's try and enjoy ourselves.

We have a night out at a top London restaurant. Let's make the most of it."

The taxi pulled up at the restaurant on Bury Street. Merlin's last visit to Quaglino's had been on police business. The Italian maître'd who was now hurrying up to greet them had made an important identification in a murder case.

"Chief Inspector, *che piacere!* A pleasure to see you again!"

"Likewise, Ernesto. This is Sonia."

Ernesto brushed Sonia's hand delicately with his lips. "Enchanted, *signorina*, enchanted. I think you are dining with *Signor* Gatehouse? He and his wife are already here. Follow me, please."

As they made their way to the table, Ernesto whispered to Merlin. "*Molto grazie*, Chief Inspector. It came through, no problem." Like Tony the café owner, Ernesto had faced difficulties because he was Italian. Merlin had put in a word in support of his British citizenship application.

"Frank, so glad you could make it." The AC rose. "And this must be your young lady." He beamed a brown-toothed smile at Sonia. "Darling, you remember Frank, don't you? And this is Sonia. That's the name, isn't it? I'm Edward and this is my wife, Felicity." After various nods and bows of greeting, the party settled at the table.

Gatehouse was in black tie while Felicity Gatehouse wore an elegant, long, green dress. Merlin knew she had been quite a beauty in her youth and traces of those good looks lingered on. Sonia was concerned that she and Merlin were not in evening dress but her concern evaporated as Felicity instantly put her at her ease. It turned out that Mrs Gatehouse had travelled in Poland before the war and was full of informed interest in Sonia's homeland and her former life there. As Sonia relaxed so did Merlin.

Menus were read and food orders placed and the conversation meandered pleasantly along, Merlin and the AC being careful to avoid talking shop.

"I understand you have two teenage boys, Mrs Gatehouse?"

"Oh, call me Felicity, please, Sonia. Yes, two teenage boys. Thankfully they are in boarding school in the country and well away from all the bombing."

"Do you think the bombing has really ended now?"

The AC tapped his nose knowingly. "Hitler has other things on his plate now, my dear. He needs all the *Luftwaffe* pilots he can get. I doubt we'll see the bombers back here in any force for a long time. I think the Germans have given up on the idea of bombing us into submission. It is true that we appear to be on the back foot on nearly every other military front but I think this battle of the air in defence of Britain has been won."

Felicity patted Sonia's hand. "And I understand that your brother is one of those we have to thank?"

Sonia's cheeks reddened a little. "Yes, Jan is a fighter pilot with the RAF. He has flown many missions. I am very proud of him."

"And so you should be, dear."

The best London restaurants could still offer meals up to pre-war standards. There was a comprehensive menu and the two couples ate well – Dover sole for the ladies and lamb for the men. A fair amount of wine was drunk and all were a little flushed when the desserts and cheese plate were removed. Felicity suggested that Sonia accompany her to the lounge area of the restaurant for coffee, leaving the men to their cigars and port at the table.

"You are a lucky man, Frank. She's a beautiful girl."

"Thank you, sir."

"Charming and intelligent as well. Thinking of making her an honest woman?"

"Perhaps."

"Forgive me if I'm saying the wrong thing here but I hope you won't allow loyalty to your poor late wife to prevent you from seizing a new chance of happiness."

Sensitivity was not one of the AC's strongest cards and these words of advice surprised and touched Merlin. "Fair point, sir. Thank you. And no, I won't. I am sure Alice would have approved of Sonia."

The waiter arrived. "I hope you don't mind, sir, but I haven't got much of a head for port. Nor cigars."

"How about a brandy, then?" Merlin nodded and the waiter scuttled away. Gatehouse lit his cigar. "It's been a jolly pleasant evening, Frank. I can see that Felicity is quite taken with Sonia. My wife needed a good night out. She finds it hard, you know, being at home without the boys and me working the hours I do. The hours you and I both do."

The AC sent a small cloud of smoke off behind him. The waiter returned with two balloon glasses of Courvoisier. "I'm very sorry to sully the evening with work for a moment but, as we're here together, I would appreciate a quick report on today's sad events and any other case developments."

Merlin held the brandy to his nose and savoured its aroma. "The body found today, as you know, was that of my friend, Edgar Powell. The initial medical findings suggest he was held down and drowned in his bath. I talked to you about him the other day. He had just returned from Crete and, you'll remember, brought back a letter from Simon Arbuthnot. I had advised him, in line with your suggestion, to give it to Arbuthnot's solicitor but he obviously never got a chance to do so. We found the letter this morning in Powell's safe. It contains some sort of coded message. It's my theory the murderer or murderers wanted to get hold of that letter, Edgar refused to cooperate, the murderer overdid the violence and my friend died."

"Appalling! Any idea what the code means?"

"No, but Constable Robinson told me that one of your nephews is a cypher expert of some sort. She is trying to get hold of him."

"Ah, yes. Robert. Clever chap."

"On other matters, as regards the abortion case, we've been able to identify two men we believe knew Bridget Healy, although they deny it. One is a French officer and the other a young solicitor. We are going to bring them in for questioning. There is one odd coincidence. The solicitor, a South African called Vorster, works at the firm that acted for Arbuthnot. The firm to which Edgar was going to entrust the letter."

"Ah, Frank, you hate those odd coincidences, don't you? Well, if there's anything in it, no doubt know you'll dig it out. What about de Metz? Did you get anything from Swanton?"

"Yes, he was open and helpful. MI5 first heard of de Metz when he tried to gain access to that secret government operation in Bletchley. They pulled him in. He said he was trying to visit a nephew who worked there. This checked out and they believe he was just there to tap his nephew for money. In the course of their interrogation, de Metz did, however, make insinuations that he had some intelligence information of value. Nothing to do with his nephew or Bletchley but concerning France."

"As he'd told the French. Did MI5 get to the bottom of what he knew?"

"No. He wanted money and they decided he was just trying it on. The same view taken by the French. They let him go and his parting comment was that de Gaulle was surrounded by snakes."

"No doubt he is. The whole French nation is a band of vipers as far as I am concerned, though don't tell anyone I said so. So what do you think?"

"At the moment, it seems most likely that his murder is related to the illegal abortion practice rather than security matters. However, I'm going to continue to keep an open mind."

"Quite right, Frank. Always keep an open mind." The AC stubbed out his cigar and finished his brandy. "Drink up, Chief Inspector. I think it's time to go and rejoin the ladies."

CHAPTER 11

Sunday 15 June

London

Sidney Fleming was dabbing his eye with a flannel in the bathroom when he heard someone at the door. "Hang on a second!" He had been enjoying a grapefruit, a rare delicacy these days, for breakfast and had managed to squirt juice into his eye. Sight restored, he went to see who his visitor was. It was Pulos with Marco, as always, in attendance.

"You can come in, Alexander, but he can't." Marco bristled but did as he was told.

They walked through to the drawing room. "You don't seem very friendly this morning, Sidney."

"Can you blame me after your awful behaviour yesterday?"

"Really, my friend, you can't blame me. As Tomlinson put it, we find ourselves in a legal morass."

They sat down by the open balcony door. It was going to be another hot day. Fleming impatiently flicked some fluff from his trousers. "In such circumstances, colleagues like us should stick together." Church bells started ringing in the distance. "Been to mass, yet?"

"I gave up religious observance long ago, Sidney. If ever there were a God above, I believe he deserted us a long time ago."

"You might be right there." Fleming looked Pulos up and

down. He was wearing brown trousers, a green checked shirt, a tan jacket and a yellow silk cravat.

"Looks like you've been shopping."

"I went to Savile Row late yesterday to take my mind off our problems. What do you think?"

Fleming thought Pulos looked like a South American pimp. A successful one but a pimp nevertheless. "Very flamboyant. Did you buy anything else?"

"A couple of suits. Some ties, some shoes. Of course, we have some very good shops in Buenos Aires."

"I know. I remember Simon saying he picked up some very nice shirts there on one of his trips."

Pulos looked down admiringly at his shiny new Church brogues. "Ah, Simon." He pursed his lips. "What a situation he has left us in. And now, on top of everything, the Meyer business has returned to haunt us. You knew Franzi Meyer and his wife, Adele, didn't you?"

"I did."

"A beautiful woman, I was told. I never had the opportunity to meet her myself. Simon liked her very much, he told me. You know they had a little thing for a while?"

"Of course."

Pulos eyed Fleming warily. "So, Sidney, Simon did what he did all those years ago. He screwed the husband just as he did the wife. To our mutual benefit."

"He did, and now the chickens have come home to roost."

Pulos snorted with laughter. "I love you English and your stupid English phrases. 'The chickens have come home to roost'. What the hell do chickens have to do with the Meyer boy in New York issuing legal proceedings for ownership of the share capital of Enterprisas Simal? I remember Simon often used the phrase, 'The early bird catches the worm'. I told him it was rubbish."

"You think so?"

"Of course, because sometimes a bird that is patient and bides its time can get the fattest and juiciest worm late in the day."

Fleming lit a cigarette. "So, Alexander, Anton Meyer issued proceedings against Enterprisas Simal in Buenos Aires. You omitted to report this significant fact to the Sackville board before now."

"I reported it to Simon, the chairman of Sackville. He used that other English phrase he liked. Said it was 'a storm in a teacup'. Whatever the merits of the case, he thought the right result in the Argentinian courts could be bought. He said the judicious application of bribery in appropriate quarters could stall and then kill Meyer's case. In the circumstances, he remained sanguine and didn't want to worry you and your colleagues."

"And were you also sanguine?"

Pulos smiled a little uncomfortably. "I have lived in Argentina. It may not be perfect but, like everywhere, there is good and bad – and there is good and bad in the legal system. Despite what Simon thought, there are honest judges. If such a judge…"

"Into which category does the current judge in Meyer's case fall?"

"He is the second so far. Up until two months ago it was Judge Rodriguez – he was happy to be influenced by us. Unfortunately, he has been taken ill with cancer. The replacement is Manuel Lopez. He has a reputation as an honest man but we think he will play ball in due course."

"You have something on him, then?"

A flicker of a smile passed Pulos's lips. "Perhaps. He is certainly not as pure as he pretends. In any event, going to law in Argentina is a long, drawn-out process. I doubt Anton Meyer would have the financial stamina even if the system were straight. Naturally, Simon had Meyer's circumstances investigated. He is a poorly paid junior clerk in a mediocre New York accountancy firm."

"Perhaps his brother, Felix, has resources? He certainly has the spirit, as he showed yesterday."

Pulos fanned himself with his hand. Beads of perspiration trickled down his face and into the yellow cravat. "We must remember, Sidney, that while we may be on the wrong side of the case morally, the law favours us. This issue concerns bearer certificates for which possession is…"

"Nine-tenths of the law, I know."

"No. In this case, possession is ten-tenths of the law. However Simon got them, once he possessed them he was legally entitled to exercise rights of ownership."

Fleming took a long draw on his cigarette and looked up at the ceiling. "But Simon doesn't have the certificates, unless they are with him in his Cretan grave, and neither do we. If the certificates are missing and continue to be missing, what is the position in Argentinian law?"

"I don't know, Sidney. It was never considered because there was no question as to Simon's possession of the shares."

"Well, you'd better find out. And I hope you are going to be more constructive about the Sackville Bank problems than you were yesterday."

"I am the senior executive of Enterprisas Simal. I cannot ignore my fiduciary duties. The legalities are complex."

"Bollocks! Get on side or there will be hell to pay."

*   *   *

Northamptonshire

The gardens of Sackville Hall were bursting with colour under the bright morning sun. Bees buzzed around the roses and hyacinths bordering the path from the kitchen garden to the large pond at the south of the house. Birds chirruped and, in the distance,

Lucinda Cavendish could hear the contented lowing and bleating of the neighbouring farm's livestock. When she got to the pond with her young black labrador, Archie, she disturbed some frogs basking in the sun on her favourite stone bench. They bounded into the water and disappeared from sight.

Lucinda sat down, remembering the unusually warm day last October, when she and Simon had last shared this view. It had been clear to her for some time that Simon was not himself but she had not been able to persuade him to confide in her. In the past, he had always shared his major problems with his sister. On that October day, he had sat silently gazing out over the water for a long time.

Eventually, Simon had said in a whisper: "You're the only one I can rely on, Lucy. If something happens, it will be for you to pick up the pieces and look after the family." Moments later, without another word, he had got up, hurried off to his car and returned to London. That was the last time she had seen him.

Lucinda had, to date, taken his words at their face value. Simon knew she had a fine commercial brain and had used her frequently as a sounding board as he had built up his empire. Lucinda had not condoned everything he had done and his methods, she had often felt, left much to be desired. But she had given her brother the support that she would now offer his son. She was more than capable of giving Philip the guidance he would need as he took up the reins of the family business.

However, sitting as she was in the place where Simon had uttered those words to her, Lucinda began to worry whether he had meant something more by them.

Philip had called her earlier to say that he wouldn't be able to come up as arranged for Sunday lunch. There were some pressing matters to deal with and he thought it better he remained in town. When asked what these concerns were, Philip had been vague in response. He had muttered something about "missing papers" and "problems with South America" before abruptly ringing off. She would have to find out what these pressing matters were.

Also playing on her mind was the correspondence Lucinda had opened yesterday. Most of her brother's correspondence went to his flat in London or the office but some came to Sackville Hall. Having received no instructions from Simon, Lucinda had allowed these letters to pile up, trusting that none of them could be urgent and would be read by Simon when he came home on leave. Now she knew he was dead, she had felt obliged to open them.

It had taken her a couple of hours to plough through them all. Most were of little account. People asking for charitable donations, product circulars, letters from the local golf and tennis clubs, and so on. There were only two letters of interest, of keen interest in fact, to Lucinda. They were from the Martins Bank branch in Northampton. The first had been sent last November, just after Simon had left for the army.

> Dear Mr Arbuthnot,
>
> I am writing to apologise for – and to correct – a small error in our letter of 10 September. In our summary of the mortgage loan arrangements agreed between Martins Bank and yourself on 26 August, we said that accounts statements would be sent to you at the mortgaged property, Sackville Hall, on a quarterly basis on the first working day of every month. You will no doubt recall that the loan agreement provided for six-monthly statements unless otherwise agreed. Accordingly, you will receive your first statement on 26 February 1941 and subsequently on 26 August, and so on. I apologise profusely for this clerical error.
>
> I remain, sir, your obedient servant.
> E Hardy esquire
> Manager

The second letter was the February account statement, which showed a balance owed to the bank of £20,489.12 after the deduction of capital repayments and interest for the six-month period.

Lucinda Cavendish was a measured, unemotional woman. She refused to allow herself to become upset by the endlessly challenging behaviour of her elderly and demented mother. She had hardly ever been seen to cry by friends or family, even after the sudden deaths of her husband and son. She seldom raised her voice in anger. Her initial reaction on reading these bank letters, however, had been emotional. Tears had flowed. She was surprised and shocked. Her beloved brother had mortgaged what was now her home without a word to her. He had mortgaged it to the hilt. She had almost fainted at the desk. Her mother, sitting in her wheelchair at the other end of the room, had noticed something was wrong and, in a rare moment of lucidity, asked if her daughter was all right.

Now, in the peace of the garden, with Archie nuzzling his nose against her, Lucinda calmly tried to imagine what circumstances had driven her brother to such desperate measures and she considered again his last words to her. Eventually, with thoughts none the clearer, she resolved to put her brother out of her mind for the day. No doubt there would be funds at Simon's bank to clear the debt and she would speak to Philip or Sidney Fleming about it on Monday.

"Come, Archie." She led the dog back down the path to the house, stopping for a moment by an ancient oak. Archie's father had been buried in the shade of that tree the year before. She and Simon had loved that dog so much. For the second time in 24 hours, tears fell from Lucinda Cavendish's eyes.

*   *   *

London

Devlin spent all Sunday morning monitoring Beaulieu's lodgings. Rougemont had told him that Beaulieu would be back in London by Saturday. There was, however, no sign of him and Devlin began to think that he was still out of town. At one o'clock, hungry and thirsty, he decided to catch a taxi and grab lunch in his Holloway local.

Half an hour later, he was seated in his favourite corner, a pint of Guinness and pork pie in front of him. Devlin rejected the invitations of his pub cronies to join them. He wanted to be alone with his thoughts, which, for the moment, revolved entirely around the French, whom he desperately wanted to help. He was a Francophile, hated the idea of the Nazis lording it over his beloved Paris and felt disgust for the cowardly sell-out politicians in Vichy. If there were a Vichy spy in London, Devlin wanted to help find him. He was disappointed, however, at the lack of progress being made. He sipped his stout then opened the tattered black notebook in which he recorded his case observations at the end of every day. He turned to his most recent entry: the entry for Saturday.

Devlin had followed the taxis of Pulos and Meyer to a large commercial building off Fenchurch Street in the City. Pulos and his companion had gone in and then, after 45 minutes of nervous pacing outside, so had Meyer. After going up to check the nameplate by the door of the building, which announced Sackville Bank, Devlin had taken up position in an alleyway across the street and waited on events.

At just after three o'clock, Meyer had emerged from the building and disappeared in a taxi. Devlin decided not to follow him but to wait and see who else would appear from the building. Half an hour later, Pulos and his sidekick left, followed shortly thereafter by two more well-heeled City types. Devlin still stood his ground. He wanted to know more about this place and why Meyer had gone there.

His chance came at half past five, when the security guard he'd seen opening and shutting the bank's doors came off duty. Devlin had followed the man through the City, past St Paul's Cathedral and on into Fleet Street. Just before the Law Courts, the guard had ducked into a pub. The place was almost empty and it had not been difficult for Devlin to strike up a conversation with Bert Perkins.

After a couple of pints, Perkins was happy to tell Devlin all he knew. Thus Devlin had learned the identities of the people meeting at the bank, the story – as Perkins knew it – of the Arbuthnot family and Sackville Bank, of Simon Arbuthnot's death and of the young officer who had barged into the directors' meeting shouting out something about his family being defrauded.

Devlin realised, as he closed the notebook, that his long day's work on Saturday had not been completely wasted. One thing he now knew for certain – Meyer was not the spy. No spy would draw the attention of others to himself in the way Meyer had at the bank. The young man obviously had a bee in his bonnet about a wrong done to his family. Devlin would bet his life that Meyer was not passing secrets to Vichy.

He considered Beaulieu again. The Irishman had found a note waiting for him at his digs when he finally got home on Saturday night. It read: 'Be quick. Nail the redhead. Ignore the others. Definitive new orders'. The note was unsigned but probably from Angers, he thought. Devlin knew the commandant's weaknesses. Drunk when he dropped it off, most likely, and forgot to initial it. Rougemont would have waited to speak to Devlin in person. The note only served to confirm his view that the officers were not serious about the investigation. For whatever reason, they wanted to make a show that they were investigating while simply pinning the guilt on the least congenial of the officers. Or that's how it seemed to him.

Devlin polished off his pie and washed it down with some beer. One of Devlin's strongest characteristics was stubbornness. Now that he'd started on this job, if there were a spy, regardless of what the officers thought, he wanted to catch him. After ruling out Meyer, the choice was now between Beaulieu and Dumont. He thought again about Beaulieu. Was there something fishy about his late return from Oxford? Probably not. Devlin had never been to the place himself but he understood it was beautiful. Beaulieu had probably just decided to grab another day's leave in a lovely city.

And what about Dumont? He knew he liked to drink at the Ritz. He knew he was friendly with Vorster, as were they all. Perhaps Vorster and Dumont were closer than the others? They had been drinking together on Friday. Then they had gone with that other fellow to the flats in Arlington Street. Devlin had now solved the mystery that had been bugging him about those flats.

On the way home the previous night, he'd bumped into an old friend. Billy Craig, a small-time bookmaker, had cracked a big smile when Devlin asked him the question. "That's where our old friend Percy Bishop lives. Very hoity-toity now. Changed his name to Peregrine Beecham but a nasty piece of work under any name. He's done well, though, fair play.

"Runs the biggest poker game in London in his penthouse up there. Gets all sorts of rich punters in. He has a few runners, who keep a steady flow of customers coming in from the Ritz and places like that. Very high-stakes games. I think he runs a few other games as well as poker.

"He's hard as nails, of course. Tough luck to anyone who doesn't pay his bills. He has a gang of roughhouse collectors. You wouldn't want to meet any of them in a dark alley. If you haven't got the cash to pay your debts, they'll take whatever you've got, your balls

if they are in the mood, and if the circumstances require…' Billy
Craig had run a finger across his throat and laughed. "Best not
get on the wrong side of Percy Bishop or Peregrine Beecham or
whatever he wants to call himself these days."

Devlin had known Percy Bishop in his boxing days in London
before the move to Paris. Bishop had been a bookie then, like
Craig, and had tried to persuade Devlin to throw a fight. A nasty
piece of work and doubtless up to no good but did he have
anything to do with the investigation? Dumont hadn't gone
into the block and who was to say the other two had actually
visited Beecham's flat? No, he didn't have anything worthwhile
on Dumont either.

He rose to get another drink but time was called as he did so.
Devlin shrugged. It was probably for the best. He should get back
to work. He'd go and check on Beaulieu one more time. In this
type of work, persistence was everything. Something might break
at any time. You never knew what might be just around the corner.

*   *   *

Sonia had arranged to go out to Northolt to see her brother for
the day, so Merlin had no feelings of guilt as he headed into the
Yard on a Sunday morning. He decided to walk in because it
was another lovely day. There were several bomb-craters along
the King's Road where buildings had stood. As he passed one he
found himself struggling to remember what exactly was missing.

He stopped, chewed thoughtfully on his Fisherman's Friend,
then remembered it had been some sort of non-conformist church.
Most of the rubble had been cleared but, in what remained, he saw
a small black-and-white cat scavenging for whatever it could find.
Two young boys, short-trousered and shirtless, suddenly appeared
and chased the cat away. Merlin heard their high-pitched laughter
receding behind him as he walked off towards Sloane Square.

His walk took him through Eaton Square, around Buckingham Palace and into the Mall. In March, a police officer he knew had been killed when the North Lodge of the palace was demolished by the *Luftwaffe*. Several bombs had landed in the vicinity of the royal residence and its grounds and a few outbuildings had been seriously damaged. However, the main structure had survived, suffering only blown-out windows and the partial destruction of a ground-floor bedroom.

Merlin cut across to Birdcage Walk and passed the spot where Goldberg's uncle had died. There had been some strange characters involved in that case. The face of one, Morris Owen, the grotesquely obese nightclub owner, came to him and Merlin shuddered at the memory.

When he got to the office, Merlin was surprised to find Bernie Goldberg lounging on his chair reading a copy of the *New York Herald Tribune*. Goldberg was embarrassed and jumped to his feet. "Apologies, Frank. I was just waiting here on the off-chance you might come in this morning. I guess I should have waited in the room along the corridor but I sat down here for a second, starting reading, then…"

"Don't worry. I'm glad to see you. I was worrying you might have been shipped back to the States." Merlin fell into his chair.

Goldberg tucked the newspaper away inside his jacket. "As it happens, Frank, I am being sent back. Not straightaway but at the end of the week."

"Oh, I'm very sorry to hear that, Bernie. I was just getting used to you. Missing you back home, are they?"

"I doubt it but there is a new organised crime task force and my name has been suggested."

"A promotion?"

"Theoretically, but more likely another way for the precinct bosses to keep me out of their hair. Obviously, I can't say no."

"No." Merlin lifted his feet up on to the desk and loosened his collar. The room was hot and humid. "Do you think you could open that window, Bernie? It's quite stiff. I tried yesterday but my shoulder was playing me up and I couldn't…"

"Of course." Goldberg went to the window and opened it wide. "You were shot, weren't you? How'd that happen?"

"I was arresting a murderer around this time last year. Chap called Harrison. He'd murdered four prostitutes. Slit their throats. He shot me when he was trying to escape. The doctors said I was lucky as the bone was only slightly chipped but I still get twinges and haven't got the full strength of my arm back yet." He put a hand to the damaged area and rubbed it.

Goldberg nodded sympathetically. "What happened to this guy, Harrison?"

"He was hanged by our most famous executioner, Mr Pierrepoint. The dear old AC insisted on my being present 'to represent the victims', as he put it. Dreadful. I'm not going to do that again. Have you witnessed an execution?"

"One. At a placed called Sing Sing in New York State. A gangster I knew was electrocuted there. Before I saw it, I somehow had the idea that electrocution was a clean, modern and efficient method to use. Let me assure you it is not. It is barbaric."

"Hmm. Best spare me the details. So when will you be leaving us?"

"Saturday or Sunday, depending which day is more convenient for the military."

"We'd better get our skates on then, if we are to settle these cases before you go."

*   *   *

After lunch, Pulos went for a stroll in Green Park with Marco trailing dutifully behind him. He was surprised to see that a considerable area of the park had been dug up and planted with vegetables. The sign next to it read: 'Dig for Victory'. In other areas, there was evidence of military works, the purpose of which was unclear to Pulos. There were still, thankfully, plenty of places in which to sit and enjoy fine weather amidst the greenery.

Pulos eased himself on to an unoccupied bench in the shadow of an ash tree against which Marco leaned unhappily. Pulos could see that Marco was not himself. Perhaps he had been too harsh on him. Marco had proved himself an excellent fixer back in Argentina. Pulos couldn't remember any failures. In London, he had given Marco one major task and he'd failed. This clearly sat heavily on him.

The Greek looked up at the clear blue sky and decided that the view he had formed after he had seen Fleming that morning was the correct one. It was time to go home. There was nothing more he could achieve here. He doubted whether the damned share certificates would ever turn up. If Pulos remained in England, he'd be under intense pressure to transfer money. It would be much easier to resist that pressure if he were back in Buenos Aires.

His trip to London had been very brief but he didn't consider it a wasted journey. Pulos had been able to get the lie of the land in person and to appreciate better the positions of Fleming and the others. But he'd be much better off back in Buenos Aires. If the bearer certificates were not going to fall into his hands, he could at least be back in control of the underlying businesses. Argentina was a long way away, there was a war on in Europe and, as they had discussed the day before, possession was ten-tenths of the law.

It was clear that the situation at Sackville was fraught. The problems Simon Arbuthnot had bequeathed were going to be very difficult to cover up. If the City caught wind of the problems, the bank would be in deep trouble and if Fleming thought Pulos was going to provide a solution with Argentinian funds, he could go whistle. It was every man for himself now.

As for the Meyers, it had been a shock to encounter one in the flesh but Pulos remained confident he could fend them off. A little money here and a little money there. Simon had never been prepared to consider such an approach but it probably wouldn't even take that much to buy off the Meyers.

Perhaps everything that had happened had been for the best. The best for Pulos, at least. The Greek would have liked to have known what Powell's letter contained but there it was. He turned to Marco. "Come, we are going home. Let's get back to the hotel and make the arrangements."

*   *   *

Merlin arrived home just before seven in the evening. The flat was quiet. He had spent all day trying to make progress with Simon Arbuthnot's code. He had attempted to reach Robinson to get her cryptologist brother's telephone number but she had obviously gone out for the day.

Goldberg had managed to track down a US Embassy acquaintance, who was in the encryption section, and had hurried off to Grosvenor Square with a copy of the code. However, he had called four hours later to say his friend had got nowhere with it.

Merlin himself had spent several hours in the Scotland Yard reference library looking at books about the history and science of codes. By the end of the afternoon, his head was full of a multitude of alternative code systems – transposition and shift ciphers, monoalphabetic substitution, *Vigenère*, true codes and more. It was all very interesting and educational but of little practical use to a layman like him. He had made no progress at all on understanding the meaning of 23918174933238222849 23 31313383X.

He opened the bedroom door. The curtains were drawn and it was dark. He whispered Sonia's name.

A bedside lamp came on and Sonia's head emerged from beneath the bedclothes.

"Oh, hello, darling. Sorry, did I wake you? Is everything all right?"

"Yes, fine. I got back here an hour ago and felt a little dizzy so I decided to have a lie down."

Merlin sat on the bed and squeezed her hand. "Still feeling bad?"

Sonia sat up. "I'm not dizzy any more but my stomach is a little unsettled. Probably the spicy Polish stew my brother gave me for lunch. I'll be all right soon. Just let me have another hour's rest, then I'll get up and make you some tea."

"Don't worry about tea. I'll make myself a sandwich or something. Jan all right?" Sonia nodded then snuggled back down in the bed.

Sonia had left the radio on in the living room. Merlin turned the volume down and then twiddled with the dial. He found he was too late for the main evening news bulletin and wandered into the kitchen to make himself a jam sandwich and a cup of tea.

There was often a poetry programme on the Home Service at this time of night and Merlin returned to his chair in hope. To his disappointment, the announcer introduced the Sunday evening religious service. He switched off the radio, finished his sandwich and picked up a book from the table next to him. It was a collected volume of Kipling poems. Merlin and his friend Jack Stewart were great poetry enthusiasts. Their pub get-togethers always involved an exchange of their respective poetic repertoires. Merlin had felt deprived of this pleasure since Stewart's departure to Manchester.

The book fell open at a dramatic seafaring poem. Merlin had been unaware of *The Ballad of the Bolivar* until he'd heard a rousing reading of it on the radio earlier that year. He read the closing lines quietly to himself.

Just a pack of rotten plates puttied up with tar
In we came, an' time enough, cross Bilbao Bar.
Overloaded, undermanned, meant to founder, we
Euchred God Almighty's storm, bluffed the Eternal Sea!
Seven men from all the world, back to town again,
Rollin' down the Ratcliffe Road drunk and raising Cain:
Seven men from out of Hell. Ain't the owners gay,
'Cause we took the 'Bolivar' safe across the Bay?

Merlin pictured the mountainous seas of the Bay of Biscay to the north of his father's Galician homeland, and wondered again what on earth 'euchred' meant. He closed his eyes. It had been a long and mentally strenuous day and he couldn't help drifting off.

He awoke with a start three-quarters of an hour later and automatically switched the radio on again. A story was being told and a beautiful female voice was telling it. Merlin recognised the narrator. It was the actress Wendy Hiller, whose performance in the film version of *Pygmalion* he had enjoyed so much before the war. It had been the last film he'd seen with his late wife. He dozed off again and inevitably dreamed of Alice. When he awoke, Sonia was standing over him.

"Come to bed, Frank. It's late and you obviously need a good night's sleep as much as I do."

Merlin felt a twinge of guilt that he had been dreaming of Alice when he opened his eyes to Sonia. "Are you all right now, darling? You still look a little pale."

"I'm fine now."

"Come on then." Grasping Sonia's hand tightly, he led the way to their bedroom. He realised there was no need for guilt. Alice was dead. One lovely woman had left him and another had appeared in her place.

Chapter 12

Monday 16 June

London

"What news, Sergeant? Did you get him?" Merlin set aside the turgid Home Office policing report the AC had sent him.

"Disappointingly no, sir. I went directly from home to the solicitors' office, only to be told that Vorster was away on business in Birmingham and wouldn't be back at work until tomorrow."

"Who did you speak to?"

"A partner. Mr Reginald Tomlinson."

"Did you ask him about Powell?"

"I did."

"And?"

"He said Mr Powell had come to see him but wouldn't say what they had discussed."

"Client confidentiality?"

"His exact words. I then told him that he would not be meeting Mr Powell again. That Powell's dead body had been discovered in his flat and there were suspicious circumstances. He was pretty shocked. And disappointed, I'd say. When he composed himself, he asked whether my desire to interview Mr Vorster was somehow connected with Powell's death. I told him not."

"Very well. It's not the end of the world. We'll get to Vorster tomorrow. Meanwhile Robinson is bringing her brother in this morning. After we've talked to him, let's see if we can get hold of Dumont. Given his status as a Free French officer, I suppose it would be diplomatic to call him first and ask him nicely to come and see us."

"Is Detective Goldberg coming in?"

"No. I saw him yesterday and asked him to keep away today in case Vorster and Dumont were here. I thought it might be wise to maintain his cover as regards those two. Just in case it might be of further use."

There was a knock at the door and Robinson led in a smiling young man, whose face bore a close resemblance to his sister's. He was Merlin's height but extremely thin and the suit he was wearing looked at least two sizes too big. "My brother, Robert, sir."

"Good of you to come and see us at such short notice, Mr Robinson."

"Not at all, Chief Inspector. It's a pleasure to meet you. I have heard so much about you from Claire." His sister blushed.

Bridges rearranged the office chairs so everyone could sit around Merlin's desk.

"Have you been offered refreshment?"

"Oh yes, don't you worry. Already had a quick cuppa and a natter here with Claire. I have received all the mental stimulation that a strong mug of Liptons can provide. Claire has explained you have a little piece of code you'd like me to advise on. I've no doubt you're a very busy man, Chief Inspector, so I'm ready when you are."

"I understand you are something of an expert in this area."

"Been keen on words, clues, codes and that sort of thing since I was a nipper. Modesty should forbid but I'm afraid I can boast that I completed my first *Times* crossword at the age of seven. It's a knack, of course, and I seem to have it, though I know many who are better at it than me."

"And code breaking is your job?"

Robert Robinson looked embarrassed. "Can't comment on that, even to as eminent a police officer as yourself. I'm sure you understand."

"Sorry, of course." Merlin pushed the letter across the desk. "This is our little problem. If you can help, I'd be very grateful."

Robinson moved his chair closer to the desk. "Let me just say at the outset that if there is any complexity at all, it is unlikely that I shall be able to decode it here and now. I may be able to recognise what type of code it is. After that – well, we shall just have to see."

"Any help at all will be welcome. We have no idea what we are dealing with."

"Perhaps before I study it, Chief Inspector, you could tell me about the originator of the code, assuming you know who that is, and the context of the investigation in which it features?"

Merlin quickly explained the story behind the letter. Robinson caught his breath as Merlin told of Powell's drowning and of the police suspicion that the letter had been the motive for his murder.

"An important letter then." Robinson reached inside his jacket. "Reading glasses. I hate to admit to needing them but…"

Merlin smiled sympathetically. "Not at all. I didn't like admitting it either but I've got over it now."

Robinson bent down and concentrated on the code sequence. The others remained silent as he did so. He continued his study for nearly a quarter of an hour. Eventually he looked up at Merlin, then closed his eyes and slowly recited the sequence from memory: "23918174933232382228492331313383X." He opened his eyes.

"Hmm. You say this code was put together by a gentleman whose life, before his brief stint as an army officer, was spent in big business. I doubt that as a newish army recruit he had any involvement in secret intelligence work. He was a line officer on the battlefront. I suppose he might have had some rudimentary knowledge of battlefront codes but..." Robert Robinson paused and looked up at the ceiling for a moment.

"What I mean, Mr Merlin, is that if Mr Arbuthnot were something of a cryptographer, he was more likely to be an amateur rather than a professional one. Perhaps, like me, he was a crossword enthusiast when young."

"Does knowing that help us in any way?"

"It might. If Arbuthnot were an amateur, chances are that the premise of the code is relatively simple. I do not mean that the code will necessarily be simple to unlock, but that it may be based on one of the more traditional code foundations. If we know what, we are at least on our way."

"Some grounds for optimism, then. Do you already have an idea of what type of code it might be?"

"There are a number of possibilities but it is too premature to discuss these. May I suggest we adjourn for now. I would like to go away and think hard. I have memorised the code so you may retain the letter. Fortunately, I am off duty until tomorrow afternoon and have plenty of time to give this my undivided attention."

"May we know where you'll be?"

"I have a small flat in St John's Wood. Claire has the details and I, of course, have hers. Come what may, I promise to get in touch at the end of the afternoon with a progress report."

*   *   *

"Say that again, Reggie. I didn't quite catch it."

"Powell is dead, Sidney. 'In suspicious circumstances,' the policeman said. In other words, they think he was murdered. Sidney, are you there? I said Powell has been murdered. It must be something to do with that blasted letter."

Fleming had dropped the cup of tea he had been drinking and

a dark stain was spreading across the plush cream carpet of his suite's drawing room. "I am here." Fleming stroked his forehead. He felt a migraine coming on. "It doesn't necessarily follow that he has been murdered. 'Suspicious circumstances' could easily encompass a nasty accident. Nor does it necessarily follow that if he were murdered, his death had anything to do with that letter. We know nothing about the man. He might have had many enemies. Perhaps he had a colourful love life? Who knows? Even if the death is connected to the letter, what difficulties does that cause us?"

Fleming heard a grunt of irritation from the lawyer. "Well, for a start it causes the difficulty that we are unlikely to see Simon's letter and get any further in sorting out this appalling mess he's left."

"But, Reggie, if the police have the letter, it will most likely still come to you as his solicitor."

"I don't know that the police have the letter. The policeman said nothing about a letter. Perhaps the murderer has the damn thing? Even if the police do have it, that doesn't mean I'm going to see it any time soon."

Fleming took out a handkerchief and started dabbing at the stains the spilled tea had left on his trousers. "Have you told Pulos about this?"

"I rang you first but there was no answer. Then I tried Pulos and was told by the operator that he had checked out. I spoke to the front desk, who said that he and his man had booked an early morning taxi to Croydon Aerodrome. Looks like he's done a bunk and is on his way back to Argentina."

Fleming felt his migraine intensifying. "The words 'rat' and 'sinking ship' are the ones that first come to mind, Reggie." He gave up on the stain. "So what do you advise?"

"I'm going to contact the officer in charge of the Powell investigation and see what I can find out."

"Be careful. It won't just be a question of you finding out what he knows. He will want to know what you know."

"Of course, Sidney, but what have we to hide on that score? Mr Powell was about to pass on a presumably important letter from Simon to his solicitor. That's all we know."

"Just be careful. I don't want the bank getting embroiled in this. We have enough problems as it is."

"I'll be careful."

"Is that all, as if it isn't enough?"

"There is one other odd thing. The police came to my office to interview one of my juniors. The conversation they had with me about Powell was incidental to this."

"Why did they want to interview him?"

"They wouldn't say."

Despite the early hour, Fleming felt the sudden urge for a strong drink. He had had enough of Tomlinson and his depressing news for now.

"It's no doubt some minor matter that has nothing to do with me and the bank. Let me know what the police say about Powell, won't you? Now, I have an appointment. Goodbye." Fleming telephoned housekeeping and arranged for someone to come and clean his carpet and take his trousers to the laundry. Then he poured himself a large Balvenie.

*   *   *

Philip Arbuthnot was in his flat, busily replying to the numerous letters of sympathy he had received from his father's friends and associates. He wasn't going to the office any more. It had been agreed with Tomlinson that his days as an articled clerk were over. What point was there now in pursuing professional qualifications? His father had created a huge and successful business and Philip would shortly be taking control of it, he believed, once the tiresome legal problems had been sorted out. He had just sealed a letter to an MP, who had been a regular at his father's shoots, when he heard someone at the door. Philip went to see who it was.

Arbuthnot was confronted by two large and expressionless young men, both neatly dressed in matching chalk-striped suits, dark shirts and ties. Apart from the fact that one had a small moustache, the men looked like carbon copies of each other.

"Can I help you?"

The man with the moustache spoke. "Mr Arbuthnot?"

"Yes. I wonder, did you fellows check in with the porter? He normally announces visitors for me on the blower."

A third man appeared from further along the corridor. He was a slim and elegant man of normal height. His crisply pressed light-grey suit was accompanied by a sky-blue cravat and matching top-pocket handkerchief and cufflinks. A pair of black-and-grey spats completed the ensemble. He reminded Arbuthnot of an actor he'd seen at the theatre recently.

The man was smiling. "Forgive us, Mr Arbuthnot. The porter was tied up somewhere so we just came on up. My name is Peregrine Beecham. I was a friend of your father's. So very sorry to hear of his passing. Thought I'd pop around to give you my condolences in person. I'm off to a business meeting with these chaps in the City afterwards. Sorry to turn up in such a mob." Beecham spoke with the accent of the English upper class, although to Arbuthnot's ear there was something vaguely inauthentic about it.

"Oh, I see. Well, that's very thoughtful of you, Mr Beecham. Would you and your friends care to come in? A cup of tea perhaps?" Arbuthnot opened the door wide.

"Well, that's jolly decent of you. Not much of a tea-drinker myself nor these chaps, but a glass of water would be lovely. Thank you. The fellow on the left is Mr Carson, by the way, and the other with the moustache is Mr Miller."

"Pleased to meet you all." He led the way through to his drawing room. Beecham accepted Arbuthnot's invitation to sit but his two companions remained standing. The requested glasses of water were poured and distributed before Arbuthnot took his own seat. "Did you know my father in the City, Mr Beecham?"

"No, not the City."

Arbuthnot examined Beecham properly for the first time. Although Beecham looked smart and expensively dressed, Arbuthnot thought he could discern rough edges in the man. There were two small scars on Beecham's forehead above his right eye, and there was a suggestion of another just above the chin. Beecham's hands were rough and gnarled and did not quite seem to fit their owner. "How did you know him, then?"

"He used to spend a good deal of his leisure time with me."

"A hunting friend? No, can't be that as I used to hunt with him a lot and I'm sure we'd have met. Shooting perhaps? I didn't really do that. Or boats? Cars?"

Beecham shook his head.

"I see. Well, I give up. Perhaps you could enlighten me."

Beecham drained his glass of water and continued to smile enigmatically without replying. Arbuthnot began to feel irritated. "Well, if you…"

Beecham raised a hand. "Gambling, Mr Arbuthnot. Your father always enjoyed a good gamble, as I'm sure you know."

"Well, I didn't really."

"Your father was an inveterate gambler. I understand he took many risks to get his business empire off the ground. A great success, his business empire. Worth a lot of money, I believe. Risk can be a bit of a drug, of course. Your father just loved risk. So despite his success, your father never could shake the gambling habit."

"And you gambled with him?"

"In a manner of speaking, yes."

"What do you mean?"

"I maintain a discreet little operation that affords wealthy people like your father the opportunity to enjoy games of chance at very high stakes."

"Sorry if I'm being a little slow on the uptake. Do you mean you run some sort of gambling den?" As he asked this question, the initials in his father's mysterious note came back to him. PB. Peregrine Beecham.

The smile left Beecham's face at last. "Not a description I really care for but you may call it a 'gambling den' if you wish." Beecham spat out the unacceptable words with disgust and began to drum his fingers on the arms of his chair. Beecham's companions took a step forward, their features still impassive. To his surprise, Arbuthnot felt a twinge of fear.

"Yes, Mr Arbuthnot. Your father was a regular at our 'gambling den' over the past few years. Baccarat, *vingt-et-un*, poker and the rest. He loved them all. Sometimes he won. Sometimes he won big. Other times he lost. Other times he lost big. Unfortunately, latterly, before he disappeared off into the army, he mostly lost big."

The smile reappeared. "I understood your father to be an honourable man. For a long time, he met his losses as the house met his wins. He was a very wealthy man. We were not, I know, the only outlet for his habit, but I believe we were one of the more significant. It mattered not to me how your father met his liabilities as long as he met them.

"However, I believe his gambling habit eventually strained even his huge resources. Perhaps he had to mortgage some of his extensive property portfolio? Perhaps he had to sell some? Your father managed money for other people. Perhaps…? One can speculate on how your father met his liabilities but meet them he did until at the last he found he could not or would not."

Arbuthnot suddenly realised his hands were clasped tightly together. So tightly that the blood flow had stopped and his fingers were numb. He unclasped and shook them to restore circulation. Beecham watched, still smiling, then resumed.

"When your father signed up and disappeared into the army, he owed me a very substantial sum. Prior to his departure I had a number of meetings with him. At our final meeting, your father was, I'm afraid to say, a little drunk. He said something about certain valuable share certificates he could use to realise or raise funds and settle our account. Soon after he shipped off to the army and I heard no more.

"Your father was a very good customer. My best. He might have had temporary cash-flow problems but he still presided over a huge and thriving business, as far as I could see. I decided to be patient and await his return. I could have chosen to contact you earlier to apprise you of the situation but I held off. Simon would get back home and sort everything out amicably. That is what I told myself – foolishly as it turns out."

Beecham shook his head ruefully. "Because your father is not coming home and he is beyond settling his debt. And so I have come to you, Philip, his son and heir. Along with all the good things you will inherit, there may be the odd bad thing. This is one such and I look to you now for my money. I doubt you have yet the ready cash to pay but I can consider taking the share certificates he mentioned, once you have your hands on them. I have done some investigating. I believe I know what he was talking about. Bearer shares relating to your South American business. Inferior to cash, of course, but needs must."

"I don't know what you are talking about and, in any event, the South American businesses are owned by Sackville Bank, not by my father or the family."

Beecham's smile disappeared again. "Is that so?"

"It is."

Beecham turned and nodded at his companions before getting to his feet. "A pleasure to meet you, young man. I am glad to have had a chance to educate you about your obligations to me."

"I have no obligations to you, Beecham."

"There you are wrong. I don't care how you pay your father's debt but pay you will – with cash, property, shares or whatever. Or you will regret it. I shall contact you shortly with details of the amounts owing. Now my friends and I shall bid you good day." As he went out of the door Beecham turned his head again, briefly, to give Arbuthnot one last glimpse of that infuriating smile.

*   *   *

"Any luck, Constable?"

Bridges and Robinson had interviewed as many of Powell's neighbours as possible in the immediate aftermath of his murder on Saturday but had not gained any leads. Robinson had now just returned from Flood Street, where she had been trying to speak to any neighbours who had not been around at the weekend.

They were standing in the corridor outside Merlin's office. Bridges was carrying a pile of paperwork that his boss had finally got around to dealing with.

"Yes, Sergeant. People were seen."

Bridges nodded and led the way to the junior officers' cubby hole. He dumped Merlin's files on to the table with a grunt of relief. "I've been trying to get him to sign off on these for ages." He sat down. "All right. What have you got?"

Robinson took out her notebook. "There is an elderly couple in the first-floor flat above Mr Powell's. They went away early Saturday morning to stay the weekend with relatives in Kent. They arrived back this morning. They have a cocker spaniel called Lottie. She went missing on Friday evening. After a bit of a panic they found her in the garden of a house on Cheyne Walk where she'd got trapped."

"The gardens are behind the flats, aren't they?"

"Yes. It took Mr and Mrs Wilcox some time to find the dog. They wandered up and down Flood Street and the adjoining streets for a while."

"What sort of time was this?"

"Mrs Wilcox – she did pretty much all the talking by the way – wasn't completely sure but she thinks it was some time between eight-thirty and nine-thirty. They always walk the dog at around eight-thirty and that's when they discovered she was missing. Mrs Wilcox says she saw a number of men in the vicinity of the flats and asked them all if they'd seen her dog."

Bridges finally gave way to temptation and took a ginger nut from the biscuit tin someone had left on the table. "How many men?"

"Mrs Wilcox saw two men standing a few yards from each other at the corner of Flood Street and Royal Hospital Road opposite Rossetti Garden Mansions. She thought they might have been together although they weren't talking to one another. A third man was standing in the yard behind the block where the rubbish bins are. And there was another man further up the street, standing outside the off-licence. None of them had seen her dog."

"Did they speak when she asked about the dog?"

"No. They just shook their heads."

"How long were the various men around?"

"She couldn't say. She was in such a flap about the dog that she could think of little else. Then when they found the dog it took all their attention."

"Did the husband see the men, too?"

"He saw the two men on the corner but not the other two. He went searching in the opposite direction to his wife. Up the Royal Hospital Road."

"You say this couple are elderly. Do they have all their marbles?"

"I think so. Mrs Wilcox let drop she had been a school headmistress, only recently retired."

"Would she be able to recognise any of these men again?"

"Three of the four men were well covered up, wearing hats, collars up and so on. Apart from being able to say that none of them was small, she thought it would be difficult to provide much of a description of three of them to a sketch artist. But she'd be happy to try. She did, however, have a good view of the man by the bins because his face was lit up by light from one of the flats when a curtain was opened. He wasn't wearing a hat, apparently."

Robinson looked down to consult her notes again. "Oh yes. Mrs Wilcox also remembered that although the man by the off-licence didn't speak to her when she asked about the dog, she did think she heard him swear to himself as she walked away. Swear to himself in Spanish. Anyway, she's coming in to see the artist tomorrow morning."

"Let's hope that gives us something. Well done, Constable." Bridges got up and, with a supreme effort of will, resisted a second biscuit. "Let's go and tell the chief inspector."

*   *   *

Devlin was in position on Carlton House Terrace all morning. The previous night he had witnessed Beaulieu return to his digs, looking strained and perturbed. This had given Devlin pause for thought but, when he got up on Monday morning, he'd decided he had not changed his mind. He was going to keep to the plan he'd resolved on in the pub. Meyer was in the clear and, from now on, Devlin was going to concentrate on Beaulieu and Dumont. This was still contrary to his new orders but, bugger it, that's what he was going to do and Dumont was to be the target for Monday.

It was midday when Dumont first appeared at the door of Three Carlton Gardens. As he came out, his eyes were fixed on the pavement and Devlin could see the man was lost in thought. He confirmed this by almost walking into two pedestrians in quick succession. Devlin was not to know that Dumont was anxiously reflecting on the call he'd received earlier from Sergeant Bridges, asking him to present himself at Scotland Yard for questioning.

Devlin followed Dumont on to Lower Regent Street. Halfway up the street, Dumont suddenly turned and scanned the crowds as if checking for anyone following. Devlin was safely concealed in the shadow of a shop awning. After a moment, Dumont resumed his walk then 20 yards from Piccadilly Circus, jumped into a taxi that raced off around the boarded-up Eros and into Shaftesbury Avenue.

Devlin cursed. He quickly found his own taxi but thought he must have lost Dumont. He told his cabbie to drive up Shaftesbury Avenue and kept an eye open. He was not optimistic but his luck was in – something had caused the traffic to back up suddenly. Part of a building had collapsed into the road ahead, the driver thought. Devlin told the driver he was just getting out to look and ran 20 yards ahead. He'd noticed that the taxi Dumont picked up had a bad dent in the boot and he saw the taxi nine or 10 cars ahead of his own. He ran back, paid the driver, then got into another taxi he'd seen turning into Shaftesbury Avenue only a couple of cars behind Dumont's.

The traffic sat stationary for 10 minutes before the rubble ahead was partially cleared and cars could move again. Now he was close enough to keep in touch. Dumont's taxi turned up Charing Cross Road then went along Tottenham Court Road. Devlin's taxi followed and turned right after Dumont on to Euston Road. Eventually, Dumont's taxi pulled into Euston Station and Dumont got out. This time, Dumont gave only a cursory glance behind him. Devlin sensed he thought he was clear of any followers.

The station concourse was very crowded and Devlin initially lost Dumont again but, after a quick moment of concern, he spotted the soldier entering the main station restaurant. He dashed over and found himself a table a good distance from the one Dumont had chosen but with a relatively clear view. The Frenchman ordered a whisky. After the drink arrived, he took what looked to Devlin like a folded newspaper from his jacket pocket and set it down on the table. Strangely he did not read it.

After 10 minutes, another man in a light summer overcoat sat down opposite Dumont. The man had his back to Devlin so he couldn't see his face. Another whisky was ordered and Devlin could see the men talking. Ten more minutes and the drinks were finished. Devlin saw Dumont push the newspaper across the table. Seconds later, the other man got up, put the paper inside his coat, nodded to Dumont and turned towards the restaurant exit. Devlin caught only a brief glimpse of the man's face but it was enough for him to recognise who it was. His heart began to pound. Things were moving at last.

*   *   *

"Well done, Constable. Let me know where you get to with Mrs Wilcox. Now Mr Tomlinson, the Arbuthnot solicitor, is here and wants to see me. This might be interesting. Stay, both of you. We'll see him together."

Moments later, Reginald Tomlinson was easing his substantial posterior into one of Merlin's chairs. "Are you all right there, Mr Tomlinson? I can find a… a more comfortable chair if you like?"

"No, thank you. I'm fine."

"How can we help?"

Tomlinson loosened the buttons on his suit jacket. "As you will no doubt know, Chief Inspector, Sergeant Bridges here visited my office this morning in search of one of my juniors, Rupert Vorster. I don't yet know why." He paused and looked enquiringly at Merlin's expressionless face.

"No doubt you'll enlighten me at some point. The sergeant happened to mention the sad, very sad, demise of Mr Edgar Powell, with whom my firm had some dealings very recently. I am not sure if you have any knowledge of those dealings?"

"Assume we know nothing, Mr Tomlinson. Just tell us all you know about Mr Powell."

Tomlinson launched into a long and verbose description of Powell's approach to him and their discussion of Simon Arbuthnot's letter. At the end, he stated that it was his confident belief that Powell had resolved to pass the letter on to him.

"Are you sure he was going to do that?"

"I am. Powell seemed to be an honourable man of substance. It would be only natural for such a man to decide to give the letter to the writer's solicitor in the circumstances."

Merlin looked out of the window and thought of his friend. Was it just last Wednesday that he'd been sitting in this very chair advising Eddie to do exactly that? "I think you are right, as it happens, Mr Tomlinson. He was, as you say, a sensible fellow. The letter is now in our possession. We found it in his safe."

"Ah." Tomlinson's eyes lit up. "I presume that by now you have seen the contents of the letter. Can you share them with me? Clearly as the late Mr Arbuthnot's lawyer and executor, I should be made privy to the contents."

"The letter contains a coded message. We are trying to decipher it at the moment."

"Perhaps I could be of assistance?"

"Has Mr Arbuthnot ever corresponded with you or any of your colleagues in code?"

"Er… no. I don't recall any such communication."

"Then I think it unlikely you'll be able to help us. In any event, I'd rather keep the code breaking in-house for the moment. It is our current theory that Mr Powell was murdered by someone who wanted to get this letter. If this theory proves correct, the contents of the message must have high value. Any idea what it might be about?"

Tomlinson shook his head. "I am sorry." He shook his head again. "No idea at all."

Merlin leaned forward, steepling his hands together in front of him. "It is my understanding that Simon Arbuthnot ran a large and successful business in the City and abroad and that he was a very wealthy man."

Tomlinson's chair creaked as he shifted his position. Merlin sensed that he was uncomfortable for reasons other than the flimsiness of his seat. "Yes… yes, he was a clever man."

"You mentioned that you are his executor. Can you tell me who inherits?"

"Well, there are a few legal complications relating to his final will but the intention was always for his only son, Philip, to be the main beneficiary. There is a sister, too, of whom Simon was very fond. She was to be provided for as well."

"When you say 'legal complications' what do you mean?"

Tomlinson wondered why he had introduced this qualification to his response. Sometimes his legalistic brain ran away with his mouth. He had made a mistake and Merlin had picked up on it straightaway. Merlin repeated the question.

The solicitor resigned himself to revealing more of Arbuthnot's messy affairs than he had intended. "Before he went away, and unknown to me until last week, Arbuthnot removed the latest version of his will from my office. He said in a letter that he would send me a new one. The assumption was that there were some minor amendments he wanted to make. He was always making such amendments so there is nothing sinister about this but, after extensive searching, we have not been able to find a copy of the new will nor the one he removed."

Merlin raised an eyebrow. "So you don't have the will. If not found, everything would go to the son on intestacy, wouldn't it?"

"It would."

"Perhaps Arbuthnot's message is something to do with the will?"

"Possibly."

"Mr Tomlinson, your dead client was in control of a very large fortune. People have murdered for far less than I'm guessing he was worth. Can you think of anyone who might be capable of murder to acquire a letter that might affect the disposition of such a fortune?"

"No, of course not!"

"I would ask you to think on it, Mr Tomlinson. Think on it carefully, please."

*   *   *

"Someone to see you, Colonel." The commandant stood at the door, his demeanour suggesting he had again lunched well. "It's Beaulieu. He has an interesting story to tell."

The lieutenant, also looking well lunched, appeared from behind Angers, hand raised in salute. The colonel gave no indication of his surprise but simply set down the file he was reading and gave Beaulieu a curt nod. "What story?"

The commandant walked over to Aubertin's desk and leaned in close to whisper in the colonel's ear. "We were wrong about this fellow. He's no spy. You should listen to the story he has to tell. I had to give him a few drinks to loosen his tongue but he is telling the truth, I'm sure."

Recoiling from Angers' stinking brandy breath, Aubertin pulled his chair back. He looked hard at Beaulieu. "Very well. I'll listen. Sit, Lieutenant."

Beaulieu took a chair at the desk while Angers slumped into one of the armchairs behind. The lieutenant looked uncomfortable. His hand plucked nervously at his moustache.

"Come now, Beaulieu, no need to be shy. You've been on leave, haven't you?"

"I took a few days leave with the permission of my superiors at Carlton Gardens. I had not had any leave since I arrived in England."

"A well deserved break, I am sure. I have heard how diligent and hard-working you are. You had a pleasant time, I trust?"

"Yes and no. Do you recall the name de Metz?"

"De Metz? The man the police were enquiring about?"

"Yes, sir."

"What about him?"

"I'm not sure how much you know about him."

"I have been told the basic details about his unfortunate circumstances and his death."

"De Metz came to Carlton Gardens seeking financial help. He made noises about having important and valuable intelligence information. The consensus view at Carlton Gardens was that the man was desperately casting around for some sort of currency to use with us. Because he had been an eminent man in Paris before the war and could no doubt drop some big names, he thought he could make something up to his advantage. He didn't have any real information. That was the view taken and he was sent packing."

The colonel nodded. "Quite correctly."

"Last Wednesday, I took my leave and went up to Oxford to see an old English friend of my family. He is a professor of medieval history at Wadham College, specialising in French history of the 13th and 14th centuries. He used to stay with my family at our summer house near Avignon before the war. He entertained me royally until Friday, when I was planning to return to London.

"I was at the Oxford railway station at seven in the evening, waiting for my train, when two men came up to me and insisted that I accompany them. They showed me what looked like police identity cards and it was made clear that I had little choice. I was bundled into a car and driven out of town and into the country. It was not a long journey and soon we were travelling up a long drive towards an immense house, which I later learned to be Blenheim Palace, the estate of the Duke of Marlborough."

A flash of anger crossed the colonel's face. He knew MI5 had teams operating out of Blenheim Palace. "Lieutenant, are you telling me you were kidnapped by the British security services? This is an outrage. I shall make protests at the highest levels."

"Thank you, sir, but I don't think that will be necessary." Beaulieu paused to allow Aubertin's anger to subside. "To continue, they kept me there until Sunday morning. I dined well, was given a comfortable room and could walk the grounds, albeit under supervision."

"And the purpose of this incarceration?"

"They wanted to talk about de Metz. They had apparently interviewed him themselves and had reached the same conclusion as us – that his claims to possession of valuable information were spurious and designed only to get money. However, now that he had been murdered they were beginning to worry that they might have got him wrong. They questioned me to see if I could add to their knowledge of de Metz and, on a broader level, to see what I knew of intelligence leaks in Carlton Gardens."

Angers allowed himself an ironic smile, given Beaulieu's status as Aubertin's principal suspect.

"During their questioning, they told me that they had just received information about an SOE agent in France having been compromised. I presumed them to mean by this that the agent had been arrested or killed. We went over everything a second time but I had nothing to tell them that they didn't know. Except about the photograph. De Metz had an old picture of two young men, one in some sort of cadet uniform. Two girls as well, I think. Taken in a sunny garden. Somewhere in France."

"And what of this photograph?"

"I told them that de Metz had shown it to us, saying it was very important. He said he could have someone by the balls with it. The British seemed to find this very interesting although I said that we had thought this claim as spurious as the others."

"And then?"

"They gave me a good dinner on the Saturday night – well, as good a dinner as you can expect from Englishmen – and I came back to London on the morning train."

"They didn't ask you to keep their inquiries to yourself?"

"No. In fact they encouraged me to discuss this with my colleagues on my return. Said it might – what was their phrase? – put the cat among the pigeons."

Aubertin scratched his cheek. "Well, thank you for telling me about this unpleasant experience. Are you sure you wouldn't like me to complain? No? Very well. I'm not sure there is anything more to be done. We must all take note and be on our guard against our English hosts, I think. Eh, Commandant?"

"Indeed, sir."

"You'd better get back to Carlton Gardens, Beaulieu. And thank you."

The lieutenant left and Aubertin went over to sit by Angers. He could see that the commandant's eyelids were beginning to droop and so he shook him by the shoulder. "Wake up, Auguste."

Angers sat up and rubbed his eyes. "Sorry, Colonel. A heavy lunch but all in a good cause, eh? Shall I call off the pursuit of Beaulieu now?"

"On the contrary, Auguste. I presume Beaulieu volunteered this information directly to you?"

"Yes, he rang me this morning to suggest lunch."

Aubertin put a finger to his mouth and looked thoughtful. "This episode does nothing to release Beaulieu from suspicion. Whether true or not…"

"Surely you don't think he made it up?"

"Whether true or not, it is really just the equivalent of having dust thrown in our eyes. MI5 can't know anything about our suspicions. If they picked him up, they just identified him as one of the officers to whom de Metz had spoken. You must keep the Irishman on him exclusively. You have already arranged that, haven't you?"

"I left him a message, yes. At the weekend."

"And he understood clearly. That he's not to follow the others?"

"My message was clear. Concentrate on Beaulieu alone."

"When is the next meeting?"

"Rougemont's seeing him tomorrow."

"You see him. I am sending Rougemont on an errand today. He'll be away for a couple of days. You must meet yourself with Harp or whatever it is we call him. Make sure he understands. All right?" Aubertin could see Angers' eyelids beginning to droop again. "And for God's sake, go and get some fresh air!"

*   *   *

"Hello, Aunt. Why didn't you let me know you were coming? Come on in."

Lucinda Cavendish entered her nephew's flat, handbag in one hand and a small valise in the other.

"Cup of tea?"

His aunt started to unbutton her overcoat. "Yes please, Philip. I don't know why I wore this damned thing. It's boiling outside. That idiot butler of mine said he'd read that it was going to rain in London. Why I listen to him, I don't know. He's usually wrong about everything." As she hung her coat on a peg by the door, she realised that Philip was already in the kitchen and probably couldn't hear a word she was saying. She went into the drawing room and flopped wearily into an armchair. Philip appeared with her tea.

"I'm sorry to turn up unannounced like this, dear. I did ring for you at the office but they said you weren't there. I rang here twice but there was no answer."

"Sorry, Aunt. Must have been out on my constitutional in the park."

"Anyway, I decided to get on the train in the hope that I'd find you in when I got here, and luckily you are. As you can see, I have brought a case with me. Do you mind awfully if I stay here tonight?"

"Not at all, Aunt. Stay a few days if you like. You could probably do with a change of scene. If you don't mind my saying, you look a little overwrought. Not surprising in the circumstances but…"

"Your father's death will take some getting over, of course, Philip, but there is something else that is worrying me." Lucinda Cavendish took the letter out of her bag. "A good deal of correspondence for your father comes to the hall. As you can imagine, quite a pile has built up over the past months. On Saturday, I steeled myself to go through it all. In among it all I found this. It gave me a shock."

Philip picked up the letter from the bank and read. His eyes widened. "Well, I'll be damned. So he mortgaged the hall. That bugger, Beecham!" He threw the letter down in disgust.

His aunt appraised Philip shrewdly. "My dear boy, I sense that the mortgaging of the hall is not as much a surprise to you as it is to me. Who is Beecham and what on earth was your father up to?"

Philip closed his eyes in thought. Should he really burden his aunt with what he had learned? He opened his eyes and saw the strength in her face. Lucinda had always been a rock to his father and to him. And she was the only family he had left in the world. He looked up at the ceiling. Then he began to tell her.

*   *   *

There were far too many question marks on the case summaries Merlin had just scribbled on his notepad. He went over them again.

Case 1 – Bridget Healy (Republican rebel, good-time girl?).

Found dead – Thursday 5 June at Bedford Hotel, Fitzrovia.

Cause of death – complications from botched abortion.

Abortionist – Armand de Metz, former French surgeon – refugee in England, fallen on hard times. Also dead.

Baby's father – ?

Case 2 – Armand de Metz (abortionist as above).

Found dead – Saturday 7 June at his rented Notting Hill flat.

Cause of death – bullets to head.

Murderer – ?

Suspects – ?

Motive – something to do with abortion work?

Revenge of father or another for botched abortion?

Possession of damaging intelligence about Free French?

Other?

Case 3 – Edgar Powell (soldier).

Found dead – Saturday 14 June at his Flood Street flat.

Cause of death – drowned in bath.

Murderer – ?

Suspects – men seen by Mrs Wilcox?

Others with motive?

Motive – to acquire encoded letter of Mr Simon Arbuthnot?

Other?

He popped another lozenge into his mouth as he picked up his pencil and added to his list.

Case 4 – Simon Arbuthnot (wealthy businessman).

Cause of death – killed by Germans in Cretan retreat.

Crime – link to death of Powell.

Why his letter so valuable/desirable?

Arbuthnot's business and life in London?

As he sat back, wondering whether he could usefully add any more to the memorandum, the telephone rang.

"Hello, Frank. Harold here. Got a moment?"

"Of course, Harold. Do you want to meet?"

"I think we can risk the telephone for once. I received some information regarding the gentleman we were discussing the other day. I was wondering whether you found any photographs in among his belongings?"

Merlin paused a second to recall the items they had found in de Metz's flat. "Yes, there was a photograph. An old photograph of two young men, and two young women.."

"Do you think we could have a look at it?"

"Of course. Do you want me to bring it to you?"

"No. I'll send a messenger round. Just pop it in an envelope marked for my attention. I'll have someone at Scotland Yard within the hour if that's convenient."

"I'll have it ready."

*   *   *

Bernie Goldberg spent his morning at the American Embassy sorting out the details of his return journey to the States. As always with government arrangements, an inordinate amount of paperwork was required. After all was arranged, he made his way out into Grosvenor Square and then on to Brook Street. He got to Claridge's 10 minutes late for his lunch.

Goldberg's new friend spotted him and waved him into the cocktail bar, where he had taken two seats at the counter.

"Sorry to be late."

"Think nothing of it, Detective. I know you're a busy guy. That's why I thought it best to grab a place at the bar. If you're pressed for time, we can have a sandwich here. And a drink or two, of course."

"That would be perfect, Ed." Goldberg's lunch companion was Ed Murrow, head of news operations for the American radio network CBS in London. Murrow had become a well known and influential reporter in the United States thanks to his vivid and poetic descriptions of the Blitz and British courage under the German bombs. In the tradition of a long line of war correspondents, he was a chain smoker and hard drinker. Goldberg found him engaging and intelligent company.

"They mix a good Martini here, Bernie."

"I'd prefer a beer."

"One of those foul, warm English beers?"

"Sure. I've developed a taste for them."

"If you're sure. Ham-and-cheese sandwich do you?"

Goldberg nodded and Murrow ordered. "At least in Claridge's we know we're getting real ham and cheese rather than some disgusting substitute. So tell me, how are you finding wartime London?" Murrow stubbed out his cigarette and lit another. Goldberg had yet to see Murrow without a cigarette in hand.

"I've enjoyed my time very much. Got involved in some interesting police work and been well looked after by my friend at the Yard."

"Ah yes, your friend at the Yard. What was his name again?"

"Frank Merlin."

"Merlin, that's it. Fine name. You know I'm always on the lookout for new angles in my broadcasts. After our conversation the other day, I was thinking that a London policeman would be a great subject. You know – life goes on, notwithstanding the war and the Blitz. Criminals still commit crimes, new wartime crimes emerge, the valiant policemen battle on, etcetera, etcetera. And this one has the name of a wizard. Great copy!"

The drinks arrived and the two men clinked glasses. "Merlin would certainly make a great story, Ed, but I doubt he'd welcome the publicity."

"The modest type, eh? Still, perhaps you could effect an introduction."

"I'll try but he's very busy at the moment. Three heavy cases on the go."

Murrow drew on his cigarette. "When you can, Bernie. Perhaps in a week or two?"

"I've got to go back home at the end of the week but I'll mention you to him before I go. I've got to return for a new assignment in New York."

"That's a pity. There ain't that many companionable Yanks around for me to chew the fat with."

"Anything happening today in the great outside world?"

Murrow expelled small jets of smoke through his nostrils. "Mr Churchill is going to make a broadcast to the States tonight. In response to his being granted an honorary degree by the University of Rochester. Apparently his mother was born in Rochester and his grandfather ran one of the local newspapers. I got hold of an advance copy of what he's planning to say. Good stuff as always."

Murrow produced a sheet of paper. "Here's some – I won't attempt the voice – 'For more than a year, we British have stood alone, uplifted by your sympathy and respect and sustained by our own unconquerable willpower and by the increasing growth and hopes of your massive aid. In these British Islands that look so small upon the map we stand, the faithful guardians of the rights and dearest hopes of a dozen States and nations now gripped and tormented in a base and cruel servitude. Whatever happens we shall endure to the end'. Good stuff, huh?"

"It is. What chance of us Yanks getting more involved, do you think?"

"Involved in the war, do you mean? I am confident that Roosevelt will get us into the war somehow, despite the best efforts of the isolationists. When I think how much I admired Lindbergh for his flying feats in the 20s and for his courage when that poor child was kidnapped." Murrow's voice rose, attracting the attention of some of the other customers.

"The man's a Jew hater, Bernie. Remember all that cozying up to Hitler before the war? In a few days, he's making yet another big speech against intervention in Europe. This one's in Los Angeles. The guy makes my blood boil. Him, Henry Ford and all those other damned America Firsters."

"Roosevelt has their measure."

"Yeah, he does. Here's to the president!" He turned to toast the room then ordered another round of drinks. The sandwiches arrived and Murrow opened one to check the contents. "It's OK, Bernie. The real thing. You're OK with the ham?"

"My kosher father would have a fit if he knew, but I'll eat anything." He took a bite. "Any news about what's happening in Syria? Merlin and I have had reason to be dealing with some Free French people in London."

"Last I heard the Nazis were sending aircraft to help the defending forces. A few British destroyers got hit. It's all a terrible mess, Bernie. France, I mean. Those guys in Vichy are a pretty dire bunch."

"You said you found de Gaulle a little prickly when you interviewed him?"

"I did. He's very hard work. However, although he's not very popular with Churchill and his generals, I've got some time for the man. It takes some guts, in these dark days for France, to make oneself the rallying point for opposition to Vichy and the Nazi occupiers. He may be prickly and arrogant but those are the attributes he needs for the job. Things are not going to be easy for him but he's a symbol of hope to his countrymen. Good luck to him is what I say." He gulped some more Martini.

Their conversation turned to sports teams back in the States, the London theatre and, finally, the Royal Family. Murrow had met the King and Queen and was highly complimentary. He was clearly intent on several more drinks but, after an hour, Goldberg knew he had to call it a day. He got to his feet. "Great sandwiches, drinks and company, Ed. Sorry, but I'll have to get back to Scotland Yard now. Please let me pay."

"Don't be silly, Detective. I have a huge expense account. I'm sorry you have to leave so soon. Perhaps we can do this one more time before you go back." The two men shook hands and parted. As Goldberg went out of the bar, he could hear Murrow ordering his fifth Martini.

*   *   *

"The constable's brother is on the line, sir."

"Good, Sergeant. Put him through. Did the messenger pick up the photograph?"

"He did, sir. An hour ago at two."

"Good." Merlin settled himself at his desk. "Hello, Mr Robinson. Thanks for getting back to me so quickly."

"I just thought I'd let you know where I've got to with this code. I have made a little progress. After looking at the principal options, my best guess is that the message is formulated from a book cipher."

"I remember that from the little research I managed to do. Can you remind me exactly how a book cipher works?"

"The person sending the message uses a specific book known to the recipient as the key for his code. In this instance we find the first three numbers are 2, 4 and 1. The second two numbers are 2 and 0. The commonest sort of book code would mean that these numbers are pointing the recipient to a page number and a line number. In this case, the options would be to go to page 2, line 4, or page 2, line 41, or page 24, line 1 and so on."

"And what do the other numbers refer to?"

"Letters in the line or lines commencing with the line referenced. Quite simple if…"

"Simple if you know the book."

"Well, yes. Please remind me. Do we know who was the intended recipient of the message?"

"Unfortunately it's not clear. The main candidates are the sender's solicitor, son or sister. The most recent thinking favoured the solicitor but he has just disclaimed knowledge of any use of codes by his client. He might have been lying, of course."

There was a brief silence at the other end of the line before Robinson spoke again. "I suggest, Chief Inspector, that you speak to the sister and the son to see if one of them can remember if Simon Arbuthnot had a favourite book."

*   *   *

Rupert Vorster was sitting in pensive mood on a bench overlooking the Great Pond in Kensington Gardens. He had a handful of gravel and was idly tossing the stones towards the water. It had been a bad day. It had begun with his waking to find he had a bad water leak in his bathroom. He couldn't leave the place like that so he'd telephoned to cancel his meeting in Birmingham. This was not very popular with the client, who would no doubt complain to Tomlinson or his other superiors. He had had a hell of a time finding a plumber to come to Battersea. Plumbers were in great demand in Blitz-damaged London and it had been late afternoon when Vorster had finally got one to visit the flat.

He had rung Tomlinson's secretary at five o'clock to explain what had happened and to say that he would get in early for the next few days to make up the lost time. Vorster's day had then got even worse when the secretary told him the police had visited and wanted to speak to him. Heart in his throat, he'd slammed down the telephone and hurried out in search of fresh air and somewhere to think.

Vorster wasn't really looking where he was throwing the stones and one accidentally hit a swan. The bird reared up menacingly, made a loud hissing noise and started moving in his direction. In the distance, 50 yards behind the swan, Vorster could see a park warden hurrying in his direction. He didn't need any more trouble today. He dropped the stones and immediately bolted off towards Kensington Palace, running as fast as he could, and then on until he reached one of the gates on to Kensington High Street. He crossed the road then suddenly burst into a fit of nervous laughter.

After recovering his breath, the young man rallied. Vorster realised the visit to the pond had served its purpose. He had had time to think. He had pulled himself together. Optimism resurfaced. Making up the hours at the office was a trifling thing and, as to the police, so what if they wanted to talk to him? Let them ask their questions. He had not left any trace of his actions. He was sure he could handle some stupid English coppers. There was no reason to get into a panic.

Vorster walked off down Kensington High Street and went into a tea room opposite the Tube station, where he bought himself a bun and a cup of tea. He briefly considered whether he should have an early night for once but swiftly rejected the idea. Vorster would continue with his usual evening routine at the Ritz and then, hopefully with some new customers in tow, at Beecham's. He had hoped to make headway into Beecham's good books by giving him something he very much wanted. Things had not worked out. So be it. Perhaps he would get another chance. Perhaps when he got back to the office there might be further developments he could discover? Perhaps Philip would be back in the office with news?

Now feeling back on top of his game, Vorster stepped out on to the pavement. The sun was shining and Kensington High Street was full of pretty girls. He walked off with a cheerful smile on his face.

*   *   *

"Sorry, Frank. I got tied up at the Embassy doing paperwork then I had lunch with a compatriot. I was also worried whether it was safe to come in. You know, with Vorster and Dumont."

"Perfectly safe, Bernie. We haven't been able to get hold of either of them." Merlin was at his desk staring yet again at Arbuthnot's code. "On other fronts, Robinson found a witness who saw some men loitering around near Eddie Powell's flat on Friday night. The witness is seeing the police artist tomorrow. Also, we have an idea of what sort of code Arbuthnot used in his message. We'll need a chat with his family. And Arbuthnot's solicitor was in here earlier as well."

"What did he want?"

"The message, of course, but he did provide some interesting background information. Apparently, Simon Arbuthnot didn't leave his affairs in very good order. He took away his will and a new one hasn't been found. Also, although Tomlinson wasn't really forthcoming about his business affairs, I sensed from his awkward and nervy manner that all may not have been well with the Arbuthnot empire."

Goldberg wandered over to the open window. "Not much breeze today. It's the first time since I've been here that the London summer weather feels like New York's. Hot and humid."

Bridges entered with a jug of water.

Goldberg laughed. "Perfect timing, Sergeant." Bridges poured out three glasses. "So what happened with Vorster and Dumont?"

"Vorster is out of town, Detective, and Dumont didn't respond to our polite request this morning and has not been at Carlton Gardens since lunchtime."

"Bet you they'll be in the Ritz tonight."

Merlin leaned back in his chair and looked thoughtfully at the American. "Would you be up for a repeat performance of Friday night? Assuming they are there. Your cover isn't blown. Perhaps you'll still find it possible to get more out of those two over a drink than we'll be able to in a formal interview. What do you think, Sergeant?"

"Might be worth it. They are bound to be a little on edge now, knowing that we want to speak to them. Perhaps nerves combined with drink will loosen their tongues."

"If we proceed, I think, to avoid unnecessary suspicion you ought to have some stake money on you. What do you think is a credible amount?"

"Some of those guys were playing for very high stakes. Some had cash, some obviously had credit. I suppose I'd look just about credible with £50. I've got some travellers cheques. Not sure how much, but I could..."

Merlin shook his head. "There's no question of you using your own money, Bernie. I'll speak to the AC. It's a lot of money but I'm sure he'll go along." He rapped the desk with his knuckles. "All right, let's do it. I suggest, Detective, that you go and have a nap as you're likely to have another late night." Merlin stood up. "You and I, Sergeant, are going to see Philip Arbuthnot. I have his address in Mayfair. We'll give him the once-over and see what he knows of his father's reading habits."

*   *   *

New York

"I can't hear what you are saying, Felix. The line is terrible. Please speak up." Anton Meyer's difficulty in hearing his brother on a poor transatlantic line was exacerbated by the noise of blaring car horns outside. He looked out of his apartment window and saw that a reversing truck was blocking the traffic on Broadway. He closed the window and tugged the telephone as far away as he could from the din. "Sorry, can you say that again?"

The line suddenly improved and Anton could hear his brother's sigh of irritation at the other end. "I said I went to the bank and confronted them all. I went over the whole sorry story – how Arbuthnot volunteered to take the bearer certificates for father's South American holding company into temporary safekeeping, when the Nazi authorities began to take an interest in the Meyer businesses; how, after father's escape to France, he asked for the return of the certificates and Arbuthnot wouldn't give them back; how Arbuthnot sent Pulos to Argentina with the bearer certificates to establish his ownership of our businesses there and how Pulos procured, with the help of a few bribes here and there, court approval of that ownership."

"So you reminded them of everything?"

"Yes, everything. How our father became bitter and died in poverty in Paris. Mother too. I told them how Arbuthnot stole the Meyer South American empire from the man who was supposed to be his best friend. That the fancy bank they were running was inextricably linked to a major fraud and that Arbuthnot had as good as murdered our parents."

"And what did they say?"

"Pulos smirked at me and said I was speaking rubbish. Said that Father had pledged the shares as security for loans Arbuthnot made to him…"

Anton waved his free hand in anger and sent a lamp flying.

"What was that?"

"Nothing. Carry on."

"Well, you know his line. Arbuthnot lent Father some money…"

"A few thousand dollars, nothing much."

"Yes, well, money was lent, the shares were security, the money was never repaid, the shares were foreclosed on."

"That's a complete lie. The loan and the shares were never linked and, in any event, Arbuthnot waived settlement of the debt."

"This is me, Anton. I know the story."

"What did the others have to say?"

"The pompous lawyer rolled out some legalistic jargon. 'The bank's ownership rights must be recognised in priority, etcetera, etcetera.'"

"Fleming?"

"Kept a poker face. Said nothing."

"Did you ask them where the certificates were?"

"They said they were in the bank's safekeeping."

Anton sat down wearily on one of the two threadbare sofas that furnished his drab living room. "So you made our case and they did not respond?"

"Yes, Anton."

"Well, I wasn't so keen on your seeing them, Felix, but now you have I'm glad, even if it didn't achieve much. Anything else?"

"Before I left I said that our case in Argentina would continue and that we would publicise the facts of the case in England. They didn't like that, of course."

"Can we publicise it? Do you know people in London who can help us do that?"

"Frankly, no, Anton. I don't know any City people and I don't know any journalists. Sackville is a respected City institution. I am a serving Free French officer but we are not much liked and have little influence. I was making an empty threat."

"So I just carry on with the legal action in Argentina?"

"Perhaps there will be more new developments here now that Arbuthnot is dead. As you know, I was against your persisting with the case but now I've seen these people I think you should. I just hope your wife doesn't leave you because of it."

"Is there any prospect of getting any further with Arbuthnot's family? There is a sister and a son."

"Perhaps. Look, Anton, I have to get going. I am on duty now and there is a lot of work to get done. There is information from Syria that I need to assess."

Anton looked at his watch. "I have to get going, too, or I'll be in trouble." He had used the lunch break to hurry home for his brother's call. "Thank you, Felix. I am happy that you now approve of what I am doing. It is easier to bear the burden together."

*   *   *

London

Philip Arbuthnot's internal telephone line rang. He heard the porter tell him, in that deep bass voice that always reminded him of the American actor Paul Robeson: "A couple of policemen here to see you, sir."

Arbuthnot looked over at his aunt, who was sitting by the window, engrossed in the *Times* crossword. "Better send them up, Morris."

He went over and gently shook his aunt's shoulder. "The police are here to see me." Earlier in the day, he had told Lucinda about his father's gambling problems, Beecham's visit and the mysterious letter that had been brought back from Crete. His aunt's immediate reaction had been to tell him to go straight to the police.

Arbuthnot had thought Lucinda would be wary of public exposure and protective of her brother's reputation but her response had been firm. "He is dead, you are alive. If crooks are threatening you, get the police to deal with them."

He had said he'd rather not do that until he'd discussed things with Tomlinson and Fleming. Aunt and nephew had agreed to disagree. She had gone out shopping and he had read a P.G. Wodehouse book to take his mind off things.

Five minutes later, Arbuthnot and his aunt were sitting around the coffee table in the drawing room with Merlin and Bridges. "I am sorry to bother you, Mr Arbuthnot, at this difficult time but we are dealing with a murder that may somehow be connected with your father."

Arbuthnot looked confused. "My father is dead, Chief Inspector. How can he be connected with a murder?"

"Have you heard of a man called Edgar Powell?"

"Yes. A fellow officer of Father's in Crete. I understand he brought some message from him and discussed handing it to our solicitor. I was telling my aunt about it earlier."

Lucinda Cavendish straightened in her chair. "I thought it strange that Mr Powell didn't contact Philip or myself. I would have thought we were the most appropriate people to take delivery of the letter."

"You may be right, Mrs Cavendish. I can only tell you that Mr Powell agonised about who should get the letter and ultimately resolved, we believe, to pass it to Mr Tomlinson. He wasn't, however, able to do so. Have you spoken to Mr Tomlinson today, sir?"

"No. I rang the office a couple of times but he was out."

"I see. Then you don't know about Mr Powell?"

"What about him?"

"He was found dead over the weekend. Drowned in his bath. We think he may have been murdered for the letter."

Nephew and aunt exchanged shocked glances. "Well, that's very… that's… that's terrible." Arbuthnot paused to think.

"However, I find it hard to imagine what sort of message from my father could provoke a murder. Was the letter taken by the murderer?"

"No. We have it. There is a difficulty, however. It is in code." Merlin took the message out of his jacket pocket and gave it to Arbuthnot.

Arbuthnot looked at it carefully.

"Any idea as to what it could mean?"

Philip looked blankly back. "It's just a jumble of numbers. I have no idea at all. Aunt?" He passed it on.

Mrs Cavendish took off her glasses and held it close.

Merlin leaned forward. "Our initial expert advice is that this might be some kind of book cipher. Do you remember your father having any particular interest in codes, sir?"

"No. He never discussed the subject with me as far as I can recall."

"Mrs Cavendish?"

Lucinda Cavendish returned the message to the chief inspector and briefly looked off into the distance before responding. "I believe I can say, with some certainty, Mr Merlin, that this message was intended to come to me." She smiled. "It was during the war, when we were in our teens – 1915, perhaps 1916. There was all sorts of talk about German spies. Simon read a book by John Buchan, *The 39 Steps*."

"The one they made a film of, ma'am, starring Robert Donat?"

"I don't go to the pictures much, Sergeant, but yes, I did read that there was a moving picture made. So he read that book, then some other similar stories. Simon loved tales of espionage and became particularly fascinated by secret languages. He got hold of a cipher book and was soon making up coded messages, which I was required to decipher. He made me learn how to encode messages, too, for him to decipher. I quite enjoyed it. I have always had a good mathematical brain and I like puzzles and crosswords." She pointed at the completed crossword in the newspaper in her lap. "He tried all types of code but the book cipher was his favourite."

Merlin could feel his pulse accelerating. "Did he have any favourite books for code making?"

"He did. Books by John Buchan. The one I mentioned, *The 39 Steps*, and its sequel, *Greenmantle*."

"If you were the intended recipient of this message, your brother would have to assume you knew which book to go to. Which book?"

"*Greenmantle* was his favourite. He was always rereading it. I saw him with it as recently as last year. One of the main characters is called Sandy Arbuthnot. Not surprisingly, he identified with him. A very aristocratic hero, who was a friend of Buchan's protagonist, Richard Hannay. I believe Simon saw him as something of a role model."

"Presumably the sender and recipient have to work from the same edition. If he had the source copy with him in Crete, do you have a matching edition?"

Lucinda thought for a moment. "Our father was quite impressed by our code-making efforts. He thought we should each have copies of the books we were using. So, yes, I should have my edition of *Greenmantle* somewhere at home."

"And home is where, ma'am?"

"Sackville Hall in Northamptonshire, Sergeant. Would you like me to go and bring it back for you?"

"Do you mind if we come up to you?"

"Not at all. I shall be returning tomorrow morning on the first train."

"Tomorrow around 12.30 then, if that's convenient?"

"That would be convenient." Merlin and Bridges stood up. "But please don't leave yet, Chief Inspector. Philip, I believe there is something else you'd like to discuss with Mr Merlin?"

A pink flush appeared on her nephew's cheeks. "No, Aunt, we haven't yet finished discussing that. I'd like to talk to the others and…"

"For goodness sake, Philip, spit it out. It's for the best."

Merlin settled back in his seat, bemused. "And what exactly is for the best, sir?"

*   *   *

Bridges pulled sharply over to the kerb as two fire engines raced past him on Berkeley Square. Although the raids had stopped for the moment, the fire and rescue services still had mountains of work. There were unexploded bombs everywhere, damaged buildings in need of shoring up or demolition, and broken gas and water pipes and other utilities requiring continuous attention.

"I think I'll call off those plans for tonight."

"Sir?"

Merlin rolled down the car window. "Now we know that this dangerous fellow Beecham has a part to play, it might be wise to hold off and be a little more – what's the word? – circumspect."

The fire engines disappeared in the direction of Oxford Street and Bridges engaged gears and pulled away. "I've never really understood what that word means, sir."

"We need to pause for thought. We are pursuing Vorster and Dumont to see if they can give us more on Bridget Healey. If they turn up tonight and do as before we shall be exposing Goldberg to unnecessary danger. I don't want him going to a club run by a man who is making violent threats. And these links with Simon Arbuthnot. Eddie Powell got himself killed running an errand for him. There are connections here that we don't understand but that should make us very wary. In the circumstances, it's too dangerous to send Goldberg in."

There was another traffic hold-up on the other side of Bond Street, which Bridges tried to avoid by turning into Bruton Street.

"Arbuthnot says Beecham seemed a very hard nut. That's not surprising, given the business he's in, but we need to be very careful and find out more about him. I think we should revert to the original plan and go ahead and pull Vorster and Dumont in as soon as we can. Goldberg will be disappointed but better that than he ends up in trouble a few days before he goes home."

"Fair enough, sir." They were now in New Bond Street, which was also congested, and Bridges turned left on to Burlington Gardens to cut through to Regent Street. They passed the Burlington Arcade, where they had been involved in a shoot-out nine months before. Merlin remembered everything very clearly. Things had been too close for comfort that night. Constable Tommy Cole had been the one unlucky enough to take a bullet. Merlin and Bridges could have very easily been shot as well.

Bridges was obviously thinking about that night, too. "I had a letter from Tommy yesterday. Said he thought he might be sent back from Southampton in a week or two."

Merlin smiled. "Good! Let's hope so. Now put your foot down, Sam. The road is clear."

*   *   *

Vorster was watching a game of *vingt-et-un*. Beecham's place was not at its busiest but that was only to be expected on a Monday night. There were groans as a couple of the players got cleaned out by the bank for the fifth time in succession. Vorster decided to watch another game and was walking over to one of the poker tables when he felt a hand on his shoulder. It was one of Beecham's waiters. Vorster followed him, as requested, to the study at the back where Beecham did his business.

His host was counting a wad of cash, a cigar in his mouth and a large glass of brandy on the desk in front of him. He looked up with that supercilious smile of his and tidied the cash away in a drawer.

"Rupert, my dear chap! There you are. Can I interest you in some brandy? Yes? Pour Mr Vorster a glass before you leave us, Reynolds."

Beecham was wearing, as he usually did, an ordinary suit, this evening a brown worsted. Vorster had once heard Beecham's reply to a drunken customer who had complained that he was not wearing black tie. "But if I did that, my dear Sir Malcolm, you and your guests would regard me as a *maître d'* and I wouldn't care for that."

"So, take the weight off, as my old pa used to say." Rupert sat down and tasted his brandy.

"Not bad, is it? I got several bottles in part settlement of a debt. The Earl of… I forget where. Somewhere in the far-flung bogs of Ireland. It's a cognac from the 1900s, bottled some time in the 1920s. Produced by Gautier Frères, who have been distilling this golden nectar for several centuries."

Vorster took another sip. "It's wonderful, Peregrine."

"So where is your American friend tonight? The one who came on Friday. I thought he'd told you he'd be around for a while."

"No sign of him at the Ritz tonight, I'm afraid. I thought he might have come directly here but obviously not. He'll be back another night, I bet."

"Don't bet anything, Rupert. It's not your forte, remember? Anyway, let's hope you're right. No other likely suckers tonight?" Beecham swirled the brandy around in his glass before trickling some into his mouth.

"No, sorry."

"Hmm."

Vorster turned away from Beecham's penetrating glare. "Any more news about Arbuthnot?"

"No, Peregrine."

"So the situation is as you said last week. The certificates are missing. This friend of Arbuthnot's – Powell, you said his name was – has some important document or documents in his possession. Entrusted to him by Arbuthnot as he lay dying."

"Yes. I wasn't in the office today so I have no more information. I don't know whether Powell gave what he had to Tomlinson. I…" There was some sort of racket outside. They heard raised voices.

"An unlucky customer, I presume." Beecham gave Vorster a lizard-like smile. The commotion, whatever it was, swiftly subsided.

"I think…"

Beecham put a finger to his lips and Vorster fell silent. "I, unlike you, Rupert, have not been idle. I have some new information. I made a point of finding out Powell's address."

"Actually, Peregrine, so did I."

"Did you now? And are you aware that Powell's place was swarming with policemen on Saturday?"

"Oh?"

"Powell is dead. After you told me about this last week, I was wondering about what Powell had. The certificates? Probably not. It would be very odd of him to have carried those into battle with him. A message about their whereabouts? Much more likely. In any event, we are not going to get hold of anything now. The letter is most likely in the hands of the police." Beecham topped up his brandy.

"You know, Rupert, I have been looking to you for a little creativity in helping me sort out this quandary. Arbuthnot has died, owing me a very large sum. Somehow or other, the debt must be settled. I don't have to remind you that your own debt to me, while not in the same league as Arbuthnot's, is still quite substantial."

"Of course, Peregrine, I have tried. I've…"

"I have been patient. I have avoided causing you embarrassment. I have not approached your father. I have allowed you to work off some of your debt by the provision of services. I like you, Rupert, I really do. But you'd best keep on the right side of me."

"Of course, Peregrine. I am at your full disposal." Vorster lit a cigarette with a shaking hand and avoided Beecham's eye.

Beecham drew on his cigar. "I suggest you make sure you are in your office tomorrow. Keep your ears to the ground. Report any new developments to me immediately. Is that understood?"

"Yes, Peregrine."

Chapter 13

Tuesday 17 June

London

"I don't care about Dumont and who he's seeing, Mr Harp. I thought it would have been clear from my note that you were only to concentrate your efforts on Beaulieu from Sunday onwards. If the colonel knew you had still been following Dumont or Meyer…"

"I have dropped Meyer, Commandant. He is in the clear as far as I am concerned."

"Good, but Aubertin insists that we come up with the goods on Beaulieu. He is convinced that Beaulieu is the leak."

"But Aubertin…"

"Aubertin wants Beaulieu and if you can't nail him then I'll have to do it myself, somehow."

Devlin took several drags on his cigarette. The Holborn café had its usual sparse scattering of late-morning customers, the nearest of whom, a bearded old man, was noisily slurping tea from a saucer. Angers clucked his disapproval. "*Quelles cochons, les Anglais!*"

"Where is Rougemont?"

"Rougemont has been sent to interview some newly arrived French émigrés in Kent. He is going to be out of town for a few days."

"And what about what I have just told you? Shouldn't you relay that to Aubertin?"

Angers closed his eyes. His head was throbbing and he wished fervently that he'd never been dragged into this operation. "I think the colonel has some sort of inside information on Beaulieu. He thinks it inevitable that he will make a slip any moment. I can tell him what you say but I don't think it will change his mind."

Devlin stared hard at Angers. "I monitored Beaulieu again from four until midnight yesterday. Nothing untoward. You tell me there was a legitimate reason for his late arrival back from Oxford so nothing untoward about his Oxford visit. He seems as straight as a die to me so far. Yet when I have something fishy to report on one of the others, you aren't interested. It seems to me that you are not particularly interested in finding out who the real culprit is. You just want to frame a specific officer."

The commandant's mouth twisted in anger. Devlin liked Rougemont. He thought Rougemont was an honourable, intelligent man. All he could see in Angers was stupidity, bluster and naked ambition. Aubertin had no doubt made it clear to Angers that his career would prosper if he followed his orders unquestioningly.

The Irishman shook his head. "I'm afraid I can't do what you ask, Commandant, and I can't carry on with your commission. You entrusted me with an important job, which I was happy to carry out. You know that I am as much a French patriot as an Irish one. If there is a Free French spy, I want to help you find him. I have told you where my suspicions lie. You are not interested." Devlin got to his feet. "Accordingly, I bid you farewell and good luck. Don't worry about the money but I'll leave the bill to you." He tapped the brim of his hat and turned to the door.

"Dev… erm… Harp! Come back. Come back here right now!" The door banged shut and the Irishman was gone. Angers sat in morose contemplation of the empty chair opposite for a while then requested the bill. He'd better get back to Dorset Square to brief the colonel. He knew what was coming. In the absence of Rougemont and Devlin, who else could do the colonel's legwork?

*   *   *

Northamptonshire

Merlin had originally intended to take Bridges alone with him on his trip to Northamptonshire but Goldberg was so disappointed at the cancellation of his undercover assignment on Monday that Merlin didn't have the heart to exclude him. Robinson had also been keen to come but Merlin had insisted on someone staying in London to man the fort.

Mrs Cavendish was no longer travelling home by train because her nephew felt he should be with her in Sackville Hall for the police visit and so was driving her there. Under the circumstances, Merlin had suggested they travel in convoy. And so the police Austin followed closely behind Arbuthnot's Morgan as they winded through the Northamptonshire country lanes and neared their destination.

It was perfect open-top weather but Arbuthnot kept the Morgan's hood on to protect the expensive Mayfair perm Aunt Lucinda had acquired the previous afternoon. "My reward for enduring such a terrible day," she had told Merlin. It was just after one o'clock when Bridges saw Arbuthnot turn off the road and through a high stone gateway. He trailed the Morgan up a winding drive lined with oak and beech trees. Halfway up the drive, the hall came into view.

"Beautiful house, gentlemen."

"Sure is, Frank. How the other half live, eh?"

"Early Georgian, I think, or perhaps even Queen Anne."

Bridges drove into the front courtyard and parked beyond the Morgan, which had pulled up in front of the main door. An elderly male servant tottered out to assist Mrs Cavendish into the house. Once inside, she issued a string of commands to the servant and a waiting maid before turning to Merlin. "Jackson here will escort you to the library. Philip, you accompany them. If you'll kindly allow me a moment to refresh myself after the journey, gentlemen." As she ascended the grand staircase ahead of them, the policemen followed Jackson and Philip into a gloomy room off to their right.

"Open the curtains please, Jackson. Looks as if no-one's been in here for a while. My aunt finds the library a little depressing although it was always my father's favourite room. There is a drawing room to the rear, facing our flower garden, which she much prefers."

The curtains opened to reveal a spacious, high-ceilinged, wood-panelled library coloured in hues of claret and brown. All the walls were covered with books at various levels and there were a number of comfortable-looking leather armchairs. Two large, antique partners desks faced each other near the window and a selection of old prints hung in the few odd spaces devoid of books. At the far end of the room was a large, old, stone hearth, which appeared not to have been lit for a long while. Merlin loved it all. He had often dreamed of possessing such a room. He breathed in and savoured the delightful smell, a melange of old book bindings, leather upholstery, paper and ink.

At Arbuthnot's invitation, he sat in one of the leather armchairs by the hearth. There was an old book on the table beside his chair. It had a protective cloth cover and a small cloud of dust rose into the air as he picked it up and opened it. Merlin caught his breath as he saw the title page – *The Posthumous Papers of the Pickwick Club* by Charles Dickens, published by Chapman and Hall in 1837. A first edition of Dickens' first novel, in what appeared to be excellent condition.

"This was very much my brother's room." Lucinda Cavendish reappeared and took a seat beside Merlin. "When he first came into money, Simon went about the antiquarian bookstores and auction houses with a keen will to furnish it properly. Our father had been an avid collector of books before he encountered financial difficulties. He had to sell most of his collection but Simon was delighted, years later, to successfully track down nearly all of father's first editions and buy them back. That Dickens' book is one of them, Mr Merlin. There are several other Dickens' first editions. Simon concentrated on the Victorian greats. Dickens, Thackeray, Trollope, Collins, Hardy, the Brontës and so on."

"I can see you have a very fine collection. I could no doubt spend many happy hours here if I had the time but unfortunately…"

"Of course, Chief Inspector. You have work to do. I'll try to find that book for you." Mrs Cavendish walked to the bookshelf immediately to the right of Merlin and started searching. It did not take her long. The book she held up had a grey-green hard cover. "The dust cover has long gone, of course, but otherwise it's not in bad condition." She handed the book to Merlin.

"I should think you have a lengthy task ahead of you. May I suggest you sit at the desk over there? The natural light is better and there's a good lamp. I'll get Jackson to bring some other appropriate chairs. Naturally, if you would like to make use of my own rather rusty deciphering skills, I would be happy to remain and help."

"Thank you, Mrs Cavendish, but I think we'll try to manage on our own. Perhaps if we get stuck…"

"Very well. We shall leave you to it then." Jackson brought the chairs then departed with aunt and nephew.

As the men sat down, Bridges cleared his throat nervously. "Just to remind you of what I said at the Yard this morning, sir. I don't think I'm going to be of much use to you on this. As the wife says: 'Natural cunning is what you have, Sam Bridges. Not a brain for wordplay.'"

"That's all right, Sergeant. None of us is claiming any expertise at this, are we, Bernie? It would obviously have been helpful to have Mr Robinson with us, but at least we have his crib."

Robinson had been too busy to join them on the trip but had given some pointers on how to proceed, which Merlin had noted down. He placed the note, on which he had also written the code, next to the book.

"So the code is 23918174933232382228492331313383X. This is how Robinson says we are to start – go to page 2 of the main text, line 3, then see what letters match the subsequent numbers, such numbers being the positions of the letters in the line. There are special rules for zeros but we don't have any of those so let's not worry about them for now. If page 2, line 3, doesn't give us a coherent meaning, we have to see if there's a line 39 on page 2 and do the same. If that doesn't work, we are to try again on page 23, line 9, and repeat the procedure. And if that doesn't work, try page 239." He turned to the last page of the book. "Not surprisingly, there is no page 2,391 so those are our four options."

"Good job we are not dealing with the Bible."

"It is indeed, Sergeant. Have you got the stationery?" Bridges took several large sheets of paper and pencils out of his briefcase.

"I'll read out the letters attached to the respective numbers. Both of you take a sheet and a pencil and take note. Then we'll see where we get to." Merlin looked again at his guide. "Robinson says, logically, I suppose, that numbers may be designed to work as single numbers or as combinations. A 1 and 3 may be two single numbers or 13. This is not going to be an issue with all numbers as some will be too high in terms of the normal length of a line." He opened the book and counted the letters in a random line. "This line has 61 letters so I think we can take it that we aren't likely to have combination numbers in the 70s or above."

Goldberg scratched his forehead. "Whatever you say, Frank. Let's get going."

"I suggest we take our jackets off. This is going to *trabajo en caliente* as my father used to say. That's 'warm work', Sam. Everyone comfortable? Good. Here we go."

Merlin opened the book at the second page of the main text. "Page 2, line 3 reads: '*Try my tailor, said Sandy. He's got a very nice taste in red tabs. You can use...*' Sandy is presumably the Sandy Arbuthnot with whom Simon Arbuthnot liked to identify. So the next few numbers are 9181749. Letter number 9 in this line is a... an L. Number 1 is a T, number 8 is an I, number 1 again is a T, letter number 7 is an A, letter 4 is an M, letter 9 is another L." He paused and looked across at his companions. "I have to say this doesn't sound very promising but what have you got so far?"

"LTITAML," Goldberg and Bridges read out in unison. Merlin groaned. "I hope it doesn't turn out that the deciphered message is itself in code. Let's complete the sequence of single numbers and then, if the message is still, as seems likely, gibberish, go over it again, allowing for combination numbers." He returned his eyes to the line and counted. "There are a total of 58 letters in the line. We can alternate singles and combinations for numbers from the 10s to the 50s. Then we'll see where we are."

*   *   *

"I really must question, Aunt, whether we are doing the right thing here. It's clear that my father was involved in some murky business. Not only the gambling but now this possible fraud I told you Fleming mentioned. However, here we are, allowing the police to have first sight of his last private wishes as expressed to you, assuming they can break the code. God knows what he wanted to tell you. The family honour may be at stake."

Lucinda Cavendish nibbled delicately on a custard cream. She adored the biscuits and wasn't going to allow Philip's tiresomeness to ruin this little pleasure. Only when she had finished the last crumb did she speak.

"You know, Philip, much as I loved your father, the fact is he became rather pompous in his last years. I don't like to speak ill of the dead but your father's success eventually went to his head. This talk of family honour is typical of the high-blown nonsense he filled his head with latterly. You no doubt had to listen to him on the subject a few times, so I understand and forgive you, but… really." She looked out onto the garden and saw some squirrels scampering in and out of the bushes.

"I know that Simon used to pretend that our father was a very successful businessman who had a bit of bad luck. He was in fact a glorified plumber, then a dealer in industrial machinery and cars. Yes, he came from quite a good family but he had an unjustifiably high opinion of himself and spent far more than he earned. He was also a keen gambler and drinker and it was, according to mother, no great surprise to anyone when he went bust."

"Was he…?"

Mrs Cavendish raised a hand. "I don't really want to say any more about your forebears for now, Philip. Perhaps another time, when we are under less stress. The reality is that there is little family honour to protect."

"Fine but even if that's the case, what about Father's business reputation? Shouldn't we try to protect that?"

"I doubt we have a hope of doing that. The bank is going to find it very difficult to cover up this fraudulent dealing we've just learned about."

"Fleming and Tomlinson are clever men. And they say Pulos is as sharp as a pin. They're bound to find a way."

Philip's aunt reached out for another biscuit and munched it thoughtfully. "Mr Pulos is very sharp indeed. As is Sidney Fleming. It was with the assistance of those two that Simon perpetrated his worst fraud."

"What do you mean 'his worst fraud'. You mean there have been others?"

"You poor boy. You have no idea of the sort of man your father was, have you? Of course there were other frauds. As Simon always loved to say about his business competitors: 'Behind every great fortune there lies a great crime'. Simon certainly had several crimes behind his fortune but there is no doubt which was the greatest."

Lucinda Cavendish reached out for the photograph she had shown Philip on his last visit. "You remember this picture? Your father and his friend in tennis gear?"

"Yes. Remind me, who is the friend?"

"Franzi Meyer. Simon met Franzi in London, just after the last war, in 1919. Simon was just starting out in the City. Franzi was from a very rich family in Frankfurt. His father had built up a large conglomerate with interests in finance and industry in Germany, some other European countries and overseas in South America. It survived the Great War intact. So Franzi was a rich German boy and Simon a penniless clerk.

"They met in a pub or café and for some reason hit it off, despite their difference in years. Franzi was a little older than Simon and had been sent to London to re-establish one of the family businesses. Your father was quite a charmer in those days, as was Franzi, and they enjoyed themselves in London. Of course, your father sponged off Franzi and then got him to chip in financially to a couple of his early ventures. When Franzi went back to Germany to assume control of the whole family operation, the two remained best friends and kept in close touch."

"Please get to the point, Aunt. What was the crime?"

His aunt gave Philip a withering look. "You are as impatient as your father sometimes." She looked out again onto the garden. The squirrels had disappeared. "In due course, Hitler came to

power in Germany. Fairly soon it became apparent that Franzi
and his family were going to have difficulties."

"Why?"

"I neglected to tell you that the Meyers were Jewish."

"Ah."

"Franzi decided to take steps to protect the family's wealth as
a preliminary to getting out of Germany. He had to operate very
carefully and stealthily as by now he was being closely watched.
Ultimately, if Hitler chose to annex the Meyers' businesses in
Germany, there was little that could be done. However, they had
their very substantial South American interests. With help they
could be protected. Franzi asked your father to look after the
share certificates for those businesses. Those certificates were in
the form of bearer shares."

Philip shook his head slowly. "Bearer shares, I see."

"Obviously, he could no longer trust the German banks with
which the certificates had been deposited up to that point. Franzi
would have been wiser to deposit them in a British bank but he'd
reached a point where he didn't trust any banks. He chose to enlist
your father's help. Your father agreed to look after them.

"Shortly after he had entrusted the certificates to Simon, Franzi
and his father were arrested by the Nazis. Eventually, after much
hardship, he was released. His father was not so lucky and died
in a German prison. Once he was out, Franzi arranged to get his
immediate family to Paris, where he joined them shortly after the
Nazis confiscated the Meyers' German businesses. From Paris, he
contacted your father to get back the certificates in anticipation
of the family emigrating to Argentina."

"Hmm." Philip looked down at his feet.

"Your father refused to return the certificates. He argued that
he had lent Franzi money that was secured on the certificates.
As Franzi couldn't make immediate repayment, Simon had
foreclosed on the security. The amount owed was piffling in

comparison with the value of the shares but 'business was business' he said.

"Simon sent Pulos out to Argentina with the certificates to establish Arbuthnot control of the operations. He managed to do so, spreading substantial bribes around to ensure he got the right result. Without access to South American funds, Franzi was penniless and in no position to fight his case."

"So everything we have in South America was effectively stolen from this Meyer fellow?"

"It was. Unsurprisingly, Simon and Franzi spoke no more. I heard later that Franzi and his wife had died in poverty in Paris a few months before the war started."

"But as I understand it, Sackville now owns those shares, not my father. How did that come about?"

"Sackville was Simon's business vehicle. He decided these assets would substantially enhance the standing of the bank. All he had to do was to make a simple declaration of trust. He declared that he held the bearer shares, which Pulos had returned to him in London, in trust for the bank."

Nephew and aunt sat in silence for some time. Eventually, Philip spoke. "No family honour and no business honour, then?"

"If I were a religious woman, I would be inclined to attribute recent events to divine retribution for past sins. I am sorry to burden you with all this knowledge, but you are the head of the family now and you need to know. Honour is neither here nor there but do not think that I am unconcerned with preserving the family fortune. That is our major task. If the bank's problems become insurmountable, and we find that your father has hocked everything else he owns in England, those bearer shares become even more valuable to us."

"Notwithstanding the fact that they were stolen."

"Franzi Meyer is long dead. I have no intention of ending up penniless like him. I agree, on reflection, that it might have been

wiser to be more reticent with the police. I was worried about this
Beecham fellow and everything else you told me and wasn't really
thinking straight. However, what is done is done. We'll wait and
see if the police can manage to decode the message. Then we'll play
it by ear. The important thing is to keep our family ship afloat."

*   *   *

The police officers had been at it for more than three hours. They
had painstakingly worked their way through the various answers
presented by the lines 3 and 39 on page 2, line 9 on page 23, and so
on. They had counted along using single numbers and combined
numbers as alternatives. They had looked to see if the reversal of
the resulting letters provided a solution. All to no avail. An air of
despondency had fallen on the three men.

Merlin loosened his tie. "There is no line 91 on page 23 and so
our next, and perhaps last, option is page 239 line 18. Here we are:
'… *steep walls and made monstrous shadows. The wind swung the flame
into*…' So after 23918 we have 17493323822284923331313383X.
Number 1 in the line is an S, number 7 is A, number 4 is E, number
9 is L, number 3 is E. What does that give us?"

Goldberg read out: "SAELE."

"No good then. Let's look at double numbers. In this result,
single 4 and single 9 give us EL, which makes no sense after SA.
What if we put them together? There are more than 49 letters in
this line, so the 49th letter is… bear with me… F. That gives us
SAFE. That's more encouraging, isn't it?"

Bridges and Goldberg murmured agreement.

"The next number 3 is E, then number 2 is T, 3 is E again. After
ETE we have 8, an L, then another T. Something tells me we are
barking up the wrong tree again. Let's try 32 instead of 3 and 2 – 32
is W. Then 38 instead of 3 and 8 – that's I." They continued doubling.
"22 is T and 28 is H. That gives us 'with'. So we have SAFE WITH."

Goldberg rubbed his eyes. "Frank, there's a T earlier than 22nd in the line. The second letter is T. Isn't it the rule of this code that the letter takes its earliest number?"

"That would give us two Ts – WITT – and ruin the word." Merlin thought for a moment. "Robinson said that some codes are, by their very nature, anomalous. Let's treat this as an acceptable anomaly for the moment, as we seem to be getting somewhere."

"OK, Frank. You're the boss."

"So SAFE WITH. Safe with whom or what? I'm going to continue with double numbers for the rest. So number 49 is F, then 23 is R, 31 is O, then another O, 33 is S, there is no 83, so number 8 is L and number 3 is E."

"FROOSLE." Bridges laughed. "Sounds like something in a fairy tale."

Merlin chewed a fingernail. "Let's try again with the F and the R remaining in place. If we go 3 on its own we get E so that's FRE. If we take the next four numbers 1313 individually, we get SESE. Obviously that doesn't work. So let's try 13 and 13 – 13 is, um, D." Merlin could feel his heart beating faster. "Now we have FREDD. I recall from earlier that number 38 is I and then the last number 3 is E."

Goldberg raised his eyebrows. "SAFE WITH FREDDIE. What about the X, Frank?"

"A kiss?"

"Why not, Sergeant? The simplest solutions are often the best. If we accept, as I now think we must, that this is a message from brother to sister, why not a kiss? The message to Lucinda Cavendish from her brother Simon Arbuthnot is SAFE WITH FREDDIE followed by one kiss." Merlin leaned back in his chair with a loud sigh of satisfaction. "Sergeant, go and ask Mrs Cavendish to join us. Let's find out who Freddie is."

*   *   *

London

"There's a letter, Constable, addressed to you and Sergeant Bridges. It was hand delivered."

"Thank you, Sergeant. When did this arrive?"

Sergeant Reeves stroked his double chin. "To be honest, Robinson, I can't tell you. I found it on the duty desk when I came on shift an hour or so ago. Normally the duty officer marks the incoming delivery details on the envelope but this one is clean. It was a very busy night last night. Perhaps he forgot. Occasionally mistakes get made. There is a…"

"War on. Yes, I know, sir. Thank you anyway." Reeves disappeared and Robinson opened the letter.

> Dear Sergeant Bridges and Constable Robinson,
>
> Please forgive me for not being completely truthful at our interview and for not providing the fuller information contained in this letter in person. I have had a few unsatisfactory experiences with the police in the past and I'd prefer not to have any more.
>
> I am taking a little break from London. It won't be long before my call-up papers arrive at Mrs Lafontaine's house and much as I love my country, I don't think I will do it or myself much good by putting on the khaki uniform. I have had reason to disappear in the past and am quite good at it, so please don't waste your time by trying to track me down.
>
> I am very sorry about Bridget Healey and what happened to her. I think you suspected we had a fling together. We did not although I would have jumped at the chance. I believe I was not unattractive to her but she always had her eye on the main chance. Why waste time on a chauffeur when there are bigger fish to catch?

I told you that I last saw her briefly by chance in Piccadilly Circus in April. In fact, we went for lunch and had a bit of a heart-to-heart. She told me that she'd met someone who had got her in the family way. Bridget was very keen on this fellow and felt he was going to do the right thing by her. She didn't mean marriage but she thought he would stand by her and support her and the baby. She wouldn't tell me who he was but gave me the impression he was quite well-to-do. I offered to help in any way I could but she said there was no need.

A few weeks later, she telephoned me in floods of tears and told me that the man in question was insisting she have an abortion. She was distraught. I didn't really know what to say but again I offered my support. We arranged to meet. When we did, she had calmed down and become more philosophical – "What would I be wanting a baby for, anyway?"

We met again at the Lyons Tea House in the Strand. She told me the father of her baby had arranged for some French fellow to perform the abortion. Said she'd been told he'd been a very famous doctor back in France and would do a good job. A day or two later, she rang me in a panic. Her lover had given her the address of a hotel off Oxford Street, the Bedford, and she had been told to turn up there for the procedure the following day before one o'clock. He couldn't accompany her as he "had important work to do" although he did say he might send someone along to check that all had gone well. She was petrified and asked me if I'd accompany her. She had been told to check in to room 14 and wait.

I agreed. We got there very early. Over an hour after we got to the room, a fat Frenchman turned up.

He stank of booze. I was complaining to him about the state he was in, and saying he should arrange another time to carry out the operation, when another man arrived. He was another Frenchman. I kept trying to get everything called off but this Frenchman pulled a gun on me and told me to clear off. Bridget was naturally in a terrible state but, after a few words in French with the officer, which I couldn't understand, she calmed down and agreed with him that I should go. I hesitated but she insisted. I thought to myself that at least someone was there to keep an eye on things, even though he had waved a gun at me.

So I left. Naturally I now wish I'd stayed. Perhaps I could have saved her. I went to see a picture in Leicester Square and had a bite to eat before returning to the hotel to see if all was well. By then you fellows were all over the place. I hung around outside and heard someone mention a dead girl. I knew it had to be Bridget and went away to drown my sorrows.

I hope you can make good use of this information. If you can find the Frenchman, I am sure you will be able to get to the bottom of this. He was a good-looking young chap, dark-haired, about six feet tall. The main thing I remember about him was that he had a slight limp. Whether that was a temporary or permanent affliction, I don't know, but I hope it helps you to find him.

Yours
Peter Wilson

*   *   *

Northamptonshire

"No, I don't know anyone called Freddie, Chief Inspector. And I have no idea what the message SAFE WITH FREDDIE means. Perhaps, after all, the message was intended for someone else."

"I think that's unlikely, ma'am. Any idea, sir?"

"Afraid not, Mr Merlin. I knew a fellow in school called Freddie but haven't seen him in years."

Mrs Cavendish raised a hand to pat down her new perm. "Come to think of it, Philip, wasn't your father's regular barber called Freddie? Perhaps you should have a word with him, Chief Inspector. Back in town."

Merlin sucked in his cheeks. "Thank you, madam. We'll certainly follow that up. If anything else occurs to you both, I'm sure you'll let me know, won't you?" Merlin nodded wearily to Bridges and Goldberg. "I think perhaps we should call it a day and get back to London."

"Of course, Mr Merlin, and thank you. Is it all right if I let Jackson see you out? It's been a long day and I could do with some fresh air. Come, Philip. Let's take the dog for a walk."

Aunt and nephew said their goodbyes and the policemen went over to the desk to collect their paperwork and the book. "She's lying, sir."

"Of course she's lying, Sergeant, and she's not very good at it. The barber indeed! She knows who Freddie is but wants to keep it to herself. We'll just have to get it out of her somehow."

"It's odd though, Frank. Up until now she's been very cooperative. She identified the source book, after all. We'd be nowhere without that. Why start lying now?"

"Perhaps she thought we'd never crack the code, Bernie. Now that we have and it's a cryptic message she understands and we don't, she can clam up and act on it when we are out of the picture."

"Shouldn't we take her back to London with us then, sir?"

"What, and beat the truth out of her? No, Sergeant, I don't think that's on. Come on, I'm bushed. Let's get back home. Things might look clearer after a good night's sleep."

Jackson escorted the policemen out of the house. Merlin and Goldberg waited by the front door as Bridges turned the car round. They were just about to get in when they heard a loud shout. A labrador suddenly burst through a bush at the side of the house, chased by a grizzled and bearded old man in dungarees. "Let go, Archie, you bugger. Let go now!"

Archie had a duck clenched between his teeth. As the old man caught hold of the dog and struggled to pull the bird from its jaws, Philip Arbuthnot and his aunt appeared, both a little out of breath. The old man finally managed to get the growling Archie to release the bird, but it was dead. "The bugger! Excuse my French, ma'am, but that's the third he's done for in the past fortnight."

"Never mind, George, we'll buy some more."

"Easier said than done, ma'am. In this wartime market, ducks aren't so easy to come by. And, anyway, what's the point if Archie is going to keep on attacking them?"

"All right, George, run along now. Take Archie with you."

George put the dog back on its lead and headed back the way he had come. Just before he disappeared out of sight, he turned back and shouted: "This dog is a law unto himself, ma'am. We never had these problems with Freddie."

*   *   *

London

"Vorster. Where on earth have you been?"

"I did ring in." Rupert Vorster hovered nervously at the threshold of his boss's office.

Tomlinson frowned. "Indeed you did. That was to explain yesterday. Today is another day and it's well past lunchtime already. What's your excuse now?"

"Mr Titmus asked me to research a point of law last week. I couldn't get the answer in our library so I went straight to the Middle Temple library this morning."

"And did you find the answer there?"

"I did."

"In 30 odd years of practice together, I've not known Mr Titmus to have much interest in points of law. What was it?"

"A query about the law of estoppel, sir."

"Hmm. Very esoteric." Tomlinson gave Vorster a disbelieving look. "Very well. Now there are two things you should know, if you don't know them already. First, a policeman came here looking for you yesterday. He wouldn't tell me why. Any idea?"

"No."

"I hope you haven't done anything that will prove embarrassing to the firm."

"I am not aware of anything, sir."

Tomlinson adjusted the knot in his tie. "The second thing is that I received a cable from your father. He is in Lisbon en route to London from Cape Town. I suggest that you tidy up this police matter before he arrives tomorrow."

"Of course, sir." The thought of seeing his father so soon made Vorster's forehead prickle with sweat. "I'll deal with it."

"I intend to make sure you do."

*   *   *

Northamptonshire

They stood in a small circle around the last resting place of Freddie, Archie's late father. It was a beautiful spot. Merlin thought he wouldn't mind spending eternity under the boughs of this ancient oak himself.

When George, the gardener, had mentioned the dead dog, inspiration had failed Mrs Cavendish. Her shoulders had slumped and she had felt compelled to confirm that the previous family pet, Archie's father, was named Freddie. It had not occurred to her, she had explained, that her brother's message could refer to a dead dog. Merlin had smiled graciously at her in her embarrassment before asking George if Freddie had been buried in the grounds. The gardener, oblivious to the strained atmosphere that had descended on the group, had led the way to the oak, chattering nostalgically about the late Freddie's equable character.

Mrs Cavendish looked sullenly at Merlin.

"I am afraid, ma'am, that we'll have to…"

"Yes. Fine, Chief Inspector. Dig him up please, George."

George's face clouded over. This was not what he had been expecting and he protested vehemently but to no avail. "Just get on with it, George."

The grumbling gardener went off to get a shovel. The others waited in a silence broken only by the sound of a woodpecker at work in a nearby tree. George soon returned and began to dig. The earth under its thick layer of grass was still soft after the heavy rain earlier in the month and it did not take long for Freddie's remains to be exposed. Merlin moved forward to explore the earth around the dog. He made a circuit of the skeleton, stamping his feet on the ground. In the short space between the dog's skull and the tree, Merlin thought he detected something underfoot. He stamped his right foot down several times. There was something hollow in the sound his foot made. "Can you dig here please, George. Carefully."

George bent to his task and it did not take long for his shovel to reveal a rectangular black metal box. "Thank you. Looks like a bank deposit box. Do think you could scrape the mud off?"

George produced a large, red, spotted handkerchief from the pocket of his dungarees and wiped the box clean. The lid was secured by a small padlock. Merlin thought of asking George to find a tool so they could break it open but then thought better of it. "We'll leave it as it is and open it back at the Yard."

Lucinda Cavendish was not happy. "Come now, Chief Inspector, you must open it here. Simon left this box here for me, after all."

"This is evidence in a murder case, ma'am. As such its place is with us. We shall open it and inspect the contents. They will be released to you as and when appropriate in the context of our investigations. For the moment, I have a murderer to find and the contents of this box might help me to do so."

"But, Chief Inspector, I helped you to decipher the message that led you to this box. Surely…?"

Merlin flicked away a speck of earth that had attached itself to his trousers. "I would leave it there if I were you, Mrs Cavendish. The assistance you gave us wasn't exactly wholehearted, was it?"

"Damn it! This cannot be right. Philip, haven't you anything to say?"

Philip Arbuthnot put an arm around Mrs Cavendish's shoulder. "I think it's clear that the chief inspector's mind is made up. Come." He turned and led his grumbling aunt back to the house as George started to shovel earth back on to poor Freddie.

CHAPTER 14
Wednesday 18 June

London

M erlin was at the Yard early. There were three messages on his desk, two of which were from Robinson. One contained details of Dumont's home address in Soho. In the other, the constable said she had news of an important development, without specifying what. The third message was a duty-desk note of a telephone message from Reggie Tomlinson the previous afternoon, enquiring when Merlin would like him to send Vorster over.

Bridges and Goldberg were also early birds. Bridges brought with him the black box, which he had held in safekeeping overnight.

"We're all keen as mustard today, aren't we? Robinson's usually an early starter. Any sign of her yet, Sergeant?"

The telephone rang before Merlin got an answer. It was the AC. "Ah, Frank. I was hoping you'd be there already. I'm calling from Paddington Station. I've got a speech to deliver in Bristol about the future role of women in the police force. It occurred to me last night that it would be useful to take Claire, I mean Constable Robinson, along with me. I hope you don't mind her being out of the office for a day. I have to say that she wasn't very keen, but I said it would be…"

Merlin interrupted the AC irritably. "Sir, the constable's absence today will be most inconvenient. We are making rapid progress with…"

"What's that, Frank? I can't hear a thing with all these trains huffing and puffing."

"Can I speak to the constable, sir?"

"Sorry, Frank. Still can't hear you and I think they're calling our train. We're going to put up in a hotel in Bristol for the night and catch an early train tomorrow. We can catch up in the office then." There was a click and the connection was broken.

Merlin slammed the phone down in disgust. "That's bloody great. The AC's taken Robinson off on a jaunt to the West Country. We'll have to do without her today."

Bridges had been reading the messages on the desk as Merlin spoke to the AC. "Says here she has something important to tell us."

"I know. Looks like we'll have to wait a while to hear it. Let's hope she has time to call us when they get to Bristol. Meanwhile, we've got plenty to be getting on with. There's Vorster and Dumont to get hold of. Sergeant, call Tomlinson when his office is open for business and tell him we'll see Vorster at 11 o'clock. We'll try Dumont's home address before that. However, first of all…" he tapped a finger on the box, "… let's open this thing."

Bridges went over to an old cupboard beneath the cuckoo clock, where various odd items, such as tools, were kept, and found a chisel. The padlock was heavily rusted and it was no easy task for the sergeant to break it open. Eventually, after a lot of huffing and puffing, there was a loud cracking noise and the padlock fell away.

Merlin undid the latch and looked inside. There were three sealed envelopes, one large and thick, one large and thin and one of normal letter size. The two large envelopes were blank but the smaller was addressed in neat handwriting to Lucinda Cavendish.

"Let's look at this one first." Merlin opened the smaller envelope and found five sheets of blue writing paper, embossed at the bottom with Simon Arbuthnot's initials. Arbuthnot's hand was elegant and easily legible. Merlin put on his glasses and read the letter out loud.

My dearest Lucinda,

I know you are a clever old girl and will have remembered enough of our youthful cipher games to track down what I am entrusting to you. I apologise for the cloak-and-dagger stuff but I have got myself into a right old mess. Of course, the fact that you are reading this means that I have by now got myself into an even bigger mess – the ultimate mess, you might say – and have 'crossed the bar' as your favourite poet Tennyson puts it. So I am dead and this letter, and the things enclosed in the box with it, are intended to preserve you and poor Philip as well as possible through the storm that will follow.

The mess I have got into is not necessarily one that will surprise you, although the resultant scale of the problem might. You know how I always loved a gamble, ever since I was a young man. You will remember how I often bet the whole of the pitiful allowance Father was able to give us after his bankruptcy on one stupid nag or another.

As time went on, I managed to bring this bad habit under control, probably because my career in building the Sackville business was enough of a gamble to satisfy the urge. Although there were many ups and downs, I ended up rich and successful with a beautiful wife and son. I had to cut many corners but I always enjoyed the thrill of doing that. Yes, I lost the beautiful wife, but I was so engrossed in my business that the loss was not so difficult to overcome. I love Philip but we have been more distant recently than I would have liked, for reasons I don't quite understand. No doubt my own stupid fault.

As you know, I have done some bad things in business but have had the good fortune to be impervious to feelings of guilt. What I am trying to say, in this rambling sort of way, is that I did not return to gambling because of any particular personal pressures. I returned to gambling through boredom, nothing more. I experienced such a string of fantastic highs and lows in my life that I eventually became deadened to normal excitements. I needed something else to give my life an edge and gambling was able to provide it in these past couple of years.

But let me not digress. This letter is written more as one of advice rather than confession. Let me not bore you with all the details, but the pertinent fact remains that I have built up substantial gambling debts.

As is often the way of these things, my early gambling returns were positive and I made a lot of money. Hubris reared its ugly head, I raised the stakes and then I began to lose, and lose, and lose. All my not inconsiderable ready cash in this country was eaten up and then I had to find alternative sources. I mortgaged some properties, including, I am sorry to say, Sackville Hall.

When I had run through those funds, I thought of getting cash from Pulos but the funds in South America were bound up in business activities and working capital. In any event, transfers to me would have been difficult to cover up because of the difficulties of distance and the procedures in Argentina and the bank. I also didn't want to make myself a hostage of fortune to Pulos, who has become much less reliable in recent years.

However, there were ways I could siphon money from Sackville without detection. I am afraid that I made use of some client funds or, to be blunt, I embezzled them – and I pulled a few tricks on the banking side as well. I further compounded my situation by making speculative market investments with some of this money. While I continued to breathe I had reliable people who could cover up my transgressions and, with a bit of time, might have found a way of repaying the money. I am, however, patently breathing no more and thus the shortfall will be discovered soon enough. This will, of course, precipitate problems for the bank and our business.

No doubt you will be aghast by now at the scale of the problems I have left behind me, without my even having mentioned a financial figure. As to that, I have cleared some of the amounts owing but estimate I still have personal liabilities of over £2.5m. Some of that is owed to a rather unpleasant individual called Peregrine Beecham, some to other gambling outfits and bookmakers and a large proportion, of course, to the bank and its clients. There are also a few more modest debts owed to other banks and individuals. Being the perspicacious girl you are, you will have realised by now that when I joined the army last year, it was less to do with patriotism than with the evasion of these onerous responsibilities.

So there is the mess. What to do? Obviously you and Philip are my principal concerns. Regarding the gambling debts, my advice is to go to the police and explain the situation. Nearly all of these debts are unenforceable in law because they result from illegal gaming operations. That will not stop Mr Beecham from seeking repayment and, despite his veneer of respectability, he is a violent crook. You and Philip will need protection from him. Get the help of the police.

As regards the bank, clearly there is the potential of litigation against my estate. There is also the chance that the bank will go under because of my fraud. There are other British assets around but most, as I mentioned, are heavily mortgaged.

However, there is the one very valuable asset mentioned earlier that should prove your and Philip's salvation – the South American business. You know how I got that business and I know you weren't impressed by what I did, but there it is. Those bearer shares are worth a fortune, which should secure the good life for you and Philip. The bearer shares are in one of the accompanying envelopes. Take good care of them. You need to be clever and ensure they do not fall into the hands either of my partners or my creditors.

There are some difficulties of which you should be aware regarding the certificates. First, Sackville Bank accounts for the South American businesses as part of its holdings. It does so on the understanding that I have made a formal declaration of trust of the certificates in its favour. I have not. I sorted out a personal problem for one of our auditors a few years back and he noted, incorrectly in the bank accounts, that there was such a written declaration in place. There is not. The bearer shares belong to whoever possesses them, which is now you.

Second, one of Franzi's sons has initiated litigation in Buenos Aires for the recovery of the certificates. He is poorly funded, we have a good case – possession is everything in the case of bearer shares – and the Argentinian courts are malleable (I'm sure you know what I mean). Pulos is handling the litigation and is well on top of it.

That brings me to the third difficulty, which is Pulos himself. He has control on the ground of the businesses and I did verbally grant him 10 per cent of Enterprisas Simal, although I retained his certificate. He may well decide – in the light of my death and the imminent crisis at the bank – to assume and assert control of everything in his own right, even without the certificates.

In the envelope containing the bearer shares you will also find a card with the details of my personal lawyer in Buenos Aires. Thanks to me, he has a large file on Pulos, detailing his numerous fraudulent business dealings and associated violence and criminality. The fact that these dealings were undertaken with my approval is neither here nor there.

Excuse me, Lucinda, but there is also a voluminous record (including photographs) of Pulos's energetic and imaginative sexual life. The lawyer is confident there is enough in the file to ensure Pulos will do as you wish. This lawyer is someone you can trust and that statement bears the weight of being made by someone who, as you know, has seldom trusted anyone. If Pulos does play ball and behaves in a gentlemanly manner, you can give him his 10 per cent. If not, it is one other thing to hold over him.

One final warning on the share certificates. Somehow or other, most likely through my own indiscretion, Beecham became aware of their existence and value. I would be surprised if he is not looking for them as some form of settlement for my debts.

The other envelope in the box contains my will. I wrote it myself and it is a simple document. I leave everything to you. I feel more comfortable if you are able to assume total command in these difficult circumstances. Philip will be disappointed but I know you will look after him and, in due course, make him your heir.

It may be a good idea to send him to South America to establish a family presence there and come to an appropriate accommodation with Pulos. That would get him away from this dreadful war as well. I did briefly give thought myself to the idea of doing a bunk to South America but couldn't quite bring myself to face living with the ignominy it would bring down on our heads. Unfortunately, it now seems likely that you will have to live with the ignominy of my actions. I'm sorry.

On a minor note, Reggie Tomlinson is aware from my previous will of various small bequests I wanted to make to people. I would be grateful if you could honour those.

And so that's about it, my dear Lucinda. We are about to enter into a rapid retreat to the south-east to get away from the advancing Germans, who appear to be about to win their first major battle of the war against us. Obviously I have not made it. Think of me.

Love

Simon

Take another kiss

X

Merlin put the letter down and removed his glasses. "Quite a story, gentlemen!"

*   *   *

Devlin was treating himself to a haircut at Arnie Cohen's in Holloway. As the barber prattled on about Churchill and the war, Devlin considered yet again what, if anything, he ought to do. Worrying about it had given him a sleepless night. As he saw it, he had four options. He could keep quiet, move on and undertake something new – his partner Bill Parker had been chasing him about some juicy new divorce work that had just come in. Then again, he could stick at it freelance but find a different Free French officer in whom to confide. Meyer came to mind but he was probably too junior. The third thing he could do was to go to the police and lay everything out for them. And his final option was MI5. He had had occasional dealings with the secret services in the past and knew who to approach.

"You'd think they'd have taken some pictures of the *Graf Spee* when it was going down." Devlin realised Cohen had finished and was brushing him down.

The Irishman scratched an itch beneath his collar. "I am sure they must have. Taken photographs that is."

"If they did, then why haven't they shown them in the newsreels at the flicks? People need a boost, Mr Devlin. What with the Germans winning in Crete, the problems with Rommel in north Africa, Tobruk. If something good happened, even if it's a few weeks ago now, don't you think it would buck people up to see that famous German ship sinking beneath the briny?"

Devlin brushed a few stray hairs from his shoulders. "Perhaps they have film but it's classified."

Cohen, a chubby man with a surprisingly unkempt head of black hair for a barber, shook his head. "What can be classified about the sinking of a ship, which is public knowledge?"

Devlin had to agree. "Perhaps they are saving it up for when there's a real calamity."

"God forbid." Cohen continued grumbling about the government's public information failings as he walked over to the counter with Devlin, who paid him and added a small tip as usual. "Care for a bottle of my special hair tonic, Mr Devlin? Keep everything sleek and healthy."

"Yes, all right, Arnie. Thanks." Devlin handed over a few more coins and pocketed the small green bottle as he walked out the door. Heading north along Holloway Road, he realised that his mind had made itself up: he would go to the police. Rougemont had mentioned in passing the name of the detective who had visited the Free French office: Detective Chief Inspector Merlin. He would tell Merlin his story. If there were a Free French spy working against the allies, he didn't feel capable of just walking away. He could, however, if he unburdened himself to a responsible police officer. Merlin could decide what to do with the information and Devlin would return to the pursuit of errant husbands and wives.

He saw a telephone box. He knew the Scotland Yard number by heart, although he had a note of it in his wallet. He dialled. Disappointingly, Merlin was not available. Devlin left his name and boarding-house telephone number with an officer and a message that he had important security information and would be coming in to see Merlin later in the day.

Even though he hadn't been able to share his knowledge with the police, Devlin felt much happier now that he had committed to his decision. He smiled and as he turned into the alleyway that he often used as a shortcut to his digs, started to whistle. It was the tune of a song he had heard Charles Trenet sing in a Montmartre nightclub in '38. He was trying to remember the words to '*Boum*' as he made his way past the large rubbish bins that filled the lane. He switched from whistling to humming. Picasso had much admired Devlin's light baritone and once encouraged him to try singing professionally, to the Irishman's considerable amusement. The thought of the Spanish painter with the wild, staring eyes led him to wonder how Picasso was coping with the occupation. Perhaps he'd scarpered back home to Spain. But then he loved Paris so much. No doubt the artist would have landed on his feet somehow.

Finally, the words came back to Devlin and he began to sing but, after the first line, he was surprised to hear another voice singing along with him. It was a deep, gravelly voice that seemed to be coming from behind one of the rubbish bins he'd already passed. The song died on his lips and he turned to investigate. Then something hit him. Something heavy. Something very heavy. Blood began streaming into his eyes and his head started to pound. Through the blood he saw the glint of a knife before feeling a sharp pain in his stomach. His final sensations before losing consciousness were the smell of rotten vegetables and the sound of a whistle being blown.

*   *   *

Merlin could hear Dumont complaining loudly to Bridges and Goldberg as they brought him along Old Compton Street to the car. As he was bundled in, he turned his anger on the chief inspector. "This is a disgrace! When the general hears about this, he will…"

"Yes, yes, Lieutenant." Merlin shifted along the back seat to make more room for Dumont. "We just need to ask you a few questions. Hopefully, we won't detain you too long."

The sergeant started the engine. "He had a lady friend with him in his rooms. Not too happy about the interruption, as you can see." They made the journey back from Soho to the Yard within 10 minutes.

Dumont had calmed down by the time they'd got to the Yard and he'd taken his seat across from the policemen in one of the downstairs interview rooms. He declined the mug of tea Bridges offered him with a Gallic shrug of disdain. "Come on then, *messieurs*. Let's get this over with. Ask away. You will understand, of course, that if your questions relate in any way to my military duties, I shall not be able to answer them."

Merlin added a lump of sugar to his tea and stirred. "Rest assured, Lieutenant, that our inquiries only pertain to your personal life." Merlin asked a number of preliminary questions about Dumont's duties in London then nodded at Goldberg. "Do you remember this gentleman on my right?"

Dumont had a dark, narrow face with slightly hollow cheeks. His dark brown hair was neatly parted and combed. Small, piercing brown eyes were set above a small, thin nose and broad mouth, which turned up slightly on the left. He gave Goldberg a disgruntled look. "'Gentleman' is not the word, I think. A gentleman does not join other gentlemen for a drink under false pretences. I understood that you were a diplomat, *monsieur*, not a police – what is the American word? – stool pigeon."

"Mr Goldberg is a policeman. He was working undercover for me when he met you. We were acting on information that you and your friend, Mr Vorster, were friendly with a woman called Bridget Healy."

"I know no such person."

"Are you sure, Lieutenant? Miss Healy was an attractive young lady seen frequently in the Ritz bar, sometimes as one of your party, according to our sources." Merlin slid the photograph of Bridget over to Dumont.

After a cursory look, Dumont shook his head. "We often mix with large parties in the Ritz, *Monsieur* Merlin. Large, jolly parties. There is a war on, you know, and everyone is determined to live life to the full. But if you expect me to remember every good-time girl who attaches herself to our group, you ask too much of me. I notice, by the way, that you used the past tense in regard to this lady."

"She is dead. Miss Healy was the victim of a botched abortion."

"I am very sorry to hear that but what has it to do with me?"

Goldberg leaned forward. "You and your pal Vorster told me you knew some Irish girls."

Dumont smiled. "Yes, my American friend, I have met some Irish girls in London. And I have met some Scottish, Welsh and, of course, English girls. But no, I did not know this Miss Healy and I did not discuss her with Rupert. It is possible that she may have been in the Ritz at the same time as me but I do not recognise her. I am naturally sorry she came to a sad end but…"

"I heard you and Vorster discuss her by name and I heard one of you use the word 'pregnant' in relation to her."

Dumont's face reddened with indignation. "No, sir, you certainly did not. You misheard. We never discussed someone of that name and I know no pregnant women."

Merlin decided to change tack. "What about the gambling club to which Vorster took the detective? Run by a fellow called Beecham. What do you know of that?"

"Very little. Rupert goes there, I don't. I am not a rich man, *Monsieur* Merlin. I have no money to gamble."

"What can you tell us about Mr Beecham's friendship with Mr Vorster?"

"They are friends. That is all I know."

"Nothing more?"

"I believe Rupert runs occasional errands for Beecham."

"Like finding him customers?"

Goldberg leaned forward. "The word we use back home, Lieutenant, is 'shill'."

Dumont leaned back and looked down his nose at the American. "Use whatever word you like, *mon ami*, but why on earth are you asking me about this? I have nothing to do with Mr Beecham's operations. I have never met the man." He relaxed his shoulders and smiled apologetically.

"Really, *Monsieur* Merlin. I did not know Bridget Healy. I have no knowledge of her pregnancy and her unfortunate abortion. I would be grateful now if you could let me return to my important work. We are fighting a war together, you know."

Merlin and his officers kept on at Dumont for another half hour but made no headway. Eventually, Merlin conceded defeat. "Very well, Lieutenant. You may go, but we may want to see you again. If you are likely to leave London, please let us know."

As they were getting to their feet, Sergeant Reeves appeared at the door. "Sorry to interrupt you, sir, but there are two gentlemen here who say they have an appointment with you. I told them you were busy but one of them got rather irate so I thought I'd better let you know. Names of Tomlinson and Vorster."

Merlin thought he saw a flicker of concern cross Dumont's face. "That's all right, Sergeant. Please show them in here. We are finished with this gentleman." Reeves disappeared down the corridor and quickly returned with Tomlinson and Vorster in tow.

"Thank you, Lieutenant. The sergeant will show you out." Merlin watched carefully as Dumont squeezed past the new arrivals and avoided Vorster's enquiring eye.

*   *   *

Doctor James McGregor and Constable Vernon Price were standing in a corridor of the Royal Free Hospital in Hampstead. "Is he going to be all right?"

"He's a very lucky man, Constable. You saved his life. What exactly happened again?"

Price, a stocky young officer attached to Holloway police station, had already explained that, during his morning round, he had been alerted by a loud cry from an alleyway. "Even in broad daylight, it was hard to see clearly into the alley, which was narrow, overhung by rickety guttering and roofing, and cluttered with large bins. I didn't have a torch with me but I could just make out three men, two of whom appeared to be tipping the third into a bin.

"I shouted, blew my whistle and ran into the alley. By the time I got to the bin, the third man was already in it, one leg hanging awkwardly over the side. The two others had scarpered. I blew my whistle again and gave chase but they were too far ahead. They were out of sight when I reached the end of the alley and I knew the victim was my priority.

"When I got back to him there was another man there. An off-duty fireman who'd heard my whistle. We got the man out of the bin as carefully as we could, flagged down a van in Holloway Road and got here as quickly as possible. Tom, the fireman, used his shirt to try and staunch the bleeding."

The doctor, a plump Yorkshireman with a bushy grey beard, acknowledged the fireman waiting, shirtless, on a chair behind Constable Price.

"Well done both of you! By some miracle, the knife missed his vital organs. He took some powerful blows to the head as well, but his skull must be pretty solid as I can't see a fracture. You two and the van driver deserve a medal, but there's nowt more you can do here for now. Why don't you go back to the police station, Constable, and see if you can find out who this fellow is?"

"Did you find anything on him that might be of help in identifying him?"

"His possessions are all in this little bag. Keys and a wallet containing some money and a note of a telephone number. Also a small bottle of hair tonic with the address of a hairdresser on Holloway Road."

"Thank you." Price read out the telephone number with a look of surprise. "WHI1212 – that's Whitehall 1212."

The doctor raised an eyebrow. "Scotland Yard, isn't it?"

"Yes. I wonder why?"

*   *   *

"Sorry to keep you waiting, gentlemen. Thank you for bringing Mr Vorster to see us, Mr Tomlinson."

Tomlinson glared. "Look here, Merlin. I'm trying to be helpful but it really takes the biscuit, keeping me here, twiddling my thumbs. I'm a busy man. You've kept me waiting for…"

"There was no need for you to wait, Mr Tomlinson. It is Mr Vorster we wish to see."

"I waited because I wanted to know about your trip to Northamptonshire. I understand from Mrs Cavendish that there were developments."

There was a sound of scraping chairs as Bridges settled Vorster at the table. "We did indeed make progress – and I would be happy to discuss our visit with you at some point – but we really can't mix apples and pears. The purpose of this appointment is to interview Mr Vorster on a matter that has nothing to do with you, Mr Tomlinson, or your clients. Unless you are here with Mr Vorster as his legal representative, I must ask you to take your leave. You can wait if you wish or the duty officer can arrange another appointment for us."

Tomlinson's face flushed but he managed to suppress his anger. "As far as I'm aware there will be no need for Mr Vorster to have legal representation and, if there were, I doubt it would be appropriate for me to provide it." He looked at his junior.

"Do you require representation?" Vorster shook his head. "No. Very well, I'll do as you say and arrange another appointment at the desk. Good morning to you, Chief Inspector." Tomlinson turned and reached for the doorknob but had to jump back as an out-of-breath Robinson suddenly burst through.

"Sorry, sir."

"Hello. This is a pleasant surprise. We thought you were in Bristol."

"I eventually managed to persuade my uncle – sorry, the assistant commissioner – that I would be of more use here. I got off his train at Swindon and caught the first service back. I'm sorry if I'm interrupting something important but I really need a quick word, sir."

Merlin turned to Tomlinson, who was following the exchange with interest. "You can go, sir." The solicitor departed with a loud harrumph.

"We were just about to interview Mr Vorster, here. Can't it wait until after that?" The fraught look on Robinson's face suggested it couldn't. "Very well. I won't be long, gentlemen." Merlin found an empty room next door. "All right, Constable. Fire away."

Robinson handed Merlin Peter Wilson's letter. Merlin read it carefully. "Hmm." He paused to think. "We'll discuss this all together when we've finished with Vorster. Important as it is, Constable, I still think it could have waited until after we'd finished the interview."

"It's not just the letter, sir. I needed to speak to you straightaway because I think I just saw him."

"Saw who?"

"Wilson says the Frenchman he saw in Bridget Healy's room at the hotel was a tall, dark man with a limp. I just saw a tall, dark, French officer with a slight limp leaving the Yard as I came in."

Merlin suddenly realised what she was saying. "Dumont?"

"If that's who it was."

"Where is he now?"

"I ran after him but a taxi drove up and he managed to escape me."

*   *   *

"We are investigating the death of a young lady in a botched illegal abortion. The lady was an Irish girl named Bridget Healy. I apologise for the subterfuge but Mr Goldberg here, whom you met the other night, is in fact an American detective seconded to the Yard. In his conversation with you, he asked you about an Irish girl you had been seen with – the girl in this photograph, Bridget Healy. You and your friend, Dumont, denied knowing her but the detective here heard one of you mention her name and the word 'pregnant'. We have now spoken to Dumont. What do you have to say now?"

Vorster's eyes flitted nervously back and forth between Merlin and Goldberg as he weighed his options. Eventually, he decided on one. He tapped the photograph. "Well, now you show me the photograph, yes, I recognise her. But I only knew this girl as a pretty face in a crowd, nothing more. The name Bridget Healy meant nothing to me."

"And what about her being pregnant and having to have an abortion?"

"I know nothing about an abortion. I vaguely remember someone asking where the pretty Irish girl was one night, and someone else saying that we wouldn't see her again for a while as she was 'up the duff'. I believe those were the words used. I may have repeated that to someone."

"Can you remember who it was you heard say that?"

"No, sorry. You know what the Ritz is like at night. Loud voices, buckets of drink."

"You strike me as someone who can handle his drink, Mr Vorster."

"Perhaps the night I met you, Mr Goldberg. Not every night, though."

"It wasn't your friend, Dumont, who made the comment?"

"I said I can't remember, Mr Merlin."

"Lieutenant Dumont has a limp, doesn't he?"

"He does. I think he had a riding accident or something before the war. He disguises it quite well when he has his cane with him. You can't tell then."

"You and Dumont are good friends, aren't you?"

"We are friends. I don't know that we are necessarily good friends."

"Do you have any professional relationship with him?"

"No. Unless you call providing him and his French friends with occasional share tips a professional relationship."

"What about Peregrine Beecham?"

"What about him?"

"What is your relationship with him?"

Vorster's cheeks reddened. "I don't see what business that is of yours."

"Don't you? Beecham runs an illegal gambling den. You don't think that's police business."

"I am not involved in his gambling business. I have played there on occasion, when funds have allowed."

"Come now, Vorster. You loiter around the Ritz and find customers for Beecham, don't you? That's what you did with Detective Goldberg here, isn't it? You look out for likely punters with a view to taking them round the corner to be fleeced by Peregrine Beecham."

"Mr Beecham runs a straight operation, Chief Inspector. People win, people lose. Of course, the odds – as always – favour the house but your use of the word 'fleece' is, I think…"

They were interrupted. It was Sergeant Reeves again. "Sorry to disturb you again. I just received an urgent call for you from the station at Holloway. I've made a note of the message here, sir." Reeves handed over the note. "They said it was very important so…"

Merlin read the note to himself: 'Man attacked and nearly killed on Holloway Road. Identified as Conor Devlin. Man with that name rang for Merlin earlier, saying he had important security information and wanted to come and see Merlin. Man has just regained consciousness but in a bad way in Royal Free'.

Merlin thought for a moment then patted Goldberg on the shoulder. "Detective, something's come up." He handed over the note. "I'd like you to grab Robinson and go up to see this chap in Hampstead. Call me when you've spoken to him. Bridges and I will finish off with Mr Vorster here."

Goldberg read the note, nodded and followed Sergeant Reeves out of the door. Merlin returned to Vorster. "We know that you run errands for Beecham. Why you need to do this when you work for a respected firm of London solicitors and are, as I understand, the son of a wealthy South African industrialist, I really don't know."

Merlin noticed Vorster flinch at the mention of his father. "Whatever the reason, I have to advise you that your choice of friends or associates is extremely unwise. You say you know nothing of Bridget Healy's abortion. However, we have only just now received reliable information that your friend, Dumont, was present in the hotel room where the abortion was carried out. Do you really expect me to believe that you know nothing of it?"

A nerve in Vorster's right cheek began to twitch. "Yes, I do. Dumont told me nothing about this. I know nothing about any abortion or…"

They were interrupted yet again. Two people were at the door. One a was a short man in his 60s. Despite the heat outside, he was wearing a woollen three-piece suit beneath a heavy blue overcoat. He removed his hat to reveal dyed black hair, combed to hang like a curtain from his dome-like cranium. Bright, intelligent eyes darted around beneath the jungles of his eyebrows. He had an imposing presence notwithstanding his diminutive stature.

His companion was a heavily built man, who looked like he might have a powerful pair of fists. An angry Reeves appeared behind them. "I'm very sorry, sir. These men were at the desk when I got back there, enquiring about Mr Vorster. I started to ask them who they were but this big brute knocked me out of the way and led the little chap down here. I'm going to get some other officers and put the two of them in custody for assault and whatever else I can think of. Blasted cheek. I've never…"

"That's my son you have there," the short man interrupted, his lower lip jutting out intimidatingly.

Merlin appraised the new visitors. He shook his head at Reeves. "That's all right, Sergeant. No need to arrest anyone. The gentlemen can join us. Perhaps you could find a couple more chairs?"

Sergeant Reeves made his astonishment and dissatisfaction at Merlin's response clear but did as he was told.

The old man appraised Merlin in turn. "I presume you are the man in charge. I am Pieter Vorster. Please explain what you are doing with my son." He gave his son a cursory nod of acknowledgement.

"I am Detective Chief Inspector Merlin, sir. And this is Detective Sergeant Bridges."

Pieter Vorster ignored the proffered handshakes and examined his son's face. "The boy's looking distinctly peaky. You appear to be giving him the third degree. What's he done? Stolen the Crown Jewels?"

"Not quite."

The newcomers took their seats. "This fellow is my associate, Van de Merwe. I've just completed a long and tiresome journey from South Africa. I'd be grateful if you could tell me what is going on."

"We are asking your son some questions about the death of a woman with whom he was acquainted."

"Very slightly acquainted, Father."

"Shut up, Rupert. Anything else?"

"He has some friends in whom we have an interest – a Free French officer and a local gangster."

Pieter Vorster looked at his son with disgust. "And has he been able to help you?"

"Not yet, no."

"Do you have anything on my son? Is he under arrest?"

"No. We are just asking questions."

"If you have nothing on him then is he at liberty to go?"

"We have more questions."

"May I politely request that you save those for another time. I would like to talk to my son and assess whether he should see you again with legal representation."

"You are within your rights, of course." Merlin sighed and glanced at Bridges. "May I ask how long you'll be staying in London?"

"I shall be putting up at The Dorchester for three or four weeks."

"I would like an assurance that your son will remain within the jurisdiction. His departure for South Africa would be unhelpful."

"Don't worry, Merlin, he'll be staying here. I can assure you I have no desire to turn my son into a fugitive."

*   *   *

A brown package was waiting on Merlin's desk with a covering note from Robinson: 'Sketch of one of the men seen Friday night in Flood Street by Mrs Wilcox. No success with the others. Just arrived on my desk as received your instruction to go to Hampstead so passing unseen to you, sir.'

Merlin unsealed the envelope and looked at the pencil-and-charcoal drawing of a young man. He realised he'd left his glasses in the interview room and held the drawing closer. At first sight, the blurred image stirred nothing in him. Then, as it became clearer, something about the nose and mouth began to seem familiar.

The drawing itself gave no clue as to the subject's hair colour but there was a line at the bottom that read: 'Witness not sure about hair colour but best guess fair/sandy/blond'. The forehead was receding. The mouth was small. A not unattractive face but the artist had captured something mean in the man's expression. Merlin held the sketch away and then brought it close again. All of a sudden he realised he knew the face. By God, he knew it!

"Sergeant, come here. Sergeant!"

*   *   *

Devlin was not a pretty sight. The heavy bandaging around the top of his head was speckled with blood and the face beneath was deathly pale. One eye was covered by the bandage. Doctor McGregor had given Goldberg and Robinson a full rundown of the injuries. They knew there was further heavy bandaging beneath the bedclothes. Devlin was upright in bed but appeared to be sleeping.

"Are you sure he's all right to speak?"

"He's dosed up with morphine, Constable, so he'll be a little woozy, but his brain is all there. Obviously, take it easy with him. He is very keen to speak to you – he's been going on about nothing else since he regained consciousness. Mr Devlin, Mr Devlin… the officers are here to speak to you."

Devlin's visible eye opened and his lips parted. He spoke in a croaking whisper. "Inspector… Inspector Merlin." The doctor nodded to Goldberg, then slipped away.

"No, sir. I'm Detective Goldberg and this is Constable Robinson. Chief Inspector Merlin sent us along to speak to you."

Devlin found his voice. "My head has been a little bashed about but…" a half-smile broke on his lips, "my hearing seems to have been affected. It's really strange but you sound like a Yank."

"That's because I am one, Mr Devlin, but I work for Mr Merlin, as does the constable here."

"Hello, Mr Devlin."

"Ah, that's a proper English voice, if I ever heard one." His eye lingered on Robinson. "A Yank and a pretty English rose. An interesting pairing but if this fellow Merlin trusts you…" Devlin closed his eyes as a shudder of pain went through him. A long minute passed before his eyes opened again.

"Sorry about that. Doesn't do your insides much good, poking a blade of good Sheffield steel around inside them. Better get on and tell you my story before I pop my clogs." Devlin saw Goldberg's look of incomprehension. "Die, that is, Detective."

Devlin cleared his throat. "I'll try to make this as concise as I can. I spent much of the 30s in Paris. I learned to speak French to a pretty good standard and I made a few French friends. When I returned to London, I inevitably found there were one or two people I knew in the Free French forces. I have had several different occupations but when I returned to London just before the war, I took up employment in what is politely called the security business – but I call it snooping. Mostly snooping on cheating spouses for divorce purposes. I discovered I had a knack for it.

"In due course, my skills came to the notice of my Free French contacts and I undertook a few snooping jobs for them. Following and observing suspect French exiles, that sort of thing." Devlin paused and nodded at a jug of water on his bedside table. Robinson poured out a glass and trickled some between his parched lips. He cleared his throat again.

"In my most recent job for the French, a job on which I was engaged for the past week or so, I was to keep an eye on some of my friends' fellow Free French officers. There was suspicion on high that someone was leaking information to Pétain's crew in Vichy.

"I followed various of the officers. By the end of this week, there was one I had come to suspect. I aired my suspicions to my contacts but they weren't interested. It became clear to me that the senior officers had already decided on the culprit without any clear evidence or, at least, any evidence they were prepared to share with me. They wanted my help now to fit up the fellow they had fixed on. I declined and withdrew from the operation. This was yesterday.

"I was worried about what would happen now and didn't sleep well. This morning, I decided to give your boss a call. I had seen police officers visiting the Free French headquarters and heard his name mentioned. I knew some investigation was under way." A globule of blood escaped from under the bandage and trickled slowly past Devlin's mouth. Robinson reached out with her handkerchief to mop it away.

"Thank you, dear. This morning I had a haircut, after which I made a telephone call. I left a message for your boss. Minutes later, I was attacked."

"Is there anything you can tell us about that attack?"

"Sorry, but most of it's a blank to me, Mr Goldberg. All I can remember is the stink of the rubbish bin into which they bundled me. You'd best speak to the copper who saved me to learn more about that. What I do know is that it was a professional attack. I would guess most likely by someone who didn't like what I was saying to the French."

"What about other enemies?

"Oh, there are plenty of people around who don't like me, Constable. There's a string of deceiving husbands and wives to kick off with. I don't think any of those people would turn their hand to murder, though. And I doubt I was being robbed. I don't exactly have the reputation of a wealthy man."

"Who are your contacts in the Free French organisation?"

"Commandant Angers and Captain Rougemont but I don't think either of them would have had anything to do with this.

The key must lie in my suspicions. The man who is being fingered as the spy is called Beaulieu – Lieutenant Beaulieu. They want him out of the way either as a scapegoat or for some other reason. The officer I suspect of treachery is called Dumont."

Goldberg and Robinson exchanged astonished looks. "Why do you suspect him, Mr Devlin?"

"I saw him meeting with…" Devlin suddenly convulsed with pain and cried out. A nurse hurried in to tend to him. After a quick look, she turned to the police officers. "I'm sorry but that's enough for now. Can you please go?" Reluctantly, Goldberg and Robinson left the room.

*   *   *

"We got him, sir. Luckily there was a temporary shortage of taxis."

"Where is he now, Sergeant?"

"He's in the one of the basement cells. The old fellow insisted on staying with him and I agreed."

"Is that a good idea, Bridges?"

"I thought it might be helpful. The father is extremely domineering and clearly they don't get on. It's possible he could jangle his son's nerves and make it easier for us to get the truth out of him."

"Fair enough. You could be right. Let's leave them to stew together for a while. Has the warrant for Dumont been issued?"

"Yes, sir. Sergeant Reeves is handling the arrest with a couple of constables. They are going to his digs first. If he's not there, they'll go on to Carlton Gardens."

"Let's hope they find him. Any news from Robinson and Goldberg?"

"Not yet. I rang the Holloway police station and got a little more information. The man is called Devlin. He's some sort of private eye. He'd just had his hair cut locally. They found some hair tonic on him, which led them to the shop. The barber knew him well and was able to provide an address. They are going round to have a look now."

"What did his message say again?"

"That he had important security information for us."

"Could be about anything but I suppose I should have mentioned it to Harold when he rang me just now."

"What was he after?"

"He said they might have got something useful from that photograph of de Metz's. Some initials that appeared after scientific treatment. He said he'd be in touch with more details later."

"Tomlinson apparently arranged with Reeves to come here at 10.30 tomorrow."

"Call him to rearrange. I'd like to see him and the man who's now running the bank – Fleming isn't it? And whoever else they think should be at the meeting. I think I'd prefer to meet them on their turf. Tell Tomlinson we'll be at Sackville Bank at noon tomorrow."

Merlin glanced over at the clock. "It's two-fifteen now. We'll leave the Vorsters for another hour. Meanwhile, I'm starving. See if you can rustle up a few sandwiches from Tony's, please, Sergeant."

*   *   *

"Hello again, gentlemen. I'm afraid that you'll have to remove yourself, Mr Vorster. On this occasion we most certainly need to interview your son on his own and any objection…" Pieter Vorster raised a conciliatory hand and, to Merlin's surprise, made no argument. He seemed chastened either by whatever he and his son had discussed or the lengthy wait they had endured in this bleak room – or both.

"I've had a long chat with Rupert, Merlin. He has been an utter fool – not for the first time in his life – and I'm going to have to bail him out financially yet again, but he is no murderer. I have asked him to make a clean breast of everything." He glowered at his son. "And you will, won't you?" The young man ran a shaking hand through his hair and nodded. Vorster Senior picked up his hat and growled: "I'll be at The Dorchester if you need me."

"You've already read him his rights, haven't you, Sergeant?"

"Yes, sir."

"Very well." There were no chairs in the cell. Rupert Vorster was sitting at one end of the bunk and the policemen squeezed on to the other. "Let's get straight to the point. As has been explained to you by Sergeant Bridges here, a Mr Edgar Powell was murdered at his Flood Street flat last Friday night. We have a witness who saw a man loitering near the entrance to Mr Powell's apartment block that night, somewhere around eight-thirty to nine o'clock, within the timespan when we believe Mr Powell died. This witness described the man to our police sketch artist, who produced this likeness."

Merlin showed Vorster the drawing. "We think this is you. Now, we can go to the trouble of bringing in the witness for a formal physical identification, or you can save us a lot of time by confirming that you were there."

Vorster gave the faintest of nods. "I... I... admit that I was there, Chief Inspector, but I had nothing to do with the death of Mr Powell, I swear it."

"Why were you there?"

"It's a long story."

"We have all the time in the world."

Vorster folded his arms then unfolded them. He stared down miserably at his feet. "As you have seen, my father is quite – what shall we say? – a handful. We don't get on very well. He is a very wealthy man and you would assume, I am sure, that as his only son, I would be rolling in it. That is not the case. I am kept on a very tight leash. On occasion, Father has seen fit to loosen the leash – albeit reluctantly – when I have got into financial difficulty."

"You mean he's had to bail you out of trouble from time to time?"

"I would prefer to say help me out rather than bail me out. However, there it is. After I left university, my father insisted, before he would contemplate employing me in his business, that I acquire a profession. He left the arrangements to me and I eventually got taken on at Mr Tomlinson's firm. At the beginning, my father wanted me to subsist on the meagre income of a clerk but he relented enough to provide me with a modest flat in town and a small supplementary allowance."

"Most people would be delighted to get an allowance and a flat in London from their parents."

"That's as may be, Sergeant, but I have been raised in wealth and have expensive tastes and habits."

"And would one of those expensive habits be gambling?"

Vorster clasped his hands together and nodded slowly. "It would, Chief Inspector. I do like to gamble. Sadly, I seem to have had a run of bad luck."

"You gambled at Beecham's place?"

"I did, and I lost. Beecham was very friendly and provided substantial credit to me because of who my father is. He was not so friendly when I said my father would not cover my losses."

"You asked your father?"

"No, I couldn't bring myself to grovel to the old man. And I can assure you he would have made me grovel." His head dropped. "As he most certainly will do now."

"So what happened with Beecham? And what has all this to do with Powell?"

"Patience, Chief Inspector, I'm getting there. Mr Beecham and I came to an accommodation regarding my debts. I have good social skills. I am a good conversationalist. Some might call me good-looking. I am well educated. I get on with people. I agreed to spend my evenings in the Ritz, and occasionally in other watering holes, identifying and befriending new customers for Mr Beecham's establishment. That was how I met Dumont and the other French officers I know. It is a rather tedious way to spend one's evenings, and tiring too, but Beecham is happy with my efforts."

"All these late nights can't have been good for your day job?"

"I have stamina, Sergeant."

"Is there anything else you do for Beecham?"

"Occasionally, he asks me for stock market intelligence. Or for other information I might get through my job. He was particularly interested in any information I could get concerning Simon Arbuthnot who is, or rather was, the major client of the firm."

Merlin rubbed his shoulder. It had been a long and intense day and his bullet wound had begun to ache, as it usually did when he was bushed. "And did you have information on him?"

"Simon Arbuthnot, Beecham explained to me, owed him a hell of a lot of money. Knowing he ran a huge and successful business, Beecham had been understanding and had been giving Arbuthnot time to sort things out when, all of a sudden, the man disappeared into the army and got out of Beecham's reach.

"Before his disappearance, Arbuthnot had drunkenly told Beecham about some valuable share certificates that could cover his debts 10 or 20 times over. Beecham asked me to find out what I could about these at the firm. I approached Philip Arbuthnot in a roundabout way, but it was quite clear he knew nothing about them. I did learn, however, by keeping my ear to the ground that Tomlinson kept the certificates safe somewhere, though I never found where. After Simon Arbuthnot's death became known, I heard chat in the office about the certificates having been removed some months previously by Mr Arbuthnot, together with his will. I told Mr Beecham all about this.

"Then this fellow Powell appeared with his letter from Arbuthnot, and I heard Mr Tomlinson telling someone on the telephone that the letter would probably indicate the whereabouts of the certificates and the will. I told Beecham. Then I thought about it. It occurred to me that I might have a chance of extricating myself from Beecham's clutches. If I could get hold of the certificates – or information leading to them – on behalf of Beecham, perhaps he would wipe out my debts. I resolved to take a chance and have a go. I then managed to get hold of Powell's address from a secretary in the office."

"And how exactly did you intend to get Mr Powell to give you what he had?"

"Ah." Vorster sat up. "I hadn't exactly worked that out. I was going to wing it – I can be a persuasive chap."

"You thought you'd get Powell, an honourable man entrusted with Arbuthnot's dying wish, to entrust the letter to you, a clerk with no significant relationship to the Arbuthnots?"

"I was desperate to get out of Beecham's clutches. I thought I might tell Powell I was Philip's close friend. I'd tell him the truth about the gambling and Arbuthnot's debts. Persuade him that it was sensible and in Philip's best interests to help pay off Beecham."

"And if this unlikely and deluded stratagem didn't work, what would you do then? Threaten him? Assault him? Murder him? That's what happened, isn't it? Powell rejected your implausible request. He was not particularly well built and was still recovering from his ordeal in Cyprus. You, Mr Vorster, are a bit of a physical specimen, aren't you? Almost as solid as that ape of your father's. You overpowered him, tortured him, drowned him. Isn't that what happened?"

Vorster looked panic-stricken as he fully realised for the first time the danger of his position. He gripped the edge of the table tightly. "But… but… I never met him, Chief Inspector. I never met the man. Before I had a chance, I saw someone else gain entrance to Powell's flat. I saw a man carrying a box of some sort at the street door of the building. I heard him ring the bell and talk into the speaking tube. I heard him call out that he had a delivery for Mr Powell and then go into the building.

"I waited and watched and, almost an hour later, I saw that person come out and hurry off. While I was waiting for the coast to clear, I was churning everything over in my mind and, to put it simply, lost my bottle. I recognised that my plan was, as you say, deluded. My desperation to get out from under Beecham had clouded my judgment. I walked away, Chief Inspector. You must believe me. I walked away."

"I assume this is the story you told your father? He claims to believe you. Can he tell when you're speaking the truth, Mr Vorster?"

Vorster's face looked washed out with fear and exhaustion. He shrugged.

"And this person at the door. Did you recognise him?"

"No. I was standing in the archway of the rear courtyard of the building behind a wall. There was a gap through which I had a view of the door. I saw a man well wrapped up in a gabardine coat and wearing a large fedora hat. He was about my height but I couldn't see his face."

"So you are saying Powell himself let this man in the front door?"

"Yes. To take delivery of the box, presumably. But the man stayed there much longer than one would expect of a delivery man."

"So you are saying this was Powell's murderer?"

"If the murder took place around the time you say, he must be the likeliest candidate."

"Did you see anyone else?"

"There was a woman looking for her dog. I saw a few passing pedestrians?"

"Any men loitering nearby?"

"Not that I can remember. I didn't have much of a view of the street from where I was."

Merlin looked coldly at Vorster.

"I swear I didn't kill him, Chief Inspector."

Merlin raised his eyebrows at Bridges, who shook his head dismissively. "I'm sorry, Mr Vorster, this story seems very glib and convenient. I don't think we believe you. I think you were the man at the door who gained access to Powell's flat by claiming you had a delivery. This man you saw is an invention. I'm not going to charge you yet, but if you want to clear yourself, you're going to have to come up with something more substantive. Until you do so, you remain our prime suspect."

Merlin stood up and turned to Bridges. "Come on, Sergeant. Perhaps a quiet night in the cells will aid Mr Powell's memory. We'll revisit everything tomorrow."

Vorster's head slumped to his chest and he started to whimper. However, just as the policemen were going through the door, he called out excitedly: "Wait, Mr Merlin. I can remember one thing. The man… The man at the door of the flats. He was wearing aftershave. A powerful cologne, I think I'd recognise it again. It wasn't a run-of-the-mill fragrance."

Merlin looked back at him and nodded. "Goodnight." He slammed the door shut.

*   *   *

It was only eight but it felt later to a weary Merlin. He called out for Sonia but there was no answer and he made straight for the bedroom, where he collapsed on the bed. Not long after, he heard a key in the front door. "I'm in here, darling." Sonia appeared and joined him on the bed.

"Are you all right, Frank?"

"Just tired. I had a heavy day. No need to bore you with it, but we made good progress."

Sonia stroked his cheek gently. "Frank, you know I am always interested in your work. Please tell me your news."

"Well it seems, amazingly, that the three cases I have been working on are interconnected. And, on top of that, we may have a lead on a possible espionage plot."

Sonia squeezed his hand and inched closer. "How exciting! My brilliant detective!" She gave him a quick kiss on the cheek. "I have news of my day, too."

"Good news, I hope."

Sonia hesitated. "Good. At least I hope good." She kissed Merlin's cheek again. "I went to see the doctor today."

"About that tummy bug? Was everything all right?"

"Yes, everything is fine."

"I hope he didn't charge you an arm and a leg. You didn't settle it yourself, did you? I…"

"Shush, Frank. Don't worry about the money."

"Just tell me how much and I'll…"

"I'm pregnant, Frank."

Merlin's mouth opened wide but no words came out.

"Cat got your tongue, Frank?"

"I'm… I'm…" Merlin examined Sonia's face carefully then lowered his eyes to her stomach. "Are you sure? Is the doctor sure?"

"Quite sure. You are happy then? I thought you might be angry."

Merlin reached his arm around Sonia's neck. "Of course I'm happy. Astonished, but happy. Why on earth would I be angry?"

"Because we didn't exactly plan this. You are a very busy and important man. We are not married. This baby might be – what is the word? – an encumbrance, an embarrassing encumbrance to you."

"How could you think such a thing? I am delighted. Come, come here." He hugged her tight then suddenly pulled away. "Sorry, I wasn't thinking. I need to be more careful. Don't want to hurt the baby."

Sonia giggled. "You silly man. A little cuddle is not going to hurt the baby."

"Oh, good. Well, I don't know much about babies, do I?" Merlin's hand manoeuvred its way under Sonia's blouse and touched her stomach "I can't feel him or her."

"It's too early yet, you idiot."

He pulled her towards him again and they kissed. They lay back on the pillows and within minutes, despite the excitement of Sonia's news, Merlin was fast asleep.

Chapter 15

Thursday 19 June

London

"Mr Fleming will see you now, gentlemen." A young bank clerk led Merlin and Bridges into a room that matched almost exactly Merlin's expectation of what a City boardroom would look like.

Tomlinson, Fleming and Philip Arbuthnot were awaiting them at a grand, brightly polished mahogany table. The walls of the room were hung with old paintings and historical prints of London. Above the table were three large chandeliers, antique cabinets and tables lined the walls and a beautiful old grandfather clock occupied the far corner of the room. The picture windows offered a view of gabled City roofs and a glimpse of the Tower of London and Tower Bridge in the distance. Merlin paused to admire a print of Somerset House and the Thames in 1841.

Tomlinson waved a sedentary greeting from the table as Sidney Fleming walked over to the policemen. "Do you like our boardroom, Chief Inspector?"

Merlin turned his attention to the dapper, bow-tied man who was now extending a hand to him. "I certainly do. Mr Fleming, I presume? Beautiful pictures you have here and I see the German bombers have been kind enough to avoid ruining your fine view."

"Yes, we have been lucky to avoid damage ourselves, as have the buildings you can see going down to the river. The story is different in other directions."

Philip Arbuthnot slid up behind Fleming. "Chief Inspector."

"I thought it appropriate to invite Philip to join us, Mr Merlin, as the leading family member."

"No Mrs Cavendish?"

"My aunt was taken poorly yesterday. She has a touch of summer flu. Nothing serious."

Fleming led Merlin and Bridges to the table. "She had been keen to attend but unfortunately wasn't up to the trip down from Northamptonshire."

"That's a pity."

After everyone was seated, Tomlinson was the first to speak. "I do hope Mr Merlin that, despite Mrs Cavendish's absence, you will feel it within your powers to share the details of the box contents with us. I am, after all, solicitor to the late Mr Arbuthnot's estate, to Philip here, to Mrs Cavendish and, of course, to the bank. In the circumstances…"

Merlin raised his hand. "Thank you, Mr Tomlinson. I am not going to hand the contents over to you but am prepared to disclose broadly what they are. Given how and where we found the box, it will be no surprise to you to hear that Mrs Cavendish was the intended recipient of her brother's letter and of the box contents. You should be aware that the correspondence in the box references criminal activity that will, of course, have to be investigated."

Fleming, Tomlinson and Arbuthnot exchanged nervous glances.

At a nod from Merlin, Bridges opened his briefcase and set out Simon Arbuthnot's three envelopes. Merlin picked up one of them. "In this we have Simon Arbuthnot's final will. In it he leaves pretty much everything to his sister, Lucinda Cavendish."

Philip Arbuthnot blanched and raised his hands in the air. "That… that can't be right. He wouldn't…"

"Bear with me please, Mr Arbuthnot. Let me lay the full story before you." He picked up another, thicker envelope. "This contains 10 bearer-share certificates for a total of 100 shares in Enterprisas Simal in Argentina." Tomlinson and Fleming were suddenly galvanised. "We understand this represents the entire share capital of that company." Fleming nodded.

Merlin held up the third, smaller envelope. "And here we have Simon Arbuthnot's last letter to his sister." He paused to withdraw the five sheets of paper, then looked up at the anxious faces opposite him. "I'll summarise.

"One – in recent years, Simon Arbuthnot built up very large personal debts through reckless gambling.

"Two – while he managed to clear some of those debts, substantial ones remain, a large proportion of which are owed to a man called Peregrine Beecham.

"Three – in order to meet his debts, he ran through his liquid assets, borrowed against illiquid assets and ultimately resorted to fraud." Merlin looked at Fleming. "This fraud, he tells us, was perpetrated on clients of the bank, principally through illegal diversion of funds placed under the management of the bank. This was, of course, also a fraud perpetrated on the bank itself.

"Four – aside from his personal assets, and his partnership in the bank, which it was not easy to liquidate, the most valuable asset in Mr Arbuthnot's possession was the ownership of Enterprisas Simal as represented by the bearer shares. He mentions that these certificates were originally acquired in dubious circumstances from someone called Franzi Meyer.

"Five – there are parties outside the family with claims on these certificates. A son of Meyer's has mounted a legal suit in Argentina to recover the certificates, although Simon Arbuthnot expressed his confidence that the suit would come to nothing.

Also, he says that Peregrine Beecham has become aware of the certificates' existence and their potential as a source of repayment of Arbuthnot's gambling debts to him.

"Six – his bequest of his estate to his sister is not intended as a slight to his son. In light of the dire circumstances outlined in the letter, he decided that his sister was better placed to conserve and protect Philip's inheritance. He advises Philip to go to Argentina to take hold of the South American businesses."

Merlin returned the letter to its envelope and Bridges put it and the other two packages in his briefcase. There followed several seconds of shell-shocked silence. A very shaken Philip Arbuthnot was first to speak. "Where exactly does this leave us? I understand now why there was all this John Buchan stuff to get the certificates, the will and the advice secretly to my aunt. But here we are. We – or rather *you* – have the documents, and my father's secret advice to my aunt is secret no longer. What happens, now? What does it mean in practical terms?"

Fleming stared grimly at the young man. "What it means, Philip, is that your father's bank is in very serious trouble."

"Were you aware of your partner's fraud, Mr Fleming?"

"My partner? More my employer than my partner, Mr Merlin. And the answer is no, I wasn't aware." Fleming looked pointedly at his solicitor.

Tomlinson had gone even paler than Philip. "The information you have given us erm… Chief Inspector is erm… very shocking. Very shocking, indeed. I really must have some time with my clients erm… to consider the legal ramifications of it all."

"Very well, Mr Tomlinson. Give Mr Fleming your legal advice. He is going to need your very best. Naturally, we shall have to pass our information on Mr Arbuthnot's fraud to the appropriate section of the City of London police. They will no doubt…"

Fleming suddenly brought a hand down loudly on the table. "Dammit, Merlin, you must understand…" His voiced cracked with emotion. "This is a most delicate matter that must be handled most carefully. There are the depositors' interests to be considered as well as the people who have put funds under management. There are also the numerous regulatory and market implications. Any premature leakage of…"

"As I was about to say, Mr Fleming, the City of London fraud squad will be aware of the delicacy of the situation and no doubt will take all such factors into account. They are experienced in this sort of thing, I am not. I presume there'll have to be some level of consultation with the Bank of England, among others, but I'll leave all that to them."

Fleming stared at Philip Arbuthnot as he dabbed his forehead with a handkerchief. "I should emphasise as well that the certificates are not Simon's – or I suppose I should now say Mrs Cavendish's – to dispose of as she wishes. Simon held them, or 90 per cent of them at least, in trust for the bank and they are thus the property of the bank. If anyone seeks to dispute this, the bank will assert its rights most vigorously."

Merlin looked down at the table. It was so highly polished he could just about see his reflection in it. "Simon Arbuthnot touches on this in the letter. I think you'll need to have a careful discussion with your auditors on the subject, Mr Fleming."

"What on earth do you mean by that, Chief Inspector?"

"He says the declaration of trust never happened."

"But it was all sorted and verified by our auditors!"

"That's why you need to speak to them, sir."

Fleming banged a hand down on the table in frustration and started to say something but Tomlinson intervened. "I think it would probably be wise now, Chief Inspector, if you and the sergeant left us. There is much to consider and I need to have a long talk with my clients."

"Of course, Mr Tomlinson. We'll leave you to it. Come on, Sergeant."

*   *   *

Back at his desk half an hour later, Merlin found he couldn't get Sonia's bombshell out of his head. Was he really to be a father at last? Alice had been very keen on having children but it had become impossible once she'd fallen ill. Now it was really happening with Sonia.

Important issues would have to be resolved, principally the question of marriage. He was happy to tie the knot, but was she? Sonia gave the impression of wanting to be a free spirit. But illegitimacy was no minor thing in this day and age. Neither of them was much concerned with appearances but they would have to decide one way or another – and quickly too. Sonia wasn't showing yet but it would only be a matter of weeks. "Weeks, only weeks," Merlin muttered to himself.

"Are you all right, sir?" Bridges was at the door with Goldberg and Robinson.

"What? Oh, Sergeant. Sorry. Just thinking about something. Hello, everyone. Sit down, please. Things are happening so quickly that I want to make sure everyone's up to date. Let's go case by case, although they now increasingly appear to be linked to a greater or lesser degree." Merlin picked up the note he had made earlier.

"Let's start with Bridget Healy. We now know the identity of all three men who were at the hotel with her. The man who accompanied Bridget to the hotel was Peter Wilson, the chauffeur of Bridget's sister. Mr de Metz was the abortionist, as we have known for some time. And Lieutenant Dumont was the third man, who arrived later, threatened Wilson with a gun and told him to clear off. So the question is: can we deduce from all this that Dumont was the father of Bridget's child and that he arranged the abortion? My own view is that while a compelling case is clearly building against Dumont, we should continue to keep an open mind until we have absolutely convincing evidence."

"Or a confession, sir."

"Or a confession, Sergeant. Am I wrong in my view?"

Bridges, Robinson and Goldberg shook their heads in unison.

"Let's move on to de Metz. Sergeant, where are we with the forensics on that shell casing found at his flat?"

"I had a call this morning. They finally found the lost casing and have identified the gun it came from. They say it's a French gun, a *Modèle* 1935A. Not very common apparently."

"A French gun? Good. Another nail in Dumont's coffin, perhaps. The clearest circumstantial motive we have for the murder of de Metz still remains vengeance by Bridget's partner against the negligent abortionist. Was Dumont that partner and does he own a *Modèle* 1935A?"

"There's still the MI5 story."

"Yes, Constable, but MI5 appear to be off the hook on the basis of what Swanton told me."

"We still have the possibility of others threatened by de Metz's potential knowledge, Frank. You said Swanton couldn't say whether de Metz had attracted the attention of MI6 or SOE."

"You're right, Bernie. And now we have Devlin and his story, which in a way gives de Metz's claims some credibility. But we'll come to that in a minute. Next up, Eddie Powell." A bee buzzed noisily through the office window and hovered above the desk. Bridges got up and made a couple of unsuccessful attempts to swat it before it disappeared out of the window as suddenly as it had arrived.

"We now have Rupert Vorster's admission that he was outside Powell's flat on the night of the murder. He says he was going to try to get Arbuthnot's letter off him but bottled it and left."

"Why was he trying to get the message, sir?"

"Sorry, Constable. I forgot I hadn't explained that. Beecham knew about Arbuthnot's bearer certificates and wanted them.

Vorster surmised that the message in Powell's hands might disclose their whereabouts. He wanted Beecham to release him from his own debts and hoped to do so by getting hold of the certificates for him."

"He must have been pretty desperate if he'd kill for that."

"It appears he is in a desperate position, Constable. Owes a pile of money that his rich father won't pay for him. And let's not forget, the letter did ultimately lead to the certificates and other valuable information. But at present he denies the murder. Let's take him at his word, for the moment. He says he saw someone going up to Powell's flat and then hurrying out a while later. He can't physically identify the man but says he smelled nice."

"Pardon, sir?"

"He says, Constable, that the man in question was wearing a distinctive aftershave."

Two river barges outside sounded their klaxons noisily and at length. Merlin glared at the window in irritation until they stopped. "Finally, we have the new case of Mr Devlin, a private investigator badly beaten up and stabbed yesterday in Holloway, but, luckily, still with us. According to Devlin, and in line with de Metz's apparent claims, there is a security issue at the Free French office in London. The presence of a spy is suspected. Devlin was engaged by someone at Dorset Square to keep three officers under observation. Amazingly, Dumont was one of them. What are the other names?"

"Beaulieu and Meyer, Frank. When we went back to see Devlin this morning, he also gave us the names of the Free French officers he dealt with. They were our guys, Rougemont and Angers, under the direction of Aubertin. Devlin's story is that there was pressure to finger Beaulieu, even though there was no evidence. He liked Dumont for the part, the officers weren't interested so he pulled out. That was the day before yesterday. The day before he was viciously attacked."

Bridges raised a hand. "With respect, sir, what business is it of ours whether there are spies among the French? Isn't that something for MI5?"

"It is indeed, Sergeant, but given Dumont's involvement and what we have been told about de Metz, we have a strong interest in whatever has been going on. I am meeting Harold, by the way, after this. I'll tell him Devlin's story but he's apparently got something for us from de Metz's old photograph."

Merlin reached his hands behind his neck. "So that's where we are. Some way further down the line but still with many issues to resolve." He turned to Goldberg. "Are we any closer to finding Dumont?"

"The guy's gone completely to ground, Frank. At Carlton Gardens and Dorset Square they say he's taken a couple of days leave, no-one knows where, and there's no sign of him at his flat."

"How about the girl he was with when we picked him up the other day? Does she know anything?"

"No sign of her either."

"I see. Damn it."

"Why don't we get on and have a word with this Beecham fellow, sir?"

"Absolutely, Constable. We now know from Devlin this morning that it was Beecham whom Dumont met at Euston – this prompted his suspicion of Dumont. So Beecham's role might be critical."

"Maybe Dumont had gambling debts and that's why he was meeting Beecham. He didn't want us to know about them so that's why he lied about knowing him."

"Perhaps, Sergeant. We can ask him but first we have to get hold of him."

"By the way, sir."

"Yes, Constable."

"The clerk at the Bedford Hotel, Noakes, called me today. He'd finally remembered the odd thing he noticed about the man who came last to the hotel. He remembered he had a slight limp."

Merlin smiled. "Better late than never, eh?" He got to his feet. "Right. I'll go to my meeting now with Harold and then we can reconvene and decide exactly what our next action should be."

*　　　*　　　*

"He's in the back room, Frank. Through here." Merlin followed Tony into the café-owner's private quarters and found Harold Swanton comfortably ensconced in an armchair, sipping a hot drink, his long legs stretched out before him. "Lovely mug of Bovril your Italian friend here makes."

"Would you like one, Frank?"

Merlin detested Bovril. "No thanks, Tony. I'm fine." He took the armchair opposite Swanton and Tony left.

"Trustworthy fellow, is he?"

"Completely. He'd do anything for me. Solid as the Rock of Gibraltar."

"I'm not so sure Gibraltar's that solid these days. Hitler would love to get hold of it and Franco might help him. Anyway, thanks for arranging this cosy little meeting place." Swanton set down his drink and reached into the briefcase at his feet. "Here's the photograph you gave me. We noticed some almost invisible initials on the back. Using their magical arts, our scientists managed to make them legible. There are two sets."

"What are they?"

"Here, see… The first are ADM. Armand de Metz obviously. And here, AA."

"AA. Doesn't mean anything to me."

"You said, Frank, that de Metz showed this photograph to the French officers."

"They said he did so suggesting that it could do someone some harm."

"I guess one interpretation of that is that someone in the photograph was involved in the fishy activities de Metz was implying he knew about."

"Assuming there was any truth in his story, Harold, which I understood your agency thought not."

"I'm not an officer who is afraid to admit a mistake, Frank. Let's proceed with an open mind. So there are two young men in the photograph and two young women. I think we can discount the women. Of the young men, one is dark-haired, one is fair-haired."

"The darker one is probably de Metz."

"And the fair-haired chap in the uniform is presumably AA. So who is he?"

"You've looked through the Free French rosters for those initials?"

"Of course. We've checked all the names on the military list, as well as all the staff, secretaries, kitchen workers, everyone. We found only one person with those initials."

Merlin realised with a start that he knew that person. "Auguste Angers?"

"Yes."

"I've met the man. Not a favourite. What do you propose to do?"

"Pull him in, of course. What was your impression?"

"Good-looking chap. Vain. Arrogant. Shifty. I believe he lied to us when questioned about de Metz."

"Sounds promising."

Merlin scratched his ear thoughtfully. "I have some news that you ought to hear before you proceed further."

Swanton picked up his Bovril and took a noisy sip. "Fire away, Frank."

"Ever heard of a fellow called Devlin? A private eye of sorts."

"The name seems vaguely familiar."

"He has told us an interesting tale."

*   *   *

Back at the Yard, Merlin reported to Bridges on the meeting.

"So, Swanton agreed to wait for us to get hold of Dumont before he moves on Angers?"

"Yes, Sergeant. He wants to hear what Dumont has to say first. But he is putting Angers under immediate surveillance. Beecham as well. I said we'd hold off from pulling in Beecham until tomorrow to allow Swanton to observe his movements over 24 hours."

"So, Dumont remains our priority for now?"

"He does. Still no sign of him?"

"No. I've got several officers on the job."

"Where are Robinson and Detective Goldberg?"

"They went off to see Mrs Lafontaine. Now that we know Dumont knew Bridget well enough to attend her abortion, I thought we should see if his name rang any bells with her sister."

"Good idea." Merlin looked pensively out of the window.

"Will that be all, sir?" There was no reply. Bridges repeated the question.

"Sorry, Sergeant. I was miles away." Merlin blushed. "Do you mind if I ask you something personal, Sam?"

"Of course not, sir. What do you want to know?"

"Do you enjoy being a father?"

Bridges' face broke into a grin. "It's wonderful, sir. Babies are hard work, naturally, but Iris carries most of that burden. All I really have to deal with is the difficult nights. The bawling can be wearing but at least the toing and froing to the baby's bedroom has helped me lose a few pounds! When that giggling little bundle looks up at you with those tiny sparkling eyes, well… a man can feel like a millionaire!" He was now beaming. "Why do you ask?"

Merlin shuffled some papers on his desk as he avoided the sergeant's gaze. "Oh, no reason, in particular. Just wondered how you were getting on with the new situation, that's all."

"Kind of you to ask, sir. I'm getting on fine. Now, if you don't mind, I'd better get on."

"No, of course. Off you go, Sergeant. Let me know as soon as there is news on Dumont."

*   *   *

After mulling over what Merlin had told him of Devlin's story, Harold Swanton decided to take the question of the possible involvement of Dumont, Beecham and Angers in a French security leak very seriously indeed. While Merlin's team continued to search for Dumont, Swanton sent four men to Dorset Square to keep an eye on Angers and assigned four men to the surveillance of Peregrine Beecham. They positioned their car at the junction of Arlington Street and Bennet Street, just down from the Ritz. A porter in Beecham's building was suborned to give Swanton's men the nod as and when Beecham came out.

It was nearly five in the afternoon when the watchers saw a large black Bentley pull up outside the apartment building. Minutes later, three men came out of the building and got into the car. A little wave from the porter confirmed their man was on the move.

Beecham's car drove off, turning right into Bennet Street, then into St James's Street. The traffic was flowing freely and Swanton's agents had little difficulty keeping the Bentley well in view.

The Bentley proceeded along the Embankment, then crossed Waterloo Bridge. At the roundabout on the southern side of the bridge, it took the railway station exit, drove up the ramp and pulled to a halt opposite the main taxi rank. The agents pulled over to a loading bay some yards off. They watched as two men got out of the car, then the third. Swanton's lead agent, Peters, a calm, beanpole of a man, examined the old police mugshot of Percy Bishop that agency records had matched to Beecham.

He raised his binoculars and knew he was watching the same person, albeit a slicker and sleeker one than in the photograph, follow his men into the station.

The three men made their way through the crowds to the station buffet. Beecham quickly found a table at the back of the restaurant while his sidekicks grabbed stools at the counter.

Peters and his team took up position behind a newspaper kiosk some 30 yards from the buffet. "What do you think? Looks like a meet to me. Eric, there's a telephone booth near where we came in. Go and call Swanton. Tell him we may be on to something. I'll go in and you others find cover outside."

It was now five-thirty and the buffet was crammed with commuters. Waiters and waitresses bustled back and forth through the crowd. A variety of smells battled for dominance – body odour, cheap perfume, coffee, cigarette smoke, alcohol and engine oil. Conversation was carried on with difficulty against a background of train whistles, steam blasts and the usual succession of unintelligible station announcements. Most of the male customers seemed happier to drink on their feet so there were plenty of tables to be had but Peters chose to stand at the counter, a few places along from Beecham's men.

A frazzled-looking waitress delivered a coffee to Beecham. She spilled some of the drink on the table and Peters saw Beecham berate her angrily before she hurried tearfully away. Beecham's eyes scanned the room. He looked nervous. Whoever he was meeting was late. He had finished his coffee by the time a man finally materialised at his table. A tall young man in blazer and grey trousers.

*   *   *

"Frank? I just got a call. Beecham is at Waterloo Station. My people think he's about to meet up with someone. It occurred to me, in light of what you said, that it could be Dumont. I thought…"

"On my way, Harold."

"I don't need to tell you to be careful. I've asked the agent who phoned me to wait at the telephone box he called from. It's the one just outside the concourse next to the taxi rank. He'll tell you the score and take you to my men."

"Thanks, Harold. On my way." He found Bridges in the corridor talking to Robinson and Goldberg about their visit to Bridget's sister. Merlin hurriedly explained the situation. "It may all be a wild goose chase, of course, but if there's a chance of Dumont turning up…"

"I'll go and get the car, sir."

"How was Mrs Lafontaine?"

"She didn't recognise Dumont's name or description, sir, but she did recall Bridget asking to borrow a teach-yourself-French book."

"Well, that helps." Merlin looked hard at Robinson. "I think, Constable, on reflection, that it might be best if you stay here. Things might get a little hairy."

Robinson bridled at this. "With respect, sir, if I'm kept away from any police operation because it might be 'hairy', I'll never have a chance of becoming a good policewoman."

Merlin shook his head. "You have a point, Constable, but you're also in uniform. That will be a problem."

"Problem quickly solved, sir. A friend and I were going to a film tonight and I have a change of clothes here. I'll see you at the car in a jiffy." She raced down the corridor.

Goldberg laughed. "There's no telling a woman. You should know that, Frank."

*   *   *

"And so, Lieutenant. You have something else for me?"

Dumont leaned closer to Beecham. "I do. I appreciate your help but I must say I'm still not very keen on your choice of rendezvous point."

"My experience is that the best place to be invisible is in a crowd, as I've told you before." Beecham lit a cigarette as Dumont's coffee arrived. "Anyway, it's a pleasure to be of assistance. A lucrative pleasure, thanks to your friends in Vichy. Any news about the other fellow?"

"I just got back from Suffolk, where I went to see him yesterday. Arrangements have been made to extricate him by sea. He should be back in Paris within a day or two."

"Good. If he'd been caught, things could have been difficult for you."

"And you also, perhaps, *Monsieur* Beecham."

"Any more difficulties? You know I had Devlin dealt with?"

"He is dead?"

"Near enough. My men say that they were interrupted during the job but assure me he was beyond saving."

Dumont scratched his nose thoughtfully. "I have been interviewed by the police about the Irish girl. The one who died."

Beecham's eyes narrowed. "Problems?"

"No. They have nothing on me. However, Vorster was also pulled in."

"Poor Rupert. I may have to deal with him, too. He might become an embarrassment. This has nothing to do with the business at hand though?"

"No." Dumont paused. "The good news is my product is having a significant effect. Initial SOE operations in France are being seriously compromised. This…" he cautiously slid a small envelope across the table "… should cause further damage…"

Beecham spread his arms. "I am happy for you, Lieutenant, but while you know I have sympathies with your side, this is more of a commercial than ideological matter for me." Beecham slid the envelope into his jacket pocket. "Thank you. I think we should leave now. When you need me next, contact me in the usual way."

"Merlin and his people know about you now. You might want to consider relocating your gaming operation."

Beecham toyed with the large gold ring on his right index finger. "I don't need to worry about the police, my friend. I have the senior officers in the Vice Department in my pocket."

"I think Merlin might be a different – how do you say it? – kettle of fish."

"Well done, Lieutenant. You are picking up our slang very well! But please, do not concern yourself. My friends will look after me."

*   *   *

Merlin and his colleagues were met by a burly, balding man at the telephone box. "Eric Walters. Pleased to meet you, Chief Inspector. And your colleagues, of course." The agent smiled at Bridges and Goldberg but looked a little surprised to see Robinson. "They are in the buffet, sir."

"Who are they?"

"Beecham and his two heavies. Beecham has a table at the back and the others are watching out for him at the counter. Peters is observing from the inside while my two other colleagues are observing from out. One of them just ran over to tell me that Beecham has just been joined by someone."

"Did that someone have a limp?"

Walters shrugged. "He didn't say."

The crowd swirled around Merlin and his group. Merlin realised that if it came to it, the crowds would make escape easier for their quarry. Any move would have to be precise, quick and well coordinated. "What are your instructions, Mr Walters?"

"Mr Swanton told me that if you identify Dumont, we are to help you arrest him. If it is Dumont then it makes sense for us to pick up Beecham and his men."

"It's not going to be easy, is it?" Merlin frowned. "So we'd better see if it's Dumont."

Walters looked towards the buffet. "Do you want to wait until he comes out?"

"I think, on balance, someone should go in to make an identification. If we leave it until he comes out and it is Dumont, he has a good chance of slipping away with all these people in the station."

Goldberg patted Merlin on the back. "Let me go and make him, Frank."

"Beecham and Dumont know you, Bernie. If they see you first, they'll be alerted. Same goes for you, Sergeant, before you offer. Dumont knows you. And me for that matter."

Walters put a hand on Merlin's shoulder. "I don't care how you identify them, Mr Merlin, but, rest assured, once you've given us the nod we can deal with them. My two friends over there were respectively army light heavyweight and navy middleweight champion boxers in their time. I wasn't a champion but I'm pretty handy myself."

"Thank you, Mr Walters, but what about guns?"

Walters pulled his jacket back to show Merlin his side-arm holster. "We are fully prepared."

Robinson stepped forward. "Sir, Dumont has never seen me but I've seen him. Why don't I go in?"

Merlin contemplated for a moment what the AC would do if any harm came to his niece. He couldn't risk it. "Constable, thank you, but…" Merlin was suddenly knocked over by a man racing for his train. By the time he got back on his feet, Robinson was halfway to the buffet.

*   *   *

"You go first, Lieutenant. And good luck!"

"Goodbye, Beecham. Excuse me but you might have to wait a little. Call of nature." Dumont nodded towards the gents.

"Make it quick. Please."

"I'll do my best. *Au revoir*."

Beecham waved a hand at his men, who took this as their cue to go out on to the station concourse. Then he called a waitress over. Robinson came into the restaurant as he was settling the bill. She scanned the room unsuccessfully but then saw Dumont emerging from the toilets. Immediately she turned on her heels and ran out to find Merlin. There were a few frantic seconds when she looked for him in vain but then she heard her name called in a harsh whisper. The policemen had joined the MI5 agents behind their kiosk. Merlin pulled her in with them and gave her a stern look. "That, Constable, was very…"

"It's him, sir. Definitely him."

"All right. What do you want to do, Mr Walters?"

"Beecham's two men are now over there by the buffet door, presumably waiting for their boss. We'll roll them up while you go in for your Frenchman."

Merlin agreed and the agents acted swiftly. Beecham's men were taken completely unawares. They managed to fend off a few punches but were swiftly overpowered then handcuffed to a nearby metal railing. The scuffle went almost completely unnoticed by the swirling crowds.

Meanwhile, Dumont was making his way through the buffet to the door. Halfway there, he found his path blocked by a fat lady settling at her table and had to wait as she manoeuvred her chair out of the way. By the time she had done this, Merlin and his officers were in the restaurant.

As Dumont approached the door, Merlin stepped forward to confront him. "I have a warrant for your arrest, sir. It'd be best if you come quietly."

Dumont's eyes flared with anger. "No chance, Merlin." He reached into his jacket and brought out a gun.

Merlin stepped back. "Don't be stupid, Dumont!"

"Why not? What have I got to lose?" He pointed the gun at Merlin but there was a sudden surge forward by the crowd now gathered behind him and the gun was knocked from his hand. Before Merlin had a chance to grab him, Dumont's hand had reached into his jacket again and produced a hunting knife. There were screams and shouts as Dumont swung the knife in front of him. He thrust at Merlin but missed. He thrust again unsuccessfully and Merlin managed to grasp his arm. He tried to shake Dumont's knife free and had almost succeeded when he slipped in a puddle of spilled beer and fell headlong into a table.

The Frenchman bent down to plunge the knife into Merlin's back, but Goldberg pulled him back. Dumont managed to extricate himself from Goldberg's grip and turned to face him. He stabbed at Goldberg and sliced his cheek but the American landed a heavy punch on Dumont's face. As he reeled back, Peters joined the fray but another swing of the knife slashed his hand and he stepped back, as blood began to pour.

Merlin was now back on his feet with Goldberg beside him and Bridges, who had been struggling to find a line of attack in the narrow space, was approaching the Frenchman from the bar side with a chair above his head. Dumont realised a change of tack was required and he turned and grabbed hold of the nearest woman he could find.

"I shall slit this pretty young lady's throat, Merlin, if you do not allow me passage."

Initially, his eyes clouded with sweat, Merlin couldn't see the woman's face but then with a lurch of the stomach realised it was Robinson. He backed away. "Don't move. Don't resist. Keep still. It will be all right." Robinson's eyes flickered an acknowledgement. Merlin made way with the others to allow Dumont and his hostage through the door. He saw a small trickle of blood on Robinson's neck where the knife had broken skin.

Once out on the concourse, he looked wildly around him. As Merlin appeared through the door, he turned to him. There were 10 yards between them. "Merlin! You and your colleagues will remain here while I take the lady to the taxi rank. If you try anything she will…" There was a sickening thud and Dumont's eyes glazed over. The knife fell from his grip as he collapsed to the ground, his head hitting the concrete with a loud crack. Robinson couldn't avoid falling with him and she was momentarily pinned under his body until Bridges was able to pull her free, unharmed apart from the cut on her neck.

Walters looked down at the unconscious Frenchman with a satisfied look. He had been able to approach Dumont unseen from behind the kiosk and fell him with a pistol to the head. Peters, who now had a handkerchief tied tightly around his wounded hand, and the two boxing champions wandered over to offer their congratulations.

Merlin remembered Beecham and turned to see him squeezing out on to the concourse through the crowd that had gathered at the restaurant door. Their eyes met and Beecham gave Merlin an odd little smile before breaking into a run. Merlin shouted to the others. "Come on! Beecham's getting away!"

The route to his own car was closed to Beecham so he ran in the opposite direction towards the Tenison Way exit. Everyone apart from the boxers, who were looking after Beecham's men, hared off in pursuit with Merlin at their head. Beecham was a fit man and a good runner. Over 60 yards they made no ground on him. However, as Beecham neared the exit, he bumped into a porter and fell. He was swiftly on his feet again but had lost his bearings and began running the wrong way. Merlin and the others were now much closer.

Beecham realised his mistake and decided his best option was to get to the platforms, where he might still be able to lose his pursuers or even jump on a departing train. He hurdled a closed barrier with surprising agility and ploughed through the crowds waiting for a train to arrive at Platform 5. Merlin cleared the barrier a little more clumsily and followed. Beecham had regained the lost ground but halfway down the platform his path was blocked by a large party collecting luggage from a porter's trolley. He turned to see Merlin fast approaching but then a small gap opened for him and he was through, just as Merlin himself was held up by the same party. When Merlin emerged, Beecham was 50 yards ahead again but the platform was emptier further along and it was easier to follow his movements.

Suddenly, the whistle of the approaching train blew. It now occurred to the breathless Beecham that his best tactic would be to cross over to the platform opposite just before the train arrived. The engine was coming into sight at the far end of the platform. He had to act quickly. Beecham didn't waste time climbing down on to the tracks but jumped. It was a fair drop and, as he landed, he twisted an ankle. He grimaced with pain as he tried to lift his foot but found it was trapped under a rail. He tried to move it again. And again. He was trapped.

By now, Merlin was above him on the platform and could see the panic-stricken terror in Beecham's eyes as he looked up. The train continued its slow but relentless approach. Merlin reached out a hand and grasped Beecham's but, soaked in sweat, it slipped from the detective's grip. Bridges arrived, assessed the situation and ran towards the train, waving and shouting for the driver to stop. The driver didn't or couldn't understand and the train carried on. Merlin reached down again, this time managing to grab the sleeve of Beecham's coat but it was too late. The train was almost on them and he had to let go. The policeman watched in horror as, with a hideous scream, Peregrine Beecham was torn to pieces by the wheels of the engine.

CHAPTER 16
Friday 20 June

London

Merlin paced back and forth around his room. The adrenaline was still pumping. Goldberg and Robinson were seated at the desk, he with a bandage on his cheek and she with a sticking-plaster on her neck.

"I don't think I'm going to forget this day in a hurry."

"It's a pity we lost Beecham, Frank. He could have cleared up a lot of things."

"If Dumont cooperates we should get what we need, Bernie. And we have Beecham's men. What do we have on them, Constable?"

"Charlie Miller and Vincent Carson… Quite long criminal records for such young men. Violent assault, robbery, burglary and so on. They were both in prison until nine months ago and were let out after volunteering to join up. Both were given postings but never made it. Went AWOL."

"No surprise there. They are downstairs in the cells?"

"Yes, sir. Next to Vorster."

Merlin looked closely at Robinson. "Are you sure you don't want to see the doc? Just to double-check you're all right?"

Robinson was back in uniform and looking little the worse for her ordeal. "No, sir. This nick on my neck is nothing and I'm fine otherwise."

"You were very brave."

"Thank you, sir."

"You too, Bernie."

"Come off it, Frank. You and Robinson were the true heroes."

"Not me." Merlin sat down at last. "I'm not going to be very popular with the AC when he finds out what happened, Constable."

"He'll not find out from me, sir."

Merlin smiled. "He'll find out from someone. Is that the gun report you have there?"

"Yes, sir."

"And does it confirm what we thought it might?"

"It does. The gun Dumont dropped at the station was a *Modèle* 1935A."

"Ballistics?"

"We'll get the full report tomorrow."

"Let's hope there's a match."

"Bound to be."

"Yes, Bernie." Merlin looked at Goldberg's cheek. "You're going to have a nice little scar there as a souvenir of London."

"Might make me look more fearsome to the New York villains."

"I'm sure you can handle the job without looking like Lon Chaney." Merlin winked. "So, back to Dumont. If he murdered de Metz, was it because he feared the doctor was going to expose him as a spy or because of the botched abortion? If it was the first reason, where does the photograph come in? Dumont is too young to be one of the people in that picture. Perhaps it's a red herring?" Merlin scratched his head.

"If he killed for the second reason… well, for what it's worth, Vorster still insists he doesn't believe Dumont was the father of Bridget's baby. Says he would have known if Dumont had a girlfriend. We obviously need another session with Vorster." Merlin pondered for a moment. "In fact, why don't you two go down and see him now? Tell him we've got Dumont and more evidence. See what he says."

The telephone rang. "Sergeant. You're still at the hospital? They've told you. Good. Bring Dumont back straightaway and put him in one of the interview rooms. We'll see you in 20 minutes." Merlin looked up. "Dumont is apparently fit to come out of St Thomas's. Must have a skull of iron."

"Will the MI5 people want to sit in on our interview with Dumont, sir?"

"I had a word with Harold Swanton, Constable. He said we could have first shot at him on the criminal matters and then he'd take over. Meanwhile, his men are about to pull in Auguste Angers to see if he's the other chap in the photograph."

Goldberg shaded his eyes from the bright sunshine now pouring into the room. "If he is, what does it mean?"

"That he was Dumont's accomplice in espionage? I don't know, Bernie, but I hope we're about to find out."

*   *   *

Robinson led Detective Goldberg down the gloomy, narrow corridor giving access to the cells in the basement of Scotland Yard.

"This is where Beecham's men are, Detective." Robinson pulled open the viewing grille in the second door they came to. The moustachioed Miller was sitting on the bed, looking morosely into space. He ignored the sound of the grille opening. Carson was pacing back and forth in the small space not occupied by the bed. He turned to bare his teeth at the door and Robinson slammed the grille shut.

"Our man's next door, Detective."

An unshaven, hollow-eyed Vorster jumped up excitedly when they entered his cell. "Have you come to let me go? You know I didn't kill that chap. Surely you can't keep me in here much longer?

My father will provide a surety if that's what you need. The…"
The officers shook their heads and his face fell. The young man
slumped back down on the bed.

"We've got Dumont now, Mr Vorster. We are going to see what
light he can cast on events. Meanwhile, Detective Goldberg and I
would like to go over your story one more time. Let's start at the
beginning. Did you…?"

Robinson stopped as they heard voices at the door. The grille
went back and Sergeant Reeves' face appeared.

"Sorry about this, Constable, Mr Goldberg. It's just that this
cell is quite a bit larger than the one next door in which we're
holding those two brutes of Beecham's. I thought it would be
sensible to switch them into this cell and put this fellow into
theirs." Reeves leaned forward to whisper. "Sergeant Bridges told
me he'd prefer them to continue to share a cell so they can get on
each other's nerves. Might make them more amenable to turning
on each other, he said."

"That's fine, Sergeant. All right, Detective?" Goldberg nodded
as he helped Vorster to his feet and they all went out into the
corridor. Reeves and another constable held the handcuffed
Carson and Miller back as the detectives led Vorster to their
former cell. The young man did not seem to appreciate the change
of scene and fell with a groan on to his new bunk. He closed
his eyes, sighed and leaned back against the wall. Then, all of a
sudden, he jerked to attention with a strange, quizzical look on his
face. Vorster sniffed the air. His eyes widened and his lips opened
into a broad smile. "That's it!"

"That's what, Mr Vorster?"

"Didn't you smell it, Constable? Can't you smell it? It's still
lingering in here."

Goldberg sniffed. "Some sort of perfume?"

"It's cologne, Detective." Robinson concentrated. "Quite an
unusual one, I think."

"It's his cologne. The man I saw go into Powell's flat. He was wearing that aftershave and he's just left this cell." Vorster banged the bed for emphasis. "There is your murderer of Edgar Powell. One door away." He started to laugh.

*   *   *

They were in the same interview room as before. Dumont looked utterly drained but Merlin sensed that he was not yet broken. Merlin showed the Frenchman the letter they had found on Beecham's mangled body. It contained chapter and verse on a forthcoming SOE operation in France. Dumont gave it a cursory glance.

"So, Merlin, what do you want me to say? That I know nothing of this? That Peregrine Beecham and I were just enjoying a friendly coffee? That this letter must be a plant? Well, you can relax. I don't deny that I used my privileged position in Carlton Gardens to acquire secret information about SOE and other military activities and pass it on to Vichy. I don't deny that I believe in Marshal Pétain and the deal he has done to save France. I am a patriot, Merlin. It is just that my idea of patriotism does not coincide with yours or that of your masters."

"Nor of General de Gaulle's obviously. And your patriotism has already resulted in the deaths of several of your compatriots, Lieutenant. How do you feel about that?"

Dumont looked at Merlin with disdain. "You are stupid if you think the situation in France is black and white, Chief Inspector. There are many shades of grey. I, and millions of my countrymen, believe that reaching the accommodation we did with the Nazis was the best solution to our national predicament. For having a limited version of liberty and independence, there is obviously a price to pay. Recognising Great Britain and de Gaulle's organisation as enemies is part of that price."

"It is not my job to take moral positions, Lieutenant. Just to ascertain facts. Did you act alone or were there accomplices?"

"Obviously, Beecham was an accomplice. Before him there was another but he is safely back in France now. I had no others."

"No other Free French officers helping you out?"

"None."

Merlin looked across at Bridges then down at the letter Dumont had passed to Beecham. "Your spying activities are not my principal concern, Lieutenant. I'm going to leave it to MI5 to discuss such matters with you in detail. My interests are more mundane. Such as the murder of Armand de Metz.

"Our scientists have examined the gun you dropped at Waterloo Station. It is a *Modèle* 1935A. A shell casing from such a gun was found in de Metz's bedroom. De Metz was responsible for the death of Bridget Healy in the hotel bedroom you were seen in. It was he who hung around Carlton Gardens trying to wheedle money out of the Free French and threatening to expose espionage in your midst. Come now. Be as forthcoming as you've been regarding your espionage. You have little to lose now. It was your gun that killed de Metz, wasn't it?"

Dumont sat back in his chair, a look of disgust on his face. "In war people die. If people die because of my intelligence activities, they are as warriors fallen on the battlefield. I regret it but have no shame. I have just been doing my duty as a combatant officer.

"However, to commit a cold-blooded murder of an innocent old man, disgusting drunk though he may have been, for this I would feel shame. I am not a cold-blooded murderer, Merlin. Whatever your forensic people say, I did not kill de Metz."

"Then who did? If you didn't kill him because he posed a threat to your spying activities, you shot him because he killed your mistress and child. If you were not the father of the child then, logically, if I were to believe your story, the likeliest killer is that father. If you are telling the truth, you must know who that man is. Now is the time to tell us. Otherwise, you are going to carry the can."

Dumont looked off into the distance. After a long silence he nodded. "Very well. I'll tell you about the girl. I believe you are wrong in thinking that the father killed de Metz. I am certain he would have not been capable of such an act. Distasteful as it is to break a confidence, it seems I must if I am to preserve my own honour."

*   *   *

It was lunchtime and Commandant Angers' stomach was rumbling. He had just been about to enjoy an aperitif in his office when Peters and Walters had burst in and invited him – with a menace that brooked no refusal – to accompany them to their car.

Twenty-five minutes later, the Frenchman found himself at a table in a bare, windowless room somewhere in St James's. Harold Swanton sat opposite, flanked by Peters and Walters. Swanton waited patiently as Angers exhausted his lengthy list of complaints. Finally, the soldier fell silent and Swanton got down to business.

"You told the police you knew nothing about Armand de Metz, didn't you? That was a lie. Why did you lie?"

"I did not lie. At the time of the interview I knew nothing but later I learned that some fellow officers had met him."

"This photograph was found among Mr de Metz's possessions. Do you recognise it or the people portrayed?"

"No. I have never seen it before in my life and I have no idea who these people are."

"Do you see these initials on the back, sir? AA – your initials. How do you account for them?"

"Indeed, they are my initials. As they are of the Automobile Association. Perhaps the photographer was a member of that fine organisation?" Angers attempted a laugh in appreciation of his wit but it sounded more like a strangled croak.

"If you think this is an occasion for levity, sir, you are very much mistaken. We have become aware of breaches of security in your organisation. Classified information on SOE operations in France has been passed to Vichy and thence to the Germans. We caught someone red-handed doing this yesterday."

Angers' face managed to conjure up looks of surprise, curiosity, innocence and indignation in quick succession. "We have ourselves been investigating such matters, Mr Swanton. If you have beaten us to the gun, then very well done and I look forward with interest to learning the name of the culprit.

"However, if you are interviewing me in the belief that I have anything to do with this crime, you are mistaken. I can only assume that you are founding your suspicion on the unfortunate coincidence that you have found my initials on an old photograph in de Metz's possession. This is flimsy indeed!"

"De Metz was certainly aware of treachery in your organisation. It is clear from his behaviour that he thought the photograph, on which your initials feature, somehow pointed to the traitor. You are the only person in your organisation with those initials."

"That is both stupid and incorrect! Straightaway I can think of someone else who has those initials."

*   *   *

Dumont relaxed as he told his story. "You were right, Chief Inspector, about the relevance of the Ritz bar. It was there that Bridget Healy met her lover. She was a pretty, young and vivacious girl. If my friend had not moved on her, then I might have.

"She was, however, as you say, smitten with this man from the outset. He is an intelligent, well bred man of the world. It was all just a bit of fun to him. Bridget was staying with her sister when they first met but, after a while, he organised a little flat for her off Oxford Street, where he could visit her. He took her to good restaurants, the theatre and so on. After their initial meeting, he stayed away from the Ritz as he wanted to be discreet. She did still go there occasionally on her own.

"Then Bridget fell pregnant. The moment she told him, his first thought was to procure an abortion. She was taken aback, devastated, but there it was. The girl had romantic notions of marriage and of keeping the child. He confided in me. Someone told me that this fellow de Metz, who'd been hanging around our office, was in the abortion business. I knew of his claims to have secret information but, like everyone else, I thought he was just off his head.

"I learned of his eminence as a surgeon before the war. I suggested de Metz to my friend, who said he had heard of him in Paris. He agreed but made it clear he could not meet him personally for some reason. He asked me to handle the arrangements. I did, going so far as to attend the operation.

"Bridget brought a male friend, a chauffeur. I thought it unwise to have too many people witnessing what was, after all, an illegal arrangement and I got rid of him. The rest you know. Poor girl. My friend was upset, of course, when I told him what had happened but as I say, he was a man of the world."

Bridges scoffed. "Some might say you've made up this story to deflect us from the truth and save your bacon."

Dumont managed a hoarse laugh. "Sergeant, please. How much of my bacon will be left to save after your friends at MI5 have finished with me? I have my reasons for what I have done for Vichy. You and MI5 may not appreciate them but they are honourable ones. As I said before, I am not a cold-blooded murderer and will not carry the can, as you say, for de Metz. I am sorry to betray a friend but, if that is the only way to assert my innocence, so be it."

Merlin stared hard at Dumont. "So then, Lieutenant. Please be so good as to tell the sergeant and me the name of this friend of yours."

*   *   *

Angers swept a hand through his hair. "I'm sure if you look more closely, you'll find several people with such initials but, as I say, I can think of one immediately, although I'm sure it won't be of any use to you."

Swanton raised an eyebrow. "Perhaps you'd be good enough to share that person's name with us?"

"Why, the colonel himself has these initials."

"But his first initial is B."

"B for Bertrand, yes. That's what may be listed but I know for a fact that his Christian name is Alphonse. He couldn't stand his first name so he changed it later to Bertrand. But the name on his birth certificate, as I know from his own lips when in wine, is Alphonse. Alphonse Aubertin. Of course, the colonel had nothing to do with de Metz – and this information is useless for your purpose – but I mention it to show the absurdity of your line of investigation."

Swanton nodded. "Very interesting, Commandant. Of course, our line of investigation may indeed be absurd but nevertheless…" The telephone rang and Swanton picked it up. "Frank, hello… is that so? That's very interesting. Very interesting indeed." He sat back and stroked his chin, a strange smile on his lips. "I have also learned something very interesting. Just now. What? Oh, I'll explain when I see you. I'm heading over to you now."

*   *   *

Merlin had poured himself a whisky from his office stock. He felt he deserved one. It was nearly nine o'clock. Goldberg appeared in the doorway.

"Fancy a drink, Bernie?"

"Don't mind if I do."

Merlin poured out a glass. "*Salud!*"

"*L'chayim!*"

"Bridges has gone home to Iris. Where's Robinson?"

"Gone on a date with her boyfriend."

"Pity. I'd like to have congratulated her. What a day!"

"So, Swanton has taken Dumont away?"

"Yes. They've gone to Blenheim Palace, one of MI5's nicer outposts. Angers too. And Aubertin. Harold's view, quite rightly, was that security matters must now take priority over our criminal matters. He also believes the more robust MI5 interrogation methods will produce quicker results than our more pedestrian ones."

"They're going to rough them up, you mean?"

Merlin shrugged and drank some whisky. "We'll be in on the kill though, as Harold put it. The moment he feels the whole story is going to break open, he's sending a car for me. I'm just hoping that's not going to be three in the morning – I need my sleep."

Goldberg sighed. "You realise I'll be gone tomorrow, Frank?"

"I know, Bernie. I'm going to miss you. At least you're leaving with a major success under your belt. I'll make sure your superiors know. Tell me again how it happened."

"Really, Frank, it's your girl, Robinson, who deserves the credit. I played only a minor role. The moment Vorster told us about the cologne, she got Reeves to split Carson and Miller, removing Miller to another cell. We interviewed Carson first. It was his cologne. We put Vorster's evidence to him. He was a hard nut. Wouldn't say anything.

"Then we went to see Miller. Told him what was what. Robinson did a subtle song and dance about how, if he didn't play ball, he would be charged as an accomplice to murder for keeping watch for Carson. Banged on about how the penalty for an accomplice would be the same as for the principal – the rope. Said if he came clean we'd do our best to press a lesser charge. Eventually, after an hour or two of this, Miller capitulated and confessed everything. When we went back to Carson he went berserk. Started hitting his head on any available surface. Said he'd make Miller pay for being a snitch. Still won't admit anything but, anyway, with Miller and Vorster's evidence, you have him."

"I'm sure you had more of a hand to play than you say, Bernie. Thank you – it's been good working with you."

"Likewise, Frank."

"Vorster's been released, I presume?"

"Yes, his father picked him up an hour ago. He even seemed happy to see his son."

"Perhaps they'll turn over a new leaf?"

"I wouldn't bet on it."

Merlin refilled their glasses and the two men sat in silence for a while until Goldberg got to his feet. "Reckon you ought to get back to that beautiful girl of yours, Frank."

Merlin nodded. "Yes. I'll go in a minute but erm… wait a moment. I've got something to tell you, Bernie. You're the first to know. Sonia's pregnant."

Goldberg immediately shot out a hand. "That's wonderful, Frank. Well, as long as you're happy about it. Are you?"

"Yes, I'm happy. It's a bit of a shock but…"

"If you're happy then so am I. Go on, you'd better get home pronto. I wish you all the very best. Maybe one day you'll get out my way. It would be good to tackle some American bad guys together." The two men shook hands again. There was still a little whisky in their glasses and Goldberg raised his. "A toast to Frank Merlin Junior!"

Merlin looked coy. "Or maybe Francesca?"

*   *   *

Blenheim Palace, Saturday 21 June

Swanton's car picked up Merlin at his flat at nine, just after Sonia had left for work. The journey to Blenheim took just over two hours. As the car motored up the driveway Merlin, like any first-time visitor to the country seat of the Duke of Marlborough, was overwhelmed by the beauty and size of the palace before them. A home more fit for a king than a duke, he thought. The car pulled up to a door at the rear of the building and the taciturn young driver uttered his first words of the journey. "In there, sir." Merlin found Peters waiting for him in the doorway.

"How's the hand, Mr Peters?"

"Had to have a few stitches. They'll be out in a day or two. All in a good cause, Chief Inspector. Come. The boss is waiting downstairs."

Merlin followed Peters down a flight of stairs then along a warren of corridors until they reached a large oak door. They entered and found Swanton attempting to make his huge frame comfortable in a raddled old armchair beside a stone fireplace in which, despite the warm weather outside, a fire was lit.

"Frank, welcome. Take a pew." Merlin sat down in another equally decrepit armchair and looked curiously at the fire. "Place is draughty as hell, Frank. You'll appreciate the fire. Trust me."

"If you say so, Harold."

Peters disappeared.

"This room is normally the cubby-hole of one of the senior manservants. The senior under-butler or the junior over-butler or something like that. I'm not sure how many butlers a duke is meant to have. In any event, it seems a nice little retreat for a man when seeking relief from the onerous duties of pouring out Krug and Château Lafite for his masters."

Swanton found his best position and sank back into the chair. Merlin could see that despite the cheery bonhomie, he was exhausted.

Swanton rubbed his eyes. "You're no doubt thinking how knackered I look?"

"Well…"

"I'm looking knackered because I *am* knackered. I'm getting too old for these all-nighters. Our French friends have been very hard work. And I'm not just talking about our friends along the corridor. The Free French command in London has been up in arms about our pulling in their officers. De Gaulle has been on the blower from Cairo. The Foreign Office has been at the receiving end all night. The PM himself once or twice, too, I understand."

"What have they been saying?"

"Initially they were in denial. The chaps we have are excellent fellows and can't have done any wrong. We stupid English must have made a terrible mistake. When it was explained that, in the case of Dumont, he was caught red-handed and had admitted his treachery, the complaint changed. If a French officer was a traitor he should be handed over immediately to the French for interrogation and punishment. His treason was no matter for the British.

"Of course, with Aubertin we couldn't tell them we had anything yet so there was more palaver. Angers too. Thus it was made clear to me by the FO that I'd better get a move on in getting to the bottom of things."

"And have you? Got to the bottom of things?"

"I think we're almost there. That's why I got you here now, Frank. When we started out, as you know, Dumont had named

Aubertin the father of Bridget Healy's baby. This pointed to him as the murderer of de Metz. If that were the case, was the botched abortion the only motive or was there something else? What was the relevance of the photograph? Were the initials Aubertin's, the commandant's or someone else's?"

Swanton paused to pack tobacco into a small pipe. "Do you want to smoke a cigarette, Frank?"

"No thanks, Harold."

Swanton lit the pipe and drew on it a few times. "You know, Frank, we have methods of interrogation not open to you. I'm afraid to say that we have had to make use of these methods with regard to Aubertin. They served us well. We were also helped by the gun."

"The gun?"

"Yes, when…"

There was a knock at the door.

"That's Peters with Aubertin. We can hear the whole story from him now. He promised to be cooperative and tell us everything. Let's hope he lives up to his promise."

There was a second knock.

"Come in!"

Aubertin looked a very different man from the one Merlin had met with Goldberg 12 days before. As he shuffled into the room, handcuffed and stooped, it was hard to reconcile this figure with the elegant and assured officer who presided over Dorset Square. He was wearing a sweat-stained collarless shirt and trousers that, without belt or braces, he struggled to keep up with his handcuffed hands.

Peters brought a third chair up to the fire and pushed Aubertin firmly into it before withdrawing to a seat by the door.

Aubertin raised his head for the first time and looked at Merlin. The Frenchman was red-eyed and had three days of growth on his chin. His face was deathly pale but showed no signs of violence. His hands also seemed undamaged. The marks or scars of whatever had been done to Aubertin must have been hidden beneath his clothes. Merlin decided not to speculate on what they might be.

"You remember Detective Chief Inspector Merlin, Colonel?"

Aubertin muttered something inaudible.

"Speak up, Colonel!"

"I have had the pleasure, yes."

"He visited you to enquire about Armand de Metz, did he not?"

"He did."

"And you told him a pack of lies, didn't you? Said you didn't know the man."

The colonel's lips moved but no answer came.

"Didn't you?"

"You know I did, Mr Swanton. I…" Aubertin started to cough and was only able to stop with the help of a glass of water.

"Better? Good. Would you now care to tell us about yourself and de Metz? The whole story, please."

Aubertin sighed. "I knew Armand de Metz. I knew him very well. We were childhood friends. We grew up together in the country. In the Auvergne. Not so far from Vichy. We are the two boys in your famous photograph. I am in the cadet uniform of the military-run school I attended. The two girls are his cousins. I married one of them."

Merlin raised an eyebrow. "She is still your wife?"

"Yes."

"So you have a Jewish wife?"

"I do."

"And she is still in France?"

"Yes."

"A dangerous place for a Jew to be at the moment."

Aubertin made a throaty noise that sounded vaguely like a chuckle. "It is. And 'therein lies the rub' as Mr Shakespeare puts it. Her situation is at the heart of my predicament, as I have told Mr Swanton."

"So you have, Colonel, although I'm not sure I believe you."

Aubertin looked coldly at Swanton before continuing. "So, yes, Armand and I were childhood friends. We carried on being friends into adulthood, when we were young ambitious men in Paris. By then, of course, we were also relatives by marriage. However, our different political persuasions drove us apart. He was a man of the left, I, like many military men, of the right. He was very active in the Socialist Party. A great friend of Léon Blum. I joined an anti-socialist organisation run by a man called de la Roque. Colonel de la Roque. It was called the *Croix de Feu*. The Cross of Fire. This organisation was beyond the pale for Armand."

"I have heard of it. Wasn't it violently anti-Semitic?"

"I wouldn't say that, Mr Merlin, but it held the view that many of France's problems – and indeed the world's – were the responsibility of Jewish financiers and businessmen."

"And you subscribed to that view, even though your wife is a Jew?"

"I have nothing against Jews as Jews. I love my wife. She is not to blame for the errors of the more powerful members of her race."

"Did de la Roque and his people know about your wife?"

"They did not, but, in any event, I took measures to protect her." Merlin leaned forward. "What measures?"

"I took them not just because of my political activities. It was becoming increasingly clear that it was not a great thing to be a Jew in 30s Europe. I had a friend high up in the Ministry of the Interior. He procured new papers for my wife. She was the only child of a Catholic father and a Jewish mother, both deceased. The papers gave her a dead Catholic mother instead."

"Wouldn't there still be people around who knew she was Jewish?"

"She had no close living relatives except for Armand, whom we now never saw. Her Jewishness had never been discussed with our friends. Jeanette is blonde with a fair complexion. She doesn't look Jewish."

Merlin glanced at Swanton, who was giving Aubertin a sceptical look. "Interesting, Colonel, but going back to de Metz and you. You fell out politically in the 30s and were no longer friends. You were still married to his cousin. What next?"

"I was stationed in north Africa when Hitler invaded my country. I was under orders to remain at my post so had no opportunity to go and get my wife. Then I got called to England by de Gaulle and took up my position here in London. Some weeks after my arrival, I was approached by someone. An agent of Pierre Laval in Vichy. My first thought was to have him arrested but I decided to listen to what he had to say. He spouted the usual Vichy propaganda – resistance against the Germans is futile, Britain will fall soon, it is the duty of all Frenchmen to pull together in unity. Then he came to the point.

"He told me the Vichy authorities had thoroughly investigated the backgrounds of all de Gaulle's senior officers, including me. In my case they had discovered that my wife was a Jew. Laval's man explained that, very shortly, the Vichy government would respond to German pressure and start rounding up Jews en masse and intern them in camps in France or abroad." Aubertin looked down.

"The man told me that if I wanted to ensure my wife's safety, I would have to perform a few tasks for Vichy. He said the marshal's government was particularly interested in prospective British secret operations in France. An officer working secretly for Vichy was about to join us in London. An officer with excellent credentials, who had been approved to work in de Gaulle's office. He required me to keep an eye on this man and do my best to ensure he had access to the desired intelligence information. If I did not comply, my wife…"

"The new officer was Dumont?"

"Yes. He would not know my identity but would be aware that someone senior was smoothing his path. For purposes of security and deniability. We had a few methods of communicating when necessary. Letter drops, a go-between and others."

"Why did they need Dumont? Why not just rely on you?"

"They preferred to have someone with a lower profile than me doing the donkey work. If Dumont were to be compromised in some way, they could, if they wished, have a second bite at the cherry with me."

"Didn't quite work out that way, did it?"

Aubertin smiled bleakly. "No."

"Wasn't there some way you could get your wife out of France? Pull some strings? Get her to north Africa?"

"She is an invalid, Mr Merlin. She had a stroke not so long ago. That is one difficulty. The other is that she won't budge, anyway. She is determined to be on the spot to look after our house and animals."

"Don't you have any children, who could persuade her of the dangers and get her out?"

"No."

"So you did as the Vichy agent asked?"

"Yes."

Swanton blew a cloud of pipe smoke up to the ceiling. "Yes, Frank. The colonel ensured Dumont's safety as he passed over some very juicy stuff to Vichy and the Germans."

"We seem to have lost sight of Armand de Metz. How does he fit into this part of the story?" asked Merlin.

"Early this year, I received a letter from Armand advising me of his arrival in the country. He said he was penniless. The letter was emotional. I think he was probably drunk when he wrote it. Armand relayed the dreadful news about his family and dwelt on his numerous misfortunes. He wanted money, naturally. To my regret, I chose to ignore the letter. I had enough on my mind as it was and he was nothing to me."

"Couldn't you have given him a little money for old times' sake?"

There was a rasping noise as Aubertin scratched his stubbled chin. "I should have. I am not short of money. I was financially comfortable before the war and had the foresight to send a good sum of cash to England before 1939. I could have afforded it but I really didn't want to have anything to do with the man. My mistake."

"What happened next?"

"I received a second letter. In this, Armand made a point of mentioning my wife's little secret."

"He threatened to use his knowledge?"

"Yes. Subtly but yes."

"Did you respond to this letter?"

"No."

"And then?"

"He began, as you know, haunting the Free French office and bothering various officers. He made a point of keeping well away from me and Dorset Square but managed to speak to Meyer, Beaulieu and others at Carlton Gardens. He didn't get any money out of them either but began following officers to pubs and cafés and eavesdropping on them. Then he began claiming he had important intelligence information he could divulge for a price."

"And waving that photograph around."

"Yes. That damned photograph. Then I got a third letter. You must realise that Armand had a brilliant brain. Fuddled with drink he may have been but his mind was still as sharp as a pin in many ways. Even before Fillon launched his investigation, there was occasional gossip about the possibility of leaks in the organisation. Armand must have heard some talk of that kind, which prompted him to give the matter some thought. He devised a theory. Unfortunately, he put two and two together and came up with four. He considered from what he knew who would be the likeliest candidate as a spy. He knew I had been in *Croix de Feu*, many of whose former members are prominent in Vichy and I would know well. He knew I had a Jewish wife to protect in Vichy France. I was exposed. What better candidate for a spy, he calculated, than I?"

"And he put this in his letter to you?"

"He did, Mr Merlin."

"What was your reaction?"

"I was stunned and frightened. At the time, I was not only preoccupied with these concerns but also had my girlfriend problems."

"Ah, yes. Bridget Healy. You do not deny the relationship?"

"What point is there now in doing that?"

"What about the love you profess for your wife?"

"In France we do things differently, you know. I love my wife dearly but she has never had problems with the occasional dalliance on my part, particularly when I have been abroad. Bridget was a lovely girl. My wife would have approved. We had some fun. I set her up nicely and showed her the finer things in life, such as they are in London. Then she became pregnant. There was never any question of my letting her keep the baby and taking responsibility for it. After initial resistance, she accepted this was the wisest solution."

"Abortion."

"Yes, of course." Aubertin's voice was weakening as he approached the end of his story.

Swanton added more tobacco to his pipe. "Come on, Colonel. Speak up. Not much more ground to cover."

Aubertin cleared his throat. "Inevitably, in the course of my duties, I get to know some of the junior officers. I got to know Dumont socially. Nothing wrong with it, I thought, since he had no idea of my situation. I was probably unwise, however, to get involved in the odd drinking session with him and some other officers. I believe I was with him when I first met Bridget at the Ritz. Anyway, he knew about me and Bridget.

"One night, after several drinks, I confided in him about the pregnancy. He was one of the officers whom de Metz had got to know and, a day or two later, he told me Armand was now in the abortion business. Dumont had heard and believed Armand's stories about being a hot-shot surgeon and felt he was bound to do a competent job. When he suggested Armand, I thought there was an opportunity to kill two birds with one stone. I would retain de Metz anonymously as abortionist for a very generous fee. He would perform the operation successfully and, with my money in his pockets, there would be less pressure on him to blackmail me. It all seemed so clever at the time but now…" Aubertin put his head in his hands. "That poor, poor girl." He started to sob.

Swanton was not sympathetic. "Come on, Colonel. We'll not have any of that. Get on with it and give us the last act."

Aubertin pulled himself together. "So, Dumont agreed to go to the hotel on my behalf to keep an eye on proceedings. He told me afterwards that Armand had been drunk but had insisted on going ahead. When I learned what happened I was distraught and furious in equal measure. I drank a bottle of whisky, went to bed and in the morning I knew what had to be done. Armand deserved punishment for his drunken butchering of Bridget while, over and above that, he posed a serious threat to what I was doing for Vichy and thus my wife. He had to die."

"Just to get the chronology right, Colonel, the abortion operation and Bridget's death took place on Thursday 5 June. Dumont told you what happened in the evening of the same day and you decided on your course of action on Friday 6 June. Have I got that right?"

"I suppose so, Mr Merlin. Dates are beginning to seem rather vague now."

"So what next?"

"I already had Armand's Notting Hill address from Dumont. The following day – that would have been the Saturday, I guess – early in the morning, I went there and shot him."

"So why did you use Dumont's gun?"

"I didn't."

Swanton set down his pipe. "I can help you there, Frank. You told me Dumont's gun was a *Modèle* 1935A. After we picked up Aubertin, we turned over his office and in his desk there was a gun. A *Modèle* 1935A."

Aubertin shook his head slowly. "A strange coincidence. They are not standard issue and not very common. I didn't know Dumont had one. I have another more modern army issue gun but prefer the *Modèle*. It has seen me through some difficult situations. In this case, however, it's discovery meant…"

"That the game was up, eh, Colonel? When I told you that the police had a shell casing from the flat, you knew there would be a match."

There was a long silence that Merlin eventually broke. "But what about this internal investigation you were running, Colonel? What was going on there?"

Aubertin grimaced, closed his eyes and arched his back. He took a few deep breaths. "Sorry. A spasm – I have sciatica." He half-smiled. "I was hoping the attentions of Mr Swanton's men might have bent my spine back into shape."

Swanton growled something unintelligible.

"As to your question, Mr Merlin, after concerns expressed by the British, a French internal inquiry was launched by a Colonel Fillon, who, after some initial work, abandoned it to me when he went abroad with the general. Three officers, the most recent arrivals from north Africa, had been identified by Fillon as potential suspects. One of the suspects was Dumont. Obviously I had to protect him. I was given the impression that the general didn't take the investigation seriously and initially felt I could just go through the motions. Thus I delegated the job to Angers, who I knew was too lazy to be effective.

"Unknown to me, he in turn had delegated the task to Captain Rougemont, who is a clever young man. Rougemont then recruited Devlin, who is a competent operative. When I found out about this, I made a mistake and allowed the arrangements to stand. Despite being under renewed pressure from the British to step up the investigation, I still felt I could control things satisfactorily through Angers.

"So Dumont was one suspect and the others were Lieutenants Beaulieu and Meyer. I knew little of Meyer, save that he was a Jew, but I knew that Beaulieu was a vain and arrogant young man whose father had once vetoed a promotion I was after. If there were to be a scapegoat, it was him. Devlin had been following the three men around for a few days and I had, of course, got a warning to Dumont about this but I decided that all efforts should be concentrated on Beaulieu. If Devlin could only find out something compromising about Beaulieu I might be able to trump something up. I advised Angers to tell Devlin to focus only on Beaulieu. Devlin disobeyed, Dumont made a mistake and Devlin's suspicions fell on him. When I made Dumont aware of this, he was quick to act and arrange for Devlin to be dealt with."

Swanton leaned over to tap his pipe against the fireplace. "Dumont has confirmed, Frank, that it was Beecham's thugs who attacked Devlin."

"I see."

Swanton looked long and hard at Aubertin before nodding to Peters. "I think that's enough for now, Colonel. You and I will have another little chat later. Off you go, now."

Peters pulled the colonel roughly to his feet. On his way out, Aubertin turned to look beseechingly at Merlin. "Swanton doesn't believe me, I know, but please, Mr Merlin, I only did it for my wife, I swear…" The thick door closed behind him and any further words were lost as the men's footsteps receded down the corridor.

Merlin leaned back in his chair. "Don't you believe him, Harold? About his wife?"

"Does it really matter, Frank? I pretty much believe everything else apart from his claim there were no other accomplices in Dorset Square and Carlton Gardens. I'll be looking further into that. And then there's the go-between Aubertin inadvertently mentioned. We'll get that name out of him. The excuse about his wife makes him look better but isn't it just as likely that he was always in league with those old fascist *Croix de Feu* friends of his in Vichy? Whatever his true motivation, the fact remains that his and Dumont's treachery led to the deaths of several good men and women. For that he must pay the penalty."

Suddenly Merlin felt very tired. "It is a little frustrating that I'm neither going to be able to bring Aubertin to trial for de Metz's murder nor Dumont for the attack on Devlin."

"Sorry, Frank. There'll be no due process of law for these two. We'll milk them for everything we can get. Find any others involved. Once we've done that it'll be…" Swanton ran a finger slowly across his throat.

"What about de Gaulle and his lot?"

"We may allow the French an interview after we've finished with them but Aubertin and Dumont will remain in my custody." Swanton stood up and stretched his arms. His face suddenly brightened. "I don't know about you, Frank, but I'm absolutely parched. Peckish too. How about I organise some beer and sandwiches? They have some very nice stuff in the ducal pantry."

"I can think of nothing better, Harold."

CHAPTER 17

Tuesday 24 June

London

"Ah, Frank. There you are. Come in, sit down. I can't tell you how glad I am to be back in the office. If I had had to drink another one of my wife's special medicinal hot drinks, I'd have been ready to top myself."

Merlin made his way to the AC's desk. "Are you all right now, sir?"

"Fit as a fiddle. It was that damned trip to Bristol! When Claire deserted me for you! On the Thursday morning, before I headed back to London, I went for a walk in a park near the hotel and was caught in a torrential downpour. Just came out of the blue. I didn't have a coat on, as the weather has been so lovely, and had no change of clothes so I travelled back to London sodden. Result was that within a few hours I felt rotten, my temperature was through the roof and the bronchitis I'm prone to had made an appearance. I was pretty much poleaxed over the weekend. Anyway, the good Dr Lang and the tender ministrations of my dear wife have brought me back to the land of the living.

"But that's enough about me. What news, Frank? I managed to read the report you sent me on Sunday. Well done! Seems everything is pretty much wrapped up, although it's disappointing that we can't follow through."

Bridges had given Merlin a particularly strong brew of tea on his arrival at the Yard earlier in the morning, and Merlin's taste buds had still not recovered. "Do you mind if I help myself to a glass of water, sir?"

"Not at all, Frank. Pour me one while you're at it."

Merlin drank most of his glass in one gulp before he sat down. "Yes, obviously Aubertin and Dumont are out of our hands now. Swanton is sweating them to identify any accomplices. Apparently, the fellow with the medical recruitment agency in Putney, Renard was the name I think, may have acted as some sort of go-between. Harold has also been questioning Rougemont but is pretty sure he's done nothing wrong."

"What happened to Commandant Angers?"

"In the clear. He was released yesterday. Swanton decided he had nothing to do with the espionage but apparently he departed a much-chastened man."

The AC picked up a pencil and proceeded to tap his teeth with it, an annoying occasional habit of his. "And what about the case of your poor friend?"

"As I wrote in my report, Constable Robinson and Detective Goldberg did a superb job of pinning down Carson as Eddie's murderer. His partner, Miller, had betrayed him but we eventually got his confession yesterday. Everything was as we suspected.

"Carson was sent by Beecham to get Arbuthnot's message from Powell in the belief that it would somehow lead to the bearer shares. As Vorster told us, he gained access by claiming he had a package to deliver to Powell, who got out of the bath to let him in. Eddie wouldn't hand over the message so Carson got rough with him and gave him a dunking or 10 in the water. Overdid it. He's trying to say it was an accident, of course, but that's not going to get him anywhere. Poor Eddie. Survived the hell of Crete to die a cheap and sordid death back home."

"A brave and honourable man, Frank."

"Yes, sir. Miller has obviously admitted to keeping an eye out for Carson outside the flats. Cooperative as he's been, I'm going to see if I can nail him as an accomplice to murder. If I fail we also have the attack on Devlin to prosecute, although it's going to be difficult without Dumont's or Aubertin's direct evidence."

"How is Devlin?"

"Recovering slowly but he's going to be all right."

The AC finally stopped using his teeth as a xylophone. "Any more on Beecham?"

"Originally Percy Bishop, a small-time crook from Bethnal Green. Got involved with Oswald Mosley as a fascist organiser and thug. He started a protection racket then became a bookie. Through Mosley he began to move in higher circles. Eventually he reinvented himself as Peregrine Beecham, found some deep-pocketed backers and started his gambling operation in Piccadilly. We don't know how he got hooked up with Vichy. Presumably something to do with his Mosleyite past. Swanton is investigating."

"I don't understand why we've never gone after this chap before? The set-up in Arlington Street is or was clearly illegal. Why haven't the vice squad done anything about it?"

"A very good question, sir. Do I need to answer it for you?"

Gatehouse bit his lip and shook his head. "I have no authority over vice, Frank, as you know. I can only try to broach this with the commissioner."

Merlin sighed. "We both know there are some suspect officers in that group."

The AC echoed Merlin's sigh. "I know the commissioner won't be keen on doing anything worthwhile. He'll say: 'We can't afford to rock the boat at time of war, Gatehouse.'"

The two men sat in a long, pensive silence, which the AC eventually broke. "What about the Arbuthnots?"

"The City of London police are continuing their investigations and the Bank of England has sent some people in to help and work alongside the management. Fleming, the man who succeeded Simon Arbuthnot as head of the bank, resigned over the weekend and has apparently left the country. Word is he's on his way to South America."

"To take charge of the business there?"

"No doubt. To try at least. He won't find it easy, apparently. The man on the spot, Pulos, is quite formidable, according to Philip Arbuthnot. And there are other difficulties. The Meyer family is continuing with its litigation. Felix Meyer, the son who was innocently entangled in Devlin's investigation as I mentioned in my report, told me the full story of the fraud perpetrated on his father, which led to the South American business falling into Arbuthnot's hands. He asked if there was anything I could do about it, but I told him it all happened too long ago and I had more pressing matters to deal with."

"What of the younger Arbuthnot?"

"Doing the decent thing, it seems. He's taken over as chairman of the bank and is cooperating fully with the police investigators and the officials from the Bank of England. He says he's not going to take advantage of one of the legal sleights of hand revealed in his father's letter."

"What was that?"

"That there was never a valid declaration of trust conferring ownership of the South American business in favour of the bank. Philip and his aunt could, therefore, have asserted direct ownership of those assets. A new declaration of trust is being made in the bank's favour. The bank will still have a job to get control of the assets but still… I didn't particularly take to Tomlinson, the solicitor, but he seems to have been a good influence on the young man. And on the positive side for Philip, at least he hasn't got Beecham breathing down his neck for his father's gambling debts."

"Well, good for Philip. I'm glad he appears to be behaving so honourably. Poor fellow. Bloody awful mess to find yourself in so young. The South African is in the clear?"

"He is. His story about Eddie's murder proved true and he led us to the culprit. He's a silly young man but he's done nothing criminal."

"That's a relief. His father has powerful friends here and I was anticipating interference if things had gone the other way." The AC sipped some water. "Well, let me know when you hear more from Swanton."

"I shall, sir."

"And what do you think of the developments in Russia?"

"I don't really know what to think, sir."

"Whatever it is, it's a major new turn in the war." The AC fiddled with his collar stud. "I'm sorry I missed my chance to say farewell to Detective Goldberg."

"Yes, sir. I must say I found him a very decent and useful fellow to have around. I'm prepared to admit that I wasn't keen on the idea at the beginning but he proved a very helpful member of the team."

The AC flashed a mouthful of mottled teeth at Merlin. "I'm glad that my ideas gain your approval once in a while, Detective Chief Inspector."

Merlin smiled back. "Any news of my other officers, sir? Obviously with Goldberg gone I am a little short-handed again."

"All in hand. All in hand, Frank. Speaking of your officers, I understand that Constable Robinson handled herself well at Waterloo Station the other day?"

"She was very brave, sir. You must know that I didn't encourage her to…"

"Don't worry, Frank. Something like this was bound to happen at some point. She's a headstrong woman like her mother, not to mention her aunt. I'm just glad you were at hand. Now, anything else? If not, I don't want to detain you further from your work."

Merlin shifted awkwardly in his chair. "There is one other thing, sir."

"Yes, Frank. What is it?"

"Something personal I feel you should be made aware of."

The AC's face clouded over. "Not that stuff about wanting to join up again? I thought I made it clear last time that you are far too essential to the force to…"

"No, sir. Not that. I just wanted you to know that Sonia is… is… pregnant."

The mottled teeth reappeared. "My very heartiest congratulations, Frank. I'm sure you'll make a superb father! What excellent news!"

Merlin hadn't quite known what reaction to expect from the AC but this effusive one was a surprise. "Th… thank you, sir. I thought you might be… erm… a little…"

"A little what, Frank? Put out, censorious, disappointed? Goodness, I may have my faults but small-mindedness is not one of them. Mrs Gatehouse likewise. She liked Sonia very, very much. Told me she would be delighted to see you settle down with such a fine woman." He clasped Merlin's hand and shook it vigorously.

"Thank you, sir." There was a moment's awkward silence during which Merlin managed to extricate his hand from Gatehouse's firm grip. "It's just that, our not being married, I thought you might see as an embarrassment to you or to the service."

"Poppycock, Frank. You must do as you see fit. I assume naturally that you are standing by the young lady?"

"Of course, sir. I… I… love her."

"Good! Very good! May I be so presumptuous as to enquire if you plan to make her your wife?"

"I hope to but, er… we haven't discussed it properly yet."

"Well, you better had, hadn't you?"

*   *   *

Vichy

Admiral Darlan and Pierre Laval sat beside the open French doors in Laval's suite. In the distance a church clock was striking midnight.

"I saw your light on as I was passing along the corridor. I hope you don't mind being disturbed at this late hour."

"Not at all, François." Laval gestured towards the pile of papers on his nearby desk. "I was working, as you can see. The interruption was welcome. I'm sorry I have nothing to offer you by way of refreshment. We could call down but experience tells me that room service is not very responsive after 11 o'clock."

Darlan sank back into the plush leather padding of his chair. "Do not concern yourself, Pierre. I just thought I'd pop in to hear your views on today's news from London."

"What news in particular?"

"Come now, my friend. You know very well. The MI5 arrest and detention of two of our officers. They were your men, weren't they?"

Laval pursed his lips. "They were part of my team, yes." He sighed and shook his head. "They will be missed but there are others."

"Very embarrassing, though. What does the marshal say?"

"He doesn't know about it. Probably best kept that way."

"I'll not tell him, my friend, but there are plenty who will be happy to do so, with the appropriate dollop of poison. You are not short of enemies."

Laval stroked his moustache. "These things are bound to happen from time to time, François. One cannot expect all wartime operations to go smoothly."

"And what of the Germans? What have they to say?"

"*Herr* Abetz rang to commiserate. He said he was confident that we would be able to find alternative new sources soon and

I do indeed have other irons in the fire. He said his SS man Schmidt was particularly grateful for the contribution of our fallen countrymen in London."

"By 'fallen', Pierre, do you mean to say that they have already been executed?"

"I don't know that for a fact but if it hasn't yet happened, it will soon enough." Laval loosened his shirt collar. "Of course, one or other of the men must have become sloppy. If I had to put money on it, I'd say Aubertin. Dumont was a real professional." Laval closed his eyes for a second. "Whether it is worthwhile to carry on protecting his wife now, I really don't know."

Darlan rose. "I don't know what you are talking about, Pierre, and I don't think I want to. I can see that you are tired and I am too. I'll bid you goodnight."

"Anything further on the fall of Damascus?"

"No, Dentz has not been in communication."

Laval creaked to his feet. "What hope Beirut now, eh? I suppose it's too much to hope that de Gaulle won't fly in to Syria to gloat." The admiral shrugged wearily as Laval escorted him to the door.

CHAPTER 18
Thursday 26 June

London

"Here is the latest report on German progress, Prime Minister." "Thank you, Jock." Churchill set down his pen – he had been heavily annotating a paper on munitions sent by Commander-in-Chief Sir Alan Brooke – and took the file from his private secretary, Jock Colville. A smile appeared on the PM's face as he began to read. After battering Britain from the air for more than nine months, Hitler had apparently postponed his UK invasion plans and turned his military offensive eastwards.

Four days earlier, Germany had attacked Russia, its erstwhile ally. Of course, if Hitler defeated Russia there wouldn't be much to smile about. Most of Churchill's senior officers were pessimistic about Russia's chances. One or two thought Stalin wouldn't last more than three weeks. However, whatever the outcome, Hitler's change of direction had, at the very least, given Britain some breathing space.

The report told Churchill that the Germans were making strong progress everywhere. Hitler's forces had launched their attack on several fronts along the length of Russia's western border and were rolling rapidly through the Baltic states, Byelorussia, the Soviet sector of Poland and the Ukraine. The *Luftwaffe* had already destroyed thousands of Russian aircraft before they'd even got off the ground. The prime minister got to the end of the report and set down the file, his smile now replaced by the familiar bulldog jut of the chin.

"All seems to be going well for *Herr* Hitler. So far, at least."

"Yes, sir. But it is a huge undertaking."

"Operation Barbarossa, Hitler has called it, apparently. Redbeard is presumably a reference to the Holy Roman Emperor of that name. Brooke gives the Russians greater credit than some of his colleagues. He still thinks Hitler will win but that it will take him three or four months. If he's right, that's three or four valuable months for us to continue building up our defences against the Nazis' return."

"Or three or four months to persuade Roosevelt to get America into the war."

"Quite so, Jock. Then again, perhaps the Russian soldiers will surprise the Nazis yet, as they did Napoleon. I wonder how Mr Stalin is taking this turn of events? He must now regret executing all those talented generals of his in recent years."

"It is somewhat ironic, isn't it, sir, after the Russians cobbled together their disgraceful Molotov-Ribbentrop Pact with the Germans?"

"Indeed it is, Jock." Churchill consulted his watch. Lunchtime soon. That was why his stomach was rumbling. "Sit down for a minute, why don't you? These papers can wait for a moment." Colville did as he was bid. "What other news?"

"Arrangements are well in hand for the changeover in the Middle East. Auchinleck will take charge in Cairo next month and Wavell will transfer to Delhi as per your orders, sir."

Churchill gazed off towards the windows at the end of the room. "I still feel a little bad about Archie Wavell but things out there need a shake-up. Claude Auchinleck is a good man."

"A friend, recently in Cairo, told me that while Wavell is sorry to go there's one part of his job he says he won't miss."

"And what is that?"

"Having to babysit de Gaulle."

Churchill snorted with laughter. "He's still out there, isn't he? No doubt scheming to organise a triumphal march for himself through Damascus. Well, at least it keeps him out of my hair. And this Aubertin case must be causing him some grief."

Colville looked perplexed. "What case is that, sir?"

"Sorry, Jock. Forgot you didn't know about it. It's meant to be hush-hush. I'd better keep it under my hat or I'll be in MI5's bad books. Let's just say something very embarrassing to the general occurred. Mr Merlin at the Yard was involved. He and Swanton did a good job."

Churchill's eyes wandered to the paper he had been working on earlier. Colville took his cue and got to his feet. "Are you planning a trip to Ditchley Park again this weekend, sir?"

"I think so. Ronald told me they were hoping to have a showing of Korda's new picture about Nelson – *That Hamilton Woman* I think it's called. Laurence Olivier and his pretty new wife, Vivien Leigh. Sounds just my cup of cocoa."

*   *   *

Buenos Aires

Pulos listened as Victor gave the cleaning woman her instructions on the other side of the door. He had made it clear to his valet that he wanted a particularly thorough job done today. His wife was returning from Bariloche later and no evidence must remain of his dalliance with the two charming *chicas* Pulos had brought home from the Club Atlantico in the early hours of the morning.

The office could wait a while today. Pulos would stay at home until the woman was finished so he could check her work personally. His wife had a very sharp nose for this sort of thing. Although he knew very well about the fun and games she got up to on her trips away, he did not want to start their next period of cohabitation on the back foot.

He finished dressing and went into the drawing room. He had told Victor he didn't want any breakfast but Pulos was pleased to see his valet setting down a cup of steaming coffee on the table beside his favourite chair. The businessman sat down and drank with a sigh of pleasure. The moment he replaced the empty cup on its saucer, his desk telephone rang. He rose and went to take the call. It was his secretary.

"*Señor*, another cable has arrived. From Mr Arbuthnot again. Shall I read it to you?"

Pulos groaned. "If you must, my dear."

"As per previous wires bank in very difficult situation. Please transfer funds requested. Also still most urgent you return to London. Please arrange immediate passage. PS Fleming reported en route to BA."

Pulos groaned again. This was the fourth cable this week asking him to send money and to return to London. He had also been informed of Fleming's resignation and Philip's assumption of the chairmanship and knew that Sackville was overrun with policemen and Bank of England officials. He had been told about Simon Arbuthnot's will and of the discovery of the bearer shares, which were now in police custody. In the circumstances, surely Philip and the board must be aware that his return to London was as likely as Hitler agreeing to take tea with the Chief Rabbi of Argentina?

Pulos returned to his chair and pondered the one new item of information in the cable – Sidney Fleming was on his way to Argentina. Pulos could hardly blame the man for clearing out. The difficult question was whether Pulos should welcome him as a potentially useful ally or as an unwanted ship-boarder to be repelled. The Greek had considered his position at length and continued to feel it was a strong one – no, he didn't have the bearer shares in his possession and was unlikely to ever enjoy such possession, but he did have physical control of the businesses. That was the crucial thing.

Pulos called out for another coffee. The shares came to mind again – and then Marco. He realised now that it was a good thing Marco had failed in the task Pulos had given him in London. If Marco hadn't held back and allowed someone else to muscle in, his bodyguard might have been Powell's murderer. And from what he now understood, possession of Powell's message wouldn't have led Pulos to the shares. He had heard there was some complex code involved, which he doubted he'd have been able to crack. So it was good that Marco hadn't got blood on his hands. Good that he had walked away from Flood Street. Pulos resolved to be a little nicer to Marco than he had been since that night.

Victor appeared with fresh coffee and a plate of biscuits. The Greek picked up a chocolate confection and munched it thoughtfully. What could the people in London really do? Would Philip travel out to see him? Would the police or the Bank of England officials make the journey? He couldn't really see it, given the wartime situation. If Philip did come, Pulos was confident he could make mincemeat of him. Would the British authorities try to intervene somehow in the Meyer litigation? Surely that would be counterproductive to any assertion of ownership of Enterprisas Simal by Sackville or the Arbuthnots? If the Meyers were in the right, then the shares and underlying business were theirs and theirs alone.

He picked up another biscuit, a coconut one this time. Perhaps Fleming's keen intellect would be of use? But if Pulos had to make room to accommodate him, it would cost him money. A lot of money. That thought reminded him that there were more transfers to arrange today. Whatever happened, he was going to make sure his personal cash reserves were significantly boosted through the siphoning of company funds. He had some loyal, malleable accountants who would cover his tracks.

Second coffee finished, he rose and went over to his desk. Among the pile of papers was yesterday's letter from the company lawyers appraising him of the disturbing news that Manuel Lopez, the second judge in the Meyer case, had suffered a serious heart attack. Pulos's lawyers had only just managed to get him onside a few days before. For the right amount of money, he too had been for sale. Now they would have to work hard again to ensure his replacement was similarly amenable.

Pulos sighed. There was a lot on his plate but first things first. He would go and see how the cleaning was coming along. Some ladies' undergarments were bound to have lodged themselves in hidden crannies and his help might be required.

*   *   *

London

"Hello, darling. You managed to get home early as you promised. How wonderful. I've made us a stew. Rabbit stew."

Merlin closed the door. "One of my favourites."

"I knew that would please you. And there's a nice bottle of red wine. But first I have a bottle of beer for you. A light ale. I'll just go and get it."

Merlin went to sit in the living room. He had walked back from work on what was a very warm night and was perspiring. The windows were open and he was happy to feel the caress of a light breeze. Sonia reappeared with his beer. He took the drink then reached out with his free hand to grasp her hand and pull her gently on to his lap. "And how was your day, darling?"

"Oh, you know, the usual. Very busy. Some nice custome Some horrible ones. An argument about clothing coupons. usual. How was yours?"

"All right. No, sorry. Better than all right. The investigat into Hess is going nowhere so Peter Johnson has been sent b to us and the AC has finally relented about Tommy Cole a allowed his return from Portsmouth. Both look fit and we was able to fill them in on all they've been missing."

Sonia stroked his cheek then gave it a peck. "Perhaps you co do the same for me later. You've been so busy and I've lost trac

"I'll tell all over dinner. How long will that be?"

"Another 20 minutes or so."

"Are you not having a drink?"

"I'll just have a small glass of wine with the food."

Merlin set down his beer and hugged Sonia close. "Darling, really need to talk about things."

Sonia pulled back and smiled coquettishly. "Things? Wh things?"

"You know very well, Sonia. We need to discuss what to regarding the baby and us."

"And what is it you propose regarding the baby and us, Fran

"Well, I suppose that's the key word, isn't it? Propose, I mea

Sonia extricated herself from Merlin's arms, stood up a moved to the armchair opposite. She arched an eyebrow Merlin. "Very well, Frank. I believe there is a traditional w of doing this in England and you know that I am a tradition kind of girl."

Merlin couldn't help but splutter with laughter as he got and walked over to Sonia, arms outstretched. Sonia took hands in hers. He dropped to his knee. "My dear darling Son would you do me the honour of becoming my wife?"

Sonia looked very serious for a moment. Then her eyes beg to well up. She stood and pulled Merlin to his feet. Putting h